…a Crouch is the author …
…blished novels: *Cuckoo*, *Ever*…
…l *The Long Fall*. Before becom…
…ector/playwright and then a …
…es in Brighton with her husba…

…ise for *Her Husband's Lover*:

…chological thrillers don't come much better than this' Clare
…kintosh

…eliciously dark psychological thriller that challenges your
…ainties right up until the explosive final twist' *Sunday*
…*or*

…ulia Crouch coined the term "Domestic Noir" it's hardly
…sing that she is one of the most adroit practitioners of the
…*Financial Times*

…liciously disturbing . . . Crouch is one of those writers who
…evitably keeps one up too late, and *Her Husband's Lover* is
…o exception' Alex Marwood

'A brilliant and compelling thriller from the Queen of Domestic
Noir' Helen FitzGerald

'Thoroughly enjoyable read that makes you want to lock the
door' *Woman's Way*

'Totally unputdownable – until I got to the twist that made me
drop the book' Erin Kelly

'Taut and twisty, and full of surprises. I loved it' Sarah Hilary

'Nothing is what it seems in this brilliant novel by Julia Crouch.
What a clever, unsettling, absorbing book' Elly Griffiths

'A fantastic, fast-paced and riveting read. *Her Husband's Lover*
is addictive, dark and disturbing. I struggled to put it down
and it stayed with me long after I'd finished' Lisa Cutts

'A perfect mix of intriguing characters and unexpected surprises,
compell…ng because the ground beneath our feet is constantly
shifting … she makes her readers think' Ruth Dugdall

HER HUSBAND'S LOVER

JULIA CROUCH

HEADLINE

First published in Great Britain in 2017 by
HEADLINE PUBLISHING GROUP

First published in paperback in 2017 by
HEADLINE PUBLISHING GROUP

1

Cataloguing in Publication Data is available from the British Library

B format ISBN 978 1 4722 0670 1

Typeset in Sabon by Avon DataSet Ltd, Bidford-on-Avon, Warwickshire

Printed and bound in Great Britain by Clays Ltd, St Ives plc

Headline's policy is to use papers that are natural, renewable and
recyclable products and made from wood grown in well-managed
forests and other controlled sources. The logging and manufacturing
processes are expected to conform to the environmental regulations
of the country of origin.

HEADLINE PUBLISHING GROUP
An Hachette UK Company
Carmelite House
50 Victoria Embankment
London EC4Y 0DZ

www.headline.co.uk
www.hachette.co.uk

For Sarah and all at Booky

1

'Get back. Get *back*!'

In the roar of the night, her blood-red eyes flick to the rear-view mirror. Behind, the scarlet Porsche bears down on her, the headlight dazzle blinding her, even through thick sheets of rain. She takes a sudden turn onto the unmade track that leads to the clay pits. But he follows, stuck to her like the devil. Stones ricochet against the side of her little white Fiesta, whose worn wheels lurch in and out of potholes, which, brim-full of water, are deeper than they appear in the darkness.

The children, blanket-wrapped and strapped snug in the back, do not stir.

Thank God.

Thunder cracks the night. Her head pounds as if Thor himself were swinging a hammer around and around inside her brain. Her heart is so fast, so big in her chest that it seems as if there is no room for her lungs.

She floors the accelerator, but it is not good enough. She has got this far, but she knows he won't let her make it away.

The lane widens slightly and he takes his advantage, roaring up against her, barging her off, off towards the dark side of the track.

Unannounced, as if suddenly placed to meet her, the giant, solid oak presents itself.

The nose of the Fiesta meets the trunk of the tree, the

Porsche piles into the back of the little car, crumpling all of its safety zones, activating airbags, bringing everything to a sickening, juddering, slap of a crash of a stop.

Black. Silence. Tick of hot exhaust.
Hiss of steam where rain meets hot metal.

Louisa twists her head against the press of the airbag and turns her wild eyes to the furthest edges of their sockets to check on the children. They look like sleeping angels.

Where is *he*, though? Are they still in danger?

Somehow she manages to squeeze herself out of the remains of the driver's door. Her legs don't seem to work, but whatever pain she will feel has not yet surfaced from the adrenaline surging through her sinews. She drags the rubble of her body towards the smoking ruins of the Porsche, which appears to have ingested the rear of her car through the maw of its windscreen.

In her way, in the road in front of her, a football.

A football?

No. Something else.

A black lump in an oily puddle, the headlights catching a flame of hair.

Sam's eye, glinting blankness at her.

The horror.

But all she feels is relief.

All she thinks is: *So it's all over, then.*

So. She and the children are free.

Knowing this, she drags herself back to the Fiesta.

Her shaking hand – three fingers broken, and that's the least of her woes – grasps upwards for the back door handle.

But before she can even begin to yank the jammed thing open, something bright and loud and hot lifts her body and blasts it away, up, and twenty feet through the blue-black, sodden night.

She doesn't know it, but she lands on a soft, mossy patch.
Out, they tell her much later, of harm's way.
She is, they tell her, lucky.

2

The distant long, flat beep wakes her. Or she thinks she's awake. Her eyes are open, so she supposes that must mean she's not sleeping.

Rapid footsteps hurtle past her bed, heading in the direction of what has now turned into a shrill alarm. Out of the edges of her fixed gaze, she detects movement, urgency.

Then all is still again, except for the constant, steady beep that she instinctively knows is to do with her – her companion beep, she calls it – to tell the others that she is doing fine.

Immobile, incoherent, unable to communicate, but fine.

She has no idea who she is, or where she is, but she has a sense that, someday soon, things will be clearer.

People come to her from time to time. The women she thinks of as her attendants – there is a word for them, but she can't quite find it – check things, do things, put things in her to stop her hurting. Others come, too. Someone who calls herself Fiona, who says she is acting for her. She comes quite a bit and sits by her side, tapping away at something. Another woman with grey hair appeared once: a lined, worried face looming over her.

'Can she hear what I'm saying? Does she know who I am?'

She knew that she had some connection to this person, but beyond that, nothing.

'I said something like this would happen at some point,

didn't I?' the woman said, looking at her with weary eyes. 'Didn't I?'

'Now then, Celia,' a male voice said from somewhere outside her field of vision. 'Don't go upsetting yourself.'

'It's all my fault,' the woman said, and as she leaned over her, a fat tear dropped from her eye.

She tasted its salt as it trickled between her dry lips, around her breathing tube.

'It's not your fault, hen,' the man said. 'Everything that's happened is down to her.'

Is it? she thought. Is it really?

What has happened?

And now, in the silence following the beep and the footsteps and the flurry, she drifts away again to the greyer part of her world.

But just as her eyelids are beginning to droop and block out the half-light of her clinical surroundings, the pale face of a girl floats over her. It's thin, with dark-ringed, bloodshot eyes and a downturned red gash of a mouth. Black, gauzy pieces flutter around the face, long, dark hair trails onto her face, annoying her.

She can't even flinch, let alone brush it away.

This face, too, is familiar. Something about it stirs a heat deep inside her, in the part of her that is hidden, beyond thought.

Her companion beep picks up pace.

The red mouth opens. The voice that comes from it is deep, croaked. 'What did you do, Louisa?'

Louisa? Is that who she is, then?

Something inside her lets go. Beneath her a fluid gurgles and for a moment she registers a sense of relief. But the easing is only physical. The tension inside her is still there, pricked and pointed by the presence of this face above her.

'What the hell did you DO?' The voice is harsh now, whispered, heavy with pain.

Two hands hover between this face and her vision. She has a moment to register the bitten fingernails, the worn red nail varnish, before bony fingers pinch her nostrils and a clammy palm is placed over her mouth, around her breathing tube. It only lasts for a couple of seconds, and, thanks to the ventilation tube that does her breathing for her, it poses no real danger. But the intention is clear, written on the face hovering behind the hands.

'I could do whatever I want to you right now,' the voice goes on, as the hands are removed. 'It's you who should be dead right now, not Sam. You should have got what was coming to you.'

She tries with all her might to make a sound. Every scant fibre of her strains to speak. But nothing comes out.

'It's all your fault, Louisa,' the girl says.

Nothing works.

The face disappears from above her and she thinks she has escaped. But then, a prickle of hot breath burns at her ear. 'If you survive,' the voice says, '*if* you survive, I'm not going to let you get away with it. If you survive, you'd better watch out, Louisa.'

Then the girl is above her again, pulling pads from her chest, undoing wires, tugging clips from her fingertips. Her companion beep goes flat like the one that woke her. An alarm sounds and there's a terrible clatter and a scuffle to her side as the attendants arrive.

'Out!'

'Her again. Call security.'

'Too late.'

'Is she all right?'

The familiar face of the top attendant looms into her view. Her gentle smile soothes her. 'Let's get you sorted, Louisa, shall we, then?'

The attendants busy themselves cleaning her up and reattaching her wires and monitors and drips.

The girl is gone. But she – Louisa – remembers this visit.

It marks the beginning of her recovery.

3

Paul, the doughy young orderly, wheels Louisa backwards into the coroner's court through the accessible entrance, so her first view is of pale wooden veneer doors closing behind her, bashing the foot of her extended, pinned leg so that, even though she doesn't want to appear to be a wimp, she can't help wincing.

'Ooh, sorry love,' Paul says.

She could have walked, she'd told them. It would be on crutches, slow, painful and graceless, but titanium rods and endless months of intensive physiotherapy mean that it is, with those qualifications, possible.

Her lawyer Fiona advised, however, that she should stay put in the wheelchair.

'Sympathy is your friend,' she said.

Louisa closes her eyes, and tries to breathe whiteness up through her cramping feet and into her heart and mind. It's a technique they've taught her at The Pines to deal with the panic that can, without warning, claw at her ribcage and squeeze all the breath from her.

As Paul pushes her over to the wheelchair space, she gazes up at the raked rows of metal chairs, which are upholstered in that blue fabric you only ever see in offices. He tilts and turns her – jerkily – and she takes in the raised desk, behind which the coroner will sit.

The room waits expectant, like a stage before the entrance of the actors.

But, unlike a play, here the star, the main draw, is absent. More than absent: dead, in fact. Incinerated, ashes, dust.

Louisa yearns for her peaceful room at The Pines – her home for the past three months and for the foreseeable future – with its soft feather cushions, high thread-count sheets, quality sound system: the little personal touches she has been encouraged to add to make her lengthy rehab more homey.

Money, after all, is no object. Not now.

Whatever it takes to make her better, Fiona says, her steely Rottweiler eye glinting. Fiona is now no longer pro bono.

Whatever it takes.

How ironic, though, that she should now consider The Pines – a rehab hospital, the sort of place Sam used to threaten her with – to be her sanctuary. Life surely throws some curve balls.

There will not be a big crowd today. There are very few people for the coroner to ask about Sam. His parents died before she met him, when he was in his twenties. His brother, who lives in Sweden, declined – via Fiona – to come, and Louisa would truly rather die than have her parents anywhere near her.

No. It will just be her, Paul the orderly, Fiona, the coroner and, she supposes, the police.

As good as all alone, then.

She swallows down the taste of self-pity that refluxes into her mouth.

'I'll get us both a cuppa, then, love,' Paul says as he parks her in the accessible space at the front of the bank of blue chairs.

'Lovely, thanks.'

'Bar of choc?'

Louisa shakes her head.

She doesn't like this spot he has put her in. It is overly exposed, and, thanks to the neck support of her chair – five months after the accident she is still troubled by whiplash injuries – she won't be able to turn around and see what's going on behind her. Already her scalp is tingling with the sense of uninvited presences that has plagued her since her time in intensive care, when she wasn't sure which were ghosts flitting around her bed and which real people.

She thinks again about getting to her feet and moving to a 'proper' seat. But Fiona is right. It looks better if she stays down here in the disabled spot, stuck under the coroner's nose, openly displaying the collateral damage, the fallout from Sam's rash and violent impulses.

Doors slam behind her and a shudder runs down her back. Has someone come in?

She tries to imagine herself back in her room at The Pines. She'd be playing music on that sound system. The old, familiar, calming structures of a Bach piano concerto, perhaps. Or, more likely, the *Music to Relax to* Spotify playlist that she has, quite unexpectedly, taken to – meditations in slow guitar, or strings gently plucked to a backdrop of rainfall. Stuff she used to reject as anodyne, soppy.

Great trauma, of course, leaves its mark on a person. Particularly when it involves head injuries and coma. But for it to completely change her taste in music? And it's not just that – the transformation has also extended to food, clothes, books. Everything now points to the comfortable for her: custard, half-hour comedies, soft, fleecy garments, stories with happy endings. Lines that were sharply drawn are now softened. Pen has turned to charcoal.

It's as if she has become a completely different person.

'Two sugars, right, yeah?' Paul says, handing her a cardboard cup of scalding, pale-beige liquid. Yep. She even takes sugar in tea now, something she is trying to give up, because she is trying hard to consolidate her remarkable coma-diet weight loss.

He settles himself beside her and they wait for the others to turn up. The others. What, Louisa wonders, would you call them? Not guests – it's far from a party. Attendees? Witnesses? – Well, there weren't any witnesses except herself, and she's already here. Investigators?

Again, she shudders.

The tea smells faintly of air freshener, though when she sips it all she can taste is the mercy of sweetness. Paul unwraps a KitKat and breaks it into four pieces, which he lays out on his navy trouser leg like fat chocolate matchsticks.

'This room's too brightly lit,' she tells him.

Pushing a whole piece of biscuit into his mouth, he nods in agreement, his sparse, straggly comb-over flopping out of position.

She sighs and looks around. The functional air of this room could bring a person down. Yes, the bureaucratic unpicking of a death may be necessary, but it's so far removed from the reality, the pain that operates on every conceivable level, the stink, the blood, the blackness and horror, that it might as well actually not happen. They might as well all say: well, that's it then; they're dead, it's awful, and there's nothing to be done.

That would be wrong of course. But she is so numb at the moment, she can barely think straight. Grief – or perhaps the drugs they give her to cope with it – has not only changed her predilections, but also the way she constructs logic.

She has lost her husband and – this is the thought she can bear the least – her children. Sometimes she wonders if there is anything left of her.

The doors behind her open again, but the presence of Paul – marshmallow-textured though he is – makes her feel protected. A rustle of tights, a clop of formal high heels, a blast of too much perfume. People take their places around the room and, from the sounds they make, they must be mostly women. Women in tailoring. Louisa must be the only one here in loose-fitting clothes – a long, felted skirt to cover the alarming bolts protruding from her extended shin and a loose, soft tunic on top. It's all about textures and the way they fall when you're in a wheelchair, she reckons, ever the one with an eye for this sort of thing.

'Hiya.' Fiona takes her place beside her and squeezes her hand. Louisa's eyes prick with tears, as they do these days whenever anyone shows her an unasked-for kindness. But she's not going to let herself cry. Not now.

The coroner strides up to her raised desk, her manner as perfunctory as a teacher about to take form time. Fiona has briefed Louisa that Madam likes to keep it as relaxed as possible in this, her domain, over which she reigns absolute. As if to confirm this, she turns and beams at the assembled – what, audience, then? – before smoothing her red tweed skirt and taking her seat. Just before she speaks, she directs a sympathetic glance over at Louisa, which, like Fiona's touch, almost does her in.

She starts the proceedings and calls the detective sergeant who has been working on the case – a sure-footed woman called Pam who has been Louisa's constant point of contact throughout her ordeal. Pam goes through the details that Louisa knows off by heart now: the tyre tracks and skid marks that support the story that Sam forced her car off the road and straight into the tree; the clearly documented and medically recorded history of domestic abuse Louisa suffered at his hands. Louisa closes her eyes and tries once more to breathe the white up inside herself.

DS Pam goes on to outline the forensic evidence found in Sam's study which, though circumstantial, points to the fact that he was, in all probability, responsible for the death of his first wife Katie, who was found bludgeoned to death in a wood at the back of the marital home she refused to leave.

Louisa is certain she hears someone gasp behind her. Who else is here? Why can't she turn and look?

'Is this relevant?' the coroner asks. 'We are here to establish the facts of death.'

'It demonstrates that he was an unstable man prone to violent outbursts. That his death was due, in part, to that.'

The coroner nods and makes a note.

'You OK?' Fiona whispers in Louisa's ear.

Blood roars through her brain. This is not a good sign. Her chest now feels doll-sized, and part of her mind is floating away.

'Is *she* here?' she asks Fiona, who looks around behind where they are sitting.

'Oh, shit,' Fiona says, her brow descending. 'She is.'

'Louisa, are you all right to give us your version of the events?'

The coroner's kindly voice hauls her attention back into the room. She snaps her eyes open and nods. Paul wheels her forward and positions her at the front and to the side, so that she is facing both the coroner and the rest of the room.

And then she sees her: Sophie, sitting at the back of the room, all done up in black, draped crepe, as if *she* were the grieving widow, her dark, hollow eyes boring into her.

It's the first time Louisa has seen her in the flesh since she was in intensive care, and even then, she's not sure if she dreamed that episode – those episodes? – or not. The cruelty of Sophie's ripe belly straining at the fabric of her dress is almost too much for Louisa, when she can no longer even touch her own children. A wave of nausea hits her and she is just about to say that she can't go on when a clerk – another woman, in another suit – bustles over with a bible and swears her in.

'You are Louisa Williams, widow of the deceased?' the

coroner asks in a voice that one might perhaps use on an upset four-year-old.

'Yes,' Louisa says, feeling very much as if she is that child.

'I know you have had the worst of times, and I'm so sorry to put you through this again, my dear. But we have to have it down as a matter of record. Could you just this one last time take us through what happened on that night?'

Fiona stands. 'I have to remind you, madam,' she tells the coroner, 'that my client's recall of events, while better than it was, may well be incomplete due to the head injuries and shock sustained as part of the incident.'

The coroner closes her eyes and nods her assent.

The set of Fiona's shoulders as she turns to sit suggests to Louisa that she is giving Sophie one of her steel-laser looks. But once she is back in her chair, facing towards her, she is all gentle, encouraging smiles. Fortified by this, Louisa takes a deep breath and dives in.

'I was driving my car. We were –' she looks at Fiona, who smiles and nods at her, ' – we were escaping.'

'Escaping?'

Louisa keeps her eyes on Fiona. She must resist the temptation to look up at Sophie. 'I was scared. I was desperate. I was at the end of my tether. We had to get away.'

'How was it that Sam was behind you?'

Louisa closes her eyes and speaks. 'He came home as we were leaving. He – he was chasing us. He'd said many times before that we'd never get away from him. That he'd hound me until I died if I tried to leave him. I should have pulled over. I should have stopped and faced him, turned back, waited for another time . . .'

She has told this story so many times it feels as if it has taken a life of its own. Despite this, she has to stop talking to calm her breath.

14

'Take your time, Louisa,' the coroner says.

Louisa looks up, ready to speak again, but Sophie hooks her gaze, draws one long finger across her throat then points it at Louisa.

Louisa blinks. Her lungs shrink to the size of a foetus's curled fist, and she gasps for air.

The coroner catches her look, follows it, and clocks Sophie. 'What's going on?'

'This is the girlfriend of the deceased,' DS Pam stands and says, every tiny note of her inflection implying that this intruder is an irrelevance.

'I am a person of interest.' Sophie stands, her burning eyes still locked on to Louisa, scorching her like a match on a piece of cellophane. 'She's a liar,' she says. 'Everything she's telling you is a lie. She drove him to it. He was trying to *save* them. Sam would never hurt anyone.'

'This is all nonsense, discredited and irrelevant to the inquest.' Fiona says. 'And I want it on record that this woman has a history of drug abuse, and has served a custodial sentence for perverting the course of justice, wasting police time and possession of Class A substances. Since the accident, she has pursued a vicious social media campaign against my client. I must ask that she is ejected from this court.'

'Yes. I'm aware of what's been going on. Hard to miss it,' the coroner says.

DS Pam makes her way up the steps towards Sophie, followed by two court orderlies.

Louisa, who can barely breathe now, succumbs to a panic which engulfs her, sending a message out to the far parts of her body to shut down.

Sophie stands and puts her hands in the air. 'I'm going. You don't need to touch me. *Don't fucking touch me,*' she shouts as Pam puts out a hand towards her. She turns on her high, spiked, vampish heels and heads out of the room. At the top of the steps, she stops, and gives Louisa one long, last look, and, with her lips, outlines the words:

I'll get you.

Then she is gone.

But the effect is lost on all but Louisa. Everyone else is too busy taking care of the object of Sophie's performance, whose airways have finally shut up shop. Paul produces an oxygen mask from somewhere under the wheelchair and clamps it to her face, but despite his attentions, Louisa cannot find enough air to keep her brain running. As she blacks out, the image of Sophie's crazed expression burns on the back of her eyelids; her mouthed words, translated into a harsh whisper, echo in her head.

The coroner's verdict, Louisa finds out as she comes round from the heavy sedative Paul felt compelled to empty into her veins, is death by misadventure.

Misadventure indeed.

What a grade A, one-hundred-per-cent, undiluted bastard.

Bastard.

4

Three Years Earlier

'Fen Manor. So grand!'

'And, Mrs Louisa Williams, you are now the lady of it all,' Sam says, sweeping her burgeoning figure up into his arms. He carries her across the threshold of their new home, which smells of paint, beeswax, old and new wood.

She relinquishes her bunch of anemones, placing them on the ancient oak console in the hallway, their stems crushed from the tight clutch she had on them all the way from the registry office.

She keeps telling herself that he is a good driver, but he steered the Porsche so furiously down the narrow lanes leading here that she was afraid she would not live to see her new home.

'You're just not used to being a passenger,' he said when he noticed her pale face and knotted hands.

And he has a point. Before him, she had been entirely in the driving seat of her life. Sure, her parents, on pulling their disappearing act, had paid to see her comfortably through art school. They also bought her an apartment in the centre of Bristol, a seeming act of generosity that she knew was, in fact, born out of guilt and designed to keep her away from them. But, apart

17

from that, she has stood on her own two feet since the age of eighteen.

And then, at twenty-four, she met Sam.

She looks up at him in the entrance to their new home. Even two years on since they first met, the sight of him still gives her a rush of pleasure.

'I'm the luckiest woman alive,' she tells him. 'I can't believe all this has happened. From design briefing to this.'

He had come to Paradigm – the Bristol consultancy where she was star designer – for a complete visual identity for his high-tech, app development start-up. From their very first meeting, the chemistry between them encompassed the whole periodic table.

'It's been a long road,' he says. 'But we've got here at last. And now you're mine, to have and to hold, for ever.'

'For ever,' she says, reaching up and kissing him.

The big problem had been Sam's wife at the time, Katie, who hadn't been too pleased. But they were powerless to stop what was happening between them. And then, tragically, poor Katie was removed from the picture.

They're trying to put all that behind them, though. Because now, here she is, Lou – or Louisa, as he prefers to call her – moving right across the country to rural Cambridgeshire to stand beside him, while his booming business, with its fresh, bold logo, typeface and colour ways, marches on to conquer yet more corners of the digital marketplace. And all this after she supported him through the fallout from the horrible, brutal murder of his first wife, the ensuing intrusion and suspicion of the police and, finally, vindication of his pleas of innocence and the dropping of all charges. He wouldn't be able to find anyone else who would love him like she does.

'You like it, yes?' Sam says, breaking away and gesturing at the wooden panels and grand, turning staircase.

'You've done a beautiful job.'

Louisa had been too busy finishing projects at Paradigm, mollifying George her boss about her departure, to have any hands-on involvement in the refurbishment. So, after selecting the architects, she was happy to let him have the reins, so long as he allowed her the occasional glimpse of photographs and drawings. After all, he was on the ground in Cambridgeshire, and she was over in the South West. 'I love it,' she says. 'I love it.'

He takes her hand and leads her further into the house. She feels like some sort of medieval princess in her empire-line cream silk and lace dress, designed to show off the breasts that appeared like a novelty to delight them both the moment she fell pregnant. Her hair, loose, long, thick and blond, decorated with flowers woven into tiny plaits, waves around her shoulders, helping to complete the illusion.

'We're going to be so happy here,' she tells him.

'We are. We deserve this.'

'A fresh start,' she says.

He stops, turns, puts his hands on her shoulders and kisses her on the top of her head. 'A fresh start.'

He flings open a heavy, wooden door to reveal a beautiful, bright room. 'The perfect kitchen for my perfect family.'

A gleaming cream Aga thrums away in the centre of the back wall, complemented by more practical ovens and a gas hob set amongst sleek, streamlined units and clean, Corian work surfaces. It is everything Louisa had hoped for, almost the exact room that, as a child, she saw herself standing in, babies all around, making cakes and presiding over bubbling pots. There's even an armchair to sit in and breastfeed.

'And here . . .' Sam steers her through a door at the far end of the kitchen – 'is your studio!' He stands back to reveal an ultra modern extension on the back of the ancient house – all window and wood and stone, still smelling of fresh plaster.

He has equipped the room with everything she needs, and

it's all top of the range – a 32-inch monitor, large scanner, laser printer, A3 digital drawing pad, Bluetooth this and that, storage, Aeron chair. And, to top it all, the view from the fold-back glass doors is a lake full of bullrushes, giving on to an endless fen, just hazing slightly in the late August afternoon.

'What is it?' Sam says, drawing her to him and wiping away with his thumb the tear that has trickled down her cheek.

'I can't believe it all,' she says. 'It's too perfect.'

'What did I tell you?'

'I know.' She shakes her head.

'You just had to trust me. I didn't want you to worry. George was pushing you too hard.'

She nods. 'He was so cross about me going.'

'It's none of his business. It's your life. Our life.' He puts his hand on her belly. 'Our baby's life.'

Louisa nods. But it had been hard on her boss. He had put so much time and effort into nurturing her. Over the five years she had been with him, he had come to rely on her skills. When she told him she was leaving, he had made her an offer which, had she not had Sam's bright future to play a part in – and the whole poor Katie business to escape – she would have found impossible to refuse.

But she has always tried to do things to the best of her ability, and she wants to do this motherhood section of her life as perfectly as she did the rising designer part. And, through almost no effort of her own, everything has fallen into place.

'Come on, just one glass won't hurt,' Sam says, popping a bottle of ready chilled champagne he has pulled from the fridge.

Louisa puts one hand on her belly, holds up her free index finger and shakes her head.

'Better not to touch a drop,' she says.

'Just wet your lips, then,' he says, handing her a tulip stemmed glass, half full.

She puts it to her pregnancy-sensitive nostrils. It smells, well, delicious. She takes one tiny sip, closes her eyes and lets the bubbles play on her tongue before guiltily swallowing.

Her heart rockets, fuelled by instant doubt. What if she has ruined her baby, after seven months of perfect eating and drinking? What if this one sip short-circuits the nervous system, blasts some tiny part of the DNA, malforms?

Stop thinking this, she tells herself. Stop it.

Sam, who has downed his glass, gives himself a refill and leads her through another door into the vast living room.

'The wedding presents!' she says, running towards the pile of beautifully wrapped gifts stacked around the fireplace.

A frown flickers across his forehead. 'We're not opening them until tomorrow, remember, Louisa? You're supposed to be admiring the work I've done on the house at the moment.' He smiles.

'Sorry. It's lovely, of course. And there's my trophy cabinet!'

'And there's your trophy cabinet.'

'Thank you. I know it doesn't really go with the scheme, but it means so much . . .'

He lifts his hand and brushes it aside. It's just a minor detail to him, so long as it makes her happy, and she loves him for that. 'Downstairs living rooms knocked together as instructed,' he goes on. 'So that we can all live with each other. No shutting away into little boxes.'

'Not like how I grew up.'

'Not how you grew up.'

'The opposite! There'll be no TV,' she says, starting the game they have played throughout her pregnancy.

'Interested parents.'

'Home schooling.'

'Well, let's see about that – you may be too busy with work, though. Umm . . . home-cooked meals.'

'Lively discussions at the dinner table.'

'Long country walks.'

'Parents who aren't alcoholics, or handy with their fists, or emotionally abusive.'

'Careful now, Louisa. Positives, remember?'

'OK, then. Errr . . . ponies when they're older – like my Star. But our children won't need their ponies for emotional support.'

'No. They'll just love their ponies because they're lovely ponies, lucky kids.'

'Lucky kids.'

'Lucky us.' He presses his nose against hers, and they absorb this picture of the new life they are going to build for themselves here, in this house.

She tries not to allow the thought, but it keeps popping up in her mind: if there's one consolation to be had from Katie's death, it's that it made all this possible.

She kisses her new husband. He smells delicious, of Eau Sauvage and champagne, with a faint, minty note on his breath. Their eyes meet; they smile.

'OK, then, Mrs Williams,' he says, his voice low. 'Let me show you the rest of your domain.'

Taking her by the hand, he leads her upstairs.

He shows her, briefly, the nursery: just one of the four children's rooms, waiting to be filled. But right now, they have exhausted their interest in interior decor and nest building.

He opens the door to the vast master bedroom, which is built on top of the studio extension. She pushes him back onto the bed and, still in her cream silk and lace, undoes his fly buttons and straddles him, laying claim, christening the room.

Much later, among tangled sheets and discarded finery, she wakes to full moonlight flooding through a roof that she now sees is mostly made of glass. The sky is velvety black, punctuated by stars so much brighter than she knew back in Bristol.

Quietly, so as not to disturb her new husband, who lies like some auburn Greek hero on the good linen sheets, she picks her way out of the bed and, naked and round as a puffball, tiptoes out into the hall and sits at the top of the stairs, where she can see out of a high window onto the blue-shadowed field beyond. All she can hear is the tick of the clock in the hall and, from time to time, the hoot of an owl, somewhere out there in the warm summer night.

This is peace, she thinks. This is my haven.

5

Now

Red.

Sophie slams into her bedroom in her high heels, kneels in front of the shrine and keens, a flood of scarlet washing up through her so that she is certain that, any minute now, she will start crying blood.

'*Fuck* Louisa. *Fuck* the police. *Fuck* that fucking ambulance chaser Fiona.'

As she spits out her litany, she fixes her eyes on the centrepiece, the one photograph she has of herself and Sam, taken on her phone as they lay in bed in this room.

There were other images – more explicit, more sexual – but they were all on his phone, and that went up in flames with him, in the car, so they are lost to her. She loves this picture though, because of its simplicity and innocence. It reminds her that there was more between them than just that extraordinary sex. He's lying on his back, his arm around her, his head angled towards her, his gaze one of adoration. She laughs up at the camera as she holds it above them both. Yes, she used to laugh. She knew then how to be happy, and – unlike Louisa ever did – how to make *him* happy.

She knew so well how to make him happy. They were so good together.

After he died – or, as she likes to put it, after Louisa drove him to his death – she had the picture printed out and framed. Sitting on a small round table covered with an Alexander McQueen skulls headscarf, it now forms the central point of this corner of her bedroom, the area she has devoted to what might have been. Among the items arranged around it are the last red roses he brought her – now crisp, browned, disintegrating, and the coiled-up leather straps she liked to use on him. A ticket for the one film they saw together lies next to the bottle of Eau Sauvage he kept here to cover up the smell of her when he left.

Sophie opens the scent, dabs it on her pulse points, inhales the lavender and citrus and wood. It calms her. For one second, it almost brings him back.

But it doesn't, of course.

Nothing will bring him back.

Closing her eyes and saying her own atheist prayer – because she, more than anyone, knows there cannot be any God – she puts the bottle back in its place.

She lights a stick of incense and sets it in a holder at the front of the shrine and breathes in the sweet smoke. Her feet tingling with pins and needles from kneeling, she levers her foreign, inhabited body upwards, and staggers backwards towards the bed, bringing the photograph with her. This baby inside her is the surprise gift he left her – on his last night on earth, if the dates are anything to go by. It means that she is special, that she will always have a part of him.

She pulls her smart shoes off her complaining feet. Four-inch Manolos are hard work when your body is carrying extra weight. It's a novel experience, this roundness. Until now, she has always been effortlessly slim, elegant, catlike. For her brief yet successful modelling career, it defined her, made her. It was also her undoing. Scouted at fifteen, she morphed too early from Mancunian council estate Sharon to huskily well-bred

Sophie, earning more money in a week than her alcoholic, unemployed old dad saw in a year, and all for being photographed in glamorous clothes in exotic locations. It was all lovely, until, like all fairy tales – and, she's coming to believe, bloody everything in her life – it went wrong. In her case, the big bad wolf was the celebrated middle-aged man – The Photographer – who raped her repeatedly until she was eighteen and so addicted to the cocaine he fed her that she gave up resisting him.

'I ballsed it up at your inquest,' she tells Sam's photo.

She had planned to go in there all ablaze and say her piece, defend her man. But the moment she set foot in that horrible, formal room, she had frozen. All she could remember was the humiliation of standing up in a different court, aged nineteen, to hear all her former so-called friends and colleagues provide character references to support The Photographer against her allegations.

Her mistake back then had been that, in a moment of sore lucidity, she had gone into a police station and reported him for the abuse she had suffered. The ensuing trial turned out to be hers though, not his, the charge perverting the course of justice, with the juicy addition of possession of a quantity of cocaine. After standing in court for two hours of humiliation and tellings-off, she was made a high-profile example and sent down – via a phalanx of snapping flashbulbs – for two years. Because of her offence – supposedly lying about being raped – the other inmates, who, to a woman, it seemed, had suffered some sort of sexual abuse of their own, viewed her as a stuck-up, spoiled little falsifying bleater who devalued their own experiences. Her policy had been to stay out of their way by hiding in her bed. This often worked, but not always, and then violence was meted out. But it did mean that her sentence was reduced to one year for good behaviour.

'No one believed me then. No one believes me now. I'm

useless, Sam, and I'm sorry.' Her reputation goes before her: she is a beautiful madwoman, an unreliable witness.

She knows that, if he could answer, Sam would tell her she's talking rubbish, that she's better than all that. When they met here in Cambridge – where she had come after prison to get away from her old haunts to start a new, cleaned-up life – she confided in him that her dream was to be a lawyer, to support women like herself, to stop more injustices happening. Instead of laughing at her as she had feared, he had been amazed, brilliant. He even supported her through college – where she had to start with the GCSEs she failed to take at sixteen – so that she didn't have to work behind a bar, as she was doing when they first met.

When he died, she was moving on to A levels. But she has jacked in all her courses now. The untouched books sit on a shelf in the living room. Grieving, pregnant: how could she think of going on? Another bit of wreckage of her life.

Another piece of hope Louisa stole from her.

The red rises again.

She massages the cramp from her toes. Along with the vintage YSL crepe jacket worn over a Moschino shift that stretches neatly over her bump, the shoes had been a currency, a tactic for the inquest. She had looked fucking serious, not to be fucked with. It was the sort of outfit she imagined herself wearing in court, had she managed to become a lawyer.

But she blew it today. She clammed up. In that poisonous setting, her grief at losing Sam – still raw and bloody after just five months – coupled with her desire to see Louisa annihilated, overwhelmed her. And then that policewoman said something about some bullshit evidence proving that Sam murdered his first wife.

Bringing that up again.

'They've always been desperate to frame you for that,' she says to Sam's picture. 'And now you can't argue with them, poor love; they want to get their hooks into you again. I tried to speak out, but that Fiona started on about my past. She made me out to be worse than a piece of shit on her shoe.'

She had been a fool to think that she would have been taken seriously in that room full of dull women in cheap tailoring, with their clean hands and their clipped nails, all creaming themselves with sympathy for poor Louisa, all looking out for Poor Tragic Louisa. Not one of them is considering for one moment what happened to *her*, Sophie.

And with that thought of Louisa, the swell of anger bursts. She had it all, Louisa did. The man, the house, the children, the money, even the looks – or so Sam said, although it was hard to see them under all the blubber.

Louisa all but pushed Sam away. Was it any wonder he found his way into Sophie's slender, toned arms, which were, as he pointed out to her on several occasions, made for wrapping around him, pinning him down in bed.

Yes. *She* held *him* down. For the first time in her chequered sexual history, she was in control. After the shit and the fallout from her nightmare in fashion, Sophie had been *so close* to her first ever chance of happiness – to being with Sam, in that beautiful house in the countryside. She would have made a wonderful wife, the third-time-lucky Mrs Williams. And she would have looked fantastic, too, in a retro fifties pinny and little else, the little baby at her feet, her briefcase full of worthy, knotty case files in her study.

Maid in the living room, cook in the kitchen, whore in the bedroom. With the piquant addition of tiger in the courtroom, Sophie had been so ready for her Jerry Hall moment.

And then instead she went all limp kitten at the inquest.

What a failure.

She has to do better.

Taking her own cue, she stretches over to her bedside table and picks up her iPad. Time to get to work, patrolling the

Internet for mentions of Louisa, using her multiple online identities to put the truth across, to help the world to see events from her point of view, the point of view of truth, the point of view of the woman who really loved and knew Sam. It's working, too. She has already garnered a generous handful of replies supporting her and condemning Louisa. And not from people who know her or Louisa, but complete strangers who can view the facts objectively – about how Louisa is just making Sam out to be the bad guy, about how he couldn't have done the things they accuse him of doing. It all makes so much sense to Sophie, and she is beyond enraged that the police, the judiciary, the solicitors, the doctors, the nurses, the press and a large, insensate slab of the general public just don't see it, that they discredit her point of view just because of some stupid mistakes she made in the past.

She loves Sam.

She loved Sam.

She will go to the ends of the earth to salvage his name. For him, for his baby growing inside her.

For herself.

Evidence pointing to him killing his first wife?

Smashing his second wife and children into a tree?

She cannot believe it of him. She will not.

He is her faith.

Too agitated to sit still, she casts the iPad to one side, stands, tiptoes her stockinged feet to stretch them out, and reaches down one of the many identical *Cambridge Evening News* front pages pegged to the washing line cordoning off her shrine corner from the rest of the bedroom.

MY LIFE OF HELL: TRAGIC LOUISA TELLS ALL, the headline shrieks.

'Tragic fucking Louisa,' she says, as usual, addressing the accompanying photograph.

The headline taunts. The image – a close-up of Louisa's

miserable, bloated, bruised doll-face, taken shortly after she woke up from the coma – mocks. Sophie bought every copy she could find. Her supply, while diminished, is still quite sufficient for a good few more of these moments.

'Liar,' she says to Louisa's lost eyes on the cover.

'Bitch,' she says, as she tears the photograph from its nest of viper words.

'Cunt.'

She reaches Sam's Zippo lighter from the shrine, from its place beside the last bag of tobacco she and he had shared that very night, the night of the crash.

Holding Louisa's picture by its corner, as if it were contaminated, she lights the part furthest from her fingers. As usual, it takes immediately, and the flames lick upwards, consuming those puffy, poached-egg features, which, after extensive study, look to Sophie like those of an over-inflated Barbie sex doll.

She doesn't like to admit it, but Louisa looked better than that today – she has lost weight, started taking care of herself. She has the air now of a shabby Marilyn Monroe. It all reeks of insincerity.

She holds the paper until the flames burn her fingers and she is forced to drop it to the already scorched carpet. She doesn't care. She has no reason to be maid, cook or whore any more.

Or shit-hot lawyer.

She stamps out the flames, singeing her feet through her sheer Lycra stockings.

If it weren't for the baby, and the possibility of revenge, she'd lie down in the middle of it and let it all burn.

6

'Don't look at it,' Fiona says, her pale-blue eyes stern under her blond crop.

Louisa tries to shift her gaze, but the iPad remains firmly on the lectern on her over-bed table, the *Daily Mail* article about the inquest and verdict in full view, drawing her to it like light to a dark star. The press have been all-night partying with the new evidence, which, in the weeks since the inquest, has been made public – the bloody shirt, found hidden in Sam's study in Fen Manor, which proves beyond reasonable doubt that he not only tried to kill his second wife, but that he also, in all likelihood, murdered his first. They love it, of course they do.

So poor Katie's photograph – captioned *His First Victim* – appears above a picture of Louisa being wheeled away from the coroner's office, headed *Tragic Louisa Williams*. That prefix has been applied to her name so many times that she should probably add it to her passport.

All this intrusion into the tragedies of Louisa's life would be painful enough, but it is the comments below the line that stab her most viciously. She should have got used to them by now, should have done as Fiona has told her time and time again and stopped looking. But still, the poisonous lies, the hundreds of vile green arrows, the upward-pointing 'likes' for the most toxic remarks – those blaming everything on her rather than him, supposing she must have goaded him into it, stating that she was a drunkard, a terrible mother, self-centred and vindictive – cave her in. Making a monster of the victim is a popular sport, particularly when she's a woman.

She looks through the window at her view of a green meadow and a river. The sight often – but not unfailingly – helps her find peace. She has the best room, with the most stunning outlook The Pines can offer. It is also the most expensive, of course.

'How can so many people be so mean?' she asks Fiona. She doesn't know if she'll ever be able to face the world outside these walls again.

'They're not talking about the children in the press, though,' Fiona says. 'I've nipped all that in the bud.'

Louisa winces at the mention of Poppy and Leon. She can bear all of this horror but that, and Fiona knows it. She has locked thought and mention of them far away in the darkest corner of her mind, and the only way she can cope is by not being reminded.

'Sorry,' Fiona says.

'No,' Louisa tells her. 'I know, and thank you.'

'Sophie's got to be behind at least half of these comments,' Fiona says. 'And the rest are just other lonely, vicious, libellous shits. My team pick up on everything iffy, so it'll all be taken down within the hour.'

'What about Katie's sister?' Louisa says, taking the weekly gossip magazine from underneath the iPad and holding it up in front of Fiona's face. '"I'll Never Believe My Sister's Husband Was Her Murderer"? We can't un-print this. Old Lucy always had a soft spot for Sam, even when she was getting at him for "abandoning Katie" and "running off" with me. She always had it in for me, and I'll bet Sophie's got in touch with her and wangled herself into her favour.'

Fiona takes the magazine from her and looks at it. 'Who brought this in for you?'

'One of the care assistants.'

Fiona shakes her head. 'I didn't want you to see this. We're taking care of it. We've got the rest of Katie's family publicly disowning Lucy. I pointed out to them that if they didn't step up, their compensation from Sam's estate would be in question.'

Louisa shakes her head.

'And to hammer it home,' Fiona goes on, 'we've arranged for an exclusive interview in next week's issue of this particularly shitty little rag. It was that, or libel, I told the editor. The mother, father and brother are being paid three times more than Lucy got to put their side of the story: "I Knew My Son-in-law Was a Bad 'Un", et cetera. They've done very well out of it.'

'And Lucy took money for calling me a liar. What a cow.'

'People do the strangest things.'

'I don't know why she said that. He was a monster, Fi.'

'I know. You had a lucky escape.' Fiona squeezes Louisa's hand, then moves across the room and drops the magazine in the wastebasket.

'Lucky.' Louisa gloomily looks out at her view.

The two women have grown close over the past few months. So much so that Louisa has to remind herself from time to time that every moment Fiona spends with her is charged in fifteen-minute units.

She refreshes the view on the iPad and grimaces. 'Yet more comments. Sophie would need to make multiple accounts to do all this, have hundreds of email addresses.'

'And you don't think she's obsessed enough to do that?'

Louisa frowns.

'Of course she is,' Fiona goes on. 'She's mentally unstable. She's taken too many drugs, been in too much trouble, to remain sane. Sophie is a mess, an irrelevance.'

'A nasty irrelevance.'

Fiona presses the button on the iPad and dissolves the *Daily*

Mail. 'You don't have to look at this, either, you know. Look: don't worry about her. Soon all this will blow over and the trolls will be on to the next scandal, and even if Sophie does carry on, in all likelihood no one will be bothered. We've kept her physically away from you since that time in the ICU. And there's no way she can get at you here.'

'I know,' Louisa says. 'No better security than in a rehab unit where the other half of the occupants are sectioned.'

'We've removed you from Google, and we're on to her on Facebook and Twitter, closing down every account she tries to open.'

'I know.' Louisa closes her eyes. Fiona always makes it sound so easy, reducing pain down to bullet points.

'I could push for a restraining order so she can't get at you when you leave this place,' Fiona says.

Louisa smiles weakly. 'No, Fi. I don't want to put her back up any more. You're right. I don't have to read all this.' She gestures at the iPad. 'I just want to draw a line under it and move on.'

Fiona raises her eyebrows and inclines her head. Louisa knows she can see her point, even though clearly she is dying to get her lawyer's teeth into Sophie.

'If I ever get out of this place—' Louisa says.

'Which you will,' Fiona says, squeezing her hand.

'If I get out of here, I don't want to see her ever again. Likewise, I don't want people pointing out Tragic Louisa Williams while I'm in a shop, or when I'm having my hair cut. I don't want to be reminded, every road I walk down – if this leg ever mends and I'm *able* to walk – of what went before, what happened, what has become of me. I don't want people finding out.'

Fiona looks at her hands and nods.

'If I mean to go on—'

'Which you do . . .'

34

'Which I do, I need to make a completely clean start. Somewhere new, somewhere anonymous, where no one knows who I am.'

She revives the iPad and brings up the page she has bookmarked, with the pictures of the apartment she has found – a set of square rooms on the thirteenth floor of The Heights, a listed modernist block in Central London just south of the Thames, all concrete and steel and glass and light.

Fiona eyes the images. 'Well, that would be a change, for sure.'

'It's got a shared pool, gym and steam room, too.'

'Nice. Good for your physical therapy.'

'I want to sell Fen Manor. And I want to put an offer in on this place.' Louisa taps the screen with her index finger.

Fiona squints at the asking price. 'You don't need to sell up to buy this.'

Louisa knows this only too well. No doubt believing he was immortal, Sam died intestate. However much he wished to hurt her when he was alive, upon his death – after taking care of the necessaries – all his money, his business and his property came to her. Acting on her instructions, Fiona has already disposed of the company. When it comes to cash Louisa is, therefore, mercurially liquid.

'I just want shot of the place,' she says. 'And I want to live there, in the middle of the city, where there are so many people, I won't even be seen.'

'Sounds like a plan.' Fiona can't quite hide, however, a look on her face that suggests she isn't convinced it's necessarily the *right* plan.

Louisa forges on, regardless. 'I'll go back to my old name and no one will ever bother me about all this again.'

'Can't we just get a nice little restraining order put in place, just in case? Belt and braces?'

Louisa shakes her head.

'OK. I hear what you're saying. But we need to keep her quiet, or she could keep on resurfacing for ever.'

'We do.'

'So the other way is to do a deal,' Fiona says. Sometimes Louisa can almost hear the cogs turning in her lawyer's brain.

'What sort of deal?'

'We – I mean you – let her stay in the Cambridge flat until, say, her baby is six months old.'

'What?'

'No, hear me out. Sophie has to keep quiet or we throw her out on the street. Plus you have the PR advantage of having been incredibly, blood-lettingly generous. Tragic Louisa becomes Noble Louisa. Letting her late husband's lover—'

'I'd hardly call her that,' Louisa says, her mouth tight.

Fiona smiles. 'OK, bit on the side, then, floozy—'

'Whore.'

'Yes, that, if you like. Letting his whore stay in your flat until she has her baby and it's old enough for her to stick it in a nursery so she can bloody well go out and find herself a job.'

Louisa frowns.

'OK, so I can see you're not convinced. And yes. That woman has made your recovery a hundred times more hellish than it had to be.'

'And she caused all the grief in the first place.'

'She played her part,' Fiona says. 'But you have to remember that it was mainly down to Sam, wasn't it? Look what happened with Katie. He was bad from the get-go.'

'So the idea is that if I go ahead with this plan, I'm not only watching my own back, but I'm also showing myself to be good. Putting some goodness back into the world.'

'After everything Sam did to you and the children—'

Louisa draws away sharply, closes her eyes. 'I don't want to talk about the children.'

Fiona touches her arm. 'Yes. I know. I'm sorry.'

36

Louisa nods.

'Look,' Fiona goes on, holding Louisa's hand, her voice taking on an uncharacteristically gentler tone, 'it's a win-win. We make it clear to her what the deal is, how long she's got, and you're away.'

'And if she doesn't go when the baby's six months?'

'We'll evict her. She'll technically be a squatter if she's staying there without your permission.'

'And you'll make sure that she has no idea where I've gone or what I'm doing?' Louisa says. 'I don't want her to come anywhere near me. She scares me.'

'She scares me, too.'

Louisa looks at her steely lawyer. 'I can hardly believe that.'

'No,' Fiona says. 'There's something . . . I don't know, chaotic, unbalanced about her. I've seen it in some of the criminal-division clients. You wouldn't want to get too close.'

'You certainly wouldn't.'

'Don't worry. We can make sure she'll never come anywhere near you.' Fiona takes the iPad from Louisa and scrutinises the property particulars. 'I'd better get our property department to step up on this apartment, then.'

Louisa looks at Fiona and wonders if she is paying her enough.

'And if she ever does contact you, you have to let me know, yes?' Fiona tells her.

Louisa nods.

She *is*, of course, paying her enough. More than enough.

7

'But she can't do this,' Sophie says, scarlet still simmering under her normal pallor.

The Women's Advice Centre volunteer, whose nametag proclaims her to be Jenna Smith, looks up from the letter Sophie flung at her as she thundered into the side office in a cloud of YSL Opium, late pregnancy hormones and high dudgeon.

'I'm afraid she can,' Jenna Smith says, waving the piece of paper. 'The flat is not yours. You have no legal right to it. It was part of her late husband's estate, and, since he died intestate, she inherited it.'

'I can read,' Sophie says, unimpressed by the woman's attempt at sounding as if she knows her legal shit when, in fact, she is just parroting that Fiona broomstick-up-the-arse solicitor's jargon. Jenna Smith's is the kind of job she would have been doing, had she been able to stick with the education plan, except that Sophie would have been doing it properly, paid, rather than volunteering in a dump like this.

She folds her arms over her massive, taut belly which, right now, feels like it could burst any second. For a second she pictures it doing so, and showering Jenna Smith with amniotic mush.

She will not cry, she tells herself, biting the inside of her cheeks, setting her jaw in a grimly straight line. 'So basically, she's just going to throw me out when my baby's six months old, and there's nothing I can do about it?'

'That's more or less it.'

Sophie had thought that coming here she might get a bit of sympathy. She wouldn't dream of going somewhere regular, like Citizens' Advice, or the council or some lawyer who was going to charge her more money than she possesses just to talk. She thought it would be different here, but no. She looks at Jenna's chubby po-face. Even the Women's Advice Centre, with all their batik wall hangings and spider plants, are just The Man in feminist disguise.

'So. Sophie Hanley. I'll put my cards on the table,' Jenna Smith goes on, in her irritatingly Antipodean accent. 'I know who you are.'

'Yes?'

'And I know who Louisa Williams, the owner of the flat, is.'

Sophie looks at her with the air of a sullen teenager.

'It's unavoidable,' Jenna says, 'with it being all over the papers and all. And you were pretty well known, too, weren't you, before you got put away? And you're still, well, *identifiable*.'

'What do you mean by that?'

'Well, you do have a, shall we say, distinctive look, Sophie.'

'You think so, *Jenna*?' Compared to her with her short hair, lumpy body enclosed in a shapeless jumper and baggy jeans, then yes, possibly she does. 'Why, thank you.'

'Off the record.' Jenna sits back and folds her arms, as if she is attempting to mirror Sophie's posture. 'Given the circs, I think Louisa's being more than fair. You've got six months after the birth of your –' she nods towards Sophie's drum-taut abdomen, as if she can't bear to say the word baby – 'which should be plenty of time to find alternative accommodation. She's not even asking you for rent.'

'It's my home,' Sophie says, her voice low. 'He bought it for *me* to live in.'

Jenna shrugs.

'It's not fair.'

Jenna looks at her, one eyebrow raised. 'Fairness. I'm not going to mention anything about what you did to Louisa.'

Sophie lifts her head and meets her look, a dangerous glint in her eyes.

'I mean. It's clear he was straight-up guilty,' Jenna goes on. 'Mowing down his wife and two children. And what he did to his first wife, too.' She shudders.

'Oh, he told you all about it, did he?' Sophie says, her tone horribly calm.

'No, but—'

'Then how can you say all that with such certainty?' Sophie adds.

'The police thought so, didn't they? What with how Louisa said he'd made her lie for him about the alibi, and how he kept the shirt with the first wife's blood on it to threaten her, remind her what she had coming if she stepped out of line.'

'"Louisa"? It's as if you're best girlfriends,' Sophie says. 'So you know her, then?'

Jenna flushes. Of course she doesn't know her. The case has been the subject of so much gossip and press that if someone says 'Louisa', everyone knows they mean Tragic Louisa Williams. Sophie could kick herself for coming here and thinking she would get sympathy. Of course, at this Women's Advice Centre they'd be on Louisa's side, the side of the 'victim of domestic abuse'. Everyone's all #IamLouisa.

'Sam would never have harmed anyone,' Sophie says.

'Really?'

'He was a good man. She made it all up about him hurting her.'

'And you know this, because . . . ?'

'He told me.'

'Right.' Jenna thins her lips.

Sophie crosses her catwalk long legs and eyes the woman in front of her. 'Should you really be passing opinions here? Is that really in your remit, Jenna Smith? Is this the "impartial advice to all women" you go on about in those stickers you slap in pub toilets around town? What are you going to do about helping me with my housing situation? Or are you going to refuse me because you have some all-to-cock ideas about what my boyfriend got up to, based on the lies of his mad bitch wife?'

Jenna holds Sophie's gaze, but she only lasts a couple of seconds. With the pink thread veins in her cheeks all ablaze, she turns towards her monitor and clicks the mouse a couple of times. 'The local council has a duty to assist you with housing because you're a young, lone, pregnant woman with no means of income.'

'You make me sound so pathetic.'

Jenna throws Sophie a blank look then returns her heavily hooded eyes to her monitor.

'Age?'

'Twenty-two,' Sophie says.

'Baby's due?'

'Four weeks' time.'

'How would you describe your current housing situation?' Jenna reels the list off in a monotone. 'Council tenant; housing association tenant; shared ownership; private tenant; tied home or renting with job; supported housing; sheltered housing; residential care home; hospital; prison; probation hostel; direct access hostel; B and B; short life; any other temp housing; children's home; living with family; staying with friends or sleeping rough?'

'None of those.'

'Got to put something.'

'Prison?'

Jenna adopts a long-suffering look. 'Staying with friends?'

'Huh. Hardly.'

'I can't help you unless you help yourself and co-operate, Sophie.'

'Can't you, Jenna?'

'I'll put staying with friends. Do you have any savings?'

'What's it to you?' Sophie doesn't, in fact, have a bean. The thousands she earned when she was modelling all went up her nose, and she has just scraped the barrel of what she put aside from the generous allowance Sam paid her to save her from having to continue working as bar staff. But there's no way she's going to let this dull pudding know that.

Jenna returns to her screen with an air of enforced patience. 'Do you receive any benefits?'

Sophie shakes her head. She wants to tell Jenna to fuck off, and walk away now. She shouldn't have to be in this situation. There's another woman sitting typing in the main office, a Jenna lookalike – her girlfriend, probably – who gawped as she directed Sophie into this horrible, depressingly functional side room. She's certain to be listening in, earwigging and shaking her unattractively shorn head in disapproval.

'What do you live on?'

'Not that it's any of your business, but I sell my old dresses.'

Jenna raises an eyebrow and types something. 'You should claim benefits. You're eligible for fifty-seven pounds and sixty pence per week income support, and when the baby is born, you'll get twenty pounds seventy per week on top of that. And there are a few other special benefits you'd be able to claim as well, Healthy Start, Sure Start, Maternity Grant.'

Fifty-seven pounds and sixty pence a week. Someone's taking the piss. Sophie shakes her head, vehemently. 'I'm not doing that.' She swore, the moment she walked away from her parents' council house, that she would never, ever be like them, sponging off the state; that she'd stand on her own two feet. 'All I want to do is find out if she can actually do this to me, kick me out of the home that was bought for me in good faith by the father of my child, who she drove to his death.'

Jenna looks at her. 'That's not how it was, Sophie.' She's speaking with that exaggerated patience primary school teachers use when they talk to a lying, naughty child.

Sophie flares her nostrils. 'No?'

'It's not how the courts saw it.'

'What the fuck do they know?'

'Could you please mind your language?'

'What the hell *is* this place?'

Jenna removes her hand from her mouse, her gaze from her monitor. 'Sophie. You have to help me out here. There are things that can be done. The Local Authority can help you find a council flat, or private rented accommodation, or a housing association place. All this is possible. You could sign on and get enough money to live modestly with your baby. You need to think about your baby.'

'I do think about my baby. All the fucking time. I just don't want to be doing with all that form filling and prying and telling people all about myself. I've had enough of it.'

Jenna holds up her hands. 'I take it the father is the guy who died in the car crash?'

'Of course he fucking is. Is that my fault? Why should my baby suffer because she drove him to his—'

Jenna interrupts, waving Fiona's letter at Sophie. 'And it says here that he died intestate.'

Sophie nods, sharply.

Jenna turns back to her monitor and mouse, and scrolls and clicks.

'What?' Sophie says.

'Hold on . . .' Jenna says. 'Yes. Thought so.'

'What?'

'If you can prove the child's father is – what was his name, Samuel Williams?'

'Sam, yes, of *course* it's him.'

'If you can prove that, your baby could be due a portion of his estate.'

'What?' Sophie's eyes widen.

'It says here: "If the person dying intestate has a surviving spouse and no children, their estate passes to their spouse in its entirety."'

'And . . . ?' Sophie says. 'So?'

'"If the person has a surviving spouse and children" – and that means any children, not just the children he had with his spouse – "the spouse receives the first two hundred and fifty thousand pounds and then the balance of the estate is divided into two. One half of the remaining balance passes to the spouse absolutely and the other half of the remaining balance passes to issue on statutory trusts."'

'What the fuck does that mean?'

'It means your baby would inherit. There would be conditions, but you would be able to access cash in order to house, clothe and feed the child as he or she grows up.'

'Seriously?'

'If you can prove paternity, and if you can fund the legal process to challenge the spouse's inheritance.'

Big ifs. 'And if I can find Louisa, who seems to have disappeared from the face of the earth.'

Jenna shrugs. 'You'll be able to find her. You've certainly shown your ability to persist in the way you've hounded her since the accident.'

Sophie looks at her. 'Why are you helping me, if you disapprove of me so much?'

'Because,' Jenna says, now looking directly at Sophie, 'I don't want your baby to suffer any more than it has to.'

'Having a mother like me, you mean?'

Jenna says nothing.

'I'll get out of your hair, then,' Sophie says, levering herself and her belly to a standing position.

'You'll need representation.' Jenna turns to a shelf of neatly filed leaflets behind her and pulls out a Law Society pamphlet on finding a solicitor. 'And don't forget this.' She picks up Fiona's letter and holds out the bundle of papers for Sophie.

'Thanks, but no thanks.' Sophie turns and moves out of the office. She doesn't need Jenna's bloody leaflet or that Fiona's poxy letter. She's not going to play around with all the bastards. It's never done her any good in the past.

No. She'll do things her way.

8

Six Months Later

Eyes shut, Lou stretches out in her bed, thrusting her toes against the sticky, hot sheet, and her arms up above her head. Some bones still hurt, tendons remain tighter than they should be, but the novelty of simply drawing her body to its full horizontal length reminds her that, given time, some things do heal.

She pushes herself against the wall of window alongside her bed in her new, thirteenth-floor London apartment. But instead of meeting the expected blackout blinds, her surprised naked flesh finds glass.

Now she remembers: in the night, half-asleep, barely able to breathe in the heat, she pinged the blinds up in a futile attempt to draw some fresh air into the room.

The glass feels good. It's not cold, but it's cooler than her body. She stays there for a few moments, eyes still shut, front pressed against the window, listening to the morning traffic as it begins to clog the arterial roads that circle her building. A train rattles by on tracks just fifty metres away from her window, metal clanking on metal, full, no doubt, of bleary-eyed commuters. She looked down at them this time yesterday. They're the early ones, who sit staring at little handheld displays, bound for days staring at bigger desktop screens.

Soon that will be her heading off to work like that, but not yet. Not for a week or so.

Today, she tells herself – as she has been taught by her therapists at The Pines – is the first day of the rest of her life. Even if all it promises is another fourteen hours of cleaning, sorting and unpacking, today holds hope for the future.

Finally, she starts to peel her eyelids open. It takes a moment. Stuck down through dehydration, they are also red and swollen from the dust in the apartment, dust left – along with general filth, a chicken carcass in the oven, a turd in the toilet and a tenacious stench of stale curry – by the tenants she had to evict in order to move in.

They were angry with her, and, in a way, it was understandable. But it's her place. She owns it. It's not too much, surely, to ask for a space for yourself in the world?

Like a gaunt, flapping crow, the image of the tenant she has yet to evict from the Cambridge flat swoops through Lou's brain. She consoles herself with the thought that in two months this issue will be out of her life completely. Then that will be that. The ploy of kindness seems to have worked. As far as she knows, Sophie has been quiet. But then again, Lou has followed Fiona's instructions and no longer looks at newspapers, TV or the Internet, so if her old enemy is still kicking off, she remains blissfully ignorant.

'Forget about her,' she says, quelling the nausea that rises at the thought of this girl who, repeatedly, kicked her when she was down. 'She's history.'

One eye open.

It meets dazzling sun in a hot blue sky, on a morning which is already touching thirty degrees, even though it's not yet seven and it is only April. Yes, it's really, really, weirdly hot.

Two eyes open.

And then she sees him.

In a nanosecond she's bolt upright, reaching for the sheet,

pulling it up around her spilling breasts, her scarred front, her limping, dented legs.

There is a long-haired man, a boy – a man? – and he's standing about twenty feet outside her window, hovering in the sky like some sort of walking Jesus. Or an angel. Unlike any celestial or biblical being, however, he is holding a small video camera. Thankfully, it's not pointing at her – at least, not now. But his eyes are. He is looking right at her. The expression on his face reveals as much shock as she feels. It's as if he had expected her to lie still for ever, like some sleeping princess. She doesn't linger on the eye contact, despite the part of her brain that has already registered that this boy, man, Jesus, angel – devil? – is possibly the most beautiful human she has ever seen.

On pure reflex, she is out of her bedroom, across the hall and locked in the bathroom, where there are, thankfully, no windows. The hum of the extractor fan completes her seal against the outside world.

She sits, the sweaty sheet wound around her, on the closed toilet lid. Shutting her eyes, she puts her hands over her ears so that all she can hear is the thump of the blood rushing around her head. It has been a while since she saw things that weren't there. She had thought, what with the drugs and the therapy, the anti-anxiety training and mindfulness, that this was one of the uncomfortables that she could tuck away in that place called the past.

'Yeah, right,' she says, her voice echoing inside her skull.

She takes a few minutes – no, more like fifteen – to harness her breath, calm it all down, stop the rising sense that, once again, it's all spiralling out of control.

'Get a grip, Lou.'

Get a grip.

Shaking, she stands, climbs into the bathtub and switches on the puny overhead shower. Its feeble icy trickle is one of the many things to fix on her to-do list – while the public parts of the building might give out a plush first impression, the interior of her apartment is far from well-tended – but right now it's just the ticket.

She lets the water of London – water which, she once read, has already passed through at least six people – drizzle over her head, slowly sluicing away the dirt of yesterday's housework.

Putting off the moment when she has to go back and check if that person – or being – is still standing out there in the middle of the sky, she soaps herself down, rinses, soaps again and rinses. Then, finally, there are no more reasons to procrastinate. She wraps herself in a fluffy towel and lets herself out, across the hallway and back into her room, averting her eyes from the window until she can bear it no more.

When finally she looks up, of course, he is gone.

If, she reminds herself, he was ever there at all.

Then she sees the crane from the demolition site opposite where, according to the hoardings that surround it, they're pulling down some blighted council estate to build a mix of desirable new homes. For some reason the arm of the crane has swung right across the road to rest over the car park of her building, in the airspace around her window. The sightline from her bed had blocked it, hence the floating young man effect.

He wasn't Jesus, or an angel, or any other kind of mythical superhero. He was just a boy, standing on top of a crane.

Granted, not what you'd expect to see first thing in the morning – or any time at all, in fact – but at least it's some sort of explanation.

If, she tells herself again, he was ever there at all.

9

Sophie pushes the Bugaboo along the endless, straight road. With the kind of life she has led, she has never been in anything approaching 'condition', but she is more unfit now than ever before. The house is three exhausting miles from the nearest bus stop, and, despite the early hour, she is dripping with sweat.

A creature more attuned to dark and candlelight, she finds it almost excruciating to be out this early. Even her baby's best efforts at waking her in the wee hours have not yet convinced her body clock otherwise. Her pale skin burns too easily, so she has shielded her face with a large, floppy black hat, and her arms with palest chiffon. Her eyes – red as ever from sleeplessness and grief – hide behind big, rounded, Jackie O shades.

The sun protection will also, she hopes, serve as a disguise.

Today is an open-house event for Fen Manor. It has been on the market for eight months now, but its infamous, gruesome story goes before it and, even in an exceptionally buoyant market, it's proving difficult to sell. It has already been reduced by fifty thousand and then, on one of her obsessive visits to the website of Marsden & Hunt International Estate Agents, Sophie found the announcement: *Open House. Must be seen to be appreciated.*

They're getting desperate.

When the place first went on sale, she visited M&H's offices, imagining herself to be in a parallel world where Louisa hadn't killed all her hopes, where she was, in fact, the young, beautiful wife of a successful, wealthy man. The sweet, pimply youth who laboriously wrote down her fictional details was taken aside by a pinstriped older colleague who then stepped in and challenged her. They had a photo of her, he said, and they'd been instructed by Louisa's solicitor – fucking, fucking Fiona – to prevent her from going anywhere near the property.

Which, of course makes Sophie even hungrier to do so.

Her next approach – by phone – failed as well: they also, it transpired, have tabs on her number.

Never having been in the property-buying business, this is her first 'Open House Event'. She imagines it is going to be like one of the parties she used to bowl along to in her modelling days: a house full of people, jostling each other. The big difference will be that, instead of hoovering up lines from the coffee table, they'll be noting stuff down on clipboards. In the middle of all that, she'll just be able to slip in and have a good old nose around, perhaps help herself to some souvenirs.

To make extra sure she won't be recognised, as well as all the clothing, she's wearing a blond wig. It makes her head itch like hell.

Reeds rise on either side of the road, sharp like nails. The endless blue sky arcs over a field of rotting, stinking brassicas, where a couple of crows battle it out over something wet and stringy. A morning mist, rapidly transforming into a heat haze, gobbles up the road ahead. Sophie adjusts her hat to shield her face from the scorching sun as it climbs the sky.

Just as she's thinking the countryside can go fuck itself, there it is, appearing from the shimmer, a large lump on the horizon: Fen Manor.

Her mood lifts. She's masochistically keen to see the wealth that, with Sam's death, slipped through her fingers.

She's also interested to see if there are any clues as to where Louisa has disappeared to. She has searched and searched online. Somehow, Fiona has made sure that she is untraceable. But Sophie *will* find her. She will not give up until she has rubbed Louisa's face in the misery she has made of her life. She will get the truth out of her, and she has the new determination to get the inheritance that's due her little daughter, too. Sophie *knows* that she and Sam are not the bad guys everyone makes them out to be. She smells a fish as stinking as stale mackerel. She will avenge his name; she will burn Louisa, like Louisa burned Sam.

Her fingertips crackle with the possibilities. This, at least, she can do.

She is also going to keep a weather eye out for any possible traces of Sam – a stray hair, a toothbrush. There probably won't be anything remaining after thirteen months – no doubt the estate agents have had the cleaners round. But if she doesn't get what she needs out of Louisa through the informal approaches she has in mind for when she finds her, she will need to prove that Sam was her baby's father, and, despite the fact that Sami is already a dead ringer for him, a bit of DNA might come in handy.

She looks down at her sweetly sleeping baby, who arrived after a troublesome birth four months ago, sickly and weak, blue and floppy, bound to this world by a fragile thread. Sophie camped by her cot in the Special Care Baby Unit for six weeks. Six weeks that she spent praying and expressing milk under the disapproving eyes of nurses who, like everyone else in Cambridge – thanks to press hatchet jobs, no doubt masterminded by Fiona – knew exactly who she was, what she had done, who she had slept with, all her past misdemeanours. Although she has not touched anything stronger than paracetamol since she came out of prison clean three years ago, it was clear that the medics had decided that Sami's weak condition was her fault, that she'd been caning it throughout her pregnancy. What they thought about Sophie didn't trouble her in the slightest, though. All she cared about was her baby thriving. Sami – Samantha on her birth certificate – is all she has left of Sam and she desperately needed her to survive.

The house looms closer in the mist, like some Gothic castle in a horror film. It's so bloody unfair, a complete crying shame that she has to face homelessness, while the grand place she should now by rights be living in stands empty and alone.

But nothing's fair, is it, in love and war? Isn't that how it goes? If she had been able to complete the A levels she had just started when Sam died, perhaps she would have known. Another missed opportunity to thank Louisa for.

And here it is. The house. Sam's house. The house that should be hers. Scene of the alleged utter bullshit crimes against Louisa. While she doesn't have any proof as such, Sophie *knows* Sam could never have harmed her, and she won't rest until Louisa is forced to admit it.

On the other side of the open security gates, a collection of cars clogs up the driveway – a sleek black Audi, a couple of Beemers, a little Austin-Healey covered in the estate agent's livery. An incongruous, ancient purple Micra completes the group.

She stops a little short of the gates, puts the brake on the Bugaboo and ducks behind an early blooming hawthorn to reapply her lipstick and check that her big sunhat hasn't dislodged the wig.

'Richbitch,' she says to herself in her little hand mirror. 'You are some richbitch, here to buy a house for yourself and your handsome, richrichrich husband.'

53

She certainly looks the part. She can still rock a designer frock, even though her dwindling wardrobe of samples is at least three years out of date.

Fully in character now, she lifts the handle of the car seat part of the buggy and, with Sami strapped safely inside, unclips it from the dusty armature. It's a top-end bit of kit that someone left empty outside an artisan bread shop. Sophie wheeled it off smartly without wondering too hard whether it had been abandoned or just left while its owner took their baby into the shop to buy an outrageously expensive sourdough.

Why shouldn't Sami have the best, too?

She pushes the empty wheeled section deep into the hawthorn bush. Tucking the carrier handle in the crook of her elbow, she sashays on up and through the open front door as if she, too, has just arrived in an upmarket vehicle.

'Ah.' A young woman with a tight, blond-streaked ponytail and too much mascara rises from behind a makeshift desk, where she has been sitting with an almost identical colleague. 'Hello there, little one,' she gushes over Sami, before remembering herself and straightening up and holding out her hand to Sophie. 'Welcome to Fen Manor,' she says, reciting her script in a tone as flat as the landscape. 'My name's Becky. May I take your name, please?' She picks up a clipboard and an M&H branded pen. Everything about her says Saturday girl to Sophie. Easy to get past, then.

'Samantha Williams,' Sophie says. She's thought about this for a long time. As well as being her daughter's name, it's so close to Sam's that the dumb estate agents would never believe it was being used by an imposter. Hide in plain sight, that's the way to do it.

The girl scans the list attached to her clipboard and frowns. 'Did you make an appointment?' she asks.

'Oh, did I have to? I thought I could just drop by . . .'

'We normally ask you to make an appointment . . .'

'So is that where he hid the blood-stained shirt?' someone says, out of sight. Sophie prickles.

A door opens at the end of the corridor and the pinstriped man who called Sophie out on her visit to the M&H office leads a gawking, cagoule-clad middle-aged couple across the oak-panelled hallway. These have to be the drivers of the purple Micra. Sophie steps smartly back into the shadows, but the estate agent is far too busy signalling to his colleagues his distaste at his 'clients' – who are clearly only here for the tour of the murderer's home – to notice the intruder lurking by the front door.

The grotesque little group disappears through a door and Sophie peels her slightly too large, Chanel-rouged mouth into a smile for Becky the Saturday Girl.

'I'm so sorry.' She touches Becky's sleeve. 'I only saw the notice on your website this morning. I'm over looking at a couple of other properties in the area and I thought I'd just chance my arm.' She allows her vowels to stretch out a little, to suggest the mid-Atlantic drawl she found so amusing in her erstwhile fashion colleagues.

Lifting her left hand to her throat, she touches the little diamond that matches the brilliant-cut whopper on her third finger, both gifts from Sam for their half-anniversary. He told her, as he placed them on her body, that they were a signal of his intentions. She never takes them off, because to do so would be like losing him all over again.

Yes, Becky, she thinks as she sees the salesgirl's eyes goggle at her bling. Yes, I am a rich bitch.

Becky fires a questioning look at her colleague behind the desk, who nods. She straightens her too-tight skirt and turns back to Sophie. 'My next lady and gentleman haven't turned up yet, so I'm sure I can squeeze you in. Can I have your details, please?'

Sophie gives her an entirely fictional phone number and address.

'Mmmm. San Diego. Lucky you,' Becky says as she scrawls them onto a form on her clipboard.

'Sure.' Sophie smiles. 'Do you mind if I leave my baby with you?' She hands Becky's colleague the car seat with Sami curled up in it like a soft, sweet little comma. 'It's just that I don't want to disturb nap time. If she wakes, there's some milk in the changing bag.'

Too surprised to object, the girl takes hold of baby, carrier and bag, and places them down at her side.

'I'll just give you one of these.' Becky hands Sophie a glossy folder with details of the property, then leads her on towards the kitchen, striding in and holding her arms open as if she had made it all herself. 'As you can see, it's full of light, the units are bespoke, and the appliances – top-spec – all come with the property.'

Sophie stands in the middle of the room, taking it all in, her eye roving for specks and hairs and nail clippings, her guts twisting. How on earth could Louisa not have been happy here? How could she not have been entirely grateful to Sam for all of this? And yet she drove him away, drove him to his death.

She shivers. His body filled the space where she now stands. If she closes her eyes, she can feel him on her. His feet trod these tiles. His hand touched this wall; his eyes gazed out of this window at this large, grassed garden, this trampoline, this playhouse.

This should have all been hers. She wants to roar it out loud.

'Plenty of space for the little one to play,' Becky says. 'When she gets a bit bigger.'

Sophie imagines taking the fancy toaster from the Corian worktop and flinging it through the window.

Becky turns back to the kitchen. 'Fully operational Aga,

and there's an integrated fan oven and gas hob over there as back up, or for entertaining.'

'Oh, I love to entertain,' Sophie says, regaining her composure, continuing with her act, glossing over what is really going on inside her. She would have held such wonderful parties in here.

Like a proper wifey woman might, she stoops and opens a low-level kitchen cupboard. A shiny stainless-steel food mixer stands proud among cake tins and baking sheets. To one side is a transparent plastic box. Brightly coloured bottles, polka-dot cupcake cases, a tiny rolling pin and a mini Cath Kidston apron are neatly stacked inside it. Stuck on the front, a pretty label says POPPY'S BAKING KIT.

Despite herself, Sophie catches her breath.

'I thought the house was vacant,' she says to Becky, as she straightens, gesturing at the cupboard's contents.

Becky flushes and rubs the back of her neck. 'Yes. Yes it is. Some effects were left behind and we've kept them. Makes the place look more homey.' Quickly, she ushers Sophie to a walk-in pantry. 'Plenty of storage,' she says, leaning in behind her. The shelves are crammed with tins and packets of long-life food. There is a whole wall of home-made apricot jam, a neat, minimal label stuck on exactly the same spot on each jar. The room has a sweet, fermented smell, as if something somewhere is rotting.

'It looks like the owners just walked away. Why are they selling?' Sophie asks, all innocence.

'Um. Someone passed away,' Becky says.

'Oh, I'm so sorry.' Sophie has read somewhere that estate agents have to tell the truth, if asked.

'The owner's keen to sell quickly.'

'It's been on the market for—?'

'Eight months.'

'I'm surprised no one's snapped it up.' Sophie gives the girl her best smile. 'Perhaps there are ghosts?'

'No, there aren't,' Becky says. But she can't hide the shiver that passes through her.

'Of course not,' Sophie goes on, stepping back into the lofty kitchen, eyeing the abundance of chrome and stone. 'I'd know if there were. I'm very sensitive to that sort of thing.'

'Um, let me show you the studio,' Becky says, leading Sophie into a very smart, ultra-modern extension on the back of the building. Sophie's fingers twitch.

Back in the hallway, they pass another estate agent, a boy in a badly fitting suit, who whisks his clients – a woman with Charlotte Rampling eyes and a man in a brand-new Barbour – smartly in front of them and into the living room. Sophie reckons they must be the Audi drivers. Proper rich bitches and bastards who don't need to pretend. So high and mighty are they that they don't even notice sweet little Sami, who still sleeps soundly in her car seat at the feet of the other Saturday girl.

A flash of murderousness runs through Sophie at the unfairness of it all. She'd like to lob a bomb at the lot of them, really.

'I was going to take you in there, but I guess we'll go upstairs first, then,' Becky says, rolling her eyes as the door closes on the boy and his customers. They climb the grand, dark oak staircase, and Becky shows her a room with a cot, and another which must have been occupied by an older child.

Lips fluttering, Sophie keeps the smile on her face, maintaining a cool, interested exterior while scanning for traces of Sam, hints of Louisa's whereabouts.

They glance at a couple of large spare rooms and then Becky opens a double door on to what must be the second storey of the studio extension downstairs. 'The piece de resistance,' she says, with not the tiniest effort at French pronunciation. 'The Master Suite.'

Sophie stands there blinking, taking it all in. It's glorious. From its vantage point above the fen, the room looks out, through large, floor-to-ceiling windows, onto an endless view of fields, trees, water.

'Not a man-made thing in sight,' Becky says, at her shoulder.

Sophie knots her hands tightly together to stop them shaking. This supersized king bed, this pillow, was where he slept, where, he told her, Louisa spurned him time and time again until she pushed him away. Sophie fights the urge to pull back the crisp cotton bedcovers and climb in. This is where she would have slept. Here, lying in this bed, looking up through this glass ceiling. Sami would have been in the nursery. It would have been so perfect.

So. Fucking. Perfect.

'Oh, excuse me,' Becky says as her phone blasts out some schmaltzy pop song Sophie has heard coming from clothes shops she can no longer afford to enter. Becky's cheeks redden as she sees who the caller is, and Sophie knows instantly that it must be a lover illicitly contacting her at work.

'Do you mind?' Becky gestures to the door. 'If I just nip out onto the landing and take this?'

Does Sophie mind being left alone in Sam's bedroom?

As soon as her keeper is out of sight, she pulls back the duvet and checks the bed for hairs. Nothing, of course. The bedding still has creases from where it was folded in its packaging. She turns to the cupboards. The first is empty, except for a stray floral scarf scrunched in the bottom, next to a worn pair of ballerina flats. The second, though, is full. Full of *his* clothes. The beautiful, crisp shirts that she loved to peel from his perfect body, ranged above rows of his Levis. At the side, ten of the identical black suits he had made for him by a man in Jermyn Street wait in vain for his body to fill them. Draped on his tall, toned frame, they looked simultaneously rock-star cool and smart. She leans in and buries her face among it all, breathing in the scent of him, touching the fabric.

Before she knows it herself, she has a shirt – Paul Smith, tiny purple floral on white cotton lawn – off its hanger and stuffed inside her handbag. She is going to sleep in it every night and never, ever wash it.

She runs her hands over the other garments for specks of Sam, but finds nothing.

The door opens and, a little flushed and pepped-up, Becky enters, smiling to herself and straightening her skirt as if she has just returned from a fumble.

'You've seen the en suite?' she asks.

Sophie shakes her head and, ushered in by Becky, takes the opportunity to open the bathroom cabinets and peer at Sam's toiletries – his aftershave, his toothbrush, a pot of Vicks.

Poor Sam. She was the only person in the world who could have come in and looked after his things in the way they deserved, but she wasn't allowed.

Heartbreaking.

When finally she found out that the reason he hadn't been in touch was that, far from deserting her as she had thought, he was dead, Sophie had been consumed by a desperate physical need for his body. Here in the presence of all his stuff, it once again rises in her. If it weren't for this clueless Saturday girl standing at her side, she would push her groin against the basin and make herself come.

A groan escapes her lips, surprising her almost as much as it does Becky.

'We'll go downstairs, then,' Becky says, frowning slightly. 'Please don't touch,' she says as Sophie reaches out to grab the toothbrush.

Sophie has done her research: old toothbrushes aren't likely to contain any useful genetic material, so she doesn't push the issue, and lets Becky shut the cabinet.

Back on the ground floor, Becky ushers her into the main living room where, in the midst of all the chalky pastel walls, low-level soft charcoal sofas and throws, an incongruous antique cabinet of silver trophies and cups lurks like something from a different house altogether.

Affecting nonchalance, Sophie wanders over and takes a closer look. Most of the prizes are equestrian in form or decoration – a horseshoe, a horse's head. Some are adorned with faded ribbons; a couple of dusty rosettes sit to one side on the baize shelves.

She bends to read the inscription on one of the cups. It's for Louise Turner, the Acrefield Horse Show Under Fourteens Individual Jumping Champion. Others, crammed into every available space in the cabinet, are for show jumping, showing and dressage, all over the Home Counties. All feature Louise Turner and 'Star', and they date back fifteen years or more.

In the centre of the middle shelf, two items stand out for being entirely un-horsey: a stubby yellow pencil about the size of a half-litre milk carton, and a framed photograph of a Louisa far younger and thinner than the woman Sophie knows. She's smiling – not an expression Sophie has seen on those features before – and holding the yellow pencil award in one hand and a typographically quirky card in the other, which reads *Lou Turner, Kick Ass D&AD Young Designer of the Year, 2009*.

Lou Turner.

Not Louisa Williams. Her original name, before Sam, then. One Sophie hadn't known about. It would make sense to revert to the past, wouldn't it? Once you'd rubbed out your present. Not that Sophie would, in any circumstances whatsoever, ever dream of going back to her own given name of Sharon.

'Is this the owner who died?' Sophie asks. *Bingo*, she's thinking.

'No.' Becky narrows her eyes at Sophie, who realises that

her undisguised curiosity has marked her out. It's cool if she has to leave, though. She's got what she wanted.

'So this is the widow, then? It's strange that she's left all this behind.'

Becky takes a step back and puts her hands on her hips. 'What are you doing here?' she demands as, with nothing now to lose, Sophie whips out her phone and snaps the Pencil award and the photograph beside it.

'I just think it's odd, that's all,' Sophie says.

'Are you a journalist?'

Sophie laughs. 'You have my word I'm not a journalist.'

'I think you'd better leave,' Becky tells Sophie.

As if on cue to pave Sophie's exit, Sami starts crying out in the hall.

Sophie smiles. 'I'd better go and see to my baby. We'll let ourselves out.' With an unfamiliar feeling in her heart, which takes her a while to identify as hope, she steps jauntily back out into the glaring sunshine.

At the gate, she looks back at the house.

Lou Turner, then.

She will find Lou Turner.

10

As she kneels in front of the kitchen cupboard of her new apartment, her rubber-gloved hands deep in a bucket of diluted Flash, Lou can't get the angel boy's face out of her mind. It was a kind face, a good face, a face that drew her interest.

But what was he doing, up there, staring at her as she was stretched out naked and vulnerable? And he had a camera. Had he filmed her?

All her therapy, all the care that has been spent putting her back together, has taught her that she needs to be wary in future, to guard herself against the charms of intruders. The world is full of narcissists and psychopaths who, just like Sam, will reel her in with a certain look or a beguiling word and then turn her round and take her over with such stealth that she won't notice until it's too late.

She wrings out her sponge and reaches deep into the cupboard, to the part far away in the corner underneath the sink which, from the colour it is turning her pine-scented water, has never been dealt with before.

If she had known the place was going to be left in such a state, she would have stayed in a hotel for this first week and hired some cleaners and, possibly, decorators.

What were those tenants thinking? Her vendor, from whom she inherited them, described them as 'responsible young professionals', and she had therefore expected more of them. She would never leave an apartment in a mess like this. But then not everyone shares her high standards.

When finally the kitchen is as clean as she needs it – in other words, only a little short, hygienically speaking, of an operating theatre before the guts start spilling – she unpacks the two blue IKEA bags that arrived yesterday and finds perfect places for all her brand-new crockery, pots and pans.

She hasn't brought anything with her from the old place because this is to be a completely clean start. Apart from the children's room, for which she bought new stuff before she moved in, she's making do for now with the tired rental furniture and fittings that came with the apartment. Eventually, everything apart from her own and the children's personal bits and pieces – which wait in their room in cardboard boxes for the moment when she can bear to put them out – will be brand new. She wants nothing in her new life that Sam's hands ever touched. Apart, of course, from the unavoidable, her body – but that has changed so much since he last laid a finger on it that it might as well be fresh out of the box as well. Parts that used to work – the memory and the right leg, mostly – now don't so well. Other areas have seen improvements, though. Thanks to a sustained effort of diet and exercise, there's a lot less of her. And, while she has accrued enough scars to make parts of her look patched together, the stretch marks that troubled her before all of this happened have faded to a pale, silvery trace work.

She works on. Deciding that the microwave is the source of the old curry stink, she unplugs it and lugs it down the corridor. She hefts it into the lift then out across the car park where a stack of furniture and appliances dumped by the occupants of the other four hundred apartments in her building – no doubt also 'responsible young professionals' – lies baking in the hot morning sun.

As she carries the oven, her hands squelch in a layer of grease on its bottom. Hoping that it is only the by-product of cooking, after putting the thing down, she wipes her hands on an old sofa at the edge of the pile of discards. As she walks away, a middle-aged woman in a lightweight parka just a little too cutting edge for the rest of her outfit strides up to her and points at the dead silver machine she has just dumped.

'Have you arranged for the council to take that away?' she says, coming a little too close for Lou's liking.

'Sorry?' Lou looks at the woman, whose face seems a little sunken. Hungover, perhaps.

'You speak English?' the woman says slowly, frowning at her.

Lou nods.

'You can't just dump stuff here,' she says.

'But . . .' Lou gestures with her hands at the mound of stuff.

'Yes, everyone else does. But it doesn't mean it's right. It's technically fly tipping. You have to arrange for the council to come. Imagine what it would look like if everyone put everything they didn't want on the pile.'

Lou looks at the junk and thinks it would look pretty much like it does, but she doesn't say anything.

The woman looks at Lou as if she is addressing the village idiot. Her coarsely pored forehead glistens with sweat.

'The phone number's on the building website. You know the website? W w w dot the heights dot com?' She says the address as if it is in a foreign language.

'Yes,' Lou says. 'I'll call them. I promise.'

'Good.' The woman stands back, folds her arms and stares at the pile, as if willing it to disappear. 'If it's still there at the end of the week, I'll have to report you to the managing agents. You're yet another tenant, I take it?'

'No. I own my flat.'

'Hmm.' The woman raises an eyebrow, as if she can scarcely believe this.

'Well. I'd better be getting on.' Lou deliberately ups her limp as she moves away, hoping that the woman will feel ashamed for attacking someone with an obvious disability. She doesn't look back to check, but enjoys the silent moral victory.

Yeah, welcome to The Heights.

She is quite pleased that, in the forty-eight hours since she moved in, her encounters with her fellow inhabitants have not been overly welcoming or warm. She bought her apartment sight unseen, basing her decision purely on the website photographs and the word of her solicitor and surveyor. When she first stepped into the courtyard at the centre of the development and looked up at the four interlinked blocks rising around her like space-age fortifications, she had been alarmed at the proximity of her neighbours, worried that it might lead to a villagey sort of closeness – the very thing she wanted to avoid for this, her fresh start.

But no. Parka Woman is the first person to have actually made eye contact. The two people Lou has shared lift journeys with didn't even acknowledge her presence. It's the London effect, she supposes – the way to survive city life is to insert yourself in a bubble. Phones, headphones and hoods all help, but it's more a state of mind than anything else. Lou likes all this. She just wants to keep her head down and get on with things. Anonymity will, she hopes, be a blessing.

She goes back into her tower – called South Block – using her fingertip on the two sets of biometric security doors that stand between her and the lift. As she waits for it to arrive, she enjoys the cool of the marble-clad lobby. At one end is a wall of modernist stained glass – the colours of a Klimt encased by the geometry of a Mondrian. A photograph of it on the property website was what drew her eye in the first place. It makes her want to make something beautiful, to organise shape and light and colour.

And very soon she will be doing just that. Her new job starts in less than a week and she will have every opportunity in the world to get back to what she once considered to be her big vocation in life, her area of excellence. Once, a whole lifetime ago.

The lift arrives. As the doors swipe open, they unleash an almost visible miasma of stale fart.

Ah, people.

Mouth-breathing, she rides up to the thirteenth floor, then uses her fingertip one last time, the biometrics having filtered access privileges right down to the occupants of the six apartments on her corridor. It is nothing here if not secure – another deal-clincher for her. With the nightmares she suffers, she couldn't live in a place where intruders could let themselves in from the street or climb through a window.

And this is why, beyond the surreal nature of the encounter, she found the boy on the crane so disconcerting. She had thought that, up in the sky, she would never have to worry about someone looking in from outside.

She lets herself back into her apartment, and is pleased to discover that the curry smell has gone. To celebrate, she makes a cup of tea in the shiny new kettle and a virgin mug, and takes it over to sit in a worn easy chair by the window.

So concerned had she been with the security and privacy aspects of being so high up, she hadn't even considered that she would also probably have a nice view. But she certainly does: each of the four main rooms of the apartment has a wall of windows looking out on to the most stunning cityscape. On top of that, while she can peer down into the windows of the East Block of her building – which finishes on the tenth floor – when she looks straight out there are no nearby buildings at her level. So she is not overlooked by anyone who doesn't have binoculars – or a crane to climb up.

In the distance straight ahead, Canary Wharf stands proud in the comic-book Metropolis of Docklands. Beyond that, what she supposes must be Kentish hills stretch into the hot haze of the morning. To the left, The Shard pierces the smog layer, and she can just see the golden tops of Tower Bridge. Arcing above all that are acres and acres of blue sky criss-crossed by aeroplanes and helicopters and too few birds. The railway line passes just beyond the car park of her building, and, directly opposite, there's the demolition site where the crane lives, a slowly opening wound on the body of the city.

The crane, she is relieved to see, has swung back round to where it belongs.

The thought returns of being watched by that boy.

A bead of sweat drips down her back.

The big drawback of all this glass is that on unseasonably hot spring mornings like this – HEADING FOR ANOTHER SCORCHER! the *Standard* headline shouted yesterday from the pile she has to avoid every day in the lobby of her building – the easterly aspect of the apartment turns it into a greenhouse from dawn until at least midday, after which the stored heat radiates and stagnates.

She can live with it, though, after all those months of being invaded by a coldness that made her pull all those loose, comforting clothes around herself.

On the other side of the living-room wall, next door's baby starts crying, as it has done on and off since her arrival. Lou knows how babies can play up, so she bears no animosity to the child's parents. But she does wish it would shut up. It cuts her deeply, that sound.

To distract herself, she gets up, fetches a spiral-bound notebook and pencil and writes neatly, underneath her already overwhelming to-do list:

SHOPPING:
Binoculars
Fan
Sofa and chairs
Earplugs?

And then, as it did the day before, it starts: a drilling from a machine so loud that it that must require its operator to wear ear defenders, underscored by what she thinks must be chain-saws, and the dull, repetitive thud of a pile driver that makes her sturdy concrete building shudder. Metal clangs on metal, men shout, dust clouds rise. The demolition site has started up its daily activities. She had hoped that the weekend would bring respite, but it seems not. This is clearly something she will have to learn to put up with. In amongst the tons of junk mail she picked up when she moved in were several classy brochures, jointly produced by the council and the developers, explaining and extolling the work. Two years it will take before Phase One is complete, and there are six Phases in all.

It's a far cry from Fen Manor, where the silence was some-times deafening. Perhaps at night she'd hear the scream of a tiny creature being snatched by an owl, but that was about it. Here, the twenty-four-hour backdrop of traffic noise never dims, and a nearby nightclub kicks its patrons out at three in the morning, who then shout and roar car engines and break bottles for an entire hour.

Lou hopes this clamour will work better for her than all that hush. But even now, she feels the clench and creep of a headache.

She'll get used to it, though. She's a survivor.

She is just necking a couple of her prescription painkillers when, unbelievably, the noise outside is topped by someone in the building playing AC/DC's 'Black in Black' on an amplifier turned up to eleven. She climbs on a chair and holds her ear up to the window, which, like all the others in the apartment, is open the full three inches permitted by a health-and-safety limiter. The noise is coming from the apartment directly above her.

'TURN IT DOWN!' she yells through the small gap, but of course, the offender doesn't hear.

She clambers down to the floor and thinks. She can't close the windows – she would melt or suffocate within an hour. To distract herself, she pushes all the furniture to the edges of the living room and mops the horrible laminate floor – the replacing of which is near the top of her to-do list. The liquid evaporating on the ground cools the room, and when she tips it down the sink, the cleaning water is black. This could be enough to make her happy, but still the music wallops on. It's now Black Sabbath, Ozzy Osbourne screaming something dark and satanical.

One of her counsellors at The Pines once asked her what she would do if something didn't feel right.

'I'd speak up about it before it got out of hand,' Lou had replied, feeling like the girl she had been at school: the swot, the one who always got the answers right.

'Good girl,' the counsellor had said, as if confirming this.

'Speak up before it gets out of hand,' Lou says to herself into the hot, dusty air of the apartment. She picks up her keys, marches out to the stairwell and climbs up to the next floor. But of course the entry pad onto that corridor doesn't accept her fingerprint. The music thunders towards her through the locked door, taunting her.

Agitated now, she turns to go back down the stairs to her own floor. But just as she passes the lift, it opens and a youngish woman steps out. Noting her fierce manicure and expensive handbag, Lou follows her back to the inaccessible corridor, where she touches the pad and holds the door open. A little alarmed at how easily she has just breached security, Lou mumbles her thanks and follows on through.

The noise coming from the other end of the corridor assaults them both. Without making full eye contact, the other woman tuts and shakes her head, before letting herself into the first apartment. Lou moves on past her to the door that stands above hers on the floor below. It looks exactly the same, except that it's practically pulsating with the heavy metal beat coming from behind it.

Lou steels herself. She knows her blonde, small, curved appearance is far from fearsome or authoritative, but, channelling the civic bossiness of the woman who accosted her over dumping the microwave, she holds up her fist and raps firmly on the door.

No one comes. Probably because they can't hear.

She fights the urge to run away, and knocks again, but much, much more firmly. Hammers, really.

The door opens. A man fills the whole frame with his massive, muscled, lycra-clad bulk, an aura of medicinal talc surrounding him.

'What?' he says, all aggression, his mouth barely moving in his sculpted face, his American-accented voice barely audible above the racket coming from behind him. Lou eyes the heavy kettle bell dangling from one of his ham fists. He could so easily swing it in her face.

She swallows. 'Could you turn your music down, please?'

'What?' he says. 'Speak up.'

'COULD YOU TURN YOUR MUSIC DOWN, PLEASE?'

'The fuck?' he says, with a joyless laugh.

'You see, I live just underneath you and I can barely hear myself think,' Lou says, aware that she is already making herself sound apologetic, already weakening her position.

'You want me to turn my music down?' His voice slurs, the words running into each other, as if the muscles around his face are so pumped they prevent his mouth from fully opening.

'Yes?' she says, hating the involuntary question mark.

71

'How about no.' He shuts the door in her face and she is left, on the threshold, trying to contain the rage she feels at this dismissal. She can't stop it: her fists are back at the door, pounding now.

The only reaction she gets, however, is from the woman who let her onto the corridor, who opens her door and fires a torrent of what sounds like Russian at her.

Unable to deal with any of this, Lou puts her hands over her ears and flees back to her apartment, where she shuts all the windows, takes a couple more pills, then hurls herself into the one space she has filled with all new furniture – the children's room. She dives past Leon's cot onto the lovely little bed she has installed for Poppy – all brightly coloured, with carved parrots sitting on the four corner posts – wraps her arms around Poppy's favourite Mary Doll, covers herself with the moon-and-stars duvet she picked out for her, and sobs until sleep claims her with its temporary release.

11

Adam

Adam crouches behind the base of the crane, squinting through his video camera viewfinder at the builders who have just started their working day. Their task today is cutting down a row of healthy – if somewhat parched – trees that have stood on this site for forty-five years. He's been waiting to get this footage for some time.

He can't quite believe what he saw earlier. It stirred him in a way he hasn't experienced since Charley left. That white, soft, scarred body, pressed naked against the glass, full, round breasts flattened, nipples . . .

Beauty. It's beauty, he tells himself, guilty about where his blood shot when he saw her. Where it still goes even just thinking about her.

The builders perch in cherry pickers protected by helmets, goggles, hi-vis jackets, big boots and gloves. They could be warriors going into battle, but instead they are preparing to wield their weapons against helpless trees.

So pale she was, soft-focused where her breath misted the glass. Blonde, tiny.

The chainsaws fire up and the air is full of roaring, grating and whining as they rip branch from tree, limb from trunk.

Chunks of wood thump to the floor. Even from where he is, at a safe remove of fifty metres, Adam can smell the sap, the sweet sawdust scent of freshly cut wood.

He zooms in on a digger slowly making its way to the scene of destruction. As a visual metaphor for what has been done to the community who used to live here, this sequence couldn't be more perfect.

The look on her face when she saw him. The shock, the fear in those round, pale blue eyes. It woke something in him, a yearning, a need.

He has to see her again.

Forcing himself to concentrate, he pans around the base of the trees where, along with other members of the community, he helped plant a vegetable garden as part of a defiance against orders to move out. Little remains now, just the vestiges of last year's kale, bolted into woody weeds, and a few bamboo pyramids tangled with papery, long-dead bean plants.

The branches stop falling. The men in the cherry pickers have done their bit, and the amputee trees stand to await the coup de grace.

It doesn't take long to come. The cherry pickers back off.

Adam holds the vegetable garden in shot. At the back of the frame, the caterpillar tracks of the digger trundle along to the furthest tree. The vehicle looks sinister, like some hostile alien searching for food.

Then something in a nest of weeds and vegetable plants at the bottom of the fourth tree in the line catches his eye. He zooms in on it and sees that it is the large, black-and-white cat; he has seen him so many times before on this site that he has christened him Heydon, in honour of the estate that used to stand here.

Despite all the noise and bother going on around him, Heydon seems to be staying put. Adam knows him to be a particularly chilled dude, but even so.

He zooms in more and sees why. Heydon is no he. She is, in fact, giving birth, and it looks like she's in trouble. A kitten has got stuck on its way out, and poor mama Heydon is casting around wildly, no doubt freaked out not only by what is going on in her own body, but also by what is happening all around her. Having already ripped three trees out of the earth by grabbing the trunks and tugging, the digger is closing in on her poorly-chosen shelter.

For a second, Adam is torn. Here is the making of a great sequence: poor, innocent creatures destroyed by the greedy grip of the developers. If he stays put, the film could go viral, completely discredit the builders, possibly even – and this would be the ultimate outcome – bring the work to a halt.

The digger gets closer. Adam films as the stuck cat cowers, struggles, tries to stand, fails, then nervously licks the two kittens she has already given birth to, who are already nuzzling on her full dugs of milk.

Adam continues to film.

The cat moves its mouth in a meow and looks desperately, straight into the camera. At that instant, Adam doesn't see a cat's eyes any more. Her look is exactly that of the naked girl in the apartment window: she is terrified, bewildered.

He is powerless in the face of this.

'HEY!' He jumps out from his hiding place, risking arrest, risking having his precious camera taken from him.

'STOP!'

He runs towards the digger, all muscle and power and hair streaming behind him, yelling at the top of his voice. An alarmed, high-vis man in his path jumps out of his way and speaks urgently into a walkie-talkie.

The digger roars, stutters, stops in its tracks, and Adam throws himself in front of it, his whole body shielding Heydon and her kittens.

'STOP!' he cries. 'STOP.'

At that moment, the stuck kitten pops out. Freed, Heydon jumps away from her litter and clears off, and Adam is left, surrounded by bemused builders, his hands full of mewling, blind, cat babies.

12

Sami is asleep far earlier than normal. Must have been all that fresh, fenny air. During the long last feed and cuddle, Sophie turned this evening's two exciting projects over in her mind, wondering which she should get on with first.

Warmed by the contact with Sami, she chooses the love option.

She puts Frankie on her iPad and plugs it into the speaker on her bedside table. 'Strangers in the Night': their song. She lights a stick of Nag Champa and places it in front of the shrine. Their incense.

Lying on her rose-pink vintage satin bedspread, as far away from the cot as possible, she crumples Sam's shirt over her face and inhales his essence. In the same way, she had clung to the pillows he slept on after he went. She had wrung them of him until they were so filthy that, despite her bitter grief and partiality to dust and shabbiness, she recoiled at the state of them. She wept as she washed away the last traces of him.

But here he is again, as much of him as she will ever have now.

She empties her lungs and breathes in, filling every last little branch inside them with the scent of her dead lover. Closing her eyes, she tries to bring him back.

Her left hand strays downwards and she remembers the last

time she was with him, when he was stretched out here on this very bed, attached to the four metal rings on the corner posts with the strips of leather she now keeps coiled on the shrine. She squatted over him, teasing him with ostrich feathers, making him kiss her, pinioning herself on him, covering every inch of him with her mouth.

'Look, steam rising,' she said, looking up at him.

'And so it should,' he said, his voice hoarse.

She nipped him in the way he liked and he flinched just a fraction, to let her know this was still the pleasure side of pain. Her finger worked into him and he gasped with surprised delight. It was nearly time for him, but she wanted to draw it out as long as possible.

He deserved every minute he could get.

More, she thinks, with hindsight. He deserved many more minutes, hours and years.

She scrolls back to the beginning of that night, which had been the worst through all of the horrors Louisa had piled on them both.

He had arrived at the flat rattled, wild-eyed, drenched from the rain, and told her that he had finally and unequivocally told Louisa that he was leaving, that he would no longer put up with her whining, her threats, her cold withdrawal, her mad ramblings, her paranoia. Just as he and Sophie had planned, he'd told his crazy wife that he was going to look after her financially, that he'd let her see the children. She could live here in the Cambridge flat and see the private therapist he had lined up for her. He'd even given her a gym membership.

'Then she launched herself at me,' Sam said, outrage and shock still in his voice. 'She punched me, swiped at me with a carving knife. It was only down to luck that she missed, or I'd be in hospital now, or worse.'

'Shhh.' Sophie went to him and curved her hand into his hair. 'You've been so patient with her, so kind. You don't have to be so good to her, but you are, because you're a good man. The best man in the world.'

Louisa should have been grateful that he was going to let her live here in this beautiful flat. Should have just said yes to him. What did she expect? You can't just shut up shop to your husband, rant and rave at him, attack him, and expect him to stay.

You have to work at being a wife, and that includes keeping some sort of life going outside the relationship, not giving up everything and turning all needy and whiney and doughy.

Sophie would have been a perfect wife.

'I mean, what more does she want?' she asked Sam, adjusting her silk dress so that the deep neck plunged down just beyond respectable, skimming her flawless, bra-less breasts. She knew that even in his distress he wouldn't be able to keep his eyes away.

'She still thinks it can all be perfect again.' He reached out to touch her nipple through the slippery fabric, just as she knew he would. 'When in fact it was always wrong.'

'Unlike how it is between us. Between us it's perfect.'

'Between us everything's perfect.' He drew Sophie to him. 'Oh God, Soph. You've saved my life.'

'And you mine.'

She undid his fly, he lifted her skirt, pulled her up to straddle him and, quickly, furiously, they had each other. This quick coupling was always necessary, to clear the air for slower, more considered pleasures.

When they were done, Sophie peeled herself away from him and gently pushed him down by the shoulders until he was sitting on the bed. She climbed behind him and pinioned him between her legs. Pulling off his shirt, she unleashed his scent into her bedroom.

Scent she inhales now, their child asleep in the cot beside her. The child who, she likes to think, they conceived that very last night, here where she now lies, in this same room.

Kissing the nubbly bit at the top of his spine, she worked her fingers into the flesh of his neck and shoulders, undoing the knots, loosening him until he was fluid in her hands. She loved the way she could do that for him, the way her fingers knew exactly what to do, where to go . . .

Then she sat up abruptly, leaving him hanging there, the tease that she was to him.

'Drink?' she said, swinging herself off the bed and reaching over to her dressing-table for the bottle she had pulled from the fridge when she heard his key in the door. It was Pavlovian for her to go for the champagne when he came round. It was something to do with the intensity, the otherness, of their time together. She wanted to lift it even further out of the ordinary, demarcate it, and being a little flossed on bubbles just seemed to be the right way of achieving that. Had she been able to use it without fear of sliding back into addiction, a line of coke would have fitted the bill even more perfectly. Indeed, Sam had suggested it once or twice. Liked to have it moved around on the end of his dick, he said. But she told him that it was out of the question, and he respected that.

He really respected her.

The only drugs they used, other than themselves, were alcohol and the tobacco he was pulling out of his pockets as she popped the champagne. A nice little roll-up, shared.

No tobacco any more, though. Not with Sami. The smoke from the incense on the shrine curls around the bedroom.

Sophie strokes herself and remembers how she used to see-saw the scalpel blade on the mirror, chopping the tiny lumps and crystals out until they were a fine, uniform powder. Then the deep inhale, followed by the bitter trickle down the back of the throat as she came up for air. The feeling that, whatever shit she had been through, whatever she was facing, she was, briefly, utterly invincible. Is it any wonder that, as soon as the buzz faded, she wanted more?

She wants more, now.

Think of better things, Sophie.

She holds his flowered Paul Smith shirt, breathes in once more in an attempt to force a stirring inside. But she is dry. Dried out by the loss of him. It's the first time she's tried since his death, and there's nothing there.

Not even the distant edge of a thrill.

It's hardly surprising.

Sami whiffles and stirs and Sophie thinks *oh no*, but then she settles back down again in her cot, and her mother tries some more.

They downed the champagne and looked at each other, she and Sam, wild eyed, as they always did at this point, holding back the moment of reconnection. She could see into his head, read what he wanted her to do to him today, to eclipse all the horrible things Louisa had said and done, had been saying and doing, for months.

He sheltered Sophie. He didn't go into full details because he knew it upset her. But she could picture it all too well. She knew exactly what went on back in that house in the flat fields that, back then, she believed would be hers so soon.

Before they could touch, his phone rang. Not his regular phone. He always switched that off when he was with her. It was the white iPhone, which, until recently, only he and Sophie had known about.

He glanced at the screen, and on seeing the incoming number, he angrily pressed the red button, rejecting the call. 'It's bloody her.'

The phone rang again. Again, he refused the call.

Her mouth tight, Sophie stood and reached out for the champagne bottle. Once again, Louisa had wedged herself right between them. Oh, she had such form on that score.

The phone dinged with a text message. 'Unbelievable,' Sam said, his voice weary.

'What?' She refilled their glasses: beautiful long tulip stems. Like everything else Sam and she had bought for the flat, top notch, best quality. It wasn't like they were saying Louisa would have to slum it.

'Just some bullshit about it all being my fault not hers.' Sam fiddled with the phone. 'I'll put it in Airplane Mode.'

'Oh, forget about her,' she said, handing him his glass. 'You've made the big announcement. She'll get used to it in time. Let's just enjoy now.' She knocked back her drink, took hold of his hair at the nape of his neck. 'You're mine for now.'

'I know it,' he said, smiling as she pushed him backwards onto her bed.

She was tying his wrists to the metal rings when her own mobile rang. She leaned over, picked it up and looked at the number, which she recognised immediately. It was Sam's landline, back at the house.

'It's her again,' Sophie said. 'How the hell did she get my number?'

'From the white iPhone,' Sam said, wearily. 'You're the only person I call on that number.'

Sophie lifted her phone and, unthinking of the cost or consequence – and anyway, Sam would buy her another one – dashed it onto the wooden floor, where, its screen cracked, it flashed and died in front of her eyes.

'Good,' she told Sam. 'Now it's just you and me.'

She picked up his deactivated phone and started taking pictures of him. Pulling off her clothes, she snapped him doing things to her as she ordered, making glorious images for him to enjoy when they were apart.

She still took a good photo. She still knew how to put herself to use.

'It's my gift to you,' she said, snapping his point of view of her as she lowered herself onto his mouth.

Sami stirs, and settles again.

Sophie shivers and something opens up inside her like a sea anemone. She licks her fingers, and, lightly, she strokes herself again. The smell of his shirt, the taste of herself, it's all coming back.

She still works!

An hour or so later, she was at that point when she was just about to let him come when a shrill beeping made both of them jump. At first Sophie thought that perhaps they might have set off the fire alarm, but then she realised it was the landline, which, since she moved in, had never rung.

'Ignore it,' she said. 'It'll only be a cold caller.' She carried on with what she was doing. But Sam had tensed up, and not in the way she was expecting, that tightening before the release. As the phone continued to ring, the ardour leaked from him until he was limp in her hands.

She looked up and saw his face, tight with anger.

'It's her, I know it,' he said, his teeth gritted. 'She won't leave me alone.'

'She doesn't know my landline,' Sophie said, drawing herself up to his face, kissing his cupid's-bow lips, stroking his cheeks.

'It's on your mobile voicemail,' he said.

'But my phone broke before it went through to voicemail.'

'It'll still go through.'

'Will it?'

The landline stopped ringing.

'Don't worry. It's not her.' Sophie propped herself up on one arm so that a nipple stroked his mouth.

She was just getting him back to where they had been when the landline rang again; again it had the same effect on him.

She threw herself backwards onto the bed, exhaling in exasperation.

'Is this what it's always going to be like?' she said, waving her hands in the air. 'Always haunted by her, no matter what you say to her?'

The phone rang and rang, its high-pitched electronic beep making her skin crawl.

If only there were some way of getting rid of Louisa for good.

Sam pulled at the ties around his wrists. They weren't serious, and he easily slipped his arms free. Leaning over Sophie, he dug the phone out from under the piles of scarves, paperbacks, empty wine glasses and pots of cream on her bedside table.

Untangling his feet from their bonds at the same time, he dispensed with the niceties of phone-answering. 'Look, Louisa, will you leave us the fuck alone?'

Sophie couldn't make out what was being said from the other end. She only heard the white noise of a female voice ragged with distress.

'What?' Sam jumped up and started pacing the room, tracking his free hand through his hair, parting it in five places. '*What* have you done?'

There was a long pause while he listened.

'No,' he said. 'No, you can't do that.' Then, after another tense stretch: 'Look, just calm down. Don't do that. No. Stay there. No. I'm on my way. Listen. Stay there. Don't move.'

Before he had even put the phone down, he was untangling his Levis from the pile they had landed in on the floor.

'Jesus Christ,' he said, struggling to pull them on.

'What is it?' Sophie said.

'I'll kill her,' he said.

'What's she done?'

'I need to go.'

'What do you mean?'

'She's going too far.' He threw on his shirt and stepped into his shoes. 'I swear, one of these days . . .' Preoccupied, he bent to kiss Sophie on the head. 'Later, my love,' he said, and then he was gone, and that was that.

And that thought spoils everything.

The only wet on Sophie right now is the tears on her cheeks. Sulphurous tears sprung from anger and grief. She breathes in the shirt one more time, gets up and carefully hangs it in her wardrobe for another day, for when it's not all so raw, so fresh.

If that day ever comes.

She looks at herself in the Victorian mirror on her dresser. Even in the tiny, dust-encrusted section not hidden by the hundreds of strings of beads and the armfuls of floaty scarves draped around it, she can see that she looks a sight. Always slender, she's too thin now, and her make-up is smeared, giving her panda eyes.

'How have you got like this?' she asks herself.

There are many answers to that one. But most of them are out of her reach. Except one.

Louisa.

It is time to turn her attention to the other project, the one fuelled by hate, anger, despair, revenge.

She yanks her iPad from the speaker, cutting Sinatra off mid 'Something Stupid', and, only briefly pausing to look at the photograph of Sam she has on the wallpaper, she opens up

Safari and Googles 'Lou Turner' and 'D&AD'.

And there, instantly, thanks, to the modern marvel of pushy online PR, is the article celebrating the 'Kick Ass Designer's return to the field' in just over a week from today. There's a clickable link to the swanky Soho company she'll be joining, and even a photograph of a creature who, while in no way resembling the Louisa Williams Sophie knew, is a dead ringer for the woman whose picture she snapped in the trophy cabinet display.

Who would have thought it would be that easy?

She decides that she'll play it cool. Her first approach will be to appeal to the better nature of 'Lou Turner'.

If, indeed, that crazy bitch *has* a better nature.

13

Lou stands in the insanely hot lift lobby on her floor, feeling sharp in her neat office suit. It's the second time she has worn it in the past year – the first being for the Skype interview she did for the job she is on her way to right now. Or the job she would be on her way to if the lift ever arrives.

She has allowed forty-five minutes for the journey, door to door. If the lift doesn't come soon, she's going to be late. Thinking that it's perhaps out of order again – which would make it the fourth time since she moved in – and forgetting for a moment that she can't yet walk all that easily, she toys with the idea of taking the stairs.

To see what thirteen storeys of steps looks like, she opens the door to the stairwell and peers down. Endless, that's what. Hundreds and hundreds of steps – too many for her. But not enough to deter the man who, about four flights beneath her, is sprinting up, taking them two at a time.

'Wow,' she says out loud, impressed.

But, as he rounds the final corner towards her and she sees that it's Steroid Boy from upstairs, she folds her admiration away, instead exchanging dagger stares with him as he thunders past, all testosterone and fresh sweat underscored by the pong of unwashed wicking fabrics.

Shuddering, she heads back to the lift lobby, where, at last, her carriage awaits her. An elderly woman stands inside, leaning on a shopping trolley, and the doors are just closing. Lou jams in her hand to hold them open.

'I thought it was never going to arrive!' she says cheerfully to her companion as she jumps in.

The woman tuts and scowls at her. Lou can feel the resentment coming at her for stopping the doors and delaying her journey down to ground level by all of, what, thirty seconds?

In the hum of the lift, Lou closes her eyes against the reflections of herself in the mirrored lift disappearing into the distance, no end in sight.

The woman tuts again.

Lou keeps her eyes shut. She's not going to let anything get in her way today.

The Tube journey to work is more of a challenge than it had been when she tried it for size a couple of days earlier, in the middle of the day. She had completely failed to imagine the press and thrust of the full-on London rush hour.

If walking were less painful, she would have gone on foot. But it's two miles, and anything over a couple of hundred metres has her back, hip and leg protesting in agony. It will get better, she has been told, and she is armed with the number of a great physiotherapist not far from her apartment, given to her as a leaving present by the guy who treated her at The Pines. But she hasn't phoned her yet, and wonders if she ever will. The pain feels right, somehow. Like a badge for surviving the loss of everything and everyone.

The Tube ride is six stops of challenge. Sweating in her suit jacket, she's one of too many people squeezed into a metal cylinder, rushing through hot, dark tunnels, the space around them ripe with the stench of unwashed, exposed armpits, brittle with constrained aggression, eyes evading eyes, festering germs.

One small, wayward gesture from someone and chaos could begin.

It has been such a long, long time since she's been out in the world.

She keeps as still and as untouched as possible. Does her breathing, stays calm. Pulls out her hand sanitiser and rubs it in.

Eventually she is squeezed up onto the pavement of Oxford Circus as part of a thick ooze of commuters. The hot air on the street – how on earth can this still only be early May? – hums with the smell of bad drains and ersatz vanilla-scented coffee. Oxford Street is a solid red block of stationary buses, so she decides to risk the final part of her journey on foot. Even at her own limping pace, she's going to beat public transport.

She forges on, partly humiliated, partly heartened by the way people part to let her, the crip with the gammy leg, through.

It's the first time in years that she has been out among so much humanity. Is everyone staring at her? Do they know that she's Tragic Louisa Williams?

Of course they don't. No one looks up at faces in London. And if they did, they wouldn't recognise her. Not now she's out of those awful soft clothes, her weight gone, her hair styled and newly blond, her eyeliner drawn on straight.

She's safe here.

'Relax, Lou,' she says under her breath.

Breathe.

On the pavement outside the building that houses A.R.K. Design Consultancy, she pauses, pulls a tissue from her bag and wipes the sweat from her brow and her upper lip. It's an impressive edifice: a large converted warehouse on a tiny Soho street, beautifully reconstructed into a sleekness that celebrates rather than obliterates its past.

She pulls her phone from her bag and, for courage, looks at Poppy and Leon's lovely little faces beaming up at her on her phone's wallpaper.

The sight of them, all innocence, all oblivious of what's coming, twists her guts. But it renews her determination. She's not going to let things slide.

She doesn't have to do this job for the money. She has to do it for the creative satisfaction, the chance to shine in a world that once threatened to dull her down to nothingness. And she will do this. She will do it to perfection. She owes it to her children to make something of her life without them.

Girding herself, she marches through the revolving door into the air-conditioned calm of the reception area. A security guard greets her, his sharp suit bulky with muscles and, possibly, she thinks, with a tiny frisson of excitement, weapons. With chivalrous control, he filters her through a metal detector. Satisfied she is clean, he touches his hand to his temple, military style, and passes her over to the cool, yet smilingly beautiful receptionist, who signs her in and tells her that someone will be along shortly to take her up.

Waiting on the uncomfortable kind of art sofa that only allows you to perch, Lou feels like a yokel up from the country, like she has clods of earth stuck to her shoes. Her Hobbs suit, which, when she got dressed this morning, had made her feel so firmly formed, just seems limp. It's over four years old, bought for face-to-face meetings with clients when she started out on her ill-fated freelancing career in the Fens. So, hardly worn, then. But it's not exactly up to the minute, and, compared to what even the receptionist here is wearing, it's cheap and high street.

She feels like an office girl rather than the Kick Ass Designer she is supposed to be.

It's only clothes, though. Nothing that some serious shopping can't sort out. It's not like she can't afford it. And they didn't hire her for her outfits, did they?

But she should have thought about it in advance. She fights away the voice telling her she has messed up, let herself down.

'It's all good,' she tells herself. 'All good.'

The glass and steel lift doors swish open and a woman in leather leggings and a light cashmere tunic strides across the pale wooden floor, her right hand extended. Lou recognises her as Cleo, the owner of the company, who, believing her to be living in New York, Skype interviewed her. Her edgy look makes Lou feel even more frumpy. She must be at least fifty, but she dresses like a woman half her age.

'Lou, hi.' Cleo clasps her hand and leans forward to kiss her. Lou tries not to flinch at the touch of lips on her cheek.

'We're so excited to have you with us.' Cleo puts her hand on her shoulder and guides her to the lift. 'I'll show you around before we settle you in. How's the relocation going? How was your journey in today?'

Lou mumbles something about everything being OK as the lift whisks them up several floors and lets them out onto a large space that looks like a cross between a youth club and an art gallery.

'Coffee?' Cleo asks.

'God, yes please.'

'This is what we call The Pantry,' Cleo says as she leads Lou past pinball machines, a ping pong table, and sociable arrangements of sofas and beanbags. At the far end of the space they arrive at a kitchen area with glass cupboards stocked with all kinds of free snacks – from Tunnocks Tea Cakes to hemp bars – and a large display fridge containing beer, wine, Coke, probiotic yoghurts and assorted boutique, hipster beverages.

'Hey, Si, Drew.' Cleo nods to a couple of twenty-something men in skinny retro T-shirts and big black glasses, who are necking sodas and getting very heated about a game of table football.

'Hey, Cleo,' they chorus.

'Flat white?' Cleo asks Lou, who nods.

Cleo sets about making coffee, expert barista-style on a shiny silver robot of a machine. 'I like to treat my designers well.' She points to a curtained-off area. 'That's the tech-free chill-out zone, and downstairs there's a health club. You get full free membership.'

'Does anyone ever manage to do any work?' Lou asks.

'Oh yes.' Cleo smiles and hands her a creamy cupful with a delicate leaf shape on the milk-white top. 'It's like letting people in a bakery eat the cakes. They get sick of it after a while. But what's good for me is that, if you've got all this laid on, you won't feel bad if you need to work through the night on a deadline.' She taps the side of her nose and winks.

Back in the lift, they go up, past the account management floor and what Cleo refers to as the geek deck, where all the IT and web development goes on.

The lift deposits them on the studio floor – a vast loft space with work areas demarcated by tree ferns and other foliage. It looks more like a tropical rainforest than a workspace.

Cleo claps her hands and everyone looks up from their Mac screens. 'Crew! Let me introduce Lou Turner, hot from NYC.'

'Hi, Lou,' Lou's fellow designers chorus, like schoolchildren bidden to greet a newcomer in assembly. Everyone is in denim, leather, cotton. No one has a suit on.

As Cleo leads her across the studio, Lou wonders which would be the least mortifying: spilling her coffee down her front so that she has to go out to buy something more in keeping with the company style, or carrying on for the day feeling and looking like a fusty square.

Her worries all but vanish as Cleo pushes aside a screen of foliage to reveal a vast wooden table. 'I thought you'd like this spot,' she says. The desk surface is entirely clear except for a lovely Apple monitor, wireless keyboard, mouse and Wacom pad. After so long without, the sight of the kit makes Lou itch to get to work. The vast, winged, ergonomic chair that is to be hers sits in front of an industrial steel window, which provides a bird's-eye view of the busy street below. It's a perfect spot to perch and dream.

Cleo tugs on a metal chain to draw down a mesh blind. 'You can use these if the sun gets too much, though you may be surprised: the windows may look old, but they're made from super-insulated, eco warrior blah blah glass. And here,' she says, opening a retro wooden cabinet like something you might find in a grammar school science lab, 'is all you need for old-style visualising.'

Inside the cupboard, rows of marker pens, pencils, inks, different sorts of paper and layout pads all wait to be picked up and played with. Lou feels her first rush of excitement in months. No, years.

'We're so glad to have you, Lou,' Cleo says, as she closes the cupboard. 'You with all your D&AD Pencil Awards . . .'

Lou waves it away. 'It was a long time ago.'

'George at Paradigm speaks very highly of you,' Cleo goes on. 'He was dead pissed off, he said, to lose you to breeding.'

Lou flushes. She should have expected this, of course. It was good of George to speak up for her. When she contacted him for a reference, he had understood and respected that, in order to help her move on without any damaging stigma, he was not to mention anything about the Sam business. But he clearly couldn't help himself going into unnecessary detail about the reason she left Paradigm.

'When we moved to the States I found it easier to freelance from home.'

'Did it myself back in the day. I'm all about returners getting back into the world of work. How many have you got?'

'Sorry?'

'Children. Nearly five years out suggests more than one.'

'Two,' she says, automatically. 'I've got two children.'

'Ah, tinies. It's quite a thing coming back, isn't it? Mine are in their twenties now, but I remember it well. It hits you, doesn't it?' She waves her hands in the air and rolls her eyes. 'What are their names?'

'Oh, um Ben and Willow.' Lou flushes. She has no idea why she's just told that lie.

'Lovely names!'

'Is this the latest Mac Pro?' Lou breaks away and gestures at the desk, under which she knows there will be a computer humming away.

'Of course,' Cleo says. 'Nothing but the best kit for our new top designer.' She lays a hand along the back of the desk chair. 'It's a back-friendly chair, but it's just struck me. Do you need anything extra for the, uh . . . ?' She gestures at Lou's leg.

'Oh no. No. I'm fine with this.'

'A footrest?'

'No, honestly. I'm OK.'

'Is it a permanent thing?'

'What? Oh, no. I mean – it should get better, with physio and that.'

'Ah, that's good. What happened, then?'

'I was in an accident.'

'Ouch. Car?'

Lou nods. 'Idiot ran a red light on Seventh.'

Cleo makes a face. 'New York drivers.'

'I know. Maniacs. Tell me about it.' Lou locks her fingers together and flexes them, as if to push away the subject. 'So, then. What do I get started on?'

'We'll give you your brief in a bit, down on the second floor. You'll meet Rich, the account manager for a new bottled water client. We'd like you to lead on the look and feel.'

'Great.'

'So I'll let you settle in, and I'll see you down on the account floor in fifteen. Oh, and there're some forms and mail and shit in your top drawer. You're free to do what you like, but I like to suggest a clean-desk policy.'

'Oh, there's nothing better than a clean desk,' Lou says.

Cleo bustles away across the studio floor, stopping to chat with one of the other designers on the way.

Lou takes off her awful suit jacket and hangs it neatly on the peg on the wall by the window. She tugs her white, cotton shirt out of her skirt waistband and, loosened, feels she has edged towards a style more in keeping with the other occupants of the studio. Balancing her bag on her knee, she pulls out her notebook, pen and pencil tin and places them to the left of her on the wooden desk surface, aligning them to the edge, leaving a ten centimetre margin.

She adjusts her chair so that her feet are flat on the floor and her elbows perch on the armrests, forearms extended at right angles from her upper arms to reach the keyboard, which she lines up with her notebook, pen and tin.

The magic she hoped for is taking place. She is, at last, calm and in control. Closing her eyes, she lets the noise and bustle and various discomforts of the morning settle inside her, as she says a little prayer to her own private goddess of clean starts.

She's ready. Positioned. Good to go.

She can do this.

She opens her desk drawer and pulls out a folder full of new employee forms she has to fill in. With them are three letters. Using the quaint A.R.K. branded letter opener lying beside them, she opens each in turn, taking care to slit along the tops, keeping it neat.

The first is a handwritten note on beautiful embossed card. It's signed by Cleo and the company directors, welcoming her to the A.R.K. Family – a nice touch, which instantly makes her feel valued for the first time in years. The second is a letter from the tax office, confirming her reversion to her maiden name. She puts it in her bag to file back at home.

She pulls the third from its envelope. It is handwritten, in a beautiful script, like that of an art teacher. But when she focuses on the words, the content of this lovely framework is something very different to its form.

> *Louisa.*
> *Lou.*
> *I know you've changed your name.*
> *I know where you are, too, as you've probably guessed from this letter.*
> *I need to talk to you.*
> *None of this is fair on me or my baby.*
> *Call me. I know you have my number.*
> *I'll give you one week from today*
> *(your first day at work – I even know that).*

It's not signed, but Lou knows, of course, who it's from.

Damn, damn, *damn*.

Instinctively, she throws the note across her desk, as if it is too hot to touch. As it flies from her hands, she gets a whiff of Sam, of his aftershave, and her throat catches as she tries to suppress the retch the scent induces.

She sits and stares at the piece of paper, as if it is a beast cornering her. She thought she had escaped all this. She had thought she was going to be able to start again, cleanly, clearly, untrammelled by loose threads hanging from her past.

> *None of this is fair on me or my baby.*

Bloody Sophie.

How dare she talk to her about fairness?

Lou's guts twist with anger. How dare she have Sam's baby

96

– if it even is Sam's baby – when her own arms are so yawningly empty?

And, and . . .

Realising she is biting her lip so hard she is in danger of making it bleed, Lou takes a couple of deep breaths and tries to think.

What is this about one week? Is it some sort of threat?

Is it about the flat? Or is it more than that?

She has already given that jammy little thief over a year's free board. It is more than enough. Sophie should be thanking her, rather than threatening her.

With shaking hands, Lou reaches across the desk and picks up the note. She tears it from top to bottom, side to side and up and down, then she scoops the hundred tiny pieces into the empty buff envelope from the tax office.

Taking a deep breath, she stands, picks up her notebook and pencil and, holding the envelope as if it were a bag containing the leavings of a dog, she asks one of her design colleagues where she can find the nearest ladies'.

It takes four flushes, but in the end, every last piece of Sophie's note goes down to where it belongs.

Lou returns to her desk and tries to move on.

Perhaps, she thinks, if she ignores it, it will go away.

After all, this strategy has worked very well for her in other areas of her life.

14

Then

Louisa hears the turn of Sam's key in the lock. From her perch among the detritus in the Fen Manor kitchen, she knows that, once again, he will be disappointed with what he finds.

Today, particularly, he will be upset, because he had taken steps to make the situation better. Typically for Sam, it was by throwing money at the problem. But, as also seems typical these days, she has managed to thwart his efforts.

'Do you want me to clean the bathroom for you after I have been bathing baby?' The young Slovakian woman he drafted in had asked, only about half an hour after she arrived this morning.

It was the look on her face as she asked the question, the tone of her voice as she said 'bathroom' that got Louisa. She might as well have asked her if she knew how badly she was coping, if she knew what a terrible mother and wife she was, what a pigsty her house was.

No, Louisa can't face being subject to this sort of scrutiny and criticism every day while Sam is out at work. No matter that he believes it will help her. It doesn't. It only makes her feel worse, less in control, more imperfect, more unable to cope.

So she sent the Slovak packing after her first hour. With two weeks' pay in cash – she hadn't wanted to seem unfair.

Things *will* get better. She will be able to cope. Just as soon as Poppy lets her sleep for more than two hours at a time. Just as soon as she gets over this most recent milk fever that has finally given her the excuse – on doctor's orders – to give up breastfeeding.

This failure has hit her very hard indeed. She's read the news reports about breastfed babies being brighter, more likely to succeed, more likely to be higher earners. She tried for nearly ten weeks, but it was so painful that, every time Poppy latched on, Louisa had to bite her knuckles to stop herself from screaming. And, as most mothers manage to breastfeed, so they also cope without extra help. Indeed, she had sent the health visitor packing, saying she was perfectly able to manage. Sam asking her to accept a mother's help is like him asking her to admit to a double failure. It isn't fair of him.

But now that evening has arrived, and there is mess and she is exhausted, she finds herself nearly regretting having sent the girl away.

All day, Poppy has given her the run around. Colicky from the formula milk, she wouldn't take a bottle, but cried endlessly with hunger. Every time Louisa got her washed and dressed in something fresh, she managed to explode her nappy with stinking yellow poo. And, of course, she refused to be put down to sleep.

'For HELL'S sake, Poppy,' Louisa said, the third time she tried to lay her daughter in her cot. She had to take a cushion into the kitchen and scream and throw it on the floor.

It was that or the baby.

At least there are no neighbours within earshot of the shouting and the yelling.

In between these adventures, all Louisa could do was sit there holding her tiny daughter and staring at the television.

Daytime TV has become the only way she has of knowing that some sort of life actually goes on outside these four walls.

Despite all this apparent inactivity, somehow cups and plates, crumbs and smears, dirty nappies and babygrows have piled up, seemingly of their own volition. By late afternoon, Poppy had finally given up her day-long fight, falling asleep on the rug on the living-room floor. Louisa lay by her side for an hour, hand on her tiny chest, because every time she tried to break contact, her pint-sized tormentor woke and started bawling.

In the end, she was able to gingerly peel herself away and reclaim her own body. What she should have done then, if she were the perfect new mother of her intentions, was clear up, clean, tidy, put things away, cook a meal for herself and Sam, and bathe and change out of the sick-, sweat- and baby poo-stained pyjamas she had been wearing for nearly twenty-four hours.

She did manage to unwrap a chicken from its thermally sealed plastic and put it in the Aga. But the lure of a bottle of red wine standing on the worktop was far greater than that of peeling potatoes, or tackling the scum-filled sink-load of washing-up she couldn't fit into the already over-full dishwasher that she couldn't bring herself to switch on.

So, instead of busying herself as she should, she sat at the table and poured herself a bucket of a glass of red and ripped open a large, family-sized packet of Kettle Chips and sat sipping and picking and gazing out of the kitchen window thinking how much she had in common with the empty, featureless landscape outside.

It is just as she is finishing her fourth glass – the last of the bottle – and the second big bag of crisps that the sound of Sam's key intrudes into what she had taken to be silence. Nicely muzzed by the alcohol, she imagines that she will be able to charm him round as she used to, employ her wiles to lift his mood. But, as he enters the kitchen and she gets up to greet him, her body betrays her and she stumbles and splays on the dirty floor. The shock of the fall kicks her senses into play. She smells the burning chicken, hears her baby screaming and clocks the look of dismay on her handsome husband's face.

'Where's Maria?' is the first thing he says, but before Louisa can pick herself up off the ground and explain, he is gone, into the living room, to pick up Poppy.

'Where is she?' he says again, as he re-enters clutching a red-faced, bawling, fists-and-indignation baby.

'I'll get her a bottle,' Louisa says, stumbling over to the steriliser, which is empty because every single bottle is stacked, dirty, in that dishwasher which, had she set it going, would be reaching its drying cycle now.

Sam sighs and reaches up to the cupboard, where there is a rapidly diminishing stash of pre-filled disposable bottles. Cuddling Poppy to his chest and jiggling her up and down, he unwraps one with his free hand and slips it into the bottle warmer. As he waits for the milk to heat up, he leans back against the counter and faces Louisa, who stands in the middle of the room, her arms wrapped around herself, looking at her feet, which are encased in stained sheepskin slippers.

'Well?' he says. 'Maria?'

She tells him about how she had found the young Slovakian woman intrusive, judgemental, impossible to like. About how she had sent her away.

Sam looks at her. She lifts her eyes to meet his and knows exactly what he is thinking.

He is wondering how this creature, his wife – who, on more than one occasion, had been mistaken while out with him for a particular blonde, curvaceous, desirable Hollywood star – has come to this.

Pregnancy was not kind to her. She put on around half her own body weight again. Alarmingly, the baby, coming early, had only accounted for five pounds of this mass. Enforced inactivity after the birth, coupled with a diet of crisps, wine and cake, has resulted in the rest of the fat refusing to shift. None of her pre-pregnancy clothes fit her any more, so she lives in maternity pyjamas, leggings and baggy tunics. On top of this, her body is covered in livid red stretch marks, which – she reads in mindless parenting magazines – might or might not fade in time.

Because of this, and because of the stitches put in her perineum to repair the second-degree tear Poppy inflicted on her, and, well, just because of being exhausted all the time, she and Sam have not had sex since the birth. The months before had been pretty devoid of all that too, thanks to the difficulty Louisa had with reconciling her maternal instincts with her sexuality. By the time her baby let her know that she was ready to come out, Louisa had mostly consisted of fat and anxiety.

It's a good job, she thinks, as the weight of all these thoughts pushes tears onto her formless cheeks, that she has stopped worrying about make-up. The idea of black mascara streaks coursing down her blotchy flesh would make her want to finish herself off.

The bottle warmer dings, making her jump.

'Look,' says Sam, guiding her to the armchair in the far corner of the kitchen, to the spot where she had imagined she would spend many happy hours breastfeeding a contented child – all of her children – while somehow simultaneously smiling at their beaming faces, reading a book, and gazing through the window at the glorious countryside. 'You sit here and feed Poppy and I'll clear this lot up and rustle up some pasta.'

'There's a chicken in the oven,' Louisa says blankly as he hands her the baby and the bottle.

He inclines his head towards the Aga, which is leaking black smoke. 'Like I said, I'll rustle up some pasta.'

Louisa winces. She knows he prefers not to eat carbs, and that she, the whale, should avoid them, too. She puts the bottle to Poppy's lips and tries to hold it firm against her furious sucking.

Sam raises an eyebrow as he takes the empty wine bottle from the kitchen table to the recycling bin, then he sets to in the kitchen, clearing, sweeping, wiping, washing, chopping, grating, frying, boiling and tasting. The whole process lasts all of thirty minutes. It's all it would have taken her, too, had she set her mind to it. And he does it after a twelve-hour day running a rapidly expanding business developing and selling cult-status apps around the globe.

She is useless, lazy, hopeless. She can't even get herself dressed, let alone do any work. The door to her studio remains as steadfastly shut as it has been ever since she entered her seventh month of pregnancy. Her Mac must be outdated now, her software obsolete, her skills ossified.

As if he can read her mind, Sam stops setting the table and looks over at her.

'Don't you think it might be time for you to get back to work, Louisa? Wouldn't that make you feel a little better?'

Solutions, he is always suggesting solutions. Sometimes she wants to scream and dash a cushion on the floor just for him.

Her first and only two freelance clients so far – an over-stretched local accident-claims solicitor and a failed rock-chick-turned-jam-maker – had been somewhat different to the blue-chip accounts she had handled back in Bristol. Both customers displayed an annoying combination of being both woolly and precise about what they wanted, throwing penny-pinching and late-paying habits into the already frustrating mix. Louisa has a suspicion that it isn't just mood-hijacking hormones that make her feel like curling up and hiding under a duvet whenever she thinks of returning to work.

And anyway, she wants to be a perfect mother, doesn't she? She doesn't tell Sam all this. He'd only pick holes.

Just before the baby drifts off to sleep, Sam takes her from Louisa's arms, changes her nappy, and puts her down in the pretty wicker Moses basket that Louisa can't settle her into without a massive fight. Of course, for Sam, she goes straight to sleep, no protests, no fists, no tears from anyone.

As they eat a beautifully prepared Pasta Puttanesca, Sam is, once again, full of suggestions for how to make Louisa happy, how to bring his old wife back. He'll ask around for work for her. A few of the high-tech start-ups on the industrial estate where he's sited his business on the north side of Cambridge could really do with some strong visual input.

Yes, well, perhaps that could work.

She nods and eats, nods and eats, and sips the water he has poured her, wishing it were more wine.

'We'll get a cleaner in,' he says, replenishing her glass. 'That's the sort of help you need. I was wrong with the mother's-help idea. You're a natural with Poppy. Look at the way you got her off to sleep.'

'That was you.'

But he ignores her, or perhaps doesn't even hear. 'Then we'll get a nanny in to look after her just a few hours every day,' he goes on. 'And you can slip off to the studio to get on with a bit of designing.'

A cleaner and a nanny. Doesn't sound that much different from a mother's help, except that she'll have two strangers in her house instead of one. But she continues nodding and eating, and reaches for the salad bowl to get her greens, like a good, good girl.

15

Now

'You off?' Cleo calls out as Lou passes her office at six. 'Fancy a first-day drink?'

'Sorry,' Lou says quickly, desperate to get back to the sanctuary of her apartment. 'Can't.'

'Ah. Don't want to miss bedtime?'

Lou nods and smiles.

'But see if you can get an evening off one night. It would be good to spend some social time with us. Meet the crew. Friday night is club night.'

'I'll try to work something out.'

'Can't their dad help out?'

'He's not around . . .'

Cleo touches her fingers to her lips. 'Oh. Sorry.'

'That's OK.' Lou smiles sweetly up at her, but winces internally at the hint of pity in Cleo's voice. She's not here for that. 'It's just, you know, you can only do so much when you're on your own.'

It's a good excuse. And Lou isn't sure if she's ready for 'social time' yet. She's out of practice. Also, there's the vexed question of exposure. She has already told Cleo more than she ever intended about her situation. Who knows what she might be drawn into saying on 'club night'. Things could get very complicated.

Jesus, if they aren't enough already.

She rides down in the lift. She has had a good day, back at the designer coalface, concentrating, researching and visualising ideas around water. It was *almost* possible to forget the earlier part of the day.

But when she steps onto the hot street, having said good evening to a different but identically dressed security guard, the stark fact of Sophie's malevolent little letter comes back to her like a punch to the head, and she almost retches.

She pauses on the pavement and scratches her head, furiously digging her nails into her scalp.

Sophie has found her.

Sophie wants to talk to her.

That *thing*, that girl and her baby worming their way into her life?

She pulls the clips from her hair and shakes it out.

No. She'd rather die.

So should she do what Fiona told her and let her know about this? Tell her to put a stop to it?

But she's destroyed the evidence.

And, even if she hadn't, would that letter constitute harassment?

Even thinking about going back and dealing with all that past business makes her indescribably weary. She liked Fiona and all that, but she doesn't ever want to see her again. There are no hard feelings, but she has told her she won't even open any letters from her. She just wants her to put the money from the house and the flat into her bank account when they are sold and then she can fully move on, draw a line.

Is that too much to ask?

It seems that it is. Somehow, Sophie has found out where she works. She could be watching her now. Lou surveys the street. A few arty filmy types heading home, a hipster on a fixie, and a couple of chubby little blonde women teetering on heels, dressed tightly for a night out. There's no Sophie here, thank Christ.

Head down, she makes for the Tube station. At each turn, she glances behind her. She touches in her Oyster card, slips through the ticket barrier and sighs with relief, as if she has reached safe cover rather than the entrance to the hot, dark tunnels that seemed so hellish this morning.

On the train, she works at not throwing up as a man next to her devours a stinking burger with onions and barbecue sauce. How can people live so publicly? But then, no one else on the train seems to mind or notice. There's a lot of London behaviour she's going to have to get used to.

At her stop, she has a wobble as she sees a tall, pregnant, dark-haired woman step off the train a couple of carriages down from hers. But of course, Sophie has had her baby. And, when she turns, this woman's face is nondescript, small featured. The opposite of Sophie.

She folds her hands in front of her and stands for a second until the train is gone and the platform empty.

'Just put it all away,' she says quietly, a mantra of her own devising that has been more useful to her than anything they taught her in her therapy sessions at The Pines.

'Put it all away.'

Bracing herself for bright lights and the smell of stale popcorn, she slips into the shabby shopping centre that sits on top of the Tube station. According to the redevelopment brochures, it's going to be pulled down and replaced with something far glossier – a Westfield is being hinted at.

It's hard to see how that would work. The current clientele is far from what she imagines to be the usual Westfield crowd. Elderly West Indian women amble slowly towards Meet 'n'

Meat the butchers to buy goat and cut-price chicken. Corn-rowed and back-combed schoolgirls in minuscule skirts gaze at a blindingly bright display of saris and gold jewellery in a shop called H&K Imports.

'Innit, though,' one of them is shrieking. 'Innit?'

Groups of men with the bewildered gazes and shabby clothes of newly arrived refugees gather on the public seating, talking loudly, gesticulating, ignoring the No Smoking signs. A couple of boys in gold chains and baseball caps play ping pong on a graffitied table, and, just before she turns into Tesco, Lou sees, tucked away behind one of the broken-down escalators, something being passed over in a dodgy handshake between a grey-skinned young woman and a tall white boy in baggy trousers and a straggly goatee.

The boy catches Lou looking and stares back at her with carefully crafted, personalised menace. She turns away and hurries into the shop to buy something for her supper.

It's all so very different from Cambridgeshire.

And, she has to say, thank God for that.

Outside, her healthy, ready meal supper tucked in a carrier bag, she faces the decision that has vexed her every time she makes this journey. Does she take the diversion up the ramp to run through the traffic on one of the busiest roundabouts in Europe – no mean feat with her leg and today's smart but uncomfortable good shoes? Or does she use the subway where, even in the daytime, the grimy, urine-tanged depths and the out-of-it vagrant occupants fill her with a kind of horror?

'You are better than this,' she says out loud, as she stands at the threshold of the two options.

No one around her bats an eyelid. Such behaviour is commonplace in this shopping centre.

Bracing herself, she sets off down the underpass, latching on to a threesome of bosomy elderly ladies who, with their bulging shopping trollies and bright Ghanaian headscarves, look like they'll brook no nonsense from anyone or anything.

At this time of the evening, it's busy down here with commuters and shoppers making their way under the roaring roundabout. Huddled halfway through is the usual clump of destitute, drunk and drugged city human jetsam, who pass their days and nights in this most public of shelters, dangling their scrawny dogs on pieces of string, asking for spare change from passers-by, many of whom are barely any better off.

This evening, the gathering is bigger than Lou has seen before. Even her unwitting escort of elders has to move over to get past. Pushed to the back of her group, Lou hugs the wall, as far away as possible from the vagrants. It's not noble of her, but she finds their chaos threatening, as if she might somehow catch it if she gets too close. She also feels guilty about not giving any money, or not giving enough money. Once you start, where do you stop? And shouldn't you give food, rather than coins that will be spent on the very substances that have got them into this sort of mess?

There is no perfect answer to any of these questions, and that's what makes it so uncomfortable for her.

As she gets closer, she realises that what she took to be a heated discussion verging on an argument is, in fact, a group of the street people speaking animatedly to a man holding a camera and asking them questions.

'We 'ent got nowhere to go,' one of them is saying through a big black gap where his teeth should be, his words underscored by the whine of a miserable life. 'Where the hell will we go if they fill this lot in?'

As Lou passes, the cameraman turns as if he expects to see her there and, just a couple of feet apart, their eyes meet.

'Hi,' he says, his voice full of pleased surprise, as if he knows her.

And, indeed, he does look familiar.

Then it clicks. Brown skin, long, curled dark hair: it's Angel

Boy from the crane. The beautiful boy from her waking/ dreaming moment, who had stared at her as she lay naked on her bed.

He *is* real.

He really stared at her as she lay naked.

She looks away, holds her Tesco bag to shield her and, like a beetle hurtling for shelter after its covering stone has been lifted, she hurries onwards, out of the underpass, towards her building. She runs so fast on her limping leg and stupid shoes that she trips on the concrete steps up to the pavement, tearing her tights and bloodying her knee. Shaking off the hand of a concerned passer-by, she scuttles for her biometrically secure haven.

All told, her fresh new life project isn't going quite as planned.

16

Lou cleans her knee, puts on a plaster and kisses it better. She spends a while in the children's room, curled on Poppy's bed, dreaming of how it would be if they were here now – all joyful little faces, fun and laughter. The thought brings her a kind of peace, helps her forget about Sophie and that letter, and that boy on the crane.

Finally composed enough to sit up, she unpacks one of the boxes of the children's belongings. It takes a while, but she gradually finds herself happy again, putting the things away in their rightful places, arranging Poppy's pencils and paints in the drawers of the little rocket-ship desk she had delivered from Heal's. She puts her daughter's drawing book – an album of scribbles representing people and houses, with *Poppy* written on the cover – on her bedside table for her, and sets all Leon's cuddly toys out along the edge of his cot. She always liked to think that, laid out like that, they soothed him as he tried to get to sleep. But of course she was kidding herself. Most of the time he'd start crying after just a few minutes; he was never any good at getting off on his own. And then she would have to do the dance of dealing with Poppy – who never slept the whole night through – as well as her baby brother.

It's not easy, being mother to two small children.

'But it's lovely,' she says out loud. 'A blessing. I am blessed.'

And with these words she pushes the void, the darkness – the reality – back into the locked corner at the back of her mind.

When the box is empty and everything is in the right place, she pulls herself to her feet, takes a photograph of the lovely room with all the things out in it, and texts it to the children on the special phone she has bought for them, so that she can stay in touch. Certain people would say that they are too young for a phone. They would accuse her of spoiling them, but Poppy and Leon have missed out on so much and she would do anything to make it all up to them.

The thought of the work she has to do on the apartment pushes her on, and she heads to the task she has allotted to tonight: ripping up the fusty, stained carpets in the two other bedrooms. She should have done it when she first moved in, but she had thought she could live with them until she decided what was going to replace them. As it has turned out, she can't. She can't get out of her head the fact that they have sponged up the spills, exhalations and excretions of God knows how many previous occupants. They have to go.

It's hot, dirty work. When she pulls up the carpets, all sorts of stuff is stirred up. What she uncovers doesn't look great – it's just a concrete sub floor – but at least it's sealed, so after a hoover and a wash it'll produce far less dust than the carpets. It'll be helpful, too, to have a blank, grey surface. Much easier to visualise something different on top.

By the time she has managed – without being accosted by Parka Woman – to deposit both offending items on the dumping pile outside, her face is furred with sweat-plastered dust. When she blows her nose, the tissue comes away black.

She should sit and relax now, have a cup of tea, perhaps read a book or a magazine. But the baby on the other side of her living-room wall is crying again, and, upstairs, Steroid Boy is watching what sounds like full-volume, filthy pornography.

More noise comes from somewhere down below, on the street.

She presses her nose against the window and peers into the hot, dark night. There seems to be some sort of party happening on the narrow road running between the demolition site and the railway. Someone has set up a sound system. All Lou can hear above the baby, the 'Oh YESSS! Oh YESSS!' pulsating from upstairs and the ever-present traffic outside is a thundering bass line, but it's got a rabble of revellers dancing, shouting and whooping.

She squints at the flailing figures throwing wild shadows across the railway arches. It is nearly midnight on an early May evening, people are partying outside, and no one is wearing even a light jacket. What is going on with this weather?

Panning her gaze round to the left, she starts. A tall man dressed entirely in black stands at a window in the East Block, three floors beneath hers, looking directly up at her. His burning eyes – at once accusing and attacking – remind her of something from her past, something that filled her with horror, something she can't quite put her finger on any more. Heart racing, she blinks to make sure he's actually there. When he sees her clock him, he ducks out of the way, as if dodging a bullet.

Her skin crawls.

Time, perhaps, to make use of The Heights' private swimming pool.

With towel and bathing suit rolled under her arm, she descends to the ground floor. Hoping that the man in black is not at his window looking down at her, she hurries across the central courtyard and scurries over the Japanese bridge spanning the carp pond in the middle. She doesn't dare look up, but she can feel those eyes on her . . .

Using her finger on the entry pad, she lets herself in to the pool. She's pleased to find that, at nearly midnight, she has the place to herself. Her previous two visits were in the daytime and on each occasion, while not exactly full, it was certainly peopled. The second time, two very young children splashed in the shallow end with their mother, and she couldn't even bring herself to get in the water.

She changes and washes off the worst of her dusty coating in the poolside shower. After testing the temperature with her toe, she slips on her goggles and lowers herself in, enjoying the way the water takes over from gravity. To her, with her aching joints and wobbly gait, it feels like a mercy.

Setting off, she focuses on the rhythm of her strokes, the one-two-three-up of her breathing pattern. At the end of each length, she performs a roll and turn worthy of a county swimmer.

This technical skill is something of an achievement. When she was admitted to The Pines, she told her therapists that she didn't swim, that she was scared of water. But they insisted on hydrotherapy for the latter part of her rehabilitation, once the bolts and pins had been removed from her leg. Gradually, she developed a love of floating in the warm therapy pool, allowing the water to take the weight of her mending limbs. Then she met Susi, a young former Team UK swimmer who had landed up there with broken legs after throwing herself off a tall building. Susi taught Lou how to breathe, how to hold her fingers, how to move her feet. She was also only too happy to share her battle with depression and suicide, which, her therapists reckoned, had been triggered by a childhood training schedule so brutal that it verged on abusive. But whenever her turn came to talk about herself, Lou would zip off to the other end of the pool so speedily that even Susi had difficulty catching up with her.

Lou only tells her story if she has no choice. And she plans on never telling it again. Not even to herself.

She hasn't kept in touch with Susi or anyone else from her

past. Her email, phone, appearance – everything about her has changed.

A clean start is a clean start.

And that thought is instantly tainted by the image of Sophie – a gaunt, black, flapping bird, contaminating her peace.

She surges along the pool, willing the clean, chemical water to wash this pollution from her mind.

White, coming up through her, bleaching her brain.

After thirty lengths she pauses and, panting, places her hands on the pool edge. She wets her goggles to de-fog them and scoots her head back underwater, slicking the hair from her face. Then she looks up, eyes blurry with chlorine, and realises with a shock that she is no longer alone.

A man sits with his feet dangling over the edge, just a few feet away from her. She rubs the water from her face. Despite the fact that his curls are flattened against his head, the high cheekbones, brown skin and firm lines of his shoulders are unmistakable.

When she realises who he is, her jolt sends ripples through the water.

It's the boy from the crane. The boy from the underpass.

'Fancy meeting you here,' he says, smiling at her.

17

Then

The size sixteen stretches too tightly across Louisa's breasts, gaping where the buttons barely meet. Even if it weren't the largest size she could find in the younger styles in Cambridge M&S, she would never be able to bring herself to ask for an eighteen, not when she used to be an easy ten.

This is the fifth shop she has visited. It is nearly lunchtime, her blood sugar is in her shoes, and she hasn't yet found a single thing to buy that both fits and isn't something that she wouldn't be seen dead in.

She peels off the lime-green blouse with its jolly squiggles and hopes that the shop assistant doesn't notice that, in the brief period she has had it on her back, she has sweated into the underarms. It's hardly her fault, though; this changing room is far too hot, with its glaring lights shining onto mirrors that are – surely – widthways distorting.

For a moment, her head feels too heavy to hold up. She lets it drop to her chest.

This has to be hell.

She has been waiting for something – anything – to improve for over half a year now, but, if anything, everything has steadily got worse.

The changing-room lights buzz like a stuck doorbell, the sound boring into her ears. Wincing, she piles the armful of hangers and their too-small garments on top of the buggy where Poppy, now five months old, sleeps for what seems like the first time since midnight.

'Any good?' the shop assistant chirps as Louisa wheels back towards the shop floor.

The buzzing isn't getting any quieter. In fact, it seems actually to be coming from inside her.

Louisa shakes her head and hands her the pile of clothes. She tries to say 'no thanks', but the words get stuck in her throat. The idea that these bright, uplifting colours, these delicate fabrics, these playful shapes, were ever going to work on someone like her is absurd. She had even picked out a dress with two frills on the hem and a stripe of glitter running through it, for Christ's sake.

She steers the buggy through the obstacle course of chrome display stands laden with yet more bright colours and synthetic cheer. There is only just enough space to pass between them. Don't the men who lay out these places ever think about women who have to push buggies around all day? And the shop seems to have grown in size since she came in – the lights have got brighter, the floor appears to tilt as she wades across it.

The sound continues, drilling into her brain, and she has an unnerving sense of seeping beyond the boundaries of her body and blurring into the space around her. She is as dense and as dark as a black hole.

Her phone vibrates in her pocket. Partly because she needs an excuse to stop and get her bearings, to see if she is actually heading towards the exit and not further into the bowels of the shop, she pauses and fishes it out. A woman close behind her almost barrels straight into her, tuts loudly, then retraces and takes another route.

It's a text message from Sam.

How's it going? Got anything nice? xxx

Another, better wife would think: how wonderful, not only has he given me money and told me to go into Cambridge, buy whatever I like, pay a visit to the hairdresser, get a facial, but he is also taking time out of his busy day to see how I'm getting on.

But Louisa sees this message for what it is. He's fed up with having this drab partner, whose greying black clothes have bled into her shabby whites in successive poorly sorted washes, whose long-since-dyed blond hair is brittle with split ends and dark roots, whose gut hangs over her waistband, whose skin manages to be simultaneously flakily dry and shinily, spottily greasy. Seen through this lens, his text is not a signifier of concern, but rather a passive-aggressive attack, a way of checking up on her, making sure she is doing as she's told.

She knows this because these were tactics her mother employed, too. Oh, all mild on the surface, but with a centre of disapproval and, at the very kernel, disgust at her.

Getting there, she texts back to Sam, and instead of signing off with an x, she mistypes a c. She can't even get that right.

Pocketing her phone, she spies, with relief, the shop exit. Heading off, she brushes against a display of floaty headscarves, all swirling pinks and yellows and greens. One catches on the buggy and gets dragged off its hook. Just to see what happens, she carries on walking out of the shop, the acquired scarf dangling from the buggy handle.

No one stops her, no alarms go off, facts that are at once exciting and disappointing. She comes away with a free headscarf; at least *that* isn't going to be too tight for her.

Outside, in the drizzle, the buzzing subsides to a dull, tinnitus ringing, and she is brought sufficiently back into focus to remember that, unless she wants Poppy to wake up – which she most certainly doesn't – she has to put the rain cover up on the buggy.

Sheltering in a canopy outside Starbucks, she fiddles with plastic and poppers and elastic bands, and covers up her daughter, who sleeps, pale lids covering her eyes, like some despot empress, worn with the effort of ruling over her minion.

Having finally managed to wrangle the cover into place, Louisa leans back against the coffee-shop window. She knows this will annoy the customers who have positioned themselves on stools behind the glass to people-watch while sipping on expensive lattes, but she needs the window ledge to take some of her weight. She reaches inside her changing bag and pulls out a Mars Bar, which she eats, chewing, she thinks, like a great cow.

Tucking the empty wrapper in her pocket, she hauls herself to her feet and heads towards the market place and Gap, where she hopes she'll have a little more luck. She has an idea that they cut generously there, for big-boned Americans.

But after a helpful assistant has brought her, in increasing sizes, what feels like ten different styles of jeans, she sits on the faux leather cube in the changing room and weeps. It doesn't help that the brutally lit mirror in front of her shows not only the tears rolling down her blotched cheeks, but also, thanks to the rear-view arrangement, the shake of her shoulders as they do so, and the bra straps cutting into her back fat.

Poppy wakes and starts to cry. Sweating, Louisa pulls her out and tries to comfort her until the shop assistant knocks on the cubicle door and asks her if everything is all right.

'It's just my baby,' Louisa says.

Just her baby.

'Cut it all off.'

Louisa had intended just to ask for a trim, so this comes as much of a shock to her as it does to Sue, the senior stylist.

'All of it?' Sue says, her own immaculately coiffed and streaked locks moving around her face as if they have a mind of their own and they, too, can't quite believe it.

'Number three all over,' Louisa says. 'No. Number one.' She sips her complimentary coffee, nibbles on the little cookie on the side of the saucer and looks at herself in the hairdresser's mirror. She has spent her entire day encountering her own reflection and hating it. Drastic action is what's called for. All or nothing.

Sue's pencilled right eyebrow disappears into her fringe. 'Would you like it washed first?' she asks.

'Why not?' Louisa says.

She is helped into an overall and the junior – 'I'm Janine, are you going anywhere nice for your holidays?' – sets to work, sprinkling warm water over her head, rubbing in and rinsing ylang ylang-laced shampoo and conditioner. Janine is just getting busy with some Indian head massage – 'I've just been doing this course at college' – when Poppy sees fit to wake up again. She wails from her buggy, gasping, yelling, crying, punching the air with her fists.

'Oh, poor mite,' the hairdresser's receptionist says, cooing over the buggy. 'Do you want me to see to her for you?'

'Yes,' Louisa says.

From her position, head back over the sink, she watches through a half-closed eye as the receptionist unstraps Poppy and lifts her from the buggy.

'There's milk in the changing bag,' she tells her. 'Don't worry, it's formula,' she adds, just in case the poor girl is as disgusted as her by the idea of coming into contact with another woman's breast milk.

The clippers buzz and tug. Louisa closes her eyes and feels her hair tickle her forearms as it falls in great strands around her. Unlike Janine the junior, Sue has enough experience to realise that small talk is not what this particular customer requires.

'All done,' she says after just ten minutes. Louisa opens her eyes and confronts herself. Topped by a head of mousy stubble, her face looks like someone else's, which today feels like something of a result. Sue holds up a small mirror behind her and Louisa discovers that she has a deep red birthmark on her scalp. She had no idea.

Her face is rather too round to do well without the framing effect of hair, but that will change in time. Her cheekbones *will* stage a reappearance. She *will* get her body back to how it used to be. And from this tabula rasa she will grow a new head of healthy, strong, shining locks, a far cry from the sea of thirty-centimetre lengths of brittle bleached strands tangling around the base of her chair. Louisa closes her eyes again and moves her head around, as if trying to shake water from her now non-existent hair. She feels lighter, cooler.

As if sucked up by the clippers, the ringing is finally completely gone from her ears. With this new shaved clarity, her outline is visible for all to see, a declaration that she does, in fact, exist. That she does, in fact, own her place in the world.

She smiles at herself in the mirror.

On top of all this, the receptionist has got Poppy off to sleep and back into the buggy. Perhaps this is Louisa's point of turnaround. Perhaps, if Poppy can sleep like this, she can get into the studio and back to work, continue to build on her freelance career. Become a star designer again.

She pays for the haircut with Sam's credit card. As she wheels Poppy out onto the street, she hardly notices the burden of the buggy. The rain has paused and stilled puddles silver the grey pavement.

'Earrings,' she says out loud. They will complete this, her new, bold look. She thinks of a stall in the market that sells extravagant Indian silver hoops and curlicues, great dangling things that will give her an edge. It also, she now remembers, sells loose, linen-ish dresses and trousers and tops, made by Fairtrade craftspeople in Thailand to the designs of the woman who runs the stall. They're great billowing tents, really, and quite different to what she used to wear. But, accessorised correctly, they could work in a dramatic way. A new style for the woman she feels is itching to emerge from the imperfect chrysalis of her stretched skin.

Yes, she will cut a figure. A mother, designer, wife, arty, iconic. That will work.

She bumps the buggy over the splashy market-square cobblestones. Once the place where the people of Cambridge came to buy their daily staples, it is now home to craft stalls and expensive farmers' market-type set-ups. Searching for the earring/tent dress woman, she spots her ex-rock-chick-jam-maker client, who has a stall here. She's doing a roaring trade selling jar after jar to a throng of Japanese tourists, who crowd around handing over twenty-pound notes and taking photographs.

Her back sore from the unaccustomed exercise of the morning, Louisa perches on the fountain at the centre of the market square, swigs from a bottle of water, and watches the activity around the jam stall.

Poppy stirs and grizzles, but a bit of judicious rocking settles her down again.

Eventually, the tourists move away to reveal the jam-maker's banner. With a thud of blood to her face, Louisa realises that the logo is nothing like the letterform she designed. She had picked simple and clean Gill Sans, reversed out and outlined on a plain duck-egg blue ground – the whole effect hinting at wartime home economics, *Keep Calm and Carry On* without the actual overused phrase. What she is looking at now, however, is a handwritten script set among borderline-inept line drawings of hedgerow fruits, red parts picked out in faux watercolour and – oh God – a guitar. The insult to all this injury is that the business name has lost the final g she had insisted, against the client's wishes, on incorporating into the design. It now appears as *Jammin'*.

Jammin'.

Horrified, Louisa gets up and pushes the buggy over towards the stall to get a closer look. The same disaster has happened to the labels on the jars, which, in turn, have acquired little caps of red gingham. There is not one hint of Louisa's work here.

As she draws closer, the jam maker – a woman with heavily kohl'd eyes and a stringy body wrapped in a beaten-up black leather biker's jacket – spies her.

For the few seconds that they hold each other's gaze, Louisa feels herself shrink. Cheeks blazing, she turns on her heel and quickly steers her buggy through a gaggle of German Language School students heading to buy Jammin's quirky wares, no doubt for their sentimental hausfrau mothers.

She hurries back down round the Corn Exchange and shuts herself and the buggy inside the disabled toilet at the car park just in the nick of time. Leaning over the shit-striped pan, she retches and throws up all of the hairdresser's complimentary coffee and biscuits, muddied into a mess of Mars Bar.

At least, she thinks as she spits the last acidic pieces from the back of her throat, she doesn't have to worry about holding her hair back like she did throughout all her morning sickness.

Poppy wakes, protests and fills her nappy.

It takes Louisa a good forty minutes before she and the baby emerge, blinking, from the stinking toilet, by which time she has tied the stolen M&S scarf on her head, to hide her shaven, plucked shame.

And now, only now, she wonders what Sam will make of her new look.

18

Now

Has Angel Boy followed Lou into the pool?

She braces her arms, ready to haul herself up out of the water and leg it towards the exit. Would she, with her lilting gait, make it out in time? Would she reach the lobby and Umoh the night concierge – a burly type who carries himself like he knows what he's doing – before this young, fit, strong man caught her?

Not a chance. Her best bet is to stay in the water.

A brief, alarming thought flashes through her mind. Is he something to do with Sophie? A spy sent by her?

She pins a look on him, the hardest she can manage. 'How long have you been sitting there?'

'I was just about to get in.'

Something in his tone sounds like he's making excuses, like he's been caught out.

'I was in the steam room when you came in,' he goes on. 'But I didn't want to startle you, so I thought I'd wait until you stopped and saw me.'

'It didn't quite work,' she says, treading water as if she's winding her legs up ready to sprint. 'The not startling me bit.'

'Sorry,' he says.

His apology gives her courage. She stops her feet and faces him. 'Did you follow me in here?'

He laughs and puts up his hands. 'No! Not at all. I promise.' His voice is deep, with a small tint of South London, but mostly it is framed by what her mother would have called a nice accent. Deep dimples carve into each cheek, and small silver hoop earrings shine, gipsy style, at both sides of his head.

She looks away. She doesn't want him to see that she's softening.

'And, look . . .' Something in his voice draws her eyes back to his face, which has angles that can only have been shaped by smiling. 'I'm really sorry about the other morning. When I was on the crane.'

She lowers her Speedo-sheathed body a little further into the water, so that her shoulders are submerged.

'I didn't mean to stare,' he goes on. His face is so open, so clear, that to disbelieve what he is saying would be impossible for any heart softer than a rock. 'And I didn't go up there on purpose to look at you. I was filming, you see . . .'

'Filming?' she says, alarmed, thinking of the pictures that turned up in papers and online after the accident, capturing her at moments when she had no idea at all that there were any photographers present. Her at her worst, looking how she felt inside. Once again, she has to remind herself that now no one would recognise that person as her.

Seeing her consternation, he holds up his hands. 'Oh, not you,' he says. 'Please believe me. I'm not like that at all, I—'

'So why were you staring at me?'

He flushes and looks at his feet, which he swings in the water in a peculiarly childlike way.

'It's just . . .'

'Just what?'

'Just.' He takes a deep breath. 'When I saw you all stretched out like that in the morning light, all spotlit by the sun, well, you looked, so . . . well, beautiful.'

Lou, too, colours and looks away. It's the first time in years that she's heard that word applied to her. She runs her mind back. Yes, quite literally, years. It feels like a gift, wrapped in golden paper, tied with a velvet ribbon.

'You almost made me fall off,' he adds, smiling.

Despite herself, Lou smiles too. Part of her wants to carry on with her swim. But she still feels that she has to keep an eye on him. And something else, not too deeply buried, makes her want to hear more of what he's got to say about how beautiful he found her.

'I won't do it again, I promise,' he says. 'It's just that when I saw that the crane had swung round like that, it was too good an opportunity to get the whole site in one, panoramic shot.'

'The whole site?'

'The demolition site.'

'Why would you want to do that?'

'I'm documenting it.'

'Why?'

'For the five thousand people who've been thrown out of their affordable homes so that the developers can build swanky new towers and rake in their profits.'

He lets himself into the water, his beautifully defined muscles sliding underneath smooth skin. A tangling, thorned rose tattoo twists around one of his arms, and Lou has to stop herself from reaching out to touch it. She takes a small step away from him, just to keep her distance, aware – and not in an entirely displeasing way – that his body is now in the same water as hers, that molecules are passing between them.

'So: you live here?' she asks, just to say anything, to avoid the difficult – or dangerous – silence that threatens to open up between them. 'In The Heights?'

He laughs out loud. 'Nah. Couldn't afford that in a million years.'

'So how come you're using the pool, then?' She smiles, to soften the prissiness of her question.

'I gave Umoh's mum a hand when they cleared her off the estate,' he says. 'Helped her bid for one of the few council flats available round here. So he lets me in at night, when most of you proper residents are tucked up in bed.' He taps the fingers of his right hand to his temple in an informal salute. 'I'm Adam, by the way.'

'Lou,' she says, waving at him from where she stands.

'Hey, Lou. Race you!' He takes off in the water. Instinctive competitiveness kicks in and, without even thinking, she ploughs after him. He beats her, but, determined to let neither her injuries nor her sex stand in her way, she races so hard that she forgets about judging her distance or breathing, and ploughs straight into him at the other end.

Gently, he takes her arm – just stopping her from whacking his face – and she feels the surge of electricity that passes where their flesh touches. Their eyes meet, but she immediately looks away. This is going too quickly, she thinks. In the same way that she was sure when Sam stepped into her studio at Paradigm, she knows now that she will have this boy, and nothing she thinks or does is going to stop that.

This fact takes her entirely by surprise. She's not prepared for it. Her trust and faith in love has been smashed to pieces, and the idea of stepping back into all that pinches her tight with terror.

'Jumping race?' he says, letting go of her.

'What?' She loosely moves away from him.

'Put your hands down by your sides, keep your feet together, and jump. You have to touch the bottom, both feet every time, and you mustn't use your arms. First to get to the other end is the winner.'

He sets off and Lou follows. It's hard on her poor survivor's legs at the shallow end, and she has to stop herself from crying out, in her frustration, for him to stop. But as the pool gets deeper, so it gets easier. But by then she is having difficulty not choking on the water, because she is laughing so much.

Laughing!

It's almost a forgotten art for her.

He wags a finger as she catches up with him. 'You've done this before, haven't you?' He turns, puts both hands on the side of the pool and, in a riot of rippling inked back muscles, hauls himself out, twisting so that he's sitting back on the edge where he started.

His arms look almost too powerful to Lou. And as he turned, she is certain that she saw wings on his back. Wings. Like an angel. She blinks. Surely not?

'Fancy a bubble?' He nods over in the direction of the spa pool.

'OK,' she says, and *oh no*, she thinks.

With far less grace than him, she pulls herself out of the water and onto her feet. She clocks the look he gives her body as he jumps up beside her. But it's not pity at her limp or horror at the scars on her legs or her arms. It's something very different indeed. And, of course, he's seen her limbs before. And more.

He must like a marked woman.

Just as well, then.

He's taller than she imagined – a good head and shoulders higher than her. As he leads the way to the jacuzzi, rivulets of water lick their way down his back, past the wings which, now he's out of the water, she sees with relief are not some hallucination but an intricately detailed tattoo.

They slide into the warm water. She positions herself not quite opposite him, so there is no chance of accidental touching. Apart from anything else, the round, glassy eye of a CCTV camera is pointing right at them, probably routed directly to the bank of monitors on Umoh's desk. Its presence is no doubt entirely due to the water-contaminating acts people might get up to in the spa pool.

He presses the button to start the water jets. Bubbles bounce from his body onto hers.

'So where do you live, then, if not here?' she asks.

'I'm in this place on the far side of the estate. Phase Five. A row of houses and flats. All officially emptied, due for demolition in six months' time to make way for the new shopping centre. A group of us are squatting them.'

Lou has never met anyone who squatted anywhere before. His exoticism increases.

'They'll kick us out eventually, but we're making a stand. Plus it's free, and I'm not exactly rolling in it at the moment.'

'What do you do, apart from the films?'

'The films are what I do.'

'And that pays?'

He laughs. 'Not so you'd notice. I make a little money from helping out in this café down the road.'

'So how did you get into it? The film-making, I mean?'

'I was at the college across the road. Doing a course on media and cultural studies. But I got involved with the protests around the estate. And that seemed far more important. It also meant my mum didn't have to shell out to support me any more, too.'

'Was she OK with you dropping out?'

'She was cool with it. She just wants me to be happy.'

'Wow. I wish my mother had been like that.'

'What was she like?'

'Oh, you really don't want to know.' Lou slides down into the bubbles then pops up again. 'And are you?'

'Am I what?'

'Happy.'

Adam rests his head on the edge of the pool and smiles at her. 'Yeah. I think I am. Don't want to sound smug, but I'm doing something that I believe in, something that's making a real difference.'

'They're still knocking down the estate, though.'

'But we're making it difficult for them. My job is to get the issues out there; document the life people had here, the efforts they made to keep it. The community may die, but I'm doing my best to keep the stories and the spirit going. This area is special.'

His hands come out of the water, illustrating his points as if he's drawing a map in the air.

'It's half an hour's walk from the City, the West End, it's in Zone One, on two tube lines. The overground line and nearly every bus in London pass through that roundabout over there. This building – your building – was the vanguard of redevelopment, converted from sixties offices back in the nineties, sold to yuppies and foreign investors shitting themselves about the handover of Hong Kong. But apart from that, the local community around here remained steadfastly low-to-middle-income and ethnically diverse – the people who keep the city on its feet. Then, five years ago, talk of redevelopment surfaced. It had only been a matter of time, after all. The money men have had their eyes on this part of town for decades. And now, through a smokescreen of promises of affordable housing that has completely failed to appear, they've smashed up the heart of the community and forced everyone out. Council tenants have had to move all over the borough, and the poor suckers who bought their council homes have had to go even further, because the compulsory purchase price offered was a quarter of what it'd cost to buy somewhere of a similar size round here. This was one of the last places for ordinary people – and I'm not just talking the old working class, but people like teachers, nurses, IT workers – to be able to live in Central London.'

The bubbles stop, and the water jet lets out a great sigh. Adam looks over at Lou.

'Sorry,' he says. 'I go off on one when I get started.'

'You care a lot,' she says.

'I do.'

'Your mum must be proud.' The minute she speaks, she wishes she hadn't. It sounds so patronising, so maternal, so wrong, given the circumstances.

'She is,' he says, not having picked up on any of that. 'She's good, my mum. She understands struggles. My dad disappeared before I was born and she brought me up on her own.'

'Does she live in the area?'

'Nah, she's in Farnham. She's a teacher.'

'Is that where you grew up?'

'Yep.'

A Surrey boy, burning with radicalism, dropping his aitches. And she doesn't want to even guess how young he must be.

'So now you know all about me, what about you?' he says, brushing her toe with his foot. She tries to disguise the jolt his touch sets off in her by reaching over to press the bubble button.

'Not much to tell,' she says.

'Where did you live before you came here?'

'Bristol.' She can't quite bring herself to give him the New York story she has spun for A.R.K. – it would be too complicated. So she settles for a half-truth rather than an outright lie.

'Nice. And what're you doing here?'

'I've got this job in town. I'm a graphic designer.'

'Cool.'

She rests her head back on the stone edge of the pool, closes her eyes and wills him to stop asking questions. She can almost smell the fact that he wants to know what happened to her limping and scarred leg, but she suspects that he is too delicate to ask.

131

'Perhaps you could help me with the titles for my film,' he says, instead.

She secretly opens one eye just a tiny crack. He is looking intently at her, as if he is trying to read her. 'Perhaps I could,' she says.

The bubbles froth and boil around them. They fail to work their relaxing magic, though – when Adam's foot strays once more across to graze Lou's, she almost leaps from the water. It's such a long time since she was touched by a man without a medical qualification.

'I'm sorry.' She lifts herself to her feet. 'I'm feeling a bit dizzy.'

'It can do that.' He stands and reaches out to steady her. 'This hot water.'

'I'm fine,' she says, making for the step. He sits back into the pool, and she can see that he is pretending not to notice the way she shied from his touch. Climbing out, she pulls her towel from where she left it on the railing, and wraps it tightly around herself. 'Well, I'd better be off. Work in the morning,' she says.

'Would you let me buy you a drink to apologise for shocking you like that? When I was on the crane, I mean.'

She looks down at him, her lips slowly moving to mirror his smile. 'A coffee?'

'If you like.'

'I'm afraid I'm busy this week,' she says, but not entirely convincingly. She needs a bit of time to get her head in order before she sees him again, otherwise she might make a hasty mistake that she will almost certainly regret.

'How about breakfast on Saturday, then? In The Rainbow Café at the far end of the railway arches? Eleven a.m.?'

Five days. Should be enough.

'If you like.'

* * *

132

In the changing room, she throws on her clothes, then runs as best she can across the courtyard to her block, enjoying the cooling effect of wet hair around her shoulders.

Back inside her apartment, the baby next door is still crying, the porn upstairs and party outside still swinging along, and Sophie still niggles away in the back of her mind. But somehow – it could be Angel Boy, the bubbles, or simply her expertise at tuning out the trouble – she manages, almost instantaneously, to fall fast asleep the minute her head lands on her pillow.

And she sleeps well until the nightmares wake her up as they so often do, sweating into the terror of three in the morning.

19

In nothing but a long vest top that just about covers the important places, Sophie runs down the communal stairway to pick up her post. It's nothing but buff envelopes – some with her address written in red, bills that she has no intention of paying now that, with Sami nearing six months, Louisa must be plotting to throw them both out on the street.

Sophie is determined that this isn't going to happen. But in order to stop it, she has to get to Louisa, and it looks like Louisa's not playing nicely. It's five days since she will have seen the letter at A.R.K., but after Sophie has dumped the unopened bills straight in the dustbin outside, there is nothing left for her to take upstairs.

Clearly appealing to her better nature won't work. Sophie hadn't really expected her to phone, but she thought she might at least take the cowardly option and write, respond in *some* way.

It's not like Louisa doesn't know her address, with it being her property and all, with her following Sam here and standing outside all those times, looking up at her window, all pathetic, wronged wife.

Rage rising, Sophie slams her flat palm against the heritage grey-painted wall so hard that it stings like a burn.

Louisa never let go of Sam, never accepted that he didn't love her any more.

It's not fair. It's not fair.

'What the hell is all this?' Pawel, the creepy academic who lives on the other side of the wall she has just whacked, opens his door and peers out into the corridor, his belly straining against the thin fabric of his T-shirt. Having run its course, the hallway timer light has gone out, so it takes a couple of moments for his eyes to adjust to the gloom. When he sees Sophie, he rolls his eyes and goes back inside his pork-scented flat, shaking his head.

Doesn't he know how grief has torn her?

She nearly yells it out loud, but stops herself. She still knows how to act sane, just about.

She runs up the stairs, thumping her bare feet down on the treads, just to annoy him.

After sealing herself back inside her flat, she checks that Sami is still sleeping soundly in the bedroom. Aware – more than anything by the burning of her breasts – that she doesn't have long before her baby wakes, Sophie grabs her iPad and phone and positions herself at the desk by the living-room window. This is her work station, where she makes the only income she now has, selling her old dresses. It also serves as the control centre for her campaign against Louisa.

She's on Phase Two of the Louisa project now. Phase One – the hands-off approach – had all the makings of success. She scrolls to the screenshots she saved of her comments and posts before bloody Fiona got them taken down. Other voices were joining her multiple online personas in insisting that there was more to be said about Louisa's role in the whole disaster, that it was all too convenient to paint Sam as the villain and brush the whole matter away under the carpet of his supposed guilt. She brings up one of her favourite posts – written as herself – which got over five hundred likes from complete strangers before it was taken down:

How can Louisa lie about Sam's alibi for Katie's murder and get away with just a suspended sentence, when I, WHO TOLD THE TRUTH, got banged up for perverting the course of justice for accusing my rapist? Even if Louisa said she lied under duress, doesn't that one massive untruth throw every other one of her statements into doubt?

Five hundred likes! Truly, Sophie's inability to continue with her education is the legal world's loss.

All forty-five of her Internet incarnations – each crafted to have a slightly different voice – whipped her small band of followers up into a social media frenzy. Admittedly, most of the people behind her weren't the types she would have chosen as friends, but needs must.

She looks over the email Katie's sister Lucy sent her, saying that she didn't believe Sam could have killed Katie. Sophie got really excited about that and put her in touch with a magazine journalist who had been nosing around her for a story.

But when Lucy's interview came out all hell broke loose, because the rest of the family were in the process of accepting a settlement from Sam's estate – in other words, Louisa's money.

'In other words, Sami's inheritance,' Sophie mutters as she looks over a pdf of the pathetic, slanderous interview Katie's money-grubbing mother and father gave. 'We just want closure,' Katie's mother had said.

'Yeah, the closure of two hundred and fifty thousand pounds.'

She'd spit at the photograph of the pair of them if it didn't mean it would mess up her iPad.

The short-term aim of Phase One had been to shame Louisa and bring Sophie's questions about the truthfulness of her account out into the open. The ultimate goal would have been to clear Sam's name.

Too bad that Fiona was on her back every step she took, getting everything taken down, rendering her impotent.

Phase Two – the direct approach – is, despite Louisa's lack of communication to date, far more promising. Now Louisa is out in the real world again after being holed up in that top-secret rehab unit, Sophie finally has her chance to get her hands on her properly. She can go directly to the horse's mouth, Fiona or no Fiona. It's a free world.

That's not to say Sophie has given up on the Internet. She still has Google alerts set up for a variety of related terms, including all of Louisa's different names, and there are a handful of websites that have taken up the baton. Most of these are hosted in countries beyond Fiona's litigious reach, so they still have a constant presence, keeping the flame alight.

Stirred up by a passing moped, a hot wind blows in from the street. It lifts the muslin curtain and, while she waits for her email to load, Sophie watches two students cycling down her road, no doubt off to lectures, bags in their bike baskets, chatting happily to each other in entitled voices.

Hooking the curtain over her shoulder, she watches them cycle into the distance, envying them to a point of pain for their opportunities, their privilege, their freedom.

Her inbox turns up nothing of great interest. Just that she has sold a pair of unworn Louboutins for two hundred pounds on eBay, and notification that a new article has been posted on a website billing itself as calling for justice for victims of misandry.

Sophie clicks through to the article, in which the writer muses on Louisa's childhood. He – for these websites do tend to be run by men who have issues with misbehaving women – goes on to ask whether there was anything there which could point to her being not the innocent victim she presents to the world. A lazy piece of blogging, it reveals no new information. It is really just an excuse to chew over the early misdemeanours of other women who were subsequently convicted of murder, enticing visitors to click on links to pages about them elsewhere on his site.

The article has only one – not particularly edifying – comment:

> *Gr8. Ur spot on about Louisa. Sumfings rilly fishy bout dat bitch.*

That's the problem. Until she can get the truth out of Louisa, all Sophie has is conjecture. She can feed it all she likes, but it's not facts.

Nevertheless, she signs in as Avenger_Angel – one of her more forthright personas – and comments that she would be *really* interested in finding out about Louisa's early life, and that she would be willing to pay for genuine information.

Contrary to the way every tiny misdemeanour of Sophie's past life was turned over and over in the press, virtually no information about Tragic Louisa's background ever got an airing. Sophie was sure Fiona had a hand in it, dishing out injunctions to anyone she could control.

She thinks about giving out Louisa's maiden name or outing her current identity. But that would be showing one of the few aces in her hand. If needs be, she will play as dirty as it gets to uncover the truth and force Louisa to give her what she is owed. This is for Sami now, after all, as well as for Sam. She deserves her birthright from her father's estate. And, just as importantly, she should not have to grow up the daughter of a falsely accused murderer.

What Sophie needs is dirt.

A thought strikes her. She swipes her way to the photo she took in Fen Manor, of all Louise Turner's horsey victories.

Over the next hour, she Googles and bookmarks contact information for pony clubs and shows in the Home Counties, stables around the places where Louise won cups, and pony and horse chat rooms. She gathers an impressive list, a glimpse into a world she barely knew existed. Inventing another persona for herself – Trudie Stein, a social historian writing a book about English horse and pony culture in the late twentieth century – she posts and emails her question to the addresses and URLs on her list: does anyone remember a Louise Turner, who, with her horse Star, won many prizes in the early- to mid-nineteen nineties?

It's an oddly specific question, she knows, but in her experience, people are all too willing to unquestioningly share information, particularly if it can be done anonymously and without much bother. All she has to do now is wait.

In full hunting mode now, she Google-maps A.R.K., the Soho design agency where 'Lou Turner' now works, and zooms in on Street View. She has done this so many times that, although she has not yet been there, she knows the street intimately. Today the pictures have changed. The old set must have been taken early in the morning, because in them a man was crashed out in the otherwise smug and sleek doorway, his head protruding from a filthy sleeping bag. He is now nowhere to be seen. Perhaps A.R.K. insisted on the substitution. Sophie knows how important image is to those sorts of people; after all, she has done time in that world, selling her classy looks to lend credibility and luxury to all sorts of otherwise mundane brands.

And, like the street sleeper, she too has been airbrushed out. A lot of other girls got work out of her fall from grace; her former clients wanted fresher, less toxic faces for their products.

But Louisa won't get rid of her quite so easily.

She narrows her eyes, and pictures her enemy striding into the building like one of Noah's animals, headed for salvation.

She has to speak to her, and now.

With the Street View on her screen, she taps the agency number into her phone.

'Hello, A.R.K.,' the woman at the other end says, in that lazy, OK yah! drawl bred in English girls' boarding schools – the accent Sophie spent a couple of years perfecting to mask her lowly origins.

'Lou Turner, please.'

'May I ask who's calling?'

'It's her sister,' Sophie says, trying to suppress the smile that creeps into her voice at the very thought that she might be related to that monster.

'Just putting you through.'

Sophie waits while Miles Davis plays 'So What'. Not your average on-hold soundtrack. They must think they're so smart, this A.R.K. lot.

Sophie knows the type.

'Hello?'

Every hair along her bony spine stands up. That voice. It sounds so light, so girlish, so fucking carefree. How bloody dare she possess such a voice when her own sticks in her throat, strangled, throttled by her anger? She starts to say something, but an image flashes across her brain of Fiona bearing down on her, getting the police involved, hauling her in front of another court, banging her up again, taking Sami away . . .

'Who is this?' The sugary tones bore into her ear.

Feeling the acid rise to meet her stopped words, Sophie cuts the call and flings the phone onto the sofa.

She storms through to her bedroom, where, with Sami still asleep, she kneels in front of her Sam shrine.

'What should I do now, Sam?'

'Write another letter, give Louisa one more chance.' She's sure she hears him say it.

'Really?'

'Yes. What's the rush? Let her sweat.'

She takes another of the *Cambridge Evening News* front pages from the washing line, lights it and lets it flutter to the carpet.

TRAGIC LOUISA TELLS—

'Nice plan, Sam.'

Perhaps because of the smell of burning wool, Sami wakes, and starts whimpering in her cot. At the sound, Sophie's milk instantly lets down. She pulls up her vest top and attaches her nipple to her daughter's rootling gums. It is such a blessed relief – it feels as if some of the poison is being drawn from her, and she lets the love flow for her beautiful baby daughter.

She's on her way back down the stairs, Sami strapped to her front, to take Louisa's new letter to the post box, when she sees the dark shape of a man behind the stained-glass window in the front door. She lurks in the hallway while first he rings her doorbell, then knocks on the door. He doesn't give up. He opens the letterbox and shouts through it.

'Miss Hanley?'

Sophie stays pressed into a corner, hoping that, dressed as she is now in a black, floor-length lightweight shift, she can pass as a coat hanging from the wall. She's really not up to receiving surprise visitors. In her experience, the unexpected never turns up a happy result.

But Pawel's door bursts open. He stops and scowls at Sophie.

'That's for you,' he says, jerking his meaty, professorial thumb in the direction of the doorway.

'Shh.' She holds her finger up to her mouth, but he ignores her.

'Yes,' he shouts to the man outside while directing a nasty smile at her. 'She is in here.'

Sophie makes to run upstairs, but Pawel grabs her arm and drags her to the front door.

'Here she is,' he says, opening it. Having let the visitor in, he retreats back along the corridor and slams the door of his flat, wondering aloud if he will ever have any peace this morning.

'So sorry', Sophie yells after Pawel, 'to have disturbed your WANKING.'

She turns and sees that her visitor is the guy in the pinstripe suit from Marsden & Hunt.

'Miss, um Hanley.'

'What do you want?' Sophie says, showing no sign of recognition. She's not going to make his task any easier.

'As you are aware, we will shortly be putting Mrs Williams's flat on the market. We need access now, or in the very near future, to take photographs and measure up, and, once we launch, we'll need to show viewers around.'

'To make me and my child homeless.' Sophie stares at him, her teeth biting into her lips.

The estate agent blinks. He's far less assertive once he's off his own territory.

'Is there anything I can do to stop you?' she asks him.

'Not really,' he says. 'We understand you're not a bone fide tenant, as such . . .'

'Too fucking right I'm not.' She enjoys the flicker of fear that crosses his face at her snarled response.

'So we don't legally need your permission to enter. Although' – he attempts a smile – 'I do hope you will permit us to conduct our business in an amicable fashion.'

'You what?' Sophie screws up her nose and steps towards him. He flinches, the coward. She has Sami strapped to her front, for fuck's sake. What does he think she is going to do to him?

'I hope we can get on without any, er, inconvenience,' he says.

Sophie could enjoy his discomfort, make it really difficult

for him, but she knows that if she kicks up too much fuss, Louisa will only draft Fiona in.

'You've got keys, I take it?' she says.

He nods and holds up his index finger, from which the keys dangle like little knives.

'Help yourself,' she says, rolling her eyes and flouncing out of the front door, happy that she has left the place an utter tip. 'Don't steal anything.'

As she makes her way to the post box, she wonders whether, if she bought a new lock for her flat door, she would be able to put it in herself, or whether she would have to pay a handyman to do it.

More girl students pass on their bikes and she very nearly steps into the road and pushes them off.

20

Sweating in her London eyrie, Lou pulls her sheet over her face and tries to sleep, but even at six in the morning the sun burns through the blinds. Her room is airless, despite the best efforts of a very expensive, bladeless fan – one of the many things she has bought this week to make her life here more comfortable.

But all the designer chairs, espresso machines and Jo Malone candles in the world can't hide the fact of yesterday's silent phone call. A fine thing that was, to sign off her first week at work.

There's no proof, but she's pretty certain it wasn't one of those automatically dialled spam calls.

Sophie gave her one week in her horrible little note. Was this her warning that the deadline is nearly up?

As she pulls herself from her sticky bed, she asks herself what threat Sophie really poses. The court has agreed what happened in the car crash, the police have drawn their conclusions about Katie's murder, and Katie's family have been paid off. It's all over, signed off, in the past, and nothing that vindictive little girl can do or say can change that.

She steps into the shower and aims the feeble trickle over her body. Now *there's* something that's worthy of her attention. She needs to get hold of a plumber.

She soaps herself down, running her fingers over scars which have almost become familiar to her.

Could Sophie harm her physically? That's a possibility: her own soft, broken flesh wouldn't stand a chance against her enemy's hard, dark, sharp edges, her violent tendencies, her strange proclivities.

Sophie and Sam: it took one to know one. Lou has seen the evidence.

Why is Sophie hounding her? Revenge for Sam crashing his car and dying while he was chasing Lou and the children as they tried to escape? For spoiling her dreams of becoming the third Mrs Williams?

Lou flings the soap, slamming it down onto the base of the bath. It doesn't achieve much, but it makes her feel a little better. She bends to pick it up, steadying her uneven self against the tiles.

How is she supposed to move on from horror if there's always Sophie snapping at her heels, blurring the line between the past and the present, threatening to sully her clean start, the new reality that she has, with such monumental effort, created for herself?

Again, she thinks about reporting all this to Fiona. But that would be worse than merely looking towards the past. It would be turning and actively walking back towards it, arms wide open.

'Stop asking yourself all these questions,' she tells herself as she turns off the shower. 'You're going mad here, all on your own.'

Wrapping herself in a towel, she decides that she is going to continue with her policy of ignoring the problem. Perhaps she'll be lucky, and it'll just go away. If not, well then, she'll have to keep her guard up, find a way of dealing with it herself.

She won't let Sam's little whore shatter her new life, not after everything she's been through.

She has to look forward. Celebrate the now. It is Saturday,

she has enjoyed her first week at work and today she is going to meet Adam in the café. She's going to meet a beautiful, strong young man.

A man to look after her, perhaps, should the necessity ever arise.

She doesn't like to think like that, but it's best to be prepared.

Despite all her Pines therapy-induced positive thinking, she still has to force herself out from the shelter of her apartment. As she makes her way across the clogged dual carriageway and down between the railway and the edge of the fenced-off demolition site, she constantly finds herself looking over her shoulder for Sophie.

Is this going to have to be her habit from now on?

It is with some relief that she reaches the railway arch that houses the Rainbow Café. It doesn't look much on the outside – a window cleaner is doing his best with the building dust coating the glass frontage, but he's not onto a winner. Inside, though, it is calm and clean, coffee-scented and busy, filled with people Lou's age and younger. As she passes a table near the door, she catches the rolled consonants of Spanish spoken with a South American twang.

Crowds of plants cascade from baskets hanging high up in the lofty arched ceiling, filling the place with greenery. It's a welcome contrast with the world she has just left outside where, apart from a patch of brown turf into which the site developers have stuck a notice: *Buy off-plan: studios to penthouses from just £400,000*, all nature other than human has been either parched or concreted into submission.

Best of all, Adam is here, sitting right at the back. Spotting her, he stands and smiles, replacing every spark of her twitchiness with a hankering that can only be partly explained by the fact that it is eleven o'clock and she hasn't yet eaten a thing.

She threads her way past the crowded tables towards him.

It's her first chance to properly see him for what he is – their first meeting had been compromised by shock, their second by fear, and the third by swimsuits.

The most striking thing, she sees now, is how young he is – early twenties at most, so around ten years younger than her. Next are his clothes: fresh T-shirt, loose shorts, his hair caught back in a ponytail, sunglasses on the top of his head. None of this does anything to age him, but it is such a world away from what she used to know, all the Paul Smith shirts and bespoke suits, that it can only be a good sign.

As she approaches, he reaches out for her hand and kisses her, his stubble grazing her cheek, making her stomach flip. He smells clean, faintly of cedar-wood, even on this furnace of a morning, which, over the short walk to the café, has drenched Lou in a sweat she's sure she can smell as she leans in towards him. She's glad that the long linen dress she chose to wear is dark, and doesn't show the dampness she can feel between her breasts and at the small of her back.

'Good to see you.' He gestures to the seat opposite and sits down. 'I was afraid you weren't going to show.'

She smiles and takes her place, holding his gaze with a levelness that belies how uneven she feels inside.

'I hope you don't mind,' he says, 'but it's vegan here. I don't mind what other people eat, but I can't do with the smell of frying bacon.'

'Of course not.' She tries not to show her disappointment. Bacon was what she had been hoping for this morning. A big, fat, bacon sandwich.

'The beans and arepas are very good,' he says.

'Arepas?'

'Sort of cornbread. It's kind of Colombian here.'

'But vegan?'

He smiles. 'But vegan!'

'I never associated Colombia with vegans.'

'London's full of surprises, innit?'

'Beans and arepas sounds good.'

'Coffee too?'

He goes up to the counter where a pretty young woman with olive skin and wide cheekbones takes his order. His shoulders strain against the soft cotton of his shirt as he leans forward to place their order.

Lou scans the room. A dark-haired woman more his age than her own is watching her watch him. As their eyes meet, the woman smiles, raises her eyebrows, and places her thumb and forefinger together in a perfect circle.

She is right. He's really quite something.

Good genes on that boy.

'So how long have you been living in The Heights?' he asks, nodding in the direction of her building as he places a glass mug full of thick, soy-milky coffee in front of her.

'Just over two weeks.'

'I was wondering why I hadn't noticed you before.'

'It's a big building.'

'I would've noticed you, for sure.' He smiles again, his gaze dancing over her. He's certainly direct.

The space between them contracts. She scratches the back of her neck and feels a sudden urge to run away. She's out of practice at this sort of thing, and, anyway, isn't it a bit soon for her to be engaging in all this attraction business?

She promised herself never again, and yet here she is. She is fickle, weak, a sap.

The emptiness calls, though, from deep inside her. It is vast: a deep, deep well of it.

She meets his gaze and decides to stay.

The pretty young woman turns up at their table, bearing their breakfast. Thin slivers of something that looks like bacon but can't be, some fat mushrooms, thin cornbread things that must be the arepas, home-made baked beans and chilli sauce.

'The arepas need this.' He leans over and, in a curiously maternal gesture, sprinkles salt onto her plate.

She cuts off a piece and tries it. He's right. Even with salt, they are curiously bland.

They eat. He tells her about the week he has spent interviewing past tenants of the demolition site, she talks about her new job. And all the while she can't take her eyes off his mouth, which is the most beautiful combination of curve, animation and strong white teeth.

'More coffee?' he says, putting down his knife and fork and wiping those lips with a thick paper napkin. She nods and he waves at the waitress, who smiles her acknowledgement. He turns back, folds his arms and looks at her. 'Now. Tell me more about yourself.'

'Not much to say, really.' She finishes her last mouthful and pushes her plate away. 'That was really good. I loved the – what was it – bacon-type stuff.'

'Tempeh. Yeah, it's good. So: you?'

She shrugs. 'What do you want to know?'

'OK, so where are your family?'

The blood rushes to her cheeks as her heart starts to beat too quickly. 'My family?' Her voice comes out in a tiny squeak.

'Your parents, your mum.'

She breathes out. This, of course, is family to someone his age. 'They live in Scotland.'

'But you didn't grow up there – you haven't got an accent . . .'

'No. I grew up in the South. They moved when I left home.'

'Do you get up there at all?'

'No.'

He puts his knife and fork down and looks at her.

She goes on quickly. 'It's not important. We just had a parting of the ways. We don't really speak.'

'Any brothers or sisters?'

'Nah, just me.' She sips her coffee and tries to look as if she doesn't care, as if she can't see the sympathy in his eyes. 'It's OK. Really,' she says. 'We never got on all that well. I was an inconvenience to them. They never planned on having me. They weren't equipped for it. As soon as I went to art school they were off.'

Although not entirely the full story, this is the account she has built with her therapists at The Pines. Mostly about how she has already set a precedent for surviving alone, it is supposed to paint her in a positive light, but Adam clearly sees it differently. He reaches across the table and puts his large hand on hers, making it look tiny by comparison, as if she has shrunk.

She bites the inside of her cheek until she tastes blood. She will not let the tears come. She will not.

How many times has she been let down by people who should have loved her? No, force the thought away. Self-pity is pointless and unattractive.

'Tell me about your films,' she asks, grasping for safer territory.

'I'll do better than that.' He squeezes her fingers, then lets go. He knows she's changing the subject, and he's going along with it.

Lifting a rucksack from where it is stashed at his feet, he brings it round to her side of the table, dragging an empty chair over so that he can sit next to her, right next to her, their legs touching.

'Here.' He pulls a digital SLR out of his bag and switches it on. 'This is what I've been doing today.'

He fiddles with the controls and holds the camera up so that they can both see the viewfinder. The solid, reassuring weight of his shoulder invites her to lean in against him.

'This is Cynthia,' he says.

An elderly woman sits in a floral Dralon chair in a cramped living room cluttered with tiny ornaments and framed photographs of smiling schoolchildren. As she speaks, the camera closes right in on her, so that her delicate, birdlike face, outlined by a ring of grey hair, takes up the entire frame.

'What's she saying?' Lou asks.

'Hold on.' He pauses the playback and rummages in his bag to pull out a set of earphones, which he plugs into the side of the camera. Gently holding her hair back, he puts one side in her ear and the other in his own, so they are connected by the umbilicus of the cable.

He presses play.

'. . . nineteen seventy-two,' the woman says. 'We come all this way from Jamaica and we find ourself a home on the estate and raise a family and we all grow up together in a real community, you know. Community?'

Out of shot, Adam can be heard agreeing with her.

'Everyone. I knew everyone on our block. We'd watch our children play out in the courtyard. It was lovely. A lovely place to grow up.' Cynthia's eyes shine, reflecting the unmistakable outline of Adam, behind the camera he and Lou are now looking at.

'Now I'm an hour bus journey from my daughters and my grandchildren and their children too,' Cynthia is saying, the Caribbean lilt in her voice increasing as her indignation grows. 'I don't know why I had to come here. I don't know why they couldn't find me somewhere a little bit closer, you know?' She pauses to dab at her eyes with a clean, lace hanky. 'Me husband pass away, him heartbroken with the stress of it all. And now I all alone, out here where I know no one. You know? Not a single soul.'

Adam stops the camera and looks at Lou. Their faces are so

close they are almost touching. His eyes glisten like his inter-viewee's. Lou lifts her hand to touch his cheek, but at that moment the waitress arrives with their coffees and the moment is lost.

Adam puts the camera back in his bag and goes back to his seat opposite her. The heat expands from her to fill the space he has just left.

'Woolwich,' he says, picking up his coffee. 'The nearest flat they could find her was all the way out in Woolwich, when her daughters and their families had all settled round here to be close to their parents.'

'That's awful.'

'I've shot loads of interviews like that.'

'It's beautifully done,' she says. 'The colours are lovely, the light . . .'

'I'm trying to keep the production values up, even though I've got zero budget. No point in having your heart in the right place if you're making a crap film.'

'What are you going to do with it?'

'I've got a few shorts out there on websites, but I'm working on a feature-length documentary, editing it all together, telling the story of the change.'

'And the filming from the crane?'

'All part of it. The buildings were homes that contained lives. They tell their own stories. I've been following the demolition from the start.'

'Do they let you on the site?'

He laughs. 'Nah! I'm like some kind of flea on their back, some sort of irritant. But I get in. It's not as secure as they'd like to think it is.'

'Have you ever got caught?'

'Once or twice. They send me on my way, because it would be seriously bad PR if they got me arrested. But they did say the last time that I'd had my final chance.'

'Have you got any film of what it's like in there?'

'Yeah, on my computer. But I've got a better idea. Got any plans this afternoon?'

'Free as a bird,' she says. It's been a long time coming, but it's true. Apart from the little detail of Sophie, she is, for what seems like the first time ever, blissfully without any responsibilities or concerns.

'Drink your coffee, then, Lou,' he says. 'We're going on an adventure.'

He jumps up and takes her hand.

'What about the bill?' she says as he leads her to the exit.

'It's OK. I work here, remember? They let me eat for free. '*Hasta luego*, Rosa!' he calls to the girl behind the counter.

'Laters, Adam, mate,' Rosa replies in broad South London.

As he opens the café door, Lou looks over at the appreciative dark-haired woman, who smiles and winks at her.

She's jealous of me, Lou thinks. It's an unusual position to find herself in these days, and she rather likes it.

It feels like a victory, of sorts.

21

Then

The mothers sit in a circle on mismatched chairs in the village Methodist church hall, in a fug of brewed tea and Calor gas with undertones of dirty nappy. The children squirm before them on a carpet specially rolled out by the playgroup leader to save them from the dusty floorboards. Brightly coloured plastic toys litter the carpet: cubes and blobs of purple, yellow, red, blue, alternately delighting and frustrating the babies.

'Your first time?' the woman sitting next to Louisa asks.

Louisa nods.

'I'm Sandy.' The woman points over at a porcelain doll-like two-year-old who is bossing a little boy about, telling him how to fry a wooden egg on a toy cooker. 'And that's my Amy.'

'Louisa. And Poppy.' Louisa waves in the direction of her own daughter, who, teething cheeks a-flame, is making a crawling beeline for a dreamy-looking one-year-old with a green plastic brick in his mouth. There are plenty of other green plastic bricks around, but clearly Poppy has her heart set on that one.

Louisa's daughter has shown herself to be advanced in all things. Early to sit, early to crawl and now, at nine months, she is actually hauling herself up onto anything she can grab hold of, tottering a few dangerous steps, then falling down and crying.

In the pre-birth days, Louisa imagined she would rejoice at the passing of each milestone, that her daughter's excellence would burst her with maternal pride. But now, in the thick of it, every new capability just brings more dangers, more opportunities for exhaustion.

Most of the women in the room know each other – they sit and chat, dunking bourbon biscuits in strong tea, which they drink from pale-green mugs. Every now and then one will jump up to right a fallen toddler, or to rescue a baby from the grabby fist of another.

Invariably today, Poppy is that grabby other. She is going through a curious and grasping phase, and is particularly drawn to other children's noses, hair and ears. Apart from introducing herself to Sandy, Louisa's only words so far have been: 'No, Poppy' to her daughter, and 'Sorry' to other women for the damage wrought.

'Sorry,' she says to the mother of the green-plastic-brick boy as Poppy barrels him over and snatches his toy.

Louisa hopes that the other mothers have enough compassion to see the position she is in. Surely all toddlers go through these difficult phases? But it seems not. As Poppy clambers away, brick in fat fist, her victim's ensuing wail creates a wave of maternal hostility that Louisa can practically see rolling across the room towards her.

The playgroup leader plugs an iPod into a small portable speaker and one of the inner-circle mothers hauls a plastic crate out from a cupboard. It is labelled NOISY TOYS!!!

The mothers pick up their children. Those with two put babes in arms back into car seats and perch toddlers on knees. Following suit, Louisa steps her way across the carpet and takes hold of Poppy, who protests loudly at being stopped from gnawing her hard-won plastic brick. When Louisa returns with her to her seat, she notices that Sandy has taken her delicate daughter across the circle to sit and laugh with a group of other mothers.

The empty seat next to her reminds Louisa of how it was for her at school.

As the NOISY TOYS!!! – drums, tambourines, kazoos, shakers, toy trumpets and triangles – are handed out, Louisa wonders how these other women manage to make themselves look so presentable. Each has immaculate hair and make-up and ironed clothes in intact colours. Those with pukey babies protect their clothing with dazzling white muslins shoulder-thrown like a dashing pashmina. She, on the other hand, sports a slick of mashed banana on her leggings, and, although she isn't entirely certain – mornings tend to pass in a bit of a blur – she suspects that she forgot to wipe off the under-eye smudge of yesterday's mascara that she noticed while cleaning her teeth.

At least she cleaned her teeth, though she doesn't know why she bothers even with that. Dental hygiene and any sort of make-up are surplus to requirements. Sam – who is currently on his way back from a week in New York – is hardly ever at home these days. And even if he is there, he barely looks at her, hardly even makes the effort to be civil. Not since he sent her out to make herself presentable on that abortive shopping trip to Cambridge. That, she thinks, was when his patience deserted him.

'What the hell have you done?' he said when he came home late as usual, to find her, head newly shorn, dozing on the sofa.

'I thought I'd try a new look.' She smiled, knowing that in doing so she was revealing teeth stained by the bottle of red she had put away while bracing herself for his return.

'It's utterly hideous,' he said, standing in the living-room doorway, his coat still on, his bag in his hand, as if prepared to walk straight out again. Then suddenly, frighteningly, he punched the door at his side with his free hand, making her flinch.

'Why the hell do you do these things, Louisa? Is it to spite me? Is that it?'

She laughs out loud into the room of mothers and toddlers. As if everything she does is about him!

Now her hair has grown out to a bushy dark inch all over, it looks, if anything, worse than ever before. She should go and get it styled into something that could pass, perhaps – if she managed to lose a bit of weight – as gamine. But if she did that, she would be conceding defeat at the hands of his cruelty. As the mother of his child, surely she should be beautiful to him, whatever her looks.

The children start banging their instruments as soon as they get them, so by the time 'The Wheels on the Bus' starts playing on the weedy speaker, it is barely audible. The other mothers laugh indulgently, but the cacophony sets Louisa's teeth on edge. At least Poppy isn't adding to it: rather than shake her maraca, she has chosen to chew it.

Louisa's hands hang loosely around her wriggling, gnawing daughter. For a moment, she worries about lead in paint, but then, of course, that wouldn't be an issue. This is a toddler playgroup. All the toys, surely, have to be safe?

The music carries on, through 'Twinkle, Twinkle' and 'Let it Go', with which the mothers all join in. Louisa doesn't know the words, but out of some need to fit in she mouths an approximation. Bored by now with her maraca lollipop, Poppy wriggles madly in her lap, like a propeller being wound up, head thrusting one way, feet the other. She works her hands free until one little clenched fist whacks Louisa smack in the face with the shaker. There might not be lead in the maraca's paint, but the weight of it as it lands in her eye socket makes her wonder if it isn't made of the stuff.

'OW! Sit STILL, Poppy!'

She doesn't realise how loud her yell is until it is out there. It can be heard even above the combination of Queen Elsa's exhortations and the efforts of the babies on their NOISY TOYS!!!. Everyone stops singing and banging, and at that very moment, Poppy makes a final gyration and launches herself off Louisa's knee, head first to the floor, banging her skull on the edge of a tiny seesaw.

There is a brief hiatus as she draws her breath, and everyone watches and waits. Then the wail starts, louder, Louisa fears, than any this carpet has ever witnessed.

'Awww,' the other mums say, but, as she scoops up her child, grabs her changing bag and heads for the exit, Louisa knows they think this is just deserts for her little bully girl.

Outside, as Louisa is strapping a recalcitrant Poppy into her car seat, the playgroup leader bustles out, scrunching across the gravel towards her. She puts a gentle, Methodist hand on her shoulder and asks her if everything is all right.

'Yes, thank you. Everything's fine,' Louisa says, smiling painfully brightly, holding her eyes in such a way that keeps the tears inside the lids.

As she drives away, Poppy screaming from the back seat, she watches, in her rear-view mirror, the plain woman standing in the car park in brown corduroy, looking after her with concern.

Is her misery really so obvious?

Louisa braces herself. She will not take pity. She will not take charity. She will not have anyone interfering.

She is doing fine. Just fine.

22

Now

'Where are we going?' Lou asks Adam as he leads her by the hand, away from the Rainbow Café and along the dusty, closed road between the railway arches and the demolition site. He'd started off a little too fast for her to comfortably keep pace with her limp, but, bless him, he soon realised and slowed down.

'It's a surprise,' he says, smiling at her as they pass empty bottles, broken glass, discarded takeaway containers and pools of vomit and dried piss, leftovers from the street parties that have now become a feature of the heatwave nights.

'I like a surprise,' she says.

'Look inside.' Placing a hand between her shoulders, he steers her to one of the viewing holes that pepper the tall blue wooden fence around the demolition site.

On the other side, a block of flats stands precariously, its front ripped off, its interiors gaping, exposing the patterns and colours and even some of the furniture left over from lives once lived here. It's like looking at a life-sized doll's house, or some avant-garde, multi-level theatre set.

'People's homes. It's obscene,' Adam mutters, shaking his head. 'Like some dirty Soho peep show.'

Lou nods, but she can't feel it like him. She knows only too well that everyone has to move on sometime. But, even so, his passion and commitment are appealing.

'Look, see our crane?' he says, leaning his cheek against hers to get a better view.

Our crane. She closes her eyes and holds her breath. She could just turn her head and place her lips on his . . .

But he breaks away before she can make the move. 'Come on,' he says, and takes her hand once again.

They emerge onto the main road on the far side of the demolition site to Lou's building. She flinches and shivers as a train rattles over the bridge above her. Sudden noise can do that sometimes; bring back the panic of the crash as the car smashed into the tree and everything was lost . . .

As she has been taught, she shakes it out of herself and they move on, skirting the perimeter of the site. Behind the wall of wooden hoardings, which stretches far into the distance down the road, the clang, thump, buzz and drill of the demolition site provides an incessant backdrop to the roaring traffic.

A monstrous, dirty-white articulated lorry thunders past within half a metre of them and, again, she finds her shoulders tight up against her ears.

'You all right?' Adam asks.

'Yep. It's just a bit noisy out here.'

'Tell me about it.'

They carry on along the main road, following the fence.

'All this was wide open until about two months ago.' Adam gestures at the graffiti-crusted hoardings. Lou casts a professional eye over the decoration. Among the crudely sprayed tags are a couple of beautiful, vividly drawn images of plants and trees. But most of this long fence is covered in angry political slogans, including a stretch of five-foot-high letters that declare: THIS IS NOT REGENERATION, IT IS GENTRIFICATION.

'Your work?' she asks Adam as they pass.

He shakes his head. 'My mate's. I filmed him doing it, though, all masked up – they'd get him otherwise.' He touches the paint. 'As if a handful of letters on a fence are more criminally damaging than what's going on behind it.'

Whisked by a hot wind stirred up by the slipstream of a passing juggernaut, a swirl of empty crisp packets and carrier bags dances around them, then swoops away like a flurry of plastic birds.

'I've not been down here before,' Lou says.

'Why would you?' Adam says, gesturing at the endless fence down one side of the road and the phalanx of bland, new-build apartments opposite, which are almost entirely hidden by screaming marketing hoardings: SHOW APARTMENT NOW OPEN! MODERN LIVING NEAR THE HEART OF LONDON!

Adam points at a sign declaring: ONLY A FEW REMAINING! 'If that's true,' he says, 'then why are they still pushing them like this? I mean, would you want to live in that?'

'They're pretty soulless,' Lou says, eyeing the ugly, generically functional buildings, all red brick with jauntily painted metalwork, triple-glazed windows and no soul whatsoever. At least her place, for all its thermal inefficiency, has a quirky sixties charm.

'Five years ago, this road was alive,' Adam says. 'A vibrant community in the heart of South London.'

'Wasn't it a bit dodgy, though, too?' she says.

'Don't believe everything you read in the papers.'

'Oh, I don't.' Lou, more than anyone, knows how the press can get it wrong.

'They're full of filthy lies. I don't read any of them. Not ever.'

'Is it much further?' She's trying not to show it, but she is hot, dusty and sweaty. Also, the haze of exhaust fumes from the constant wall of traffic is making her wheezy, and her bad leg is beginning to protest.

'We've arrived, in fact,' he says, coming to a stop by a mature lime tree standing on a scrubby grass verge on the road side of the hoardings.

He touches the trunk of the tree. 'Lucky old lady hasn't been cut down. Not like her sisters on the other side of the fence. When the first lot went, we sat in them, but they plucked us out with cherry pickers. They say they're going to build a new park and plant more trees, but why did they have to kill the old ones?'

Lou looks up at the scabby tree. It's certainly seen better days. She'd probably have chopped it down with the others if it had been up to her.

'You any good at climbing?' he asks.

She places her hand next to his on the tree. 'This?'

He nods.

'Um, well I used to be, when I was about ten.' She looks up. The first bough is about six feet up in the air.

'Think you can get up there with a leg up?'

She looks around at the busy road. 'Won't someone stop us?'

He laughs. 'You'd be surprised how little people want to get involved.'

'I don't know . . .'

'Go on, Lou. I promise nothing will happen. Believe me. I do this all the time.'

When he looks at her with those eyes, all she can do is trust him. And it's not like she's been particularly averse to breaking rules in the past. Is she going to start playing it safe just because she's got a bad leg and a bit of trauma to deal with?

'Look.' He takes her hand from the trunk and holds it between his. 'If you move quickly and definitely, if you look like you mean business, people really won't mess with you. They're too scared of getting it wrong, or finding out you're a total head case.'

'Oh, what the hell.' She smiles at him.

'I knew you'd be up for it,' he says, and her chest fills with pride. He thought she was adventurous. Of course she's adventurous!

'You'll have to hitch your dress up a bit,' he says. Watching him watch her, she tucks her long skirt into her knickers. He drops down in front of her bare knees and links his hands near the ground. 'Put your foot in.'

She does so and he pushes her effortlessly upwards. Beyond the wrenching pain in her bad leg, and despite all the changes wrought on her body since she was a kid, the clambering instinct kicks in immediately. Before she is really aware of it, they are both up in the tree, in among leaf buds that are browning before they have even had a stab at green. The fact that she has managed to get up here despite her injuries scores her one more mark against Sam's failed attempts to obliterate her.

She looks around at the traffic thundering beneath her, then over at the demolition site, where, behind the eviscerated blocks of flats, there is a vast swathe of cleared land. The scarred earth holds tangles of rusty, twisted old pipes waiting to be scrapped, piles of rubble as high as houses, and a grave-yard of felled trees. Beyond that, a small city of Portakabins provides off-duty shelter for the dozens of men who mill industriously about the site in hi-vis work wear and helmets.

Further to the right, three blocks of flats awaiting demolition are wrapped in a white material, like some kind of artwork. For Lou, this landscape holds a strange, apocalyptic beauty.

'What do we do now?' she asks Adam.

'We just edge out along that branch, and it's a short drop to that grassy bit.'

'We're going in?'

He smiles. 'What did you think we were up here for? There's something amazing I want to show you. When you hit the ground, be sure to get behind that old grit bin over there, or you might be spotted.'

'And I don't want to be spotted.'

He grins. 'Oh, no, you don't want to be spotted . . .'

She surprises herself at how neatly and quietly she lets herself down, steadying herself with her hands on the gritty brown grass. It doesn't matter, she tells herself, about a bit of dirt on the palms. She doesn't need her hand sanitiser.

'You're a natural!' Adam drops down beside her.

They scuttle over to a patch of dandelion leaves behind the bunker-like grit bin, which is thick with pitted layers of faded yellow paint.

She feels his hand again, this time on the small of her back. He's pointing out one of the wrapped-up buildings. 'We need to steer clear of that one,' he says. 'It's where the work's concentrated at the moment, and although that white stuff looks solid from here, the people inside can see out. We've got to get past it, though, because the thing I want to show you is on the other side.'

He leads her on and they scuttle from hiding place to hiding place. Like, she thinks, soldiers in a documentary about Afghanistan.

'It's hard to imagine people actually living here,' she says, as they duck behind a pile of rubble with a Barbie sticking out of it like a tiny earthquake victim.

'Oh they did, though. Until recently. It took them four years to get the last owners out. The brave ones who refused to go until they got enough money to buy a similar place locally. They didn't win, of course. It was pretty brutal in the end. I've got it all on film. But back in the day, the estate was really buzzing. People really liked living here. It was a real community.'

'I've never lived like that,' Lou says, catching herself off guard, giving a piece of herself away too easily.

'Would you like to?'

She shrugs. She wouldn't, in fact, but she doesn't think he'd like to hear that.

They slip behind an empty oil tank. A sign on the side of one of the nearby Portakabins tells the workers that *Safety Gear Must Be Worn At All Times*, and Lou thinks how out of place she and Adam would appear if spotted, in their casual summer clothes. They press their backs against the tank as two men sweltering in fluorescents, helmets and big boots walk past with a scroll of plans, arguing about football.

'What'll happen if we're discovered?' she whispers once they have passed.

'Normally, they'd just chuck us off, but, like I say, they're a bit sick of me, so I might get arrested.'

Lou catches her breath. The last thing she wants is to get involved with the police. She doesn't want anything to do with them ever again.

'You OK with that?' he says. He has stopped and is looking at her. 'We can go back if you want . . .'

She shakes her head, but not all that convincingly.

'They wouldn't be interested in you. I'd say I forced you into joining me.'

'And make me look like a total wet? Thanks!'

'But they won't find us anyway.'

'No.'

'Not if we're careful.' He drops to his belly and starts crawling across the ground to the next piece of cover, an empty digger.

'Do I have to do that?' she says, not much fancying the idea of getting dirty.

He stops and looks back at her innocently from the ground. 'Just showing you how careful I can be . . .'

Laughing, she goes over and pulls him up.

As they make their way around the site to the other side of the wrapped-up blocks, a whole new vista opens up.

'This is what I wanted to show you,' Adam says, tucking behind a parked lorry and drawing her to him.

The sight before her almost makes her forget the fact that he is very close to her now, pressed up behind her, looking over her head.

Almost.

An area the size of three football pitches has had everything it contained erased from it. Instead of houses and flats, it is now a great pit with terraced edges stepping down at least fifty feet. A steep ramp runs up one side, allowing access for vehicles and workers. At the bottom of the pit, several diggers stand still, as if abandoned.

'It's like something out of a science fiction film,' Lou says.

Adam snorts. 'Aliens, tunnelling down to hell.'

Lou hugs her elbows tightly to herself. Something about the scale of it reminds her of the clay pits near Fen Manor. Although, where the clay pits were full of swirling brown water, alive with hungry fish and birds, here the giant hole is dark and dead and empty. But the great dwarfing size of it makes the same impression: it overwhelms her, makes her feet itch with the urge either to run, or to jump in . . .

'It's going to be an underground multiplex,' Adam says. 'Showing the same films you can see at about twenty cinemas within a half-hour walk from here. And a mammoth supermarket to keep the rich incomers happy while they knock down the shopping centre.'

'They sent a leaflet round about it,' Lou says. She rather likes the idea of a good cinema and supermarket on her doorstep.

Adam tuts. 'Over a thousand families lived in the buildings that stood on top of this hole.'

166

'That's hard to imagine.'

His sigh is shallow, as if something is pressing on his chest. 'See how quickly they can wipe out the past.'

'True.'

They stand and stare, and Lou tries to imagine people like Cynthia from Adam's film standing on balconies, watching their children play in the courtyards beneath their flats. But she can't bring the scene to life in her mind.

'Look out,' Adam says, drawing her further behind the shelter of the lorry.

Down in the far corner of the pit, so distant that it looks like a toy, one of the mechanical diggers shudders into action. Belching diesel fumes, it trundles across the pitted ground until it reaches the edge, where it starts scraping at the sides, the man inside just discernible in his hard hat and hi-vis jacket.

The sun beats down. Adam now has his arms around her, holding her protectively, as if the digger is some kind of threat. It feels as natural to her as breathing to be standing like this with him, so she leans back into him. He kisses the top of her head, and her body shimmers.

A plane arcs noisily over their heads, glinting white at them from the hot-hazed blue of the sky. Lou tries to picture the passengers on board, but here, too, her imagination fails her. It's as if she and Adam are the only two people in the world at this moment. She turns towards him, keeping her body close and, almost instantly, her lips find his.

His kiss is even better than she had imagined. Firm, clean, just a hint of what is to come . . . and the cedar scent of him is intoxicating. She closes her eyes and breathes in the possibility.

A new life.

He draws away slightly and leans his forehead against hers. 'I've wanted to do that since I first saw you. It's been driving me crazy.'

'Me too,' she says.

They're just about to kiss again when the digger in the pit cuts its engine with a small bang, startling them both. As if they have been caught out, they draw apart.

'Has he seen us?' Lou asks.

The driver jumps from his cab. He's not running in their direction but away, towards the scarred, crumbling edge of the pit, where he falls to his knees and starts scooping earth with his hands.

Adam takes off his rucksack, pulls out a small pair of binoculars, lifts them to his eyes and trains them on the man, who has stopped what he is doing and is looking over in their direction.

Lou worries that he can see Adam, who, to get a better angle on what's happening, has edged out from the safety of their shelter. But he doesn't seem to clock him. Instead, he pulls out a walkie-talkie and turns back to where he had been digging, gesturing towards the spot as he speaks. His movements are short and sharp. Frantic, even.

'What's he found?' Lou asks. 'Can you see?'

Adam peers through the binoculars. 'Not clearly – he's in the way. Something whiteish . . .'

Still speaking into his walkie-talkie, the man squats and scrapes away some more soil, working sideways, angling himself against the edge of the pit, finally revealing what he has found.

Adam whistles under his breath. 'My days.'

'What?'

'Look.' He hands her the binoculars.

A gust of hot wind whistles around her, blowing her hair into her eyes so that she has to hold it back to get it out of the way of the eyepiece.

There, packed into the earth, are layers of white lumpish things, dirtied by the soil. It looks like the digger has chopped through a giant slice of nut brittle. She adjusts the focus on the binoculars – her eyes are closer together than Adam's.

'Do you see what it is?' he asks her.

The man works at the patch, extending upwards and sideways. It seems to have no end. He tugs at something in the packed-in stuff until, with a bit of levering, he pulls it away. It looks to Lou like a greyish football.

As if he has removed a keystone from an arch, a large chunk of surrounding matter crumbles away and falls on top of him.

They hear his scream from right across the other side of the pit. As he tries to work himself free, he throws the thing in his hand to the ground. As it rolls away, she finally sees what it is.

'A skull,' she whispers, trying to blank out what the disembodied head calls to her mind, the horror of what she has seen in the past.

'Not just one.' Adam has now got his camera out and is zoomed right in on the scene, filming. 'Look at what's all around him.'

There are bones. Thigh bones, rib bones, skulls, arm bones, pelvic bones. Another coil of wind snaps around Lou and Adam and swoops down into the pit, stirring up the dust that fell with the skeleton parts. Lou's back prickles and she feels the arepas and beans rise in her belly.

She's not all that good with death and bodies.

'It's some sort of burial ground,' Adam says.

Lou scans the wall of the pit and sees layers and layers of skeletons, like strata in a cliff face. The wind-whipped dust whirls in the pit like a sandstorm. Other workers are now running down the ramp towards the scene, stirring up the dried dirt like stampeding cattle.

The first to reach him – young, strong-looking men – take one look, then instantly pile in, digging and pulling at the bones, tugging them from the earth. But then an older, slower, fatter man – a man in charge – catches up and pulls them away, almost violently. He shouts at them – words Lou can't hear with the distance and the din of the city and the wind and the demolition work going on around them.

The workers stop what they are doing and stand still in the swirling dust, bones all around them. To a man, they look up and scan the edge of the pit.

Adam downs his camera and pulls her back behind the lorry.

Taking the binoculars from her, he packs his stuff away. 'We'd better get going,' he says. 'The old guy's on the phone. He'll be calling the police, what with all those bodies, and we don't want to be here when they arrive.'

'But they're old, the bodies, right?' she says. The depth they are at, they must have been buried centuries ago, if not millennia. Long before all of this modern London stood here.

'Oh they're old,' Adam says. 'But the police will still investigate.'

She pulls away from him and retches, vomits the Rainbow Café Full Vegan Colombian all over the gritty, polluted earth.

He holds her hair and rubs her back until she is done, then offers her water from a metal bottle he produces from his bag. She gargles, rinses and spits.

When finally she is ready, he takes her hand and they run away from the scene, as if they had never been there, as if they had never witnessed it.

23

Then

Poppy screams all the way home from the Methodist playgroup, relenting only when she is put in front of CBeebies. Numbly cuddling her daughter, Louisa sinks her first glass of wine, telling herself it's perfectly OK. She's had a bad day and today, at least, it is past midday.

The second glass helps her believe herself. The hard day followed a night where she slept no longer than an hour at a stretch, thanks to teething, screaming, shitting and – when she finally gave in and took Poppy into bed with her – wriggling. She feels like a Guantanamo Bay detainee, tortured through sleep deprivation. Except being forced to listen to non-stop Barney the Dinosaur would be a walk in the park compared to submitting to Poppy's tyranny.

She looks down at the top of her daughter's head, the fontanelle pulsating through the still sparse head of near-ginger hair Poppy has inherited from her father. 'No, not tyranny,' Louisa says. 'Just teething.'

Poppy looks up at her, rests her head against her breast and stretches her face into a two-tooth smile. It melts Louisa's heart. Cracks her up. This, she realises, is how children survive the infant years.

'You're too darn cute,' she says to her daughter in her best Disney voice. 'Too goddamn cute.'

Shortly after this, Poppy starts grizzling. It is lunchtime, and the battle of the puree must, once more, commence. Poppy has a thing about textures and, so far, she has not shown much inclination for anything solid. Even the tiniest, softest pea will have her choking and gagging as if her mother has poisoned her.

After some alarming Internet research, Louisa took her to the doctor's, but was told that this was all quite normal and that at some point Poppy will eat proper food. 'Have you ever seen an adult who only eats puree?' the doctor asked her from his comfortable chair, and Louisa had to admit that she hadn't. In the end, instead of treatment for her child, she came away with a prescription for anti-depressants for herself. She hasn't picked up the pills from the chemist, though. There's nothing wrong with her that she can't deal with herself.

As she sits slowly shovelling perfectly smooth home-made apple sauce into and around Poppy's mouth, Louisa finishes the day's first bottle of wine. Only she knows the extent of her habit. As she's the one responsible for recycling and waste, she has hidden a box at the back of one of the outbuildings for her bottles. The drinking's only temporary, anyway. She'll cut back just as soon as she feels more like herself again.

The feed over, Poppy starts drooping. Her eyelids take the lead, followed by her head, as she nearly collapses into the puddle of apple slopped on her highchair table. The jolt wakes her up, and she smacks her lips before going through the whole process again.

Two glasses into the next bottle, Louisa is drunk enough to find this quite amusing.

'Silly baby.' She wipes Poppy's mouth with a damp piece of kitchen roll, takes off her plastic bib and lifts her sweet-smelling child into her arms. Little hands reach up and clasp her shoulder and, as she carries her upstairs, she inhales the apple-biscuit scent of her head.

'Up the golden ladder to Bedfordshire,' she says as she negotiates the stair gate. Her own bed feels awfully tempting too. But she will wash up first, clean the kitchen, rinse her wine glass, perhaps polish off that second bottle. On the way up, Louisa stumbles on a pile of clean clothes she left on the fourth step. Deftly, she puts out a hand and saves herself from falling on her front and squashing her daughter.

'You can do it, Louisa,' she says, picking herself up and making her way to the top.

By the time she lays Poppy in her cot, the little girl is fast asleep. Louisa steps carefully backwards, holding her breath, but, amazingly, there is none of the usual fuss.

'What, I'm free to just walk away?' Louisa says, putting her hands to her face in mock surprise. Where her fingers touch the top of her cheekbone, she feels the sharp sting of a bruise. Out on the landing, she glances in the mirror and sees, under yesterday's mascara smudge, the purple swelling around her eye. Poppy has given her a proper shiner with that maraca.

That'll be something to talk to Sam about when he gets back from New York this evening, she thinks. If he comes home before she's in bed.

'Now then, let's dance downstairs and clear up,' she says to her reflection, and she does, flicking her wrists and swinging her hips as if she is at one of the Bristol nightclubs she used to frequent when she was at art college.

It's when she is one quarter of her way down the big oak staircase that she trips again. This time, perhaps because she doesn't feel the instinctive urge to protect her young, she fails to put her hand out and instead tumbles, quite literally head over heels, down the remaining fifteen steps.

As she falls, she thinks how perfect it is – that she should suffer the same fall as her mother, all those years ago.

Is this it? she wonders. Payback time?

Then she lands, twisting her ankle badly and whacking her head on the banister. She doesn't know how long she's out for, but when she comes to, all she feels – on top of the pain in her skull and her leg, and a cold dampness between her legs where she has wet herself – is incredibly weary. She closes her eyes and decides just to let the sleep come.

'I fly in from New York,' Sam's eyes are tight on the road as he speeds across the Fens on the way to A & E at Addenbrooke's, his anger tic thrumming in his jaw, 'and I decide that, rather than going straight to the office as planned, I'll turn up early and surprise my wife and child, perhaps take them out for an early supper.'

'I'm sorry,' Louisa says, her voice tiny.

'I'm somewhat deludedly expecting to land into a scene of domestic bliss. I don't know why. I must be mad, must have forgotten how things actually *are* these days. So of course, what do I find instead? My unlovely wife, passed out drunk and bleeding at the bottom of the stairs, soaked in her own piss and stinking of booze.'

'Sorry,' she says again. She leans her head against the window and lets the tarmac blur under her gaze.

'You could have killed yourself. You do realise that, don't you?'

She nods, smearing blood from her head wound on the cold glass. The pain is like a penance.

'And what if you'd been carrying Poppy? I could have come home to two corpses. Imagine what that would do to me.'

Louisa gives a long, juddering sob. Poppy sleeps in the back like a little angel, wrapped in the soft blanket Sam thought to put around her as, fuming, he carried her downstairs to the car.

'I've just about had enough,' he goes on.

'Sorry,' Louisa says yet again, snot gumming up her words.

'When is all this going to end?'

'I don't know.' She stares out of the window at the flat, featureless fields, now full of stubble after a long, hot summer. The odd skeletal limb of desiccated cow parsley punctuates the skyline. Is it this landscape that is doing her in, draining her of what she considers to be herself? Her head aches.

She imagines riding Star across this land. He would have loved the flat openness of it. They would have galloped like streaks along the edges of the irrigation waterways, jumping where they intersected, thumping down then streaming on, her own blond mane flying behind her, nearly long enough to join with his tail.

Oh, but that was all so long ago. The horse has gone; the hair has gone. It was, almost literally, another lifetime, and not one to be revisited.

'Is it me?' Sam asks out of nowhere.

'What?' she says.

'I mean, I don't think I'm a bad husband. I look after you, I provide whatever you need, encourage you to take your own steps to be independent, yet, even with all that, you don't seem to be able to be happy. What is it with me and wives? Katie—' He catches his breath on his ex-wife's name.

'Don't talk about Katie,' Louisa says quickly.

But he ignores her. 'She was just so damn miserable all the time. Nothing was ever right for her. Yet she was so furious, so crazy when I said I was leaving her.'

'For me.'

'Yeah, yeah. For you.'

'Yes.'

'And the same thing's happening to you now. So is it me?'

Louisa swallows. A chill of fear creeps up her throat. 'She said she'd rather die than divorce you.'

Clocking her look, he turns to face her.

'Is that what this is all about?' he says. 'I thought you believed me. I had nothing to do with her death.'

'The road, Sam!' she screams. He swerves to take the bend that he nearly didn't see, screeching the tyres, burning black on the tarmac.

When the car is steadied, she turns to him, keeping her voice as calm as possible. 'I lied for you, didn't I?'

'I was in your flat, on my own all the time,' he says, flicking his eyes from the road to meet hers. 'I just needed you to say you were there too, that you'd come back from Edinburgh earlier than you did.'

'And I did,' she says, trying to keep things level. 'I told the lie and it was for you, for us—'

'Because I had all the motive, as you know. I swear to God. If all this is because, for some reason, you're doubting me, I swear on Poppy's *life* that I had nothing to do with what happened to Katie . . .'

He is almost shouting. His hands shake as, white-knuckled, they grip the wheel. One swerve, one misjudgement, and he could finish them all off. Louisa needs to get him off the subject – if nothing else, to save her own skin.

'Slow down, Sam,' she says. 'Please. Think of Poppy.'

As if coming to his senses, he does as she asks him. Back at a more sensible speed, he takes a deep, shuddering breath. 'Is it me, Louisa?'

She looks at him through the corners of her eyes and wonders if she can trust him. If he was alone in New York. No. He wouldn't do that to her. He's many things, but he's not like that.

Is he?

No.

He did it to Katie, though . . .

'It's not you. It's me,' she says, turning back to the window. Oh, the stock scripts we fall back on.

* * *

She is silent as Sam tells the doctor what happened. He does little to disguise his anger at the events, an anger which still overshadows his concern, especially now it's clear that she's not badly injured. At one point, a nurse offers to take Poppy from him, so violently does he rock her as he speaks.

'Well, let's take a look at this noggin,' the doctor says, gently laying hands on Louisa's short hair. She's a woman in her fifties, perhaps, with an open, kind face. Before she continues with her examination, she turns her clear eyes onto the nurse. 'Perhaps you'd like to take Mr Williams and baby to the quiet room. Find him a cup of tea?'

'Of course,' the nurse says, and ushers Sam from the cubicle. When he is out of earshot, the doctor turns to Louisa, takes both of her hands in her own and gives her the same, piercing look that she gave the nurse.

'Now, my dear. Do you want to tell me what really happened? How you got this black eye? How it was you fell downstairs?'

'I fell. My baby hit me with a maraca.'

'You don't want to tell me anything else?'

Louisa wonders what she wants to hear. Just how much wine she had drunk? Well she's not going to admit that.

'Nothing else. I just fell.'

'I see.' The doctor shakes her head and works on in silence, testing Louisa's eyes, asking her if she feels sick, looking into her ears.

'Minor concussion,' she says, making a note on a clipboard. 'And a nasty black eye. Let's look at that leg, now.'

The doctor sends Louisa for an X-ray.

'Can my husband come with me?' she asks the nurse.

'You sure that's what you want?' the doctor says.

Louisa nods. Reluctantly, the nurse goes to fetch him.

'Hubby and baby are both fast asleep,' she says when she returns. 'You don't want me to wake them, do you?'

'Good news,' the doctor says when Louisa returns from X-ray. 'It's just a nasty sprain.'

'Shall I fetch the husband now?' the nurse asks, when the doctor is done explaining.

'Give me four minutes,' the doctor says, giving the nurse another look.

When they are alone, the doctor turns to Louisa. 'Now, I know you've told me what you want me to hear,' she tells her, slipping a leaflet from her clipboard. 'But I see a lot in this job, and I'm not sure I'm getting the whole story from you. I'd like you to have this. You've got a handbag, yes?'

Lou nods. Sam had practically thrown it at her when he put her in the car.

'Pop it in there and have a look when you get home. When he's not around. And, if anything like this happens again, you could just note it down in a diary or something.'

Louisa's eyes open wide when she sees the title of the leaflet: *You Are Not Alone.*

'Is she ready to go?' Sam says from the entrance to the cubicle.

'I'll wheel Louisa to the car park,' the nurse says, placing herself between the man and his injured wife.

24

After Sami's morning routine of feed, bath, change and feed, Sophie puts her, gloriously naked but for her nappy, in the bouncing chair she bought as a treat after selling the Louboutins. Sami kicks and gurgles happily while her mother tickles her toes and picks up email on the Avenger_Angel account.

Predictably, Sophie's online appeal to exchange cash for information has attracted the usual band of lunatics and chancers with crazy claims, as well as the customary Cease and Desist notice from Fiona. But Louisa's arsey lawyer knows as well as Sophie that, since the anti-misandry website is hosted somewhere outside EU jurisdiction, this notice is completely unenforceable. It might have put less determined people off, but Avenger_Angel will remain undeterred.

Her pony explorations, however, have borne tastier fruit. The Trudie Stein inbox reveals an email from someone called PonyGirl who grew up in the same village as Louise Turner, and who kept her pony at the same stable. She gives Sophie her phone number, saying she'd rather talk than put anything in writing.

PonyGirl's email smells of fear, and Sophie likes that. Leaving Sami to her own kicking and gurgling, she stretches out in her tattered silk kimono on the sofa, like a cat in the sun. This is the kind of development she was hoping for.

Using Skype on her iPad, she calls PonyGirl's number. The answering, wind-buffeted voice has a rural twang that doesn't disguise its briskness. Sophie taps the red button on her phone and sets it up by her iPad to record the call.

'I know what you really want to know,' PonyGirl says, after Sophie tells her that she is Trudie Stein.

'You do?'

'It's about the fire, isn't it?'

Sophie's ears prick up. So there *is* dirt. 'You got me.'

'What are you paying?'

Sophie sighs. She hadn't counted on this. But now she knows there's a fire involved, she can't let it go. 'Fifty,' she says.

'Two hundred.'

'One, and I can pay you immediately.'

'Send a hundred and fifty to me via PayPal at the email address on my message, and, when I see it's cleared, I'll tell you what I know.'

She drives a hard bargain, this PonyGirl.

'Will it be worth it?' Sophie asks.

'You want to know about Louise Turner and the fire? It won't disappoint.'

'I'll do it now,' Sophie says. 'Hold on.' She goes to PayPal and sends the money, using the account she set up for her eBay business, under yet another assumed identity. 'Gone,' she says.

'Got it.'

'So, what's the story?'

'This money isn't from Trudie Stein.'

PonyGirl is cautious, too. Suspicious, even. 'Trudie's my pen name.'

'Really.' PonyGirl doesn't sound like she believes her, but Sophie's pretty certain this isn't going to stop her. 'You're not recording this?'

'Of course not,' Sophie says, watching the blue hairline move across her phone screen, counting the minutes already committed to the voice memo.

'I don't want her finding out I've been speaking about her. Do you know where she is now?' A raven caws in the background of the call, and a horse whinnies. 'QUIET, Trotski.'

'I've an idea.'

'What's she up to, these days?'

'Oh, not much.'

'Small mercies,' PonyGirl says. 'She's calmed down, then?'

Sophie swallows her excitement. 'So tell me about Louise,' she says, trying to keep her voice cool, like she imagines Trudie Stein's might be.

'Come on, now. Who are you really?' PonyGirl asks.

'Like I say, I'm writing a book about horses. And Ponies. Who are *you*, PonyGirl?' Sophie reaches her long, grubby foot over and rocks Sami's bouncing cradle to keep her happy and quiet. She doesn't think an author like Trudie Stein would have a crying baby in her study.

'I'm strictly anonymous. That email address was made up specially for this, and it's going as soon as I move the cash out of PayPal, so don't think you can trace me.'

Sophie is getting impatient. 'Come on. I've paid you. Now tell me what happened.'

'So Louise and I grew up in the same village . . .'

'Which was?'

'Acrefield, in Oxfordshire. Big village green, commuter belt.'

'Did you go to school together?'

'No. She went to a private girls' school in town.'

And you got sent to the local comp, Sophie thinks, picking up the note of resentment in PonyGirl's voice.

'Her family had money, and she was an only child.'

This much Sophie knows. It's what she gleaned from questioning Sam in the early days, when she saw Louisa as her rival for a place in his life, rather than a sad loser she and he had somehow to deal with.

'And you say you kept your ponies at the same stables?' Sophie says, leading PonyGirl on.

'That's how I knew her, really.'

'So what was she like?'

'She was one of those perfect girls. Pretty, blonde – though I swear it came from a bottle – slim, tiny, rode beautifully, did well at school, let us all know about it. Had the boys after her, gifted pianist. Won prizes in everything. Seemed to collect them, in fact.'

'And?' Sophie says, hoping this litany of jealousy isn't all she's going to get for her hundred and fifty quid.

'She would win at all costs,' PonyGirl goes on. 'I swear she cheated. It's not normal to win at everything you enter. Me and my pony Boy Blue – God rest his soul, poor little man – we were her closest contenders, but we never quite beat her. I'm not being funny, but Boy Blue always seemed to get colic, or go lame, or jumpy, before competitions. We were always handicapped in some way.'

And isn't this all just sour grapes? Sophie lies back and watches the wilted leaves on the horse chestnut struggling to stay alive across the street from her flat. This time last year, two months after the crash, the same tree seemed to mock her misery with its backlit greenery and fine abundance of full, waxy candles. But this year it's more in tune with her mood – leaves dropping before they are fully formed, its few flowers stunted, dead before they are alive. 'And—?' she asks PonyGirl.

'And then one day, Star fell on the fifth jump.'

'Star – her pony?'

PonyGirl gives an impatient snort. 'Yes, *of course* her pony. Star fell, Louise rolled off and in the end Boy Blue and I took the cup.'

'Congratulations.' Sophie tries not to let impatience creep

into her voice. 'So you and Boy Blue won, and—?'

'That's where the fire comes in.'

'Go on.'

'Trotski!' PonyGirl yells again. 'Let Tinka at the oats!' Sophie stretches her patience while there is, for want of a better word, a kerfuffle at PonyGirl's end. 'Sorry,' she says eventually. 'Where was I?'

'You beat Louise and—'

'Poor Star. He was such a lovely boy. He rolls himself up onto his feet – he wasn't hurt, thank God, not then, anyway. But then Louise gets up and goes properly ballistic. She doesn't even notice she's hurt – we found out later that she'd broken her arm. All she sees is that she hasn't won. She grabs poor Star by the bridle and whacks him over and over again with her crop, until he's bucking and rearing, red welts in his flank. We had to pull her off him.' PonyGirl pauses, then adds: 'We should have let him get the better of her and trample her.'

'How old was she when this happened?'

'Sixteen. It was the summer after our GCSEs. Louise got all A's, of course, and didn't hang back in coming forward about it. It was all "how did you do in your exams?" which then, of course, gave her free rein to boast about hers. But that's not the end of it. The next week there's this massive fire at the stables, and Star, Boy Blue and two other ponies are killed.' PonyGirl's voice cracks. She stops and sniffs. When she speaks again, her tone is deeper, determined, fuelled by an anger that Sophie recognises only too well. 'They never found out who did it, but it was definitely started deliberately.'

'And you think it was Louise?'

'It *was* Louise.'

'Do you have any proof?'

'No. But when you work around animals, you learn to trust your instincts.'

'What happened after that?'

'She never came back to the stables. Never saw her again. She just dropped the whole horse thing completely. Which is just as well for her, because I would have killed her if she had come back. I hated her so much for what she did. Never saw her again. Something happened with her parents.'

Sophie jumps in. 'What?'

'That's not really about ponies, though, is it? You don't need that for your book, "Trudie Stein", do you?'

'It would be good to know what happened.'

'Then you'd better talk to them about it.'

'Do you have an address? Are they still in Acrefield?'

'No. They moved away, some island up in Scotland, I think.'

'How do I find them?'

'No idea. Her mum was called Celia, and her dad Fergus.'

'Celia and Fergus Turner.' Sophie scribbles it down.

PonyGirl pauses. 'So who are you really?' she says.

'I told you who I am.'

'I don't believe you. This isn't about ponies, though, is it? Look, don't mess me around. I knew when I saw your email. The reason I got in touch was – well, perhaps *you* can tell *me* something I've been wondering about for a while now. I've been following the story and, although she's older and fatter and all that, is Louise now called Louisa Williams?'

Stunned, Sophie can't speak.

'I knew it. She is, isn't she?' PonyGirl's voice rises. 'My God. You're a bloody journalist, aren't you?'

Still, Sophie is quiet, torn between ending the call and staying connected to hear what else PonyGirl might come up with.

'Well, it looks like she attracted a husband just like herself, too,' PonyGirl says. 'A right swine to suit the damn bitch she was. Well, then, whoever you are, you can let the world know she's not all that. She got what she deserved for harming those poor, sweet animals.'

'An innocent man driven to his death equals killing a couple of horses?' Sophie says, the sudden change in her voice alarming poor Sami, who starts crying. 'What kind of fuck-up world do you live in?'

'Ah.' PonyGirl prickles down the line. 'You're that mad Sophie woman, aren't you?'

'I'm not mad.'

'I don't believe it. You're going to get at her with all this, aren't you?' PonyGirl says, her voice rising an octave. 'And she's going to know exactly who I am, and come and find me and my animals.'

'Should have thought about that before you took my money and spoke to me.'

In the background, the wind picks up and hooves thunder away into the distance.

'Tinka! Trotski!'

Sophie disconnects the call.

She's not happy that she was so harsh on PonyGirl, but at least she's got what she wanted.

25

Adam leads Lou down an alleyway hemmed by empty seventies pebble-dashed maisonettes bearing high-security metal shutters plastered with signs warning: DANGER KEEP OUT.

'Here we are,' he says, ducking into a concrete stairwell at the base of the building at the end. 'Home, sweet home.'

'Seriously?'

'It's not so bad when you get inside.'

He leads her up four flights of filthy, syringe-littered stairs to a long, featureless balcony walkway. Most of the flats leading off it sport shutters like the houses in the alley, but a couple are fastened instead with hasps and padlocks. Like the demolition-site wall, every surface is covered with graffiti.

He stops in front of one of the unshuttered doors and unlocks two padlocks.

'Ta-da.' He pushes the door open to reveal a grimy hallway. The walls are covered in ancient, floral wallpaper. This, and a dusty dark wood dresser pushed to one side, are the only hints as to the flat's origins. On top of the flowers and curlicues of the walls, someone has inscribed rambling, incoherent poems in marker pen. Streaks of silver spray paint overlay the words, looping from floor to wall to ceiling as if the person making the marks had done a cartwheel.

'Nothing to do with me,' Adam says as Lou eyes the more recent layers of decoration.

'Can I use your loo?' Her request sounds oddly formal in these surroundings.

He shows her to the bathroom, where floors, walls and ceiling are painted purple. The toilet seat is up and a stink of stale pee hangs around the yellow-stained rim. Spotting this, Adam rolls his eyes and makes a face. 'That's not me either.' He squeezes past her, squirts some bleach on a piece of toilet paper and wipes the seat. 'Some people don't know how to live, except like pigs.'

He washes his hands in the basin then leaves her. 'I'll get the kettle on.'

She closes the door behind her, squats to pee then strips off, hanging her clothes over the shower curtain rail, because she's not sure what the purple on the floor might conceal. She rinses the bath, then stands in it and washes herself down from her face to her toes, sluicing off the dirt stirred up at the demolition site: the burial pit dust, the crumbled cadaver.

She closes her eyes and passes her hand over her forehead at the thought.

Out of the shower, she picks up a badly squeezed tube of fennel toothpaste, surveys the seven or so toothbrushes in the chipped pint glass balancing on the edge of the tub and wonders which one is Adam's. They're all too savoury for her to contemplate using, so instead she does the job with her finger until every trace of vomit is erased.

She shakes the remaining dust from her dress and pulls it back on, stuffing her sweat-damp underwear in her handbag.

'Who else lives here?' she asks Adam as she joins him in the kitchen.

'Reuben.' Adam grimaces as he hands her a cup of tea.

'Why the face? What's the matter with Reuben?'

'He's a nightmare,' Adam says. 'However much I try to

keep things together, he ballses it all up.' He points out the sink where a pile of dirty plates sits in stagnant water, the bin, which overflows beer cans and eggshells onto the cracked lino, the roach end stubbed out on the worktop, leaving one of many smeary brown burn marks, and, most disturbing of all, a used and bloody syringe on an otherwise empty shelf. 'That's just disgusting.' Adam puts his hand in a plastic bag to pick it up, and jams it into one of the beer cans in the bin.

'I left this all clean yesterday afternoon. And this is just the physical mess. There's also the minging drum and bass, the randoms he brings home, the constant stink of skunk. But squatters can't be choosers. There's always some brain-fucked junkie anarchist around to make things colourful, "man". And we'll be evicted in a couple of months at most, anyway.'

'Is he around?' Lou asks, as Adam leads her back into the hallway. There are two doors at the other end. One has 'FUCK OF' daubed on it in disturbingly blood-coloured paint.

'Padlocks were on the door, so we're on our own.'

'Phew.'

'Yeah.' He unlocks the other door and shows her into a big room. 'My place.'

As if providing an antidote to the rest of the flat, Adam's room is painted plain white, and is as spotlessly clean as her own apartment. This boy knows how to live.

Like him, the room smells of amber – proper incense, not the cheap joss stick, tobacco, and fox-piss-skunk-weed stench of the rest of the squat. White blinds at the windows filter the hot sunlight, giving an illusion of coolness. In one corner, video equipment and sound hardware stand on a couple of upended flight cases, and under the window a big bed beckons, its sparkling white linen partly covered by a deep red sari shot through with metallic thread. One wall is lined by books – Lou spots what must be the complete works of Chomsky, some science fiction and a whole shelf of environmental titles. A large reproduction of a Rothko leans against the opposite wall, vibrating colour into the space. The wardrobe door is shut, the chest of drawers too. There is not so much as a stray sock on the floor.

'I'm a boy brought up by a lone, working mum,' Adam says, clocking her marvelling at it all. 'I know about standards.'

She stands on the bare, white-painted floorboards and looks at him, this brown boy in this white room. Her knees feel weak; her hands tremble. Perhaps it's the heat . . .

'Are you all right now?' he asks her.

She nods. 'I'm just not good with skeletons, graves. The idea that we're walking around on the dead.'

He smiles and shrugs. 'It's unavoidable. In London, especially. This part particularly. It was outside the city during the plague. It's where they dumped the bodies. They thought it'd keep the infection away.'

She shudders and draws her arms around herself.

'Are you sure you're OK?'

He moves towards her, puts his arms around her shoulders, and links his hands around the back of her neck.

She nods. Closing her eyes, all she can see are bodies falling out of the dry earth. The nausea starts to rise again. But then she feels his lips on hers, his hands pulling her close to him, running up her back, lifting her skirt. She hears him gasp as he finds no underwear, then her own sigh as, still in his arms, she moves backwards, leading him towards the bed, where they fall and he lifts himself onto his hands to look down at her.

'Is this cool with you?' he asks.

And she replies, telling him that yes, it is very, very cool indeed.

'Are you sorted, or do I need to—?'

'I'm sorted,' she says, kissing him again.

* * *

189

She didn't think, after all that had happened, that she would ever be able to give herself over again. But her body has proved her wrong. He is what they call in certain magazines 'a skilled lover'. Every touch is gentle, light, drawn out until just the right moment, when something stronger, fuller, more insistent is called for.

It's only when the day is done that they have finally had their fill of each other. She lies with her head resting on his chest, marvelling at how, for however many hours it has been, she has forgotten about everything. It was as if all the sharp flints and rocks that normally underpin her had been displaced. Only now, after it's over, do they begin to resume their positions.

'I'm starving,' Adam says. 'Shall I rustle up something for us to eat?'

'Sounds good.'

He kisses the top of her head and rolls out of the bed. 'Fancy a drink? I've got some wine hidden away under the floorboards.'

She shakes her head. 'Just water will do me, thanks.'

'You sure?'

'I don't drink, I'm afraid.'

'Wow.'

'I can't. I like it too much.'

He considers this for a second, then, when he realises what she's telling him, he flushes. 'Sorry,' he says.

'Don't be. It's my own stupid fault. My mother was an alcoholic and I drank to try to blot out the childhood she slapped out to me.'

'Jesus.'

'I'm over all that now, though.'

'You are an extraordinary woman,' he says. He drops to his knees in front of her, kisses her one more time, then jumps to his feet, opens one side of the wardrobe, unhooks a cotton kimono and, pulling it on, heads out of the room.

When she can hear him moving things around in the kitchen, she gets up and goes to the wardrobe, which he has left open. Inside are his clothes, neatly ranged on two rows of hangers, the top one for shirts, the bottom for jeans and shorts.

She opens the other door, expecting to see more of the same, but, to her surprise – and alarm – she finds a collection of dresses, skirts and decidedly female tops. She pulls out one of the dresses. It is lovely: ruby coloured, chiffon, flippy and tiny, a size six at most.

'Pasta OK?' Adam says, coming back into the room and startling her.

She jumps round to face him.

'Ah,' he says, seeing the dress in her hands, her raised eyebrow as she faces him.

'They're not yours, are they?' she says, gesturing to the other women's clothes behind her. A disturbing mist swims in front of her eyes. Has he lied to her? Has she once again found herself with a man who cannot be faithful?

'No,' is all he says.

She stands and looks at him. He is so beautiful in that kimono, his long hair curling around his shoulders, his tall, muscular frame draped in that thin cotton. She so wants him to be what he appeared to be before she looked in this cupboard.

'Well, whose are they, then?'

He looks to the ground. 'They're Charley's.'

'Charley?'

'Charlotte. My ex.'

'Ex? With her clothes still here?'

'She's in New Zealand now. I said she could leave them here until she came back.'

Lou stands and looks at him through half-closed eyes, holding the tiny dress against her nakedness.

'I promise you it's true,' he tells her. 'She lived here until six months ago. With me. We met at college and we were together for two years. But she got itchy feet. She's ambitious, stayed on the course, got a first and then she wanted to travel, see the world. In her eyes I was stuck here, holding her down.'

He sits on the side of the bed and smiles ruefully. 'Said I was too nice.'

Lou puts the dress back in the cupboard and turns to face him.

'So there you are,' he says, looking up at her. 'I'm unambitious, too nice, stuck in Sarf London. If you want to go, the door's over there.'

'I think you're the best human being I have met for a very, very long time,' she says, going over to him. His face is level with her pubic bone and she holds him to her.

A short while later, they are half on, half off the bed, tangled up with one another, when they are startled by a loud bang in the hallway.

'Oh, shit,' Adam says, as they freeze and listen to the staggering footsteps, hoarse laughter and slurs of what sounds like a squadron of men off their faces stumbling their way through the flat. 'Reuben's brought some mates round.'

'Fucking hell, Little Lord Fucklaroy's left the key in his bedroom door,' one of the voices says in the hallway. Without warning, the door opens and a skinny man falls in, spilling a can of Special Brew over himself, sizzling out the joint he has in his other hand.

'Fuck that,' he says as he rights himself. Oblivious to the naked lovers, he totters over to the corner where Adam's computer gear sits, gleaming expensively.

'What we got here, now, Roobs, baby?' he mutters to himself.

He picks up the laptop and, without disconnecting it from any of the wires that attach it to the other equipment, starts to make his way back across the room. 'Got a laptop here, lads,' he croaks in a hoarse voice that suggests too much heroin and not enough teeth.

But before he can pull anything from the flight cases, Adam is on his feet, pulling his kimono around himself.

'What you doing, Reuben?' he says, putting himself in front of the other man.

'Ads, mate,' Reuben stutters. 'Oh, I er, just – I um were just borrowing this to watch a film, man, yeah, right?'

'Well, you know I don't lend out my gear,' Adam says.

'Nah, mate,' Reuben says. 'Yeah, well, you know. Room was open and all that. Oh, 'ello,' he says, noticing Lou for the first time. 'Nice one, Ad, mate,' he drawls as it dawns on him that she is female and naked.

Female, naked and cowering, wishing she were a million miles away. What on earth was she thinking coming here, anyway? Lou wraps the sari around herself, so that only her face is showing.

''Ere. Don't I know you off somewhere?' Reuben says, stumbling closer to get a better look at her.

'No!' she says, a little too quickly.

'Don't you even look at her,' Adam says, positioning himself to shield her from his leering flatmate.

'Oh, she's too good for these old eyes, is she, posh boy?' Reuben spits a great lump of greenish gob on Adam's clean floor.

Adam's shoulders stiffen and he flexes his fingers. The air in the room crackles. Lou puts her hands over her ears to try to stop the whistling that's starting up in her skull.

Out in the living room, the intoxicated men mock each other in slurring voices.

'I need to get out of here,' she says so quietly that no one can hear her.

Adam faces Reuben and holds out his hands for the laptop. 'Give it back and get the fuck.'

The two men stare at each other with mutual contempt. If it came to blows, there would be no contest. Adam is at least twice the size of Reuben, and far, far fitter.

But there are the others in the living room. A whole pack of street rats. Lou's skin crawls. A smell of burning plastic weaves its way into the bedroom, cutting through the cloudy stink of stale cigarettes and spilled beer ushered in by Reuben. They're smoking something out there and it's not just cigarettes or even spliff.

'What's going on?' Adam says, turning his head, wrinkling his nose at the stench.

'Just the boys having a bit of fun,' Reuben says. 'Like what it seems you was in here with her.' He bends to one side to look round Adam, winks at Lou, grasps his groin and hitches it up.

This is enough for Adam. While Reuben is busy making his obscene gesture, he steps forward, snatches his computer and shoulders him out of the bedroom door, bolting it firmly behind him.

He stands, back to the door, and looks at Lou.

'Sorry,' he says.

But she is already standing, unwinding herself from the sari, pulling on her dress, picking up her bag, slipping on her sandals.

'Where are you going?' he says.

'I can't stay here,' she says. 'I'm sorry, Adam. I don't want any part of this. I need a hot shower, a proper meal, a clean bed and peace. I'm going home. Unlock this door, please.'

'If I do, he'll just come back in,' Adam says. He moves around the room, picking up the clothes she peeled from him earlier and putting them on. 'Let me show you out, at least. Just in case. When they're smoking, things can get a bit out of hand.'

'What is it?' she says, watching him as he covers his perfect form with shorts and a shirt.

He shrugs. 'Crack, probably. Or meth, if they didn't get lucky. Whatever, it'll mean a night of madness.'

She steps forward and takes both his hands in hers. 'Do you want to come to mine?'

He glances over at his equipment. 'I'd love to. But I just don't trust him not to break the door down tonight and trash my gear.'

'Why not bring it with you?' she says.

'You serious?'

She smiles.

It's only when they are piling the flight cases into a cab that she realises what is happening, and how wildly it deviates from her big plan.

She has only just managed to make a safe haven for herself, and now, not only is it being threatened from afar by Sophie, but this boy, whom she hardly knows, is coming into her place of sanctuary.

What kind of idiot is she being?

But, she thinks as she climbs in over all the stuff and sits next to him, perhaps it's better this way. A man around the place might be useful, if Sophie ever sees fit to come closer.

If she can trust him as much as she thinks she can.

And what if he sees the children's room? What's she going to tell him about that?

Think, Lou, she says to herself, a moth of panic fluttering in her throat. 'Think of something.'

'What?' Adam says, as the sweating cab driver lurches them around the one-way system towards The Heights, and Lou realises she has spoken out loud.

'Oh, nothing,' she says. 'Just that this is really something.'

'Isn't it?' He leans over and kisses her.

26

Then

Poppy performs a great turn in the bed and thumps against Louisa, waking her up.

They lie cocooned in the warmth of the spare-room duvet, the daughter's hot little body squirming into that of her mother. Louisa staggered in here in the night to escape Sam's complaints about having Poppy in their bed, but forgot to draw the curtains. So now, as she comes to in the half-light of the morning, she can see that it's snowing: great, soft flakes of white animate the grey sky. Just in time for the festive season.

Carefully, she peels Poppy's chubby arm from where it has come to rest around her neck, and rolls out of bed into the warm room. She lifts her phone to check the time: it's eight. The smell of toast and coffee coming from downstairs tells her that Sam will have already left for his office on the other side of Cambridge.

She thinks of him driving his red car too fast on the icy roads, and shivers, remembering how he sometimes pushes it, remembering how scared she was on that furious drive to A & E, and how she thought briefly that he might kill them all, that she might end up like Katie, another dead wife.

Shhhh, she tells herself. He wouldn't do that.

He wouldn't.

Please take care, Sam, she whispers into the still room.

When she has woken late on other mornings, she has always felt relief that she doesn't have to see him. It's not personal – it's just that she would rather not have to meet any other human being immediately after surfacing from her embattled nights.

But today, a twist of regret surprises her. She would have liked to have seen him this morning, to have shared a cup of tea before he got up, kissed him goodbye before he set off on his fifteen-mile drive across the flatlands.

She needs to put the ghosts to rest and make this marriage work. The only alternative for her is all sorts of trouble. Today, for the first time, some sort of resolution seems to be a possibility. Today, hope glimmers in the icy whiteness outside.

She crosses the room, her bare feet enjoying the warm, pure wool carpet. When she reaches the window, she gasps. The landscape – normally so dull that she has stopped throwing it even so much as a cursory glance – has been transformed into a thing of beauty. Nearby, the snow has settled into a thick, white blanket. In the middle distance, icy lines etch the empty fields, picking out the ploughed furrows so that, when she half-closes her eyes, they appear to vibrate in the cold air. The dance of the snow as it floats down brings life to the scene, turning the grey, bare trees on the horizon into characters in a wintry drama.

She turns and looks at her daughter who lies splayed on her back, arms thrown out to each side, whiffling and snoring, her thick eyelashes trembling on her peachy cheeks. So fragile. Louisa wants to wake her up, put her in a snowsuit and wellies and take her out to roll snowballs round and round until, creaking in the fresh dry snow, they are big enough to pile up, stud with coal and carrots and dress in one of Sam's woollen tartan scarves.

Let her sleep, though. And at not quite yet one year old, she's really too young for pushing a snowball around. But can Louisa wait? And will it snow like this next year when Poppy *will* be ready?

Eyes glinting, she turns again to look out of the window and sees a hare darting across the field, its strong legs thumping into the earth, springing it up and onwards, its ears thrusting up into the air, alert, ready for anything. At the bounce of its feet on the new-lain snow, a crow rises, its black wings shuddering the air. At the same time, something dark and rooted in Louisa comes away from its moorings and lifts.

Making sure the baby monitor is on, she slides her feet inside her sheepskin slippers and tiptoes out of the room and down the stairs. Glowing in the warmth from the Aga and the underfloor heating, the kitchen seems impossibly cosy against the chilly whiteness beyond the plate-glass windows.

She has marked today out for putting up the Christmas decorations, a task she has been dreading. The idea of covering the living room in tinsel and stars and colour just hadn't seemed right to her; it just seemed like a lot of effort to make a bit of a mess.

Having put the kettle on, she pads into the internal garage to look at the tree Sam brought home the night before. It is, of course, enormous. He said he wanted it in the hallway to greet guests. Not that they have any guests. For many reasons – notionally feminist, but more an inability to cook, inability to stay sober, and a general disinclination – Louisa has steadfastly refused to play hostess for Sam's colleagues and clients. And there's no one else to invite. One of the problems with starting over is that you rip up your roots and it takes a while to replant them. Although, Louisa thinks as she tears the net from the Christmas tree, letting loose its prickling branches, she rather likes that side of it. She has never really understood why people need so many friends.

The tree unleashed, Louisa fetches a small plastic crate from a rack of shelves in the garage. This being only their second shared Christmas, she and Sam haven't yet built up the statutory crumbling cardboard box of family decorations. For now, all they have is her own small stockpile of gewgaws: a few strands of tinsel; a set of silver tessellations she made at art school; shiny glass baubles she found in an antiques shop; a couple of strings of fairy lights; a plastic spiky ball given away free in a packet of washing powder, which still smells like an artificial forest glade.

Sam brought nothing of his old life to the new home. After Katie's death, he let her family take everything from the house he had once shared with her – something Louisa hadn't thought such a great idea, because it looked like the action of a man racked with guilt. The mother stripped it like a vulture at a carcass.

Unbidden, the image of Katie's body comes to Louisa, how it must have looked to the poor jogger who found her the morning after the murder. The dog she had been walking at the time died, too, its head caved in by the same piece of wood that killed its mistress. The poor creature suffered for its loyalty.

And Sam had asked Louisa, back in the car on that trip to A & E, if the same thing was happening with her as it had with Katie . . .

She shudders.

What the hell did he mean by that?

She shakes the chilling pictures from her head, replacing them with the clean, bright whiteness of what she has now. This house, this man, this child.

This future.

'You won't let anything like that happen to you,' she tells herself. 'You're not like Katie. You can look after yourself.'

'I certainly can,' she answers.

She lugs the massive tree through to the hallway where she props it up in the spot Sam had in mind. It is too big, though. It will for ever be getting in the way. He may have the business acumen – and, yes, the charm – but she has the spatial imagination.

Instead, she takes the tree to the living room, where she finds the perfect position, next to the fire, under the arched ceiling of what was once a medieval dining hall.

Bending her ear to the baby monitor, Louisa hears the regular breathing of a still soundly-sleeping Poppy. Grateful to her for letting her get on, Louisa puts on a CD that she has kept in her box of decorations since, abandoned by her parents, she attempted to create a new set of rituals for herself. A label stuck to the front states, in her own handwriting: *This music always to be played when dressing the tree.*

The sweet voice of the King's College Chapel Choir boy soloist pipes the intro to 'Once in Royal David's City'. It is extraordinary that she now lives so close to the scene of the recording. Perhaps she and Sam and Poppy should go along to the service this Christmas Eve. She pictures the three of them, all dressed in white fur and red jackets, smiling under the soaring, fan-vaulted ceiling, a gilded glow all around them.

Singing along to the carols, Louisa spends the next two hours putting up the tree. She tops it with a star and stands back to examine her work.

It's lovely, but a little sparse. Her single-girl decorations really don't do such a monster conifer justice. More is needed. Abundance is what is needed. She gets her notepad and writes a list:

Candles on clips
Silver stars (to make?)
Candy canes
Witches' hair

She lights the fire, finally makes the cup of tea she has been too busy to think about until now, and sits back in the glow of the flames, jotting new items down on her list: food for the Christmas dinner, the types of wine to buy, what canapés she might lay on for the party for Sam's staff she has just decided to throw.

It's only Poppy's crying that pulls her from her work. And she's glad she's awake, because they can now both get bathed and dressed and out there, putting plans into action.

Before she goes to comfort her daughter, she texts Sam: *How about a drinks party for the firm? 19 Dec? Here? Don't be late home tonight. Can't wait to see you. Early night? xxx*

She runs upstairs to Poppy.

This is the beginning of the future.

27

Now

Lou forces herself awake to escape the nightmare. It's horses, this time, hooves pounding, running wild-eyed with foam-flecked lips, blood on their flanks, shying as they hit a wall of flame, an explosion.

'Come on,' she finds herself saying as she comes to. 'COME ON!'

She sits up, panting in the complete darkness, sweat-drenched despite the fan she switched on before she and Adam fell asleep. Outside her building, the whoop of the nightly street party carries on, if anything a little louder than usual because it's a Saturday night. Above her, Steroid Boy's bass lines thump down through the ceiling, the cantering rhythms no doubt having provided an inspiring backdrop for her nightmare.

'Sorry,' she says, as she comes to her senses, thinking that, surely, she must have woken Adam.

There is no reply.

She puts out a hand and touches sheet, pillow, but no man.

Switching on her bedside light, she jumps out of bed and crosses the bedroom towards the open door she is sure was closed the night before. In fact, she distinctly remembers him holding her up against it as she wrapped her legs around his body.

On her way, she trips over his clothes, left in a scattered heap on the floor.

She puts a hand to her chest, closes her eyes and breathes a little prayer of thanks. At least he hasn't upped and left her in the middle of the night.

Rejection would be a disaster for her.

Perhaps, then, he's just gone for a pee.

She tiptoes naked into the corridor, but the bathroom sits in darkness. The hot, stuffy living room is empty, too. Turning back, she sees with alarm that the door to the bedroom at the other end of the apartment is partly open.

Adam is in the children's room.

She hurries towards it. She was going to work up to explaining, and now he's gone and nosed his way in and she doesn't know what she's going to tell him.

Throwing the door wide open, she finds him, sitting on Poppy's bed, flicking through her drawing book.

'What are you doing?' she asks.

He jumps and looks up sharply, caught out.

'I'm sorry,' he says, putting the book down. 'I was looking for the bathroom, and I guessed the wrong door.'

'It's down the corridor.' She leans against the door frame and points it out for him.

'It's a bit like you finding Charley's stuff at my place, isn't it?' he asks, looking up at her.

'A bit.' Lou picks at the rug with her big toe.

'These are great,' he says, breaking the silence by picking up the drawing book again and flicking through the pictures of people with big round heads, long thin arms and legs, and no bodies whatsoever.

'They're Poppy's,' she says.

'Poppy?'

'My daughter.'

'OK. And the cot?'

'It's Leon's. My little boy's.'

'Where are they?' he asks, gesturing at the empty bed, the waiting cot.

Lou looks up at the ceiling, and breathes out heavily. She has no idea what she's going to say to him.

'They're with their father at the moment.' It comes out of her as if someone else is speaking.

'Their father. And he's—?'

'Oh, we're not together any more. He's just looking after them until I'm settled in, till I'm ready.'

'That must be hard for you.'

'It is,' she says, her voice tiny, her eyes evading his. 'But it's for the best.'

'It's a lovely room you've got together for them.'

She nods. 'The only one I've finished so far.'

He pats the bed next to him, and she sits by him, putting her sex-marked body onto Poppy's brand-new moon-and-stars duvet cover.

She crosses her fingers and makes a silent promise. *Sorry Poppy. I'll wash it for you later.*

'I can't wait to meet them,' he says. 'I love kids.'

She leans her head against his chest. If nothing else, it makes it impossible for him to see her face. Outside, the party rattles on. A woman's screams escalate into either hilarity or terror; it's hard to tell which.

He's looking forward to meeting her children. Isn't this a sign that she should put the brakes on right now?

She can't do it.

For the past year she has been adrift, alone. More than a year, really. More like three, if she thinks about it. If she allowed that state of affairs to continue, she might just float away. She needs to be grounded, and, although she barely knows him, Adam here gives every impression of being a kind, good person. He could be a strong contender for the job. Also – she knows it's early days, but she can't help herself – she imagines the beauty of the child they would make together.

He reaches down a finger and runs it along the silver-threaded stretch marks on the lower part of her belly.

'I wondered about these,' he says, his voice a rumble in his chest underneath her ear. 'And this.' He traces Leon's caesarean scar, so well done by the doctors in Cambridge that it is almost invisible so long as she doesn't get carried away with the razor. But, of course, he must have touched the ridge of it many times in the past twenty-four hours.

He doesn't mention her other marks, the zipper scar along the middle of her belly where they removed her spleen, the multiple lines where they pieced her leg back together, the burn damage on her lower arms. He must be wondering about them. But he's being so delicate about asking, and for that she is truly thankful.

He moves his fingers, which have been resting on the edge of her pubic bone, further down, between her legs.

'Not here,' she says, gently moving away from him. 'Not in Poppy's and Leon's room.'

'No,' he says. 'Of course. Sorry.'

She stands up and leads him back to her bedroom, her mind tangling with the knot of lies she is weaving for him.

It's not unprecedented. She's dealt with untruths in the past. But Adam is such a good soul. He's one of those people who make her feel dirty by their goodness.

How on earth will they end up, she and Adam?

Back on her own bed, his touch helps her put it all away again.

Again, he takes her to a place where she is beyond caring.

* * *

'I'd better go, then,' he says on Sunday evening, as they lie in the bed they have barely left all day, watching the reflection of the orange sunset on the pale-grey buildings beyond the railway.

'School night tonight,' she says. 'Gotta be my best for work tomorrow.'

He runs his hand up her right thigh and gently touches one of the circular dents left by the bolts that held her leg together.

'What happened?' he asks her, moving to stroke the mottled patches over her hands and arms where the skin graft is still bedding in.

'I was in a car crash,' she says.

'Must have been pretty bad.'

'It was.' He puts his arm around her and the scent of him makes her want to take him to her again.

'You don't want to talk about it, do you?' he says.

She shakes her head.

'I'm cool with that,' he says.

Very much later, he really does get ready to go home.

'What about your stuff, though?' she asks him as they have one, final kiss in her hallway. It's all piled in the second bedroom, where they left it when they arrived in the taxi the day before.

He frowns. 'I suppose I'd better take it back with me.'

'You can't keep it there, not with that bloke and his mates.' She holds up a finger. 'Can your friend Umoh on the front desk sort you out with fingerprint access to this corridor?'

'I should think so.'

'Well, have this.' She breaks away from him and reaches for a spare key to her apartment from a hook by the door. 'You can keep your gear here and work in the middle bedroom.'

'Are you sure?' he asks her.

She nods. 'Never been surer. It'd be good to have someone around. I hate being alone.'

She watches him move along the corridor towards the lift. Just before he disappears through the fire door, he turns and blows her a kiss, and she realises that it is true. This new Lou that she and her therapists at The Pines have built really *doesn't* want to be on her own.

And Adam will be the perfect accompaniment to her new life.

28

Then

'I can't make it this morning,' Louisa says to Sandy, who has just phoned her from the playgroup. Since she started going again in January, the two women have become what almost passes for friends.

'But Amy really wants to see Poppy. Listen.' Sandy holds the phone up and, above the general chatter, Louisa hears a small child wailing. That's just the type of thing Sandy would do.

'I'm just too whacked,' Louisa says, gazing out of the living-room window. The daffodils and narcissi she planted in a fit of optimism just before Christmas barely show any yellow to this morning's brutal sunlight, having been stunted or blown flat by winds that blast these fens, uninterrupted, all the way from Siberia. 'I need to go to bed. I've got flu or something. Every-thing aches.'

She hasn't. It doesn't. But she does want to head back upstairs and hide under her duvet.

'Poor you,' Sandy says. 'Well, Thursday, then, yes?'

'Yes,' Louisa says, but she already knows she won't be going to the Thursday session, either. She's had enough of that playgroup, all those cowlike women sitting there chewing on chocolate biscuits. Even the thought of it gives her a dull pain in the base of her stomach.

'Mumeee!' Her *In the Night Garden* DVD ended, Poppy launches herself across the living-room floor and flings her arms around Louisa's legs, nearly knocking her over. One and a quarter, and the only way she seems to be able to propel herself is at high speed, like a demented little pinball.

'Careful,' Louisa says, prising her daughter's fingers from her leggings. She walks away from her to the kitchen, which, as usual at this time in the morning, looks more like a crime scene than somewhere a family of three has had their breakfast. Well, a family of two, because Louisa isn't feeling much like food in the mornings at the moment.

She is fully aware of what this may mean. But she's not allowing herself to draw any conclusions just yet.

She plucks a rusk from a packet on the counter and hands it to Poppy, who has followed her from the living room as if she is attached to her by an invisible string. As Louisa turns, a cloud passes over the sun, and the light, which had streamed in and gilded the kitchen fittings, retreats from the windows.

'Can't you just leave me alone for one minute?' she snaps suddenly, viciously, at her daughter.

The little girl, who had been wearing a smile for her mummy, looks at first shocked, then devastated at this sudden turn in mood. When it comes, her roar of despair is deafening.

'Jesus, Poppy.' Louisa sighs heavily and, roughly, picks her up. She's going to get mashed rusk on her clothes, but that's a small price to pay for stemming a tantrum. She glances up at the wine rack, which lives on top of the kitchen wall units. Having realised that alcohol wasn't really helping her state of mind, she's been off it since the day before the Christmas party she threw for Sam's firm, which is over three months ago now. She keeps bottles up there for Sam, though, who will still have a couple of glasses with the dinners he is sometimes home in time to share with her.

When Poppy has calmed down, Louisa sits her at her little desk with a stack of the tasteful wooden puzzles that are her current obsession. She will get at least half an hour's peace from her now, she reckons. Without really thinking what she's doing, she then drags a chair over the kitchen floor, climbs on top of it and reaches down a bottle of Rioja.

She shouldn't really be drinking, not suspecting what she does about the condition she's in. But how many women don't find out for months, carry on living the high life until they're certain, with no harm whatsoever to the child? It must be millions.

Besides, she deserves it, a little bit of oblivion.

'What the hell's going on?'

Louisa is shaken awake. She's on the sofa, a string of red-tinged spittle attaching her to one of the cream cushions.

Sam stands over her, holding Poppy, who has chocolate slathered around her face and appears to be covered in flour. Her fingers smear white and wet over his previously immaculate jacket.

'Your suit—' Louisa croaks.

'You left a chair by the kitchen worktop. She climbed it, opened a cupboard and pulled out flour, eggs, beans, rice, pasta and a jar of Nutella. Luckily it didn't smash. Luckily she didn't fall. Luckily, luckily, Louisa.'

'I'm sorry.' She puts her hands over her face.

'I thought all this had stopped,' Sam says, as she swings her legs round and sits up, rubbing her eyes, which, inexplicably, are puffed and wet with tears. 'Are we going to go through all this again?'

She has no answer for him. Instead, her hand over her mouth, she rushes to the downstairs cloakroom, where she spews the contents of her stomach, which are entirely liquid and all red. She kneels there, in front of the toilet, gulping and gasping, until the retching subsides. When she is ready, she levers herself to standing and splashes her face with cold water. Meeting her own gaze in the mirror she notes the downturned mouth, the unbrushed hair, the smudged make-up that makes her look like a bloated clown, the stain of red wine on her front.

Yes, Sam. It looks like we are going to be going through all this again.

She cleans herself up as best she can, then steps out to search for her husband and daughter.

They are upstairs, naked, in a bath full of bubbles. Sam is teaching Poppy how to spell her name by sticking foam bath-play letters on the tiles.

'She's too young for that,' Louisa says, closing the toilet seat and sitting on it.

'Never too young to learn,' he says. He is avoiding her gaze.

'Nor too old,' she says. 'I'm sorry about that downstairs.'

'I don't think I could go through it all again,' Sam says.

'Nor me.'

'It's not just about you, Louisa. It's me and it's Poppy, too. You have to stop drinking. You have to stop being so miserable. You have to fight whatever it is that's bringing you down. I mean, you don't exactly have a bad life, do you? It's not as if I'm some kind of bastard, is it?'

He rubs a flannel around Poppy's delighted, chocolate-smeared face, and Louisa wishes he would just go away and stop judging her.

'Is it?' he asks her again.

He's lost some of the definition he used to have. His skin, encased in suits all winter, is horribly pale against the reddish brown hairs of his body. She thinks back to Christmas and New Year, when she thought she could bring herself to desire him again. Her efforts had resulted in sex, and it wasn't too bad, but she would have far rather watched a good film, or read a good book, and she suspects that he felt the same. In any case, perhaps because of that, or perhaps because he has been away an awful lot on business, New Year's Eve was their last time.

Ignoring his question, she picks up his clothes, which he has let fall on the bathroom floor, and takes the soiled suit through to their bedroom to put on a hanger to take to the dry cleaner's. As she bundles up his shirt, she brings it to her nose. It smells of him, of his Dior aftershave, but she thinks there's something else there, another scent, something perfumed, female, sexual.

She slams it in the chute that takes it directly down to the laundry room. So that's why he's lost interest. It's clear to her: he's screwing someone else.

She sits on the bed and puts her head in her hands, pressing her palms against her eyes until she sees black spots.

Eventually, Sam brings Poppy through. All she can think, as she looks up at them, is how she is going to have to wash and tumble dry the clean fluffy towels Sam has pulled out of the airing cupboard to wrap them both up in, when there is a perfectly fine set hanging on the rail in the bathroom.

'What is it?' he says.

'Nothing.' She sighs, lies down and turns her back to him.

'You wait with Mummy, Pops,' Sam says. 'And Daddy'll get your pyjamas and bottle.'

Poppy runs round the big bed to where Louisa lies. 'Story, story,' she says, beating the bedcovers as if they were a drum.

'Daddy do it,' Louisa mutters. 'Daddy do it all.'

'What's the matter?' he asks again, once Poppy is dressed and snuggling against his chest, sucking on her bottle.

'Nothing.'

'Yes, there is something.' He reaches across the bed to touch her thigh.

She takes a deep breath, sits up and faces him.

'I'm pregnant.'

'But—' he says, and she knows he's wondering how it could be, when they last had sex on 31 December.

She puts her hands on her belly. 'Three months pregnant.'

'Ah.' He rubs the stubble on his chin. Ginger stubble.

In the silence that follows, she eyes him like a cat watching a bird building its nest. He is working out how best to react. He could tell her off some more about drinking – especially in view of the fact that she's pregnant. He'd like that. Or he could feign relief, because at least there's a tangible reason for the about turn in her emotional state. Or he could cry and rail about how she is trapping him further into this hell of a life.

But he surprises her. He looks at her with utter delight.

'That's bloody brilliant!' he says, a smile cracking his face, his eyes shining.

He reaches out and laces his fingers into hers.

'We're in this together?' she says, thinking about the strange smell on his shirt.

'We're in it together.'

Perhaps, she thinks, this is enough?

Later, when finally she has got Poppy off to sleep, she tiptoes downstairs and watches, through the crack of the kitchen door, as he clears up the detritus of her wine binge. It's only then that she catches his face unawares, not in performance mode, and sees what he is really thinking about this, her bombshell.

And there it is, on his face.

The look of a trapped man.

The cold, hard, dangerous look of a trapped man, who, if pushed, will do anything to escape.

29

Now

'Listen.'

Adam sits up in bed and gestures to Lou to join him. Since they got together, he has hardly left the apartment. He was editing his film in her spare bedroom when she came home from work on Monday. Not only that, but he'd cleaned the kitchen and had a vegetable stew bubbling on the hob. When she jumped in the shower – to wash off the city dirt before having him on the sofa – instead of its former feeble dribble, it burst forth powerfully, all fixed. It's now early Thursday evening and he has only gone back to his squat on a couple of brief occasions to fetch more clothes.

'What can you hear?' he asks her.

She tilts her head to one side. 'London. That hum of London. Traffic. The people out partying.' She focuses her listening, frowning. 'No thumping rock from our friend upstairs. Not yet, anyway.'

'True,' he says. 'But really zone in.'

'Oh, a plane . . . helicopter . . .' A train rattles past, its ancient brakes squealing like fingernails running down a blackboard. She turns and smiles at him. 'And that, of course.'

'And?'

She shrugs. 'Nothing.'

'That's right. There's nothing.'

'What do you mean?'

He just smiles at her, in the open way that she already occasionally finds unnerving.

'What?'

'Look.' He stands, the contours of his body outlined by the rosy glow of yet another shepherd's delight sky, and points to the demolition site.

She stands beside him, her uneven gait wobbling on the imprecise ground of the mattress. 'It's all dark. It's not ten yet, is it? They have to stop at ten.'

'It's not that. They've downed tools.'

'Seriously?'

'It's that burial pit. They've been told they have to stop all work until the archaeologists have had a look at it.' He presses his nose and palms against the glass, and Lou thinks of the smear he will leave. But then she remembers that she doesn't have to worry about it: he will clean it off for her.

'They've covered it with this great white dome to keep the bones clean,' he says.

She stands behind him, crossing her arms over her chest. A shudder runs through her at the thought of it – bodies piled up in mounds over there, the dust of the past gathering like a cloud.

Again, the nausea hits her. As quietly as she can, she tries to breathe it in and let it settle back underneath.

'The people of London, dead and alive, say "nah, mate" to social cleansing.' He falls back onto the bed and pulls her towards him.

'But they'll start up again as soon as the pit is cleared, yes?' she says in the morning, as he hands her a cup of coffee and a slice of sourdough bread with apricot jam. He seems to have a knack for finding the best food even here, in this most unpromising of neighbourhoods. At least, Lou thinks, when the redevelopment is finished, there will be better food shops, little delis, decent coffee bars.

'Of course,' Adam says, fetching his own breakfast. 'But it'll slow things down, cost them money, cut their profit margins. Serves them right. It's all good.' He sits opposite her, gazes out of the window, and sips his coffee. It leaves a moustache of foamed soya milk on his upper lip that Lou wants to crawl across the table and lick off. 'And anyway, the longer you can keep this view the better.'

'What do you mean, keep this view?'

'You know about the tower?'

Lou shakes her head.

'I'd have thought they'd have told you when you bought the place.'

Lou shrugs. 'There was this pile of papers, but I just said I wanted it and signed everything without really looking.'

'You know what you want,' he says, reaching out and stroking her hand. 'I like that.'

'What tower?' she says, looking out of the window. She has grown to love this view, even with the Dark Man almost permanently at his window in East Block, like a black mark on her outlook. In any case, Adam being here – her guardian angel complete with inked wings – makes it easier for her to ignore him.

Adam stands and guides her to the window. 'So, see that hole there, with the cement and pipes and steel and all that embedded in it?' He points to a spot just across the road from Lou's building. 'That's the footings for a thirty-seven-storey tower.'

'Thirty-seven storeys? That means it'll—' Lou gapes out at the window and tries to visualise it.

'It'll completely block out your view that way. The apartment will be a lot darker – you won't get this direct sunlight at all, you won't see those hills in the distance, nor Canary Wharf . . .'

'And I'll have people looking straight in at me from their own apartments.'

'Yep. That too.'

'That's a disaster.'

'It's not great.'

'I'll have to move; I can't stay here if it turns out like that.'

He looks at her, all big brown eyes. 'Will you take me with you?'

She smiles. 'I'll think about it.'

He walks with her to the Tube station, her own personal bodyguard.

In your face, Sophie.

'What are you up to today?' she asks, as they wait to cross the road.

He makes a face. 'I'm at the Rainbow Café. I'd rather be filming the empty demolition site, perhaps get in there and grab some footage of dem bones.'

'Well, why don't you just do what you want?'

He shrugs. 'Gotta make a living, babe.'

She stops and takes his hand. 'You don't have to worry about that.'

'What do you mean?'

'Don't work in the café for cash. I make enough to support us both. Make your film instead.'

He frowns at her. 'You sure?'

'Couldn't be surer. You look after us both and the apartment, and I'll go out to work and pay for everything. Suits me, suits you.' She pulls a credit card out of her wallet. 'Have this. The PIN's four eight two three.'

'Seriously?'

'I trust you, Adam. I'd like to do this for you. Don't go to the café.'

His face opens into a wide, delighted smile. 'Lou, you are the coolest girl I ever met.'

She bristles with pleasure. 'Ah, I bet you say that to everyone.'

He bends down and kisses her on the nose.

'No. You're the one I've been looking for.'

She passes through the turnstiles.

He is hers.

30

The note sits on Lou's desk, its envelope bearing an insufficient postage label which means it was probably sent some time ago. She hasn't opened it yet, but she'd recognise that handwriting anywhere. Cradling her forehead in her hands, she looks down at it through one, half-open eye.

Handing her credit card over to Adam had been a brave and glorious leap into the unknown. Buoyed by this, she had been looking forward to coming in to work this morning and getting on with refining her ideas for the water client. Her new world once again looked shining, fresh, so full of possibility.

She closes her eyes and imagines rubbing Sophie out like a mistake on a drawing.

If only it were that easy . . .

She takes a deep breath and rips open the envelope:

Louisa –

it says, in that incongruously beautiful hand,

I asked you to get back to me in a week.
And you haven't.
Have you?

I need to talk to you. My child is legally due part of Sam's estate, and . . .

Lou doesn't read on. Instead, she crumples the note and compacts it in her hands until it is a tiny ball. Legally due part of Sam's estate? As if.

She sits, biting her lip, staring down at the people criss-crossing the Soho street, dotting in and out of the cooling shade. From where she sits, they look tiny, no more than figures in motion. A couple of soignée women perch at tables on the pavement outside a café. One has her face tipped towards the hot sunlight. Behind her large, round sunglasses, she could be looking directly up at Lou.

How simple life must be for them all down there, without the trouble she has to contend with. Thanks to Sophie, right now her past feels like an oil spill drifting her way, contaminating her hopes of a clean future.

'Penny for them.'

She looks up and sees Cleo, smiling down at her, a slight frown on her otherwise expensively smoothed forehead, as if she is surprised to find her gazing out of the window rather than working. Lou shakes the daze from her head and returns her boss's smile.

'Oh, just Monday morning, you know,' she says.

'Sure.' Cleo looks at her watch – a very nice Tag Heuer. To cheer herself up, Lou makes a mental note to get one like it for herself, to go with the new wardrobe she has been assembling in her lunch hours – Acne and McCartney, a dressed-up, dressed-down look, just subtly better, a tad more expensive than those sported by the other designers in the building. Thanks to Sam, she has the money for it, after all. Might as well spend it.

'You'll have the initial ideas presentation ready for the meeting at eleven?' Cleo says.

'Of course.' Lou is nothing if not proficient at her work, however many distractions may come her way.

'Great.' Cleo lifts her watch-free hand and shakes a retro biscuit tin in front of Lou. 'And would you like to donate for Tania's thirtieth?'

'Tania?'

Cleo points to a woman sitting over the far side of the studio, who sits glued to her Mac screen, lost to the world.

Lou hasn't really got to know anyone yet. The only name she's learned is that of the woman closest to her, and that is only because she – Chen – once stopped by her desk and offered to bring her a coffee up from The Pantry. Lou just doesn't really see the point of making friends at work. Adam is enough social contact for her.

Cleo rattles the tin again, so she reaches down and, taking her purse from her handbag, fishes out a tenner and posts it through the lid.

'Is that enough?' she says.

'Plenty. I'll be bringing the card round later for signing. And we're going to celebrate in the club next Friday. You're coming. That's an order.' She pulls a pen from her pocket and scribbles a name and number on a Post-it, which she sticks on Lou's monitor. 'Orlagh. Daughter of my best friend. Excellent baby-sitter. Lives down your way.'

She breezes away, rattling her tin, leaving Lou no space to protest.

She is just firing up Illustrator when her desk phone rings.

'Hello,' she says to her caller. 'Lou Turner.'

'Louisa Williams.' The voice is female, husky, and Lou knows instantly who it belongs to. 'Just checking you're getting my notes.'

'Will you please leave me alone,' she says, as quietly as possible.

'We need to talk.'

'No we don't.'

'You need to start telling the truth.'

'I have told the truth, over and over.'

'No you haven't. Sam did not set out to kill you and the children, and I'm certain he didn't do anything to Katie. He's not a murderer. He didn't have it in him.'

'This again. You seem to be the only person in the world who believes that.'

'You'd be surprised, *Lou*. I've been digging around a bit. Talking to a couple of people.'

'Who?'

'You think I'm going to tell you that? I gave you a week to get in touch and you failed. So I have to take control of this. I need to meet you. There are a few things we need to discuss.'

'That isn't going to happen.'

'You think not? Watch out, *Lou Turner*. You think you can rub me out like you did Star and Boy Blue?'

Louisa passes her hand over her brow and feels sweat. She closes her eyes and sees flames. 'What?'

'I know more about you than you'd think, Louise. Lou. Louisa. Whoever you are today. And don't you know it's very rude to ignore a person. You owe me, big time. We could do this amicably, or I'm prepared for it to get as messy as needs be, so I—'

'I owe you nothing.'

'Oh you do. Me and my child. Didn't you read my letter? You owe us money and truth, and I'm going to—'

'Money? *You* want money off *me*? Unbelievable. Let me tell you this: there is no way you are getting a penny from me.'

Unable to control herself, Lou slams the phone down.

A great shudder runs through her body, as if she has been electrocuted. Who has been talking about her?

And money? Is that what this is really all about?

She places her hands on her desk and stares at them: the manicured fingernails of a thirty-two-year-old, the skin-graft scars of a survivor. She tells herself that she is who she is today, not what she was before.

She picks up her mobile, scrolls through her contacts and brings up the photograph attached to Fiona's details. One of her therapists did this for her back in her early recovery days when her short-term memory wasn't so good, so that she'd know who she was dealing with, so that she knew who to avoid. She runs her finger over her lawyer's determined face, her strong jaw, her clear, I'll-brook-no-nonsense eyes. Then she touches her phone number and calls her.

'Fiona Jarvis,' the clear, clipped vowels sound exactly as they did the last time Lou heard them. 'Who is this?' she asks, after Lou can't bring herself to speak.

She won't know it's Lou, of course, because, along with everything else in her life, Lou has changed her number, even her phone provider.

She shivers; a blackness shimmers around the edges of her vision. The unwelcome jumble of feelings stirred up by Fiona's voice make it impossible for her to continue with the call. It's as if, the moment she walked away from The Pines into this new life, a sealed wall closed up behind her.

There is no going back for her.

It's just unfortunate that Sophie got caught on the wrong side of the barrier. Lou only has herself to blame. She shouldn't have listened to Fiona. She should have evicted her from the flat the minute it fell into her own hands.

Damn Fiona. This is all *her* fault.

Pressing the red button on her phone, she blocks Fiona's number and deletes her details from her address book.

Itching, she unwraps Sophie's balled-up letter and reads the rest of it. At the end, she has provided a URL, which Lou types carefully into her browser. It is a solicitor's website, detailing the facts about the inheritance rights of 'issue' when a person dies intestate.

Lou reads it, fury mounting in her chest.

On what planet are rules like this fair?

There is no way Sophie is going to get a penny. Lou would rather die.

She tears the letter into tiny, tiny pieces. Looking round to make sure no one is watching – they aren't, they're all staring at their screens, lost in vectors, typefaces and pixels – she climbs on her desk, opens the top part of her window and lets the dots of poisonous paper fall down on those carefree people down below, like strange, unseasonal snow. One passer-by, an auburn-haired man in a smart suit who, for an irrational yet terrifying moment she thinks might be Sam, stops and looks up. She ducks back inside. As she clambers unsteadily back to the floor, she notices that, across the room, the soon-to-be-thirty Tania has looked up from her screen and is watching her with raised eyebrows.

Lou gives her a little wave, shrugs as if climbing on your desk is the most ordinary thing in the world, then settles herself at her Mac and opens up her work files.

It's not exactly hard to ignore a letter, if you set your mind to it. Or its sender. A phone call – with words exchanged, this time – is more of a challenge.

And all this money business.

She suddenly feels weary. Is she going to have to deal with this, now?

31

Adam

Adam lugs his rucksack into Lou's apartment. He has been all the way down to Maltby Street to get organic sourdough bread and biodynamic vegetables. He wants nothing but the best for his Lou, and now she has given him her credit card, he doesn't have to let the fact that he is personally as skint as a bean get in the way of that.

As he unpacks the shopping, he marvels at the trust she shows him. He's not going to let her down. He will view looking after her and the apartment as seriously as he did working in the café, devote at least as many hours to it and still have half of every day free for his film-making. He can't believe how he has landed on his feet. Lou is, without a doubt, the woman of his dreams.

Life is sweet.

When Charley left him, he didn't quite know what to do with himself. It's all very well being an urban activist, but there's a part of him that craves love and comfort. His mum has always gently teased him that he is too soft, that he should grow some edges. But he knows she loves him for how he is, really. He is the man, after all, that she made.

He chops a pile of the vegetables to make a curry. Lou's

knives aren't all that, and he makes a note to check if it's OK if he gets some better ones. Once everything's bubbling, chilli, cumin, coriander and coconut spicing the air, he decides he's going to clean out Lou's kitchen cupboards for her.

He runs a bucket full of hot, soapy water and climbs onto the worktop to reach the wall cupboards. From what he can see, they're pretty tidy anyway – sanitised, compared to what he had to put up with in the squat with Reuben – but he's started so he'll go on.

He reaches up to the top shelf, which is higher than he can see into, even at his height and from his vantage point on the worktop. Lou would have to get one of the cherry pickers from the demolition site to reach it – he can't imagine that she would keep anything up there.

As he sweeps the shelf with his fingers, he thinks about her lovely soft, small and slightly broken body. She brings out the protective boy in him – he wants to hold her and look after her for ever. Just as it's getting a bit steamy, his dream is interrupted by his hand meeting a box about the size of a cake tin, tucked away at the very back.

He nudges it towards the cupboard opening, lifts it out and places it on the worktop at his feet. The box is red and glossy, with angels embossed on it in gold. It doesn't really look like Lou's style, which, he has gathered, is pared down, not about ornamentation.

When he takes his soapy cloth and wipes the shelf on which the box was sitting, it comes away clean.

'To be honest, there's hardly any point in doing this,' he says to himself, imagining he is the subject of one of his films, speaking his thoughts out loud for the camera.

He clears and cleans the other shelves, then jumps down off the worktop. While he's waiting for the shelves to dry, he wipes down the pots, pans and crockery he has pulled out, all of which, he notices, are brand new.

Then he turns to the red, glossy box.

Without really thinking, he takes off the lid. Inside, nestling in a satin bed, are two small brass vases, one elaborately engraved in pink, the other in blue. Resting on top of them both is a small, cheap, black phone. He lifts the contents out and takes a closer look at the vases. The decoration on them is, in fact, writing.

The pink writing says 'Poppy', the blue, 'Leon'.

He turns his attention to the phone, but it is dead.

Frowning, he unscrews the lid of the Poppy vase. He sticks in his index finger and draws it out to examine the grey, gritty dust that coats it.

Then he realises.

His mum kept his granny's ashes in a Japanese pot on top of her wardrobe. He had always asked her to see what was inside. When he was eight, she relented and brought it down to show him. He had nightmares about that pot for weeks afterwards until one day he noticed it wasn't there any longer.

He knows what these pots are, and suddenly the truth dawns.

Poor Lou.

How has she managed to go on?

He remembers how she was when he found the children's room. No wonder she can't tell him the truth. She can't even admit it to herself.

Poor, poor Lou.

He packs the little vases and the phone back into their satin nests, puts the lid back on the box and pushes it back where he found it at the very back of the very top shelf.

She doesn't have to tell him until she's ready.

He will just watch, and wait, and give her all his love and support.

32

Then

Outside, on the fenland field beyond the garden perimeter fence, the masked man in a white Hazchem suit judders in his tractor seat, revving up and down the furrows, spraying the newly sprouted crops with something chemical.

Sprawled on the sofa, Louisa surveys her empty glass. She has taken to buying small, 187-millilitre bottles in an attempt to limit her intake to one glass a day. But today she is having difficulty.

For a whole forty minutes she has sat on the sofa, sipping what she secretly thinks of as her medicine, waiting in vain for her daughter to stop crying into the baby monitor and get her head down for her afternoon nap. And now the glass is empty and so is Louisa. Empty of patience, empty of hope that she will get the sleep she needs to make up for the disturbed and wakeful night she suffered.

For the sake of the baby, Sam has told her to give up drinking altogether, which is why she only does the wine at lunchtime – just in case he comes back earlier than usual, which, now, is more often than not after her bedtime.

Without being totally aware of having got herself there, she finds herself on top of the stepping stool in her cool, onion-scented larder, moving aside some of the hundred or so jars of jam she made out of expensive imported apricots in her energetic, upswing era between Christmas and New Year. Jam she labelled with beautiful, pared-down typography, not a piece of gingham in sight. Jam that puts Jammin' jam to shame. Jam she'll still be spreading on her toast when her children have grown up and left home.

But it's not the jam she's after. It's her stash: the bijou, mini-bottles of Rioja she tucks away behind all the jars. So small, one more can't do any harm, can it?

Sam's voice, which she can hear as clearly as if he were in the larder with her, tells her to stop. She has to keep her baby safe. Her hand falls back down at her side. He is controlling her, even though he is not here. It's for the best, for her, for her baby, for Poppy. She should be grateful. She is not to be relied upon, not to be left to her own devices.

Meekly, she steps carefully back to the flagstone floor, washes and dries her wine glass and puts it back in the cupboard. To put as much distance between herself and the alcohol, she takes the empty bottle and steps out and down to the bottom of the blowy garden where, even this early in the year, the weeds – which she has not touched since Poppy was born – run rampant. As she walks, Louisa gulps at the air, which should be fresh out here in the sticks, but which, thanks to the spraying farmer, smells something like old chip oil.

Everything can harm your baby, Sam says in her head.

So she holds her breath as she slips the bottle into her secret recycling box. Hurrying back into the house, she finds the baby monitor is still rattling with Poppy's wails. Keeping the wine-containing pantry like an old adversary in the corner of her eye, she passes through the kitchen and up the stairs.

Poppy stands in her cot, bawling, her face red and shiny with snot, her body tremulous with some imagined trauma. Louisa could be angry with her, was angry before she sees her,

her little arms reaching out for her mummy as she enters the room.

All she wanted was her mummy.

'Oh baby,' she says, lifting her out of the cot. 'There, there. Mummy's here.'

As Poppy quietens, Louisa hears a car pull into the gravel driveway. Has the unthinkable happened? Has Sam come home early? She heads towards the bathroom where mouthwash will hide the tell-tale stink of daytime wine.

On the way, she peeps out of the landing window to check, and sees, instead of the red Porsche, a grubby, pale-green Skoda sitting on the driveway. The woman inside cuts the engine and reaches a briefcase from the passenger seat. She gets out, slamming and locking the door and strides up to the porch, eyeing Louisa's little white Fiesta as she does so. She's in her mid-forties and is wearing chain-store women's work wear. Louisa doesn't like the look of her one little bit.

The doorbell rings.

'Shhh, Pops,' Louisa whispers to her daughter as she holds her tight, pressing herself against the wall, out of sight of the window.

The doorbell rings again.

Louisa carefully peeps down at the woman, who peers into the living-room window, before returning to the front door and giving it a good hammering.

'Mrs Williams?' she calls as, having got no reaction, she disappears round the back of the house. The cheek of the woman. Technically, she is now trespassing.

Eventually, she appears round the other side of the driveway. Leaning on her car bonnet, she scribbles something on a piece of paper and puts it through Louisa's front door.

Then she gets in her car, reverses out onto the road, and is gone.

Louisa waits until the rattling of her faulty exhaust fades

completely, then, very carefully – she's not going to trip again – she hurries downstairs with Poppy and picks up the note the woman put through her door.

It appears she is some sort of social worker. 'Louisa: congratulations on your pregnancy!' she writes on a council compliments slip with her contact details. 'Just popping by to see how things are going.'

Just popping by? This is clearly Sam's work. He did it with the Slovak, and now he's got Social Services onto her, to check up on her, to see if she's behaving.

She'll show him.

She takes Poppy through to the living room and, like a good mother, she reads her *The Velveteen Rabbit*. Her little girl snuggles her sweaty little body under her arm. The picture's not quite perfect enough, though. She peels Poppy away from her – setting her off grizzling again – and goes through to the kitchen to warm up a bottle for her.

Back in the ideal mother-and-child scenario, Poppy sucks on her bottle as Louisa continues to read. She's clearly not going to sleep, though. Surely at sixteen months she's too young to be giving up on afternoon naps?

As Louisa begins to bore herself with the story, she sees an endless procession of afternoons like these. And it'll go on for at least a decade, if she and Sam stick to the plan and fill all four of the smaller bedrooms with children. Her studio will continue to sit unused, until it's turned into a playroom. She will constantly be putting her own needs to the back of the queue as she juggles the demands of children and babies and foetuses.

During the short period after Christmas, when she attended the playgroup in the Methodist hall, she asked one of the mothers there how life was with two children.

'It's like having three,' the woman said, the weariness just visible behind her otherwise perfect make-up mask. 'You've got the two kids with their various needs, and then there's the dynamic between them, which is like a whole other person.'

Fed up, Louisa picks Poppy up and dumps her in the playpen, a recent addition to her battery of plastic and wooden early years equipment. She can smell Sam's disapproval as she does this. He doesn't believe that children should be hemmed in, preferring them to run free and at will.

'But have you ever spent the whole day alone with Poppy?' she asks Head-Sam as she fetches the basket of Poppy's puzzles. 'No. You haven't, have you?'

Her whole body craves another drink, but she won't give in to it.

She stands and looks at her reflection in the living-room window. The sky is blue, with little white clouds scudding through it. If only she and Poppy could go out there, she might feel less hemmed-in. But the air is poisonous with crop spray.

'You have amazing resources, amazing will power,' she says to herself, parroting something she read in a magazine. 'You are bigger than all of this.'

Keeping hands busy, that's the thing. She fetches a duster and silver polish, spreads newspaper out on the dining table and pulls all her trophies from the cupboard that Sam detests so much. True, its dark wooden Victorian curlicues certainly don't go with the other, pared-back modern furnishings that sit coolly in the beamed and vaulted living room. But she has hung on to it through arguing that it is the only reminder she has of her childhood.

The parents-abandoning-her story is one of the few areas where she still has traction in her marriage. Allowances have to be made for her, poor unloved child that she was. For her, though, the trophy cupboard is about happier memories than her parents. It is a reminder of what she once was: a winner.

She puts on rubber gloves to save chemicals entering her bloodstream through her fingertips and poisoning her baby, and she sets about buffing her prizes, lifting the taint and making them gleam under her hands.

She and Star blazed magnificently, from when she was twelve until she was sixteen. She closes her eyes and sees the blur of grass and sky, feels the lift in the heart of a good, clean jump. Apart from that last time, she and he always won, always, and she spent every spare moment with him in the paddock, going round the jump circuit, schooling him on the long rein, running him on and on, faster and faster, until he was foam-flecked and she was all sweat . . .

She runs the duster over the glass of a photograph of them both: she smiling proudly and holding a cup, he sporting a rosette on his bridle.

'Oh, Star,' she says. 'Oh, Louise.'

The things she has lost.

With only a couple of interruptions from Poppy, who, amazingly, is each time distracted by having another basket of toys handed to her, Louisa polishes each of the cups, all of the trophies. She runs a duster over the Yellow Pencil she won for her work at Paradigm, which she keeps next to the horsey prizes as a sign that she has also more recently been a winner.

She dusts inside the cupboard and rearranges the trophies in the exact same positions. For some reason, she doesn't want Sam to know that she has spent this hour running over the glories of her past. For some reason, she feels the need to keep it furtive, hidden from Sam.

She closes the doors of the cabinet on its newly gleaming contents and turns to see that Poppy, who has not made a sound for a while, is finally fast asleep, toppled sideways over Mary Doll.

'Sweet,' Louisa says, draping a crocheted blanket over her.

'You should put her in bed,' Head-Sam tells her.

'But if I lift her, she'll wake.'

He makes no comment, but again, the stink of disapproval catches in her nostrils.

She should capitalise on Poppy's sleep and lie down herself. But something's niggling at her. She's wondering if she'll ever again be a winner, or, for her, is that the end of trophies?

Also, those little bottles in the pantry are singing to her: *Drink me!*

Keep busy, she thinks.

'How about making me a lovely dinner?' Head-Sam says.

'What do you want?'

He tells her that he fancies beef stew, so she pulls some cubed meat from the freezer and defrosts it in the microwave. She browns it, fries garlic and onions and tomatoes and herbs, mixes it all up and tastes it. Wine. It needs wine.

Would vinegar do, she wonders?

But it won't. It has to be wine. She fetches three of the small bottles from the larder.

Just as she's unscrewing the caps, her hands shaking with the effort of not holding them to her lips, her phone pings with a text. It's Sam, of course. It could only be Sam, since no one else calls or texts her. Even Sandy at the playgroup – who proved to be award-winningly thick skinned about Louisa ignoring her advances – has finally given up contacting her.

Unexpected dinner with investor, the text says. *Won't be home till late. Look after yourself. S*

Louisa narrows her eyes at the last sentence. It's one of the ways he is controlling her. It's code for don't drink, don't fall down the stairs, don't let me come home and find you passed out. It's like he's some kind of hypnotist, weaving threads of his consciousness into hers.

And no x at the end. When did he start leaving off the x's?

This is the fourth night this week he's been out late, and it's only Thursday.

He's busy, he tells her. His company is going through an

expansion phase, he's talking with venture capitalists, marketing three new apps, instant best-sellers, which means he's been dealing with the media as well.

Too busy for his wife and child.

She doesn't believe the half of it. She's not met Marisa, his marketing manager – for some reason, she 'couldn't come' to the Christmas drinks party. But she's looked her up on the Internet. She's smart, sassy, well dressed, powerful, Cambridge-educated, the same age as Louisa and not bogged down with children, bagginess, perineal scars, fumble-brain and fog.

What the hell, then, Head-Sam? Hastily, before he can tell her to stop, she downs the first of the little bottles. She can forgo the taste of wine in the stew. It's only for her now, after all.

Second and third bottle in hand, she crosses the hallway to Sam's study. She pulls his cabin suitcase from where it lives in a wall cupboard and goes through the pockets and the washbag he keeps ready inside it because he goes away so much. She finds nothing. No condoms, no scented notes, no lipstick stains, nothing directly incriminating scribbled in the jotter he keeps by his computer monitor.

She should be relieved. But, as she sits back at his desk and tips the second bottle of wine down her throat, her suspicions merely deepen.

'You're a clever bastard, Sam,' she says to the photograph of him on the cover of a trade magazine that he has, in his vanity, framed and hung on his wall. Not only can he get inside her head and send old bats in dirty old Skodas round to spy on her, but he can also hide all trace of his activities from her.

And then she remembers what she knows is hidden behind the cupboard in the corner of his study. He has no idea it is there, and one day it might prove to be very useful to her.

'Not so clever after all, then, are we, eh, Sammy boy?'

Slugging away at the third bottle of wine, she makes an

unsteady progress to the living room where Poppy has finally woken and is crying for her tea.

'Don't worry. I won't make another scene when you come in,' she tells Head-Sam.

'Of course you won't,' he replies. 'You'll be passed out in the spare bedroom, with Poppy.'

She catches her hip on the door handle and winces.

'Wino,' he whispers in her ear.

33

Now

This morning, as he has every day over the week following Sophie's nasty, threatening phone call, Adam escorts Lou from the shelter of home to the Tube station. Although she has not mentioned her tormentor – what on earth would she tell him? – he seems to instinctively know that she needs protection. She then scuttles from the Tube station at the other end to the sanctuary of work. This much she has decided: Sophie is a monster; she knows no bounds.

When it gets – as Sophie threatened – 'messy', will the attack be physical? Or will her approach be more psychological? Whatever. It's only a matter of time before she turns up, and all Lou can do is watch and wait, prepare herself.

At the end of each day spent hiding behind the shield of the A.R.K. building security guards, she creeps back home, looking over her shoulder, to the unwitting protection of her strong, reliable man, who has now almost fully moved in. Each day, new things arrive from his squat. He doesn't bring his ex's stuff, though – when Lou told him, quite understandably, that she couldn't be doing with that, he boxed up all the tiny dresses and blouses and sent them back to Charley's parents' house. Lou was happy to pay the postage.

His own clothes now take up a modest amount of space in her wardrobe. His battered toothbrush has made its home sitting in a mug next to her own electric model in the bathroom, the shining sari adorns her bed, and the second bedroom now bulges with his books and sound and video equipment, with the Rothko leaning boldly against one of the walls. They've even started referring to it as his studio, which at first made Lou uncomfortable, reminding her of her own workspace in Fen Manor and the personal and professional failure it represents for her. But, after repeating 'Adam's studio' hundreds of times to herself, she has almost cleaned the phrase of its negative associations.

Adam being so suddenly and fully in her life suits her well. He looks after her as if she is a rare treasure. Her work-bound scuttle is accessorised daily with a tasty, salad-based packed lunch in a brown paper bag, and she is welcomed when she returns at the end of the day with a hot meal, a swim, perhaps, a bath, a massage and excellent, enthusiastic sex. It's worth every penny.

Also thanks to Adam, her apartment gleams. He has a way with housework that outshines even her own. Her standards are met entirely. She pays for everything, he does everything. It's a very pleasing symbiotic relationship.

There are just two problem areas.

The first is that he wants to take her home to meet his mother. Lou would rather stick pins in her eyes. She wants Adam, not his family. She doesn't want to share him with anyone, least of all his mother.

The other challenge is the children's room. She found him in there again, when she came home from work earlier in the week.

'What are you doing?' she had asked him.

'Dusting.'

'Don't.'

He looked at her, a question in his eyes.

'I'd just rather you didn't. The room's fine as it is.'

He moved towards her, took her hand and looked into her eyes. 'Any news on when they'll be coming?'

There was something in his voice that made her think he knew more than he was letting on, and, once more, she found herself asking if she could trust him.

'Soon,' she said, ushering him from the room and closing the door behind them.

He hasn't mentioned them again.

He has also kept his word about staying out of their bedroom. She knows this because the piece of thread she shuts between the door and the frame is always in place when she checks it.

And when she sits up in the night, sweating, panting, breathing heavily with panic, he holds her until the terror passes, smoothing her hair, whispering in her ear.

'I love you,' he says.

He is a million times more motherly than she ever managed to be, and that is just what she needs right now.

'You still on for tonight?' Cleo asks Lou as she does her morning check in on the design studio.

'Tonight?'

'Tania's birthday drinks, remember?'

'Oh. Oh, yes,' Lou says.

'We play as a team at A.R.K.'

'Yep.'

When Cleo leaves her, Lou calls Adam to tell her she'll be home late. She had, in fact, clean forgotten about Tania's birthday drinks.

She doesn't leave with the others at six, claiming that she would like to do an hour more at the Mac in order to sign off

239

for the week. This is something Cleo can't really complain too much about. At half past seven, half thinking that she might just head back home instead, she gathers her things together, and switches off her desk lamp. She takes one final look out of her window at the London skyscape glistening in the hot night, and breathes in the last moments of blessed air-conditioned, safe solitude.

She says goodbye to the night security guard and, after a quick glance around the street for tall, skinny, dark-haired girls, she makes her decision – it can't be avoided – and heads off towards the private members' club – 'creatives only' – where the others are drinking to Tania's thirtieth.

The pavement throbs under her uneven step, returning heat stored up through yet another sweltering day. Horn-honking, stationary traffic jams the narrow streets, belching poisonous fumes into the evening air. Lou holds a tissue to her face to shield her lungs.

In the sanctuary of the club lobby, a couple of young women sit on a silver leather faux-Regency sofa, sipping cold wine from long-stemmed glasses. A buzz of chatter and laughter filters down the curving wooden staircase behind them. Low-key, bass-heavy jazz-funk mellows out the stark, white decor.

It is the first time Lou has entered a bar for years, and it will be a test of her new, sober persona. Just the sight of that wine in those women's hands makes her fingers tingle for the cold condensation, the icy liquid, the numbing fuzz that kicks in after the second glass.

But no. She has to rein herself in. Control herself. If she doesn't, it leads to disaster. This is a proven fact.

She taps her wrist. Tap, tap, tap: another trick from The Pines. This one sort of works, or it has in the past when she has thought of alcohol. Meeting it face to face may be different, though. Is she ready for the press and buzz she imagines she will find upstairs in this club?

She thinks of Adam back at the apartment and how he is the opposite of all this, and how she much prefers his world. But if she is going to be the best – and she always likes being the best – she has to play this game, learn how to wear this mask.

She shrugs her shoulders as if donning a cloak of cool. Gripping her shiny new corporate membership card so tightly it almost cuts into her palm, she steps towards the receptionist's desk.

'Ah, so you're our new A.R.K.-ette,' the receptionist says, glancing at Lou's card and smiling up at her. 'Welcome! They're in the Library Bar. Fourth floor. Take a right when you come out of the lift.'

Feeling like an imposter who has bluffed her way in, Lou steps into the lift and is whisked up to the fourth floor with two jovially drunk men in crumpled linen suits who bitch to each other about a film premiere they attended the previous night. She enjoys staying haughty and cool as one casts an appreciative eye her way.

The bar is, indeed, a full, heaving crush. Lou edges past the press of creative types towards the A.R.K. crowd, who have noisily taken root at a long table on the far side.

Cleo rises and kisses her on both cheeks. 'So you finally managed to pull yourself away.' She turns to the assembled group of designers and tech types. 'Hey, everyone, say hi to Lou.'

'Hi, Lou,' they chorus. From the look and sound of them, the cocktails in their hands are not the first of the evening.

'Make space for her, then,' Cleo says, and they obediently move up. 'We're on dirty Martinis. Want one?'

Lou taps her wrist, takes a deep breath and guides Cleo a little away from the others.

'I'm afraid I'm not drinking at the moment.' Cleo's eyebrows flicker upwards. 'Antibiotics,' Lou adds quickly.

'Oh poor you. Sure you can't do just one?'

Lou grits her teeth. 'I'm afraid it would make me very ill indeed.'

Which is the understatement of the year.

Cleo picks up a menu from the table and peers at it through her reading glasses. 'I think they do a couple of virgin cocktails.'

'No, really, just a pint of lime and soda will do me, thanks.' The last thing Lou needs is to start poring over drinks menus. Cleo shrugs and marches over to the bar while Lou slides into a space next to Chen, her studio neighbour, who smiles tipsily at her.

'Nice to have you join us,' she says. She offers Lou her glass, spilling a drop as she does so. 'Wanna sip while you're waiting for Cleo to get them in?'

'No thanks.'

'Go on!' She holds the glass up to Lou's lips, practically tipping its contents into her mouth.

'I don't drink,' Lou says, pushing her hand away with as much grace as she can muster.

'Seriously? Are you some kind of alcoholic, then?' Chen puts her dainty hand over her pretty mouth and giggles.

Wearily, Lou closes her eyes and scratches her forehead. When she opens them, Chen's face is pained with discomfort and embarrassment.

'It's so hot, isn't it?' she says to Chen, surprising herself with her own generosity in changing the subject.

'They say it might let up in a couple of weeks.' The gratitude in Chen's eyes says it all.

'First I've heard of it.'

Luckily, Cleo turns up to intervene with a tray of Martinis and the lime and soda. Lou tells herself that her drink looks by far the nicest with its grand size and ice-mist bloom.

She takes a deep draught, only now realising how thirsty

she is. As usual, she got so lost in her work today that she completely forgot about everything, including eating or drinking. Nothing's passed her lips since a coffee this morning, which is stupid, considering how much she has sweated, scurrying around in the heat.

'Sorry about dragging you out,' Cleo says, squeezing in next to her.

'It's fun,' Lou lies.

'So I asked my friend. You didn't get Orlagh to babysit?'

'Oh. Oh, no.'

'Who did you use?'

'There's this student on my corridor,' Lou says.

'Have you got any photos?' Cleo asks.

'Hmm?'

'Of the kids.'

Lou opens and shuts her mouth. The others laugh too loudly. She registers the background music – jazz piano of some sort – and she longs to be back at home, with just simple, comfortable, unquestioning Adam for company.

Cleo rummages in her handbag and produces her iPhone. 'This is my lot. A few years back, mind.'

She shows Lou a photo of three beautiful teenage girls, pale-coffee skins blooming rosy underneath heads of proudly curling hair just like their mother's 'My rotten little mini-me's.' She beams fondly at the image.

'They're gorgeous,' Lou manages to say, around the choke forming in her throat.

Cleo looks expectantly at her.

What can she do? What sort of twenty-first-century mother doesn't have a photo of her kids on her phone? She brings up the one photo – the picture she has attached to Leon and Poppy's phone number, and she holds it up for Cleo to see.

In it, a pale Poppy perches on one of the Eames chairs Sam bought for Fen Manor, holding Leon on her knee, sitting him up as if he is her little doll. Sam took the photograph. Louisa wasn't up to doing much at the time.

It doesn't hold great memories, that photo, but it's all she's got left of her children.

Cleo takes the phone and holds it at arm's length, as if her arty, black-framed glasses aren't quite the right prescription.

'It was taken a while ago,' Lou says, realising the children are far younger in the picture than the ages she has told Cleo.

'Ah, she's a little darling,' Cleo says. 'A little mummy in waiting. They're so sweet. You must bring them into the office one day.'

'Sure.'

'I love seeing kids in the workplace. We're thinking about getting a crèche in the building. Might you be up for it?'

'Um. Possibly.'

'We've been shortlisted for this prize, sponsored by Mumsnet. It's all about being a great equal-opportunities employer for returning women. They're running a profile of us on the site, and I was wondering if we could get a nice shot, you know, of you and the kids, perhaps at your desk?'

Lou catches her breath. 'Um. I'm not sure, I—'

'It'd be great for the company.'

'It's a bit complicated. I'd have to check with their father . . .'

Lou is saved by the sound of a knife knocking on glass as Chen sways to her feet to slur a speech about what a 'top bird' the birthday girl is. One of the other designers presents Tania with a perfectly wrapped parcel, which is greedily ripped open to reveal a soft leather iPad cover with 'Slut' embossed on the front in an elegant, cursive font.

Lou pretends to look at a text on her phone, and then leans over to Cleo.

'I've got to go,' she says. 'Leon's been sick.'

'Leon?' Cleo says, quickly. 'I thought you said his name was Ben.'

'Yes,' she says, quickly. 'Ben. I meant Ben.'

She grabs her bag and runs from the club, her cloak of cool lost.

All lost.

And she scuttles home to Adam.

34

Sophie runs down the stairs in Sam's shirt. She's been rationing the nights she sleeps in it because she doesn't want to dilute his scent with her own, which is largely milk these days. But last night she craved comfort. She's not getting the sleep she needs, because poor little Sami has spent the past couple of nights mostly awake, screaming blue murder, thanks to a stomach bug. She's still quite delicate, poor lamb, after her rocky arrival in the world, and Sophie worries to death over every tiny sniffle and digestive upset.

The mail sits on the doormat, but again it is just red bills and nothing from Louisa. It has been one week now since Sophie called her, one week where that bile in her has been festering and expanding like a nasty yeast infection.

But if Louisa imagines that Sophie will go away if ignored, she's got another think coming.

What hasn't helped Sophie's mood is that, as she sat in bed trying to breastfeed a listless Sami this morning, she paid her daily visit to the Marsden & Hunt website and discovered that the inevitable has happened: her flat is now on the market.

It appears that the guy in the pinstripe suit did a great job of taking photographs around her mess when he barged his way in. The bastard must have cleared all the crap up then dumped it back down again, because he made the flat look a lot nicer in the photographs than it does in real life. The images, set as they are above the breathless prose full of estate-agent clichés – 'remarkably spacious', 'a short stroll to the city centre', 'light-filled', 'bursting with original features' – have had the annoying result of making her even angrier about the prospect of being forced to leave her home.

She could go up to London right now and make Louisa see sense, but she doesn't want to take Sami on a train when she's this unwell. Also, with her mind on other things, she has failed to put anything up on eBay for a while, so her income has dried up. She and Sami are skint, with exactly four pounds and forty-eight pence to their names. To make things worse, yesterday the cashpoint ate her card. When she went in to the bank to complain, she was told by some plump-faced boy in a disgusting suit that it was because she had exceeded her overdraft limit, and that he couldn't allow her to have access to her account until her finances were in order.

Resisting the urge to make the scene that was building up inside her, she had drawn herself up to her full, impressive height and subjected him to one of her most withering looks. Almost fainting with a fury that sucked all the blood from her head and placed it in the pit of her belly, she kicked the brake off the buggy and stalked out, head held high, knees shaking.

It is so unfair that she is so broke. Why should she stoop to claim benefits or go cap in hand to charity, when Louisa is running around with a large chunk of cash which, by rights, belongs to Sami and her? When she could just give her this flat, not even because it's Sami's birthright, but because it would be the morally right thing to do.

She flings the red bills in the dustbin on the front porch and climbs back up the stairs to her flat door, knotting her fingers around one another, thinking, thinking.

It is becoming clear to her that she will have to go to London, track Louisa down and use whatever means she can to get to her. She and Sami can't go on like this: paupers threatened with homelessness, dragging Sam's tainted name around after them. One way or another, Louisa has to be made to see sense.

Would Sophie be capable of hurting her if matters came to such a head?

She goes to the bedroom and checks in on Sami, who, thankfully, is still sleeping soundly, lying in the cot, flat on her back, her finely boned face crowned with auburn hair, a mini rendition of Sam. The sight of her stokes the furnace of fierce love that burns in Sophie's chest.

Yes. If she had to, for Sami's sake, for the name of her child's father, for the money that is due her, then Sophie would go to any lengths.

She pulls down a TRAGIC LOUISA TELLS ALL front page from her washing line. As she tears it into thin strips, she pictures herself slowly tugging out Louisa's nails one by one, ripping them from her fingertips with pliers, until she confesses to the very worst things Sophie suspects of her: that she is a liar, a violent, vicious, abusive bitch, two-faced, evil . . .

And then, as she moves the pliers to Louisa's mouth, to start on her teeth, Louisa tells her – through her screams and sobs – that she can keep the flat, and that she will give her as much money as she needs to raise Sami. Sophie imagines this would be in the region of five hundred thousand pounds. Yes, with her bleeding, ripped fingers smearing the keyboard, Louisa logs on to her bank account and moves five hundred thousand pounds to Sophie's. No. Six hundred thousand. No. A million.

That would show the bank boy in the horrible suit when she went in to demand a new cashpoint card.

That would work.

But *would* she be able to do it? Would she be able to draw blood to get what she and Sami need from Louisa?

She gathers the strips of torn newsprint together and holds them like a bunch of flowers, while, with her other hand, she grates the wheel on the Bic lighter.

Whatever it takes. The anger and grief that has consumed her these past fourteen months has surely eaten away at what she considers acceptable.

Of *course* she could hurt Louisa.

She could kill her if necessary.

She knows what would help, though, should the spirit desert her at the last minute.

She thinks of her old friend, the powder with the power to make her believe she is invincible.

The powder The Photographer first fed her to make her more pliable.

The powder that gave her the courage to limp into Chelsea Police Station four years ago to report him for repeatedly raping her.

The powder she stupidly had on her in a significant quantity as she marched in off the King's Road and demanded to make her statement.

The powder she accidentally pulled out of her handbag when, on telling her story, she reached for a tissue to wipe her eyes. The powder that helped to put her in prison. The powder that saw her spending many, many days hiding in her prison bunk, sweating out her withdrawal.

She touches the flame to her bunch of torn, lying newspaper flowers.

The paper smoulders, then bursts into flame.

The powder that she determined never to touch again.

And yet here she is, realising that she is contemplating going out to buy some.

But, surely though, it's just a practical step, a means to an end?

Colombian courage.

She lets the flaming embers drop from her singed fingers and stamps them out on the grimy cream carpet.

A plan forming in her head, she opens her wardrobe and makes a quick calculation based on what remains of the designer samples she acquired during those powder days. If she's lucky, she's got another three grand or so before she is down to the clothes she needs to keep to cover her body.

So she's not completely skint, not yet, but she knows better than most how quickly money can just disappear.

She fingers one of her two remaining Chanel dresses. Desperate for cash, she can't wait around to sell it on eBay. And even if she could, the money would only fill part of the overdraft hole in her bank account and she wouldn't be able to get at it. She won't fetch as good a price at the dress agency on Mill Road as she could raise online, but Monica there will sub her a hundred or so for this piece. It is, after all, a classic from the Spring/Summer 2011 collection, worn just once, for the photo-shoot where she accepted it in part payment, back in the days when cash was so ubiquitous it held no importance for her.

Back when The Photographer was raping her.

She tugs out the dress with almost the same level of force she had imagined using on Louisa's fingertips, sprays it lightly with a little Dior Poison, to add a touch of *je ne sais quoi*, and cocoons it in a protective garment bag.

She takes a shower and throws on a skimpy little black sundress. When Sami wakes up, she is ready. She gives her a quick feed, which is taken hungrily enough to lead Sophie to hope that her baby's sickness might be coming to an end. Then she slips on some shades and sandals and carries Sami and Bugaboo downstairs to the front door.

They're heading first to the dress agency, and then down to the Rose and Crown. Apart from the abortive trip to the bank, this is Sophie's first outing in nearly a week. She doesn't like to go out all that much because, due to her former infamy backed up by the public attempts to discredit her Phase One attacks on Louisa – thanks a bunch, Fiona – every time she does, she is recognised, harangued, berated.

She steps inside the pub, and the daytime smell of old beer and the morning's cleaning products brings it all back to her. When she came out of prison and moved away from her old London haunts – where she would be tempted back to party powders and met with hostility by the people she used to work with – she found herself a grim little bedsit and a bar job in Cambridge, a town that she hoped would nurture her serious intentions about straightening her life out, making an honest living and getting the education which has since, once more, slipped through her fingertips.

This pub, the Rose and Crown, is where she met Sam.

He cut a strange figure that night, sitting over by the window on his own, tucking into pie and chips and a pint of Adnams. He was wearing a suit that fitted so well on his tall frame that it had to be bespoke, checked the time on an unshowy Rolex and, she noticed when she handed him his change, his nails were exceptionally clean and well-tended. He was also wearing a wedding ring.

But there was something else about him – a certain sadness, the downward dog look she'd expect to see on the tired, inept travelling salesmen who were the more usual Rose and Crown punters. He had lovely eyes, though, despite a weariness that bleached their green. And glorious, thick, auburn hair.

They'd chatted a little each time he came up for a refill. By the second pint, she found out that he lived just outside Ely. By the third, he had removed his wedding ring. When one of a crowd of noisy drunk louts grabbed her arse as she came out to collect glasses, Sam was on his feet, pushing the creep off her, squaring up to him, tapping his cheeks in a manner that was more threatening because of the lightness with which he did it. The arse-grabber's mates, seeing what would happen to him if they stayed, dragged him from the pub, off into the night, for more pints and less dangerous trouble elsewhere.

Sophie was completely disarmed. No one had ever stood up for her like that before. When he offered to walk her home at the end of her shift, she didn't hesitate. When she said she couldn't let him drive home because he was over the limit, he stayed in her horrid bedsit.

It wasn't until the next morning that she gave a thought to that mysteriously disappearing wedding ring.

And by then it was too late. She was hooked.

All this is almost too much for her to bear as she stands this afternoon, swaying on the pub threshold, looking around the bar to where he had sat that night, wishing with all her might that she could conjure him up again so that he could meet his glorious little baby.

'Babe!' her dream is broken by a shout from a grimy alcove in the far reaches of the bar. The cracked, partied-out voice belongs to the person she has come to see: Snake, who, besides leery drunken boys, was her other nemesis when she worked here.

A more or less constant fixture in the pub, Snake was never disrespectful to her like the others. It was more what she knew he could furnish her with that caused her the problems. She had told him where she stood with her drug of choice and, to be fair to him, he never pushed it on her. While he would never have defended her with his fists like Sam, Snake had confessed on more than one occasion, when off his face, to having a soft spot for her. And, if the delighted way he strides across the bar to greet her is anything to go by, nothing has changed about that, despite what she has so publicly gone through.

He claps his arms around her and grins widely, revealing more black gaps in his gums than she remembers.

'Doll!' he says. 'How ya doin'? Well, you got yourself wound up with a wrong 'un, didn't ya? Liked the way you stood up for him, though.' He sings a snatch of 'Stand by Your Man', and she catches the pear-drop breath of an addict who isn't much bothered about eating. 'This the kid? Sweet, eh. Drink?' He motions towards the bar.

Sophie, who hasn't said a word during all this, nods. Might as well, she thinks. 'Gin and tonic,' she says. One will be all right for the breast milk. It might even help calm Sami's tummy. After all, gripe water was just alcohol, wasn't it? And besides, from the beginning, she has expressed and frozen a bag of milk a day, just in case something were to happen to make it impossible for her to be there for Sami. A single parent can't be too careful. The freezer full of bags will, of course, also come in handy should she ever decide to take what she's planning to buy from Snake.

Taking care to position herself opposite him, she sits in the grimy booth and, after a brief catch-up, she tells him her business.

'You sure, doll?' he says, frowning at her. 'I know you had problems with it back in the day.'

'It's just a one off.'

Snake scratches his black curls, revealing an ear with five silver rings pierced into it. 'Cos I don't want to be the one what fucks it all up for you.'

'You don't have to worry about that.' Sophie can't help smiling. A dealer with a conscience. Life does turn up surprises.

They order another drink – Sophie's round – and they step through the dance of unwritten rules between dealer and punter. In the shelter of the alcove in the otherwise deserted pub, Snake counts out the five tenners she gives him and hands her a wrap. His scruples don't extend to stopping him writing his name and phone number on it and telling her with a wink to give him a bell if ever he can help her out again 'in any way, babe, know what I mean?'

She pushes the Bugaboo out into the harsh afternoon sunlight. It has been so long since she had any alcohol that she feels more drunk than she thought she would be after just two gins. The wrap in her bag weighs heavily on her in the way she imagines a bar of chocolate might for a dieting fat girl. To resist it is going to be a big test of her resolve, but she thinks she might be up to it. It is for emergencies only.

Woozy, weary and overheated, she drags herself back home across Parker's Piece, which is dotted with sunbathers, picnickers, drinkers and dozing students. They may be pretending not to look at her, but she can feel their attention. They all know about her.

Why has her life turned out like this?

In the middle, where someone has scratched 'reality checkpoint' into the central lamp post, she stops, puts the brake on Sami's buggy, sways on her elegant pins and turns around three times widdershins, making herself dizzy. Her nostrils flare and she can still feel the outburst she put the lid on at the bank yesterday simmering underneath her skin.

'I know what you all think,' she wants to say to the good people of Cambridge and their visitors, in a clear, loud voice. 'And you can all FUCK OFF, you know? Just all FUCK OFF.'

Helped right now by too much gin on an empty stomach and the sense that, in buying coke, she has just broken one of her most sacred rules, she almost does it, too.

She imagines them all shrinking back from the crazy lady, whom they might just recognise from somewhere.

A boy – well tailored, privileged, bright – passes too close to her. Caught in her imaginings, she grabs his arm. 'It wasn't always like this,' she tells him.

He shakes her off and goes on his way, and Sophie wonders if she and Sami will ever have a normal, happy, comfortable life.

This is what Louisa owes her.

She will keep on at her until Sami is well enough to travel. She doesn't want her to get too comfortable. She needs to be reminded. There has not been a peep from Fiona in response to the attempts Sophie has made so far to contact Louisa. It's time to take things up a notch or two.

At home, Sophie puts Sami to bed. As she's going about her motherly duties, she can't get her mind off Snake's wrap – the thought of it burns on her consciousness almost as much as her hate of Louisa.

She can't resist it. She unfolds it and takes just a tiny toot, sniffing it up like snuff from the back of her hand. Instantly, she feels the tingle, the buzz, the welcome home. It is dangerous and she knows it.

'No, Sophie,' she tells herself. She tidies it all away and puts the wrap up on top of a high shelf in the kitchen. Deciding to put her chemically enhanced energy to good use, she turns on her iPad and checks her emails. A pleasant surprise greets her in Trudie Stein's email inbox.

Sophie,

You were bloody rude to me. First you lied about who you were. Then you went on at me for being so angry about what Louise did to poor Star, Boy Blue, Milko and Silver (the other two who died in the fire, God bless their souls).

You don't understand. Horses are my people, and for me, Louise is a murderer for what she did.

So I don't know why I'm doing this. Well, I do, in fact.
I'm doing it because I want to get back at her and if I tell
you this, you can do it for me, without me having to get
my own hands dirty. I've got horses to look after.

Louise pushed her mother down the stairs. That's what
they said in the village. Shortly after, she went to art
school in Bristol, and they moved away. They're in the
Shetlands. I've spoken to my mother, who used to clean
for them, and this is their address and phone number.
They gave it to her to forward mail, or, they said, to let
them know if there were 'any problems'. That's all I
know.

Copy the details then delete this email. You did not get
this information from me.

Her heart pounding, Sophie picks up her phone and dials the
number PonyGirl has given her.

35

Liar.

The emails have been coming in all day. They are brief, poisonous affairs.

You led him to it.

Each message comes from a different email address, so it is impossible to block them.

He is innocent.

It is clear who is sending them.

I'll teach you what being a victim is really about.

Each time one arrives, Lou's mind is hauled from her work and sent into a minor, hot-faced panic.

I will have my baby's money off you, no matter what it takes.

Again, she wonders if she should go to the police. But she

won't, she knows that at least. She doesn't want to go near a police station again in her entire life, doesn't want any more questions being asked of her or anyone. Sophie would love that, everything being opened up again. Lou won't give her the satisfaction.

Then the killer final message of the day arrives.

I know what you did to your mother.

Lou is so shocked that her gasp interrupts Chen, who glances over at her from her workstation.

Has Sophie been talking to her parents?

This is too much. Panic flutters in her chest.

It's not like *they're* going to tell the truth about what happened. *They're* not exactly going to put Lou's point of view across, are they? And Sophie's going to *love* what they tell her, what they show her. She'll have a whole new bag full of weapons to use against her, all false, all one-sided.

Her head still lost in the haze that comes from spending all day on a computer, Lou sits on the Tube on her way home from work and imagines command-exing Sophie, Apple-zedding her. Highlighting her and pressing the delete button. Rubbing her out, the one fly in her ointment, the one bad apple in her whole big barrel full.

Life would be so much simpler.

Life would then be perfect.

'Get your glad rags on, we're going to a party,' Adam says as Lou flops through the door.

'Seriously?' The last thing Louisa feels like is going out.

'Now they've downed tools, we're reclaiming the demolition site. Bonfire, barbecue, sound system and speeches.'

'Won't they stop you?'

'Probably, and I'll be there to film it all.'

'You're *asking* for trouble?'

'Might be. Anyway, I'd love you to come down and meet everyone. We've been setting up all evening. It's going to be really cool.'

Cool.

Lou changes out of her designer work wear and into a cotton sundress, so that she matches Adam more closely, style-wise, for this, their first public outing other than trips to the Tube station. She doesn't want to go. She's been too rattled by that mention of her mother, and all the murk it stirs up. But, for this reason also, she doesn't want to stay in on her own.

Itching to get to the party, Adam practically drags her along the corridor to the lift.

'Let me carry that, at least,' she says, taking the picnic basket from him. He has enough to lug, with his camera, sound equipment and a large nylon holdall stuffed full of bunting, which, apparently, someone dropped round earlier in the day.

They skirt the site until they reach the far side, where a crowd of people are swarming through an open gate. It's not just the ragged young protestors Lou was expecting. All sorts are here – old, young, smartly dressed and otherwise. Mothers with children, a couple of people in wheelchairs, even a few men in suits.

'We put the word right out. Half the former residents are here, by the looks of it,' Adam says, looking around proudly.

'And the telly,' Lou says, pointing to a BBC News camera crew.

'Yep – the developers have got to play it really carefully if they're not going to look like heavy-handed bastards.'

'Hey, Adam!' a tall, shaven-headed woman calls as she passes.

'All right, Neon?' Adam replies. More people greet him, slapping him on the back, high-fiving, coming up and kissing him. Lou nods shyly as he introduces her. If she felt out of place at Tania's birthday drinks, here she could be a two-headed alien.

'How did you open the gates?' she asks as they pass through.

'I've got an archaeologist insider who slipped me a key. She grew up on the estate, and her parents were kicked out to Croydon. Just think. Move from here to Croydon! She says it's all cool so long as we don't disturb the bones.'

Lou is amazed. She sometimes gets the idea that Adam exists purely to make things easier and better for her. But here's the proof that he has a whole other life while she is at work. She's not sure how much she likes it, but what can she do?

'Didn't the site security people stop you?'

'By the time they realised what was going on, it was too late. Mass trespass, innit? There are too many of us. It'd be majorly messy PR to bust up a peaceful protest.'

'Won't they call the police?'

Adam grins. 'Probably.'

Inside, they join the crowd, heading past people handing out leaflets and drinks, cakes and sweets to the children.

'The shopping centre donated those,' Adam says. 'They're affected as much as the rest of us.'

'There you go, Leroy,' he says, handing the bag of bunting to a man in baggy denim dungarees and little else. 'That'll brighten the place up.'

'Cheers, man,' Leroy says, hefting the bag away.

At the centre of where the crowd is gathering, a group of more typical protestor types – ratty clothes, men with goatees, white women with great knots of dreadlocks piled on their heads – are putting the finishing touches to a massive bonfire they have built out of old wooden pallets and broken furniture.

Hay bales are dotted around for people to sit on.

'From a friendly farmer,' Adam says as he steers her towards one.

'In Central London?'

'Amazing what you can find if you look.'

'Adam! Adam!' An elfin girl in cut-off denims, scuffed Doc Martens and a floppy red hat bounces up to him.

'Hey, Carly. Lou, meet Carly.'

'Hi, Lou.' Carly turns quickly back to Adam. 'Are you ready for the interviews?'

'Now?' he says.

'Yep, Lainey and Shaz have only got an hour before they have to be at the hospital.'

'Bloody nurses and all their "Oh I've got to get to work and save lives" bullshit,' he says, smiling. 'You OK, then, Lou, if I just go and do this bit of filming? Won't be more than half an hour.'

She looks around. Is she OK on her own in this crowd of strangers? She thinks not, but she nods anyway.

'Cool,' he says, kissing her on the cheek. 'There's food in the basket.'

Lou watches as he lopes off with the tiny girl in big boots, who keeps touching his arm as she talks to him, and looking up at him with big eyes, as if he were some kind of god. They could be lovers, they walk so closely together. She has let this boy so fully and so quickly into her life. But can she really trust him?

She hates sharing him like this.

The site starts to get pretty crowded. Beats pour out of the sound system, and pockets of partygoers stand and move to the rhythm. People jostle past her, brushing against her. Blankets are shaken out onto the ground and plates put out. Bottles of beer and wine are opened, flasks unstoppered to pour cups of tea. Small disposable barbecues are fired up, and the air starts to fill with the smell of burgers frying, spicy jerk chicken, pork sausages.

Lou looks in the basket. Adam has packed a nut roast, with a Tupperware container of carrot and bean salad, a crusty, home-baked loaf and a small pot of the vegan margarine he insists on using. It's all very wholesome and cruelty free, but the smell of charred flesh plays tantalisingly in Lou's nostrils. The temptation to go up to someone's barbecue and pinch a piece of meat is almost too much to bear. And she's not even going to think about the wine being enjoyed all around her.

She pulls a piece off the bread and chews on it, and imagines how her mother must have blabbed on to Sophie, filling her already poisonous mind with lies and one-sided views and vindictiveness; stoking her nasty fires. All against Louisa. Poor little unloved Louise, who really did her best, who conquered her inauspicious, lonely start to really make something of herself. That's the real story, but will Sophie want to hear that? Of course not.

A group of dodgy men pass by in a cloud of musky skunk smoke. White, bare-chested in dirty old khaki shorts, sporting crude home-made tattoos and body piercings, they are led by two unmuzzled pit-bull-type dogs that strain ahead of them on thick chains. Lou lowers her head as she recognises one of the men as Reuben, Adam's former flatmate. He probably has no memory of the night in the squat, but she doesn't want to chance him spotting her and focusing attention on her.

She looks around at the crowd. It's not all family fun and games at this party. An unsmiling, shifty-looking crew lurks proprietorially around the sound system. A bunch of fat white knuckleheads with very short hair and T-shirts emblazoned with St George's crosses sit eyeing the proceedings as if they are waiting for an opportunity to wade in.

Without asking, a large woman plonks herself heavily down on the other side of Lou's hay bale and sits, sweating and fanning herself. Lou surreptitiously shifts away from the touch of her hip on hers. A group of teenagers sit down on the ground in front of her and sprawl, shouting, smoking and slugging Red Stripe from cans.

Hemmed in, and still no Adam. Lou wonders what he can be getting up to that has taken him away from her for so long.

Her head pounds, and the empty lump of panic that has lodged in her throat all day since that final, frightening email starts to expand.

As daylight fades, people light candles and garden flares. Someone puts a torch to the bonfire and it whumps up, scorching flames licking the already burning heat of the evening.

One of the sly sound crew turns up the beats. Lou's skeleton vibrates with the thump of the bass.

What has happened to Adam? She doesn't think she can bear this much longer.

And then, as if she has conjured him, he returns, picking his way across the seated masses. She stands to greet him.

'You got invaded,' he says as he joins her.

'Just a tad.'

'Sorry. I had to do that. I'm going to be quite busy tonight, I'm afraid.'

'I'll head back home in a bit. Don't worry about me.'

'I always worry about you,' he says, drawing her close.

'Nice one, Adam,' a boy says as he passes behind them.

'But, hey,' he says, 'I've got a treat for you before you go.'

He rummages in his rucksack and pulls out a torch.

'We'll need this,' he tells her. He turns to the woman whose obtrusive hips seem to have expanded to fill the space left when Lou stood. 'Can you look after our stuff please, Adodo?'

'Sure, Adam, no problem,' Adodo says, smiling to reveal dazzling white teeth.

'Do you know *everyone* here?' Lou asks as he leads her away from the main action.

He stops and looks around. 'Just about.'

'Seriously?'

'Well, not quite. But most of them. It is my ends, after all.'

'Ends?'

'My manor. My neighbourhood.'

'It's mine, too, and I only really know you.'

'We're all different.'

He leads her away from the action, down a steep slope, into the depths of the site, where the sound system beats seem to be far behind them. He flicks his torch on and she realises that they are standing in front of what must be the white dome covering the dig site.

'Didn't you say your friend doesn't want you to go in here?' she asks, drawing back.

'Special access, just for us,' he says. 'She trusts me with her bones.'

Again, she feels a flash of jealousy about the women he sees while he is not with her.

He runs the torch over the dome, which is made of stiff nylon and tensioned steel. The light finds a padlock on the zipped entrance. Adam squats down and unlocks it, undoing the tent flap with a hollow, ripping sound.

'And here they are,' he says, ushering her into the tent and shining his torch around the stifling gloom. 'Our guardians from the past. They want you to know that they're your friends.'

Lou hangs back, drawing close in beside him. Twenty or so skeletons have been laid out on the ground, in the process, from what it looks like, of being pieced together. To one side a wall of skulls looms, each one tagged and numbered and staring at her through empty eye sockets. One side of the pit is as yet unexcavated. Leg bones, bits of cloth, crumbling digits and more skulls are all packed in like ghastly fossils.

'What's the matter?' Adam says, putting an arm round her. 'You're covered in goosebumps.'

'I hate them,' she says.

'What?'

'They don't like me.'

'Lou, are you OK?'

'No, I don't think so, I don't know, I—'

'They're our friends, Lou. The past is guarding us.'

'I need to go,' she says, turning her face against his shirt, trying to concentrate on the nowness of him, his warmth, his scent, his strength. 'Can we go, please, Adam?'

'Of course,' he says. 'I'm sorry I upset you.'

'It's not you—'

She can't even begin to tell him, can she? Another unfairness to add to the pile already bowing her down.

He guides her out into the now black night. As he stoops to put the padlock back on, the sky fills with a loud explosion, sparks and flames flash in the air, red and white. Again, and again, and again.

Her chest on the point of exploding, Lou falls to the ground and kneels forward, putting her hands over her head, ducking and covering like a well-drilled Cold War schoolchild, the emptiness opening up inside her, bigger than the burial pit, threatening to swallow her up.

Instantly, Adam is there with her, his hand on her back.

'Lou? Lou? What is it?'

Lou is beyond speech. Too much past is back with her now. The lights, the dazzle of the Porsche's headlights, the explosion, the flame.

'It's just the fireworks, Lou. Look.'

He tries to get her to lift her head, but she won't, she can't.

This evening – this whole day – has been a living nightmare.

'Let's go home, love,' he says to her, gently prying her hands from her head. 'Come on.'

He helps her up, and, shielding her eyes from the fire-works, he leads her up out of the pit and back to pick up their stuff from Adodo. On the way out, he hands his camera over to Carly, who, eyeing Lou with concern, agrees to film the rest of the evening for Adam.

As they are leaving the site, a police van screeches past them, comes to a halt and unloads its cargo of officers in riot gear.

Lou sees Adam looking back at the site – his other respon-sibility beside herself – full of people enjoying an evening that is shortly going to be rudely curtailed.

'Why do you have to do this?' she snaps, terror flipping over the top, turning to rage. 'Why do you have to cause all this trouble?'

Adam turns to her, frowning, but before he can say anything, a group of mounted policemen round a corner and trot towards them, horses and riders fully armoured in riot gear, perspex eye shields and leg guards. As the horses pass Lou and Adam, foot clopping, nostril braying, panting foamy flecks from their bit-chomping mouths, Lou catches the scent of hot equine flesh, and her whole body shudders as the night air shimmers like a heat haze around her. A woman screams in the background, and Lou feels herself falling, losing her footing, tumbling, as if down an endless flight of stairs, and she can't tell whether she is herself, or her mother, or someone else altogether.

She roars into the noisy night, shaking her hands as if she's trying to detach them from her arms. She fights for her breath, which is lost, mingled with snot and tears; she's stumbling, plunging down . . .

Adam leaps forward and grabs her, just before she hits the tarmac.

'Jesus, Lou. What is it?'

'You don't know a thing about me!' She yells so hard that her throat feels as if it is ripping.

He wraps his arms around her and holds her tight to his chest.

'It's too, too hard,' she says, wetting his shirt with her gasps for air.

He whispers into her hair. 'I know everything.'

Her body freezes, rigid.

'I know the truth, Lou.'

She swallows, her face blanches, then she tries to break away. But he's too strong for her.

'I'm taking you back home,' he says. 'They'll manage without me here. You won't. And we need to talk.'

The truth. Her core turns to ice.

36

Then

Sam tiptoes in and gently closes the front door behind him. Louisa knows he's trying not to wake her, trying not to let her know that he's finally coming home at four in the morning. He thinks he can get away with it, because, unable to bear being in the same bed as his lying, cheating body, his wronged wife has moved permanently into the spare bedroom. But, despite being six months pregnant with his baby, and worn ragged by his eighteen-month-old daughter, Louisa still has some wits about her.

She has kept vigil all night, here at the top of the stairs, in a nest she has built herself of a duvet and blankets. If she does drop off, he won't be able to resist waking her and asking her what the hell she thinks she's doing; he won't pass up on such a great opportunity to belittle her, to make her appear small and stupid. But, in fact, she has managed to stay awake all night, looking out of the landing window at the long straight road outside, a thread of mercury spooling out in the light of the full moon into the distance towards Cambridge. Dawn was just breaking, leaching tonal differences into the landscape, when the flashy red of his car shot through the greyness, driven too fast as usual. He turned into the driveway, the wheels crunching on the gravel, echoing into the empty fen morning.

Did he really think she was so stupid as to constantly let him get away with this sort of thing?

Silently she sits at the top of the stairs and watches him put his work bag down on the floor in the hallway. He slips off his shoes, no doubt to get upstairs quietly. Stopping and smiling at himself – smugly, she thinks – in the hall mirror, he checks his teeth, smooths his wild, night-time hair. His jacket is loose, crumpled, open. He has no tie and his shirt is improperly tucked into his trousers. She remembers him leaving her Bristol flat at three or four in the morning looking just like this, with exactly the same, sleepy air, resisting her entreaties for him to stay, saying he needed to get back because of Katie's emotional fragility. Or, as he put it, 'the woman's going mental right now'.

'What?' Sam has picked up his bag and is now peering up the stairs. Has she spoken out loud? She's so used to being on her own, sometimes she can't tell the difference. 'Louisa, is that you?'

'Is that what you told her?' she says again, just in case she had only thought it. 'Better get back for the mental bitch back home?'

'What the hell do you mean?'

'Where have you been, Sam?'

'I've been out with a client. In London.'

'Yeah, right.'

'You can think what you like, but that's the truth,' he says. He starts to come up the stairs, his tread heavy and slow.

'Show me the bill,' she says, holding her hand out.

'What?'

'Show me the bill. If you've been out entertaining a client in London, there'll be a bill.'

He shakes his head sadly. 'Marisa's got it.'

'You were with Marisa?'

'Yes. She's my marketing manager. She comes with me when I meet clients. Helps me make the money to keep you in all this,' he swings his arm around the hallway.

Louisa scrambles to her feet, an ungainly affair, thanks to the six-month bump on her front. 'It's her, isn't it?'

'What?'

'You're having sex with Marisa.'

'Jesus Christ, Louisa. I *work* with Marisa.'

'You *worked* with me. And then we slept together.'

He shakes his head. 'That was different.' He gestures at her nest. 'This is crazy. Have you been sitting there all night?'

'So what if I have?' she says. 'What else is there to do while I breed your child?'

'Are you drunk?'

'NO!' she yells. And, for once, it's true. In the past month or so, the baby has sent out messages that it can't stomach any more wine. It has turned off the alcohol cravings. Louisa even retched at the smell when she put out her last recycling load of tiny bottles. She is sober, but finds life no less confusing or difficult. If anything, it's getting worse.

She reaches out for Sam and pulls his face towards hers. He resists, but he is no match for her determination. She could, she realises, just push him now and he would tip backwards over the banister. But, of course, she will do no such thing. She is not a violent type. She is not. She puts her face near his and breathes in deeply through her nose.

'I smell a woman,' she says. 'All over your face. Cigarettes and minge.'

'I don't know what you mean.'

'Sam, you are having sex with someone else.'

'No, I'm not.'

'Who is she? Some secretary? Some little geek intern? "I did not have shex with that woman", huh?'

Sam shakes his head, prises her hands away from him, and

starts to walk along the corridor to what she now calls his bedroom.

'Bastard!' she cries as she runs along behind him and shoves him, as hard as she can manage.

He only stumbles a little, doesn't even fall over. Righting himself, he turns, grabs both her wrists and puts his dirty fag- and vagina-scented face right up against hers, his teeth showing, the whites of his eyes startling in the dawn gloom of the corridor.

'Don't you *ever* do that again,' he says through clenched teeth.

'You're hurting my arms,' she says.

'Good,' he says. 'Now let me go to sleep, and don't give me any more of this bullshit. Some of us have to go to work in the morning.'

He throws her arms down by her sides, strides into the master bedroom and slams the door.

As she stands there, smarting, rubbing her wrists, she hears him turn the key in the lock.

She scoops up her nest and takes it to her room. Climbing into bed, she draws it all around herself, then reaches into the drawer of her bedside table, which she carried through when she moved out of the marital bedroom. Under a mess of packets of tissues, books, pens and tubes of hand cream, she finds the booklet given to her by the A & E doctor back when she fell down the stairs.

You Are Not Alone.

'Wanna take a bet?' Louisa says as she inspects her wrists. The imprint of Sam's hand is very clear. Perhaps she will have a bruise. She is being abused, mentally, physically and spiritually, by her husband.

She will not let this lie.

37

Now

Adam is uncharacteristically silent as he leads her back to the apartment. By the time they are inside, Lou is crushed by the pressure. She feels about three inches tall.

He says he knows the truth. What does that mean?

'Have you been speaking to Sophie?' she asks as he closes the door behind them. Her mouth hardly works, the words barely come out.

'Who's Sophie?' he asks.

She's not sure if she believes that he doesn't know.

'Can I have a shower before we talk?' she says. Anything to put off the moment.

A horrific thought strikes her. Has her mother been in touch?

Lou might have to send him packing if he knows too much. And what would that be? Yet another failure, another let down.

'Of course.' He strokes her arm and takes the picnic bag through to the kitchen.

Why isn't he angry at her? Why is he still speaking to her?

She comes out of the shower with a towel wrapped around her and finds him standing at the living-room window, watching the people being chased out of the demolition site by baton-charging mounted police. There's a good view of the bonfire from the apartment, but its red glow is washed out by flashing blue lights. The sound system has been silenced – male shouting and female screaming have taken over, along with the crackle of walkie-talkies, smashing glass, megaphoned orders: *Move back! Clear the area now!* Dogs bark and yelp, and all the while the police helicopter swoops and judders overhead, shining lights over the scene, catching flashes of arms, legs, faces.

'Better?' he says, turning to face her.

'A bit.'

'Come on, let's talk,' he says, pulling out a chair for her like a gentleman seating a lady at dinner.

She doesn't want to, but, nevertheless, she sits.

She raises her eyes to meet his, and they hold each other there for a couple of minutes. Her stomach flips and turns inside her. She takes a deep breath. Better to get in there first.

'I need you to know this, Adam. My parents abused me, physically and emotionally. I was either neglected or beaten. They didn't want me in their lives, not ever. My mother drank too much. I'd often come home to find her passed out on the sofa. Once, pissed, she tripped and fell down the stairs and hurt herself badly. She tried to blame it on me. Whatever she says, it will be a lie, painted to make me look bad. She doesn't want to see me happy, so if she's found out about you, if she's tried to get in touch . . .'

Adam shakes his head. 'No, no, love. It's not about her, and if she ever does try to interfere, I won't give her the time of day.'

'So, then . . . what is it?' she asks him, barely able to force the words out.

He gets up and, as soon as he climbs on the kitchen worktop and reaches into the back of the very top cupboard, she knows exactly what he has found out.

He pulls out the box, takes off the lid, removes the phone and the two tiny engraved brass urns and puts them in front of her, on the table.

Poppy and Leon. One pink, one blue.

'Oh God,' she says.

'I wasn't prying,' he says. 'I just came across them, I wanted to empty all the cupboards and give them a proper clean. I'm so, so sorry.'

She closes her eyes.

'I can totally understand why you couldn't tell me,' he goes on. 'It must be the worst thing in the world.'

She nods, silently.

'How long have you known?' she asks him, at last.

'A week or so.'

She is aghast at this, ashamed that he has let her continue her pretence. The grey, biting feeling eats right through her.

'They died in the car crash, didn't they?' he asks her.

She looks sharply up at him. 'How do you know that?'

He shrugs. 'Kind of sort of guessed.'

She looks at her hands and speaks, and it all comes out of her, almost the exact speech she rehearsed with Fiona so many times. 'Their father – Sam – used to beat me up, regularly. He had affairs just to upset me. He abused me. Some of my scars were caused by him. Well, all of them were, in fact, because the car crash . . . I – we – we were trying to get away.' Her voice has become so small that Adam has to bend forward to hear what she is saying. 'He said he'd rather see us dead than free of him. He was obsessed. He hunted us down in his car. It was much faster than my little Fiesta. He drove us off the road . . .' she holds her hands over her eyes – 'and Sam, and they – Poppy and Leon – well, they didn't survive. Only me.'

Adam is silent for a very long while.

She doesn't dare look at him. Perhaps he is thinking this is all too much for him. Perhaps he doesn't believe her. She has lied so much to him already, why should he take this to be true? Perhaps he's wishing he could just go off with that nice uncomplicated girl with the scuffed Doc Martens. Perhaps he's making a list of things to report back to Sophie about. Perhaps he was lying about not looking at newspapers, and, in fact, he has read up all about her on the Internet and knows exactly what she is.

She closes her eyes and senses the heat of him at her side. He takes her hand and leads her to the sofa, where he sits her down and wraps his arms around her, and, at last, he speaks.

'Do you see why I know I've got to be with you, rather than over there, facing the police? You are so, so brave, Lou. You have been through so much, and you have survived. I know you didn't want to talk about it, but I needed to know what had happened so I could look after you properly. Your husband, what a lowlife. Poor children. Poor, poor you, Lou.'

She rests her head on his shoulder. 'Can we put them back in their box and up on their shelf and never talk about them again, please?' she says.

'Of course.'

'I'd just like them to be left up there in peace.'

'Yes.'

'And never touched again.'

'Of course. You have my promise. I want to help you heal from all that horror. I don't know how you lived through all of that. It must have been unbearable for you.'

He strokes her hair like she is his child. He brings her to peace and to rest, until all she feels is blessed, cherished, at home.

Home.

She allows the two serpents in her paradise – Sophie, and today's realisation that her period is nearly a week late – to settle back down under the layer of calm and relief of knowing that he is happy that he has no more to find out, no more questions to ask.

'What's the phone for?' he asks, gesturing towards the box.

'I send them text messages and photographs. Tell them about my new life.'

'Oh, Lou,' he says, kissing her hair. 'Are you sure you don't want to talk about it more?' he asks her, his fingers working at her shoulder.

She nods her head against him. 'Yes.' She reaches up and tangles her finger in his hair and pulls him down so his lips meet hers. 'I'm sure.'

38

Then

A hot pain wakes Louisa, like boiling water stirring around deep in her belly.

She levers her big, pregnant self out of the lonely spare bed and waddles to the bathroom to pee. She is dog tired, Poppy hasn't woken for a couple of hours, and she should really go back to sleep. But she knows she will just lie there, waiting and waiting for nothing to happen and suffering heartburn. So she pads back to her bedroom and, as quietly as possible, pulls on her dressing gown and heads downstairs to make a cup of peppermint tea.

Having dropped a teabag in a mug, she leans back against the counter, waiting for the kettle to boil, and watches herself in the reflection of the kitchen windows.

'Big whale,' she says to herself. 'Big blubbery fatso whale-face.'

Behind her reflection, a white, lost, night bird flies splat into the window, making her in-utero baby jump, flipping around her insides. The unfortunate bird flops back, stunned or dead – she's certainly not going out in the night to find out which – against the stone patio.

The kettle flicks off, and she pours the water onto the

teabag. Cradling her hot cuppa, she lumbers through into the living room. At the size she is now, none of the resting places look appealing. Sitting on the sofa would only mean she'd have to get herself up again, which would involve an ungainly rolling down onto her knees then hauling herself to standing. The other chairs look just as uncomfortable, and she fears a couple – the bendy Danish designer models in birch ply – might even buckle under her appended weight.

She moves back to the entrance hall. She could go outside and sit at the patio set, but that would be ridiculous. The air has not quite cooled down after the summer, but it's so quiet out there that she just wouldn't be comfortable. Moreover, there's a full moon; it's a time when ghosts stalk the earth. If they were going to go for anyone right now, it would be her, no doubt about that.

And there's the matter of the dead bird. She'll leave that job for Sam to deal with, as atonement.

And boy, he could do with a bit of that.

It's three months since she first accused him, and still he denies any affair. He never comes home now before she's in bed. He says it's because of work, because things are still expanding, still progressing, still growing. Well, how long, she thinks, can he spin that out? The firm can't expand infinitely, can it? It's not like her waistline, is it?

He's avoiding her because, whenever they meet, there's a scene. He can't face the conflict he's created. She has a collection of bruises on her arm. The most recent, blue and fresh, are five finger dabs – a sure sign, should anyone ask, that, quite recently, he grabbed her.

At weekends, if he's ever around, he holes himself up in his study or concentrates entirely on playing with Poppy. He has withdrawn himself completely from her, his wife.

And what has she done to deserve this treatment? Just because she has become cow-like and waddling again, her body and mind given over to bearing HIS CHILD, he has lost interest, gone off somewhere else.

Does she have to look like a pole dancer to command his attention? Or is it that she no longer has the professional patina of a smart young Kick Ass Hotshot Designer?

In her distress, she spills tea all down her front.

'Fuck,' she mutters. She doesn't like to swear, but she's all riled now.

She'll go into his study. At least she'll be comfortable in his thousand-pound, back-friendly desk chair.

As she crosses the hallway, her eye is drawn by his jacket which, probably worse for wear, he hung so badly on the coat pegs last night that it has fallen to the ground. She picks it up and, out of habit, goes through his pockets. She knows that he doesn't like to spoil his line with possessions, so, as she expects, they are entirely empty. She brushes the jacket down and hangs it back on the peg.

When she takes her hand away she finds, caught in her engagement ring, a long, coarse dark hair. It is about as unlike any of her own – mousy, baby fine, and still, thanks to the shearing sixteen months ago, barely reaching her shoulders – as a hair could be.

Her baby decides at this moment to have a real old go at her with its feet, kick-kick-kicking her up in her diaphragm.

'Shhh, baby, shhh,' she says, rubbing the spot under her ribs where she is sure she has an internal bruise as big as all her finger dabs put together.

She carries the hair through to the kitchen so that she can have a proper look at it under the worktop lights. But, beyond its foreignness, it offers no answers. Marisa, his sales manager, has long hair, but hers is blond.

Then she sees his bag, sitting on a kitchen chair. He always says it would be the last thing he'd let a burglar take from him, but last night he was too careless. Instead of taking it up to rest by his bed as he usually does, he just dumped it down with all its expensive equipment in it.

She lifts the bag from the stool and takes it over to the table. It's one of those computer rucksacks – high end, buttery black leather – with a compartment for every imaginable accessory and office or personal need. She starts at the front and systematically works her way around each pocket, emptying contents onto different areas of the table so that she can replace them exactly where she found them. She wouldn't want Sam to think she was the mad kind of wife who went through her husband's bags. She wouldn't give him that ammunition.

She has no idea what she is looking for – a letter, a photograph, an email, perhaps. She opens his laptop and tries to log in, but she has no idea what the password might be. She tries a couple of the obvious: his name, date of birth, hers, even – although she thinks that unlikely. But she's only half-hearted about it. Fanatically cautious about his company's intellectual property, Sam probably uses a string of indecipherable symbols to protect his data.

So, even if she finds no incriminating evidence in the bag, the laptop could have it all. She thinks about how she could get the password from him. She spends a couple of minutes working out how to rig up a camera in his study to film him making keystrokes, but of course it's an absurd idea.

So she carries on, emptying the bag. She knows the passcode to get into his iPhone, but it reveals absolutely nothing whatsoever. He doesn't use it for email, and his text messages, which he keeps meticulously up to date – if it's dealt with, it's deleted – reveal nothing other than work-related business and those she sent last night, the usual thing, asking him where the hell he was, when he'd be back. They are unread, she notices, which is as much as she suspected. He will no doubt get rid of them in the morning.

His wallet reveals nothing other than restaurant bills, which he would say were for entertaining clients, to be put in for an expenses claim. She takes out his notebook and goes through it page by page, but it just contains notes from meetings, marketing ideas, pages of doodles of interconnecting circles. Geekery.

How his mind works, she thinks, almost fondly.

At the very bottom of the bag, there is not even a crumb or a speck of dust. It is as if he cleans it out every day. She holds the empty rucksack up to her pregnancy-sensitive nose. It doesn't smell how she expected. There's the leather, yes, and his own scent, his aftershave. But there's something surprising in there too, a sort of musk that reminds her of the joss sticks she used to burn in her bedroom as a teenager, a habit she nurtured almost entirely to enrage her mother.

There's something wrong, too, about the weight of the bag. Even taking into account its leather and chrome fittings, it's just a little bit too heavy. She gives it a vigorous shake. Something else is in there, moving up and down. But she has emptied all the pockets.

She puts the bag on the table and works her fingers around it, pressing down until she finds a slim, rectangular object. She slips her hand inside and, feeling around, finds a neat slit in the leather lining, cut carefully near the seam to make a discreet extra pocket. She reaches in and draws out a white iPhone.

Her fingers shaking, she turns it on and waits as it comes to life. The screensaver bears the face of a woman with long, dark hair. She has deep brown, heavy-lidded, almond-shaped eyes, a too-large mouth opened into a smile that reveals white teeth with a distinctive but not unattractive gap at the front, and the kind of cheekbones only found on the very slender. Her beauty is the first thing Louisa notices. The second is the look in her eyes. It's all sex.

She knew it. She bloody knew it.

With shaking hands, she clicks through to the other photos

on the phone, which leave her in no doubt that Sam and this woman are lovers. Lovers in ways she never dreamed he'd be into. Lip curling, she scrolls through graphic text messages full of intent about what this woman – 'Soph' appears to be her name – plans to do to him, ideas he reciprocates and elaborates on.

Soph.

There's something about the face that looks familiar. Louisa has seen her somewhere before, but she can't place it. Ignited, her baby kicks and punches inside her. She *knew* he was being unfaithful, but this graphic confirmation of her suspicions is like being beaten with an iron bar. Her first thoughts – first, that is, after a sudden and violent desire to kill both Sam and his whore – turn to revenge. She could publish this on the web. Or email the photographs to his colleagues who, she is sure, would like to see him bound like this, erect, ecstatic.

But then she thinks again. She scribbles both numbers – the white iPhone and *Soph* whore's – on the pad she used to use for shopping lists, back when she was a proper housewife. She takes one last look at the bitch, memorising her face, then switches off the phone and slips it back in its hiding place. Then, carefully, she replaces everything where she found it, doing up zips, fastening buckles, as if packing all her anger back inside.

She will wait, she decides. She will bide her time. But she will not let him get away with this. She will make him pay, and pay again.

She feels another tightening across her belly, a rising pain, hotter than the one that woke her earlier. It reaches a peak and then fades away, leaving nothing but anger and shame and disappointment.

'Poor baby,' she says to her unborn child, who is coming into this world of sorrow. 'Poor, poor baby.'

Everything has gone all wrong.

She stumbles into her unused studio. A stark contrast to

Sam's study, it has, over the past twenty-two months, become more of a dumping ground than a workplace. Empty cardboard boxes vie for attention with a stack of large bottles of the mineral water Sam insists on drinking; baskets of clean washing wait to be sorted next to stacks of the parenting and interiors magazines Louisa has bought and only half read because of the way they make her itch with inadequacy. There are several bags full of old clothes, which, in an upswing of mood, she sorted to take to a charity shop. They've been there for nearly three months, standing by for the next upswing to give her the energy to move them out of the house.

She reaches into the back of a drawer full of her unused business stationery and pulls out the notebook she bought as suggested in the *You Are Not Alone* pamphlet handed to her by the A & E doctor. The time is right to start filling it in.

She opens a couple of the new boxes of pens and selects a few different colours and thicknesses. Over the next hour, she carefully fills in a few minor incidents:

14 May: Tripped me up during argument, sprained (?) wrist. Black eye.
23 June: Chased me with kitchen knife due to burned supper. Luckily managed to lock myself in the bathroom.
12 August: Slap on face, no mark once hand print faded.
2 January: Punch to stomach, circular bruise just above navel.
17 June: Grabbed my wrists and tried to push me down stairs: bruises.
15 September: Grabs arms and pushes: bruises.

She looks at her arm and draws a diagram of the five smudges.

With a feeling of satisfaction, she tucks the book back in the drawer and takes herself upstairs where she looks in on Sam in what used to be the marital bedroom. Clearly thinking he's getting the better of her, he sleeps quietly, as if he hasn't a care in the world.

He hasn't even bothered to lock the door.

She will make him think again.

She watches him, his contours highlighted by cold moonlight slicing through the curtains he must have forgotten to close when he stumbled in.

Was he ever happy with her?

He must have been.

Will he ever be again?

She tries to picture herself in Soph's porn star poses and can't quite imagine it. Not any more. Not with this body, blasted by bearing him children.

As if by way of an answer, her huge, distended stomach draws itself in, as if it is being hugged from inside. She has to stand still for a few minutes, staring at her errant husband, silently panting away the pain.

Hating him.

As she lies in the spare bed, she searches her thoughts for crumbs of comfort.

One speck she finds is that she can congratulate herself on her instincts. She had been right about Sam dipping his dick into foreign parts.

Yay!

Then there's the *You Are Not Alone* dossier she's compiling on him. That makes her feel like she's actually achieving something.

And then she remembers the glorious mess of the Paul Smith shirt stuffed at the back of the cupboard in his otherwise ship-shape study. Suffused with his DNA – she plucked it from the dirty laundry – it is also crispy and crackled with Katie's dried blood.

This soothes her. This is where she can unabashedly applaud her instincts. Because, even in happier days, when she was so in love with him that she never ever dreamed he would turn out so evilly against her, she cleverly had the forethought to tuck the shirt away, just as an insurance policy, just in case. You can never be too careful.

As a piece of evidence it is perfect, unassailable, beautiful.

And what she will say, if – when – it is found, is this: 'Oh, he used it to threaten me, to make sure I behaved, make sure I kept my mouth shut. Or else, he said, I would end up like poor Katie. I was so scared of him . . .'

And, with this double-decker devil's food cake-load of comfort, she finally claims her well-earned sleep.

39

Now

Adam pulls open the door to the developer's marketing Portakabin and holds it for Lou to enter.

They are the only visitors. As soon as she sees him, the young woman behind the sales desk looks down at her blinging nails, then at her computer screen, then at the ceiling. Anywhere other than at Adam.

'What?' he says as he strides across the air-conditioned salesroom, holding out his hands. 'Don't I even get a hello, Jazmin?'

'Oh, Adam man,' she says, standing and straightening out her slightly too-tight red pencil skirt. With a matching jacket and white, high-collared shirt, it makes up a uniform, which, Lou notes, picks up on the livery colours of the developers in a coherent, if cheaply executed manner. Jazmin smiles, revealing a large mouthful of perfect, white teeth.

'Come here, you idiot,' Adam says, holding out his arms, and this Jazmin crosses the floor in her shiny courts and puts her solid arms around him.

As this stranger embraces her man, Lou shifts uncomfortably, pretending to look at a video of simulated people walking through a virtual-reality imagining of the finished development.

Music, which sounds as if it has been composed to a brief along the lines of 'Vision for the Future', pipes into the sales-room at a subliminal level. In fact, Lou notices, the word VISION is repeated over every surface of the jazzed-up Portakabin. It would make even the most cynical visitor believe that what's on sale here is all for the good. Only a few, along the lines of Adam, could remain immune to its seductions.

'I thought you'd be dissing me for selling out,' Jazmin says, hugging him tightly.

'Jaz, man. You gotta make a living.'

Lou raises an eyebrow. Adam's accent has taken a bold turning into 'street'.

He steps back and puts his arm around Lou. 'Ah, and look, this is my new lady, Lou.'

'Nice one. Good to meet you, Lady Lou,' Jazmin says, shaking her hand and dropping a mock curtsey.

'Likewise,' Lou says, not quite sure how to pitch it.

'Jaz grew up here,' Adam says. 'But her family got turfed out. They were the lucky ones, got a flat in, where is it, Jaz?'

'Off Tooley Street.'

'Yeah, just a hop, skip and a jump from here.'

'Not here, though,' Jazmin says, shaking her head. 'We wanted to stay here.'

'Yeah. And now look, she's working for the enemy,' Adam says.

'Quiet, Adam. I need this job.'

'It's not like there's anything else round here, innit?' he says, rubbing his hands together. 'They've seen to that.'

'There'll be jobs when it's all finished, though,' Lou says. 'In the new shops and cafés. The cinema . . .'

'Yeah, and no one on those sorts of wages will be able to afford to live anywhere nearby, because it's just homes for the rich and—'

'So!' Jazmin claps her hands, cutting across him and turning on a five-thousand-kilowatt smile. 'Before our Adam goes off on one against my employers and gets me sacked . . . What can I do for you, then?'

'Is it all right if I show Lou what's going down? She's just moved into The Heights. South Block, facing east,' he adds significantly.

'Oh, man, Lou.' Jazmin tuts and shakes her head. 'You are not going to like it, my dear.' She guides them over to a perspex case containing a model of the finished development.

Lou lets out a whistle. 'It looks like a whole town!'

'As big as,' Jazmin says. 'Three thousand new homes when it's finished.'

'Aw. See those nice little people down there, enjoying the lovely new park areas,' Adam says.

'It is going to be the largest new public park built in Central London for a century,' Jazmin says.

'You know the spiel, don't you, Jaz?' Adam says. 'And this little street market, all fancy stuff, no doubt.' He points to a grid of what look like square gazebos. 'Like another Borough Market, but neater, cleaner.'

'That's the idea.' Jazmin chuckles. 'That's exactly what I'm supposed to tell you.'

'Look at all the planted roof terraces,' Lou says. She has been half listening to their banter, but mostly she's thinking how lovely it looks, how covetable.

'They call them sky gardens,' Jazmin says, pressing buttons on the edge of the model to light them up. 'There'll be mini allotments for residents to grow their own veggies. And there are going to be green walls, too, full of plants and that.'

'Where's my place?' Lou asks Adam.

'Here.' He points to an area in the shadow of a massive tower.

'They haven't done a model of my building,' Lou says.

'Why would they?' he tells her. 'You're not important to

them, as the scale of the building they're dumping right in front of you shows.'

'It's the tallest in the whole development.' Jazmin raises her pencilled eyebrows and inclines her head. 'And yes, it will be right in the way, if you're on that side of The Heights. It passes all planning regs, though.'

'So this is the highest apartment in the whole development?' Lou points to a wrap-around roof terrace at the top of the tower. It is bursting with model greenery, and a tiny couple – he black, she white – lounge in a wood-clad hot tub.

'It's the thirty-seventh-floor penthouse, darling,' Jazmin says, shaking her head, clattering her beaded braids. 'And' – she points to the couple in the hot tub – 'these two will be stealing your view big time.'

'Could be me and you,' Lou says to Adam, and he cracks up. She turns to Jazmin. 'How much do all these apartments go for?'

'Well, we've got affordables from three hundred and fifty for a one-bed—'

'Affordable!' Adam snorts.

Jazmin rolls her eyes. 'And the others—'

'The unaffordables,' Adam butts in.

'Range from five hundred for a studio to over three mil. for the penthouses.'

'Three million!' Adam says.

'Over,' Jazmin says, nodding.

'What's the square footage?' Lou asks.

'For the affordables?' Jazmin asks.

'No. For this one.' Lou touches the penthouse on the tall block.

'We've got a special marketing pack for that one,' Jazmin says, sashaying back to her desk. 'Want a look?' She hands Lou a thick, glossy brochure.

'Seriously?' Adam says, frowning. 'Seriously, Lou?'

'No skin off my nose,' Jazmin says.

'I'm just interested in the marketing angle,' Lou says, putting her hand on his lovely, inked upper arm. 'From the design point of view.'

'Phew,' he says. 'You got me worried, there.'

'We've also got this.' Jazmin hands her a USB stick encased in eco-friendly wood, with the developer's logo branded into it. 'It's got details on the history of the site – and before you tell us all, Adam, yes, it is biased – the developer's vision for the future, and plans for each of the units. You'll also find us online, and' – she hands her a red card with her details reversed out in white – 'these are my details.'

Adam looks at Jazmin in amazement. 'You don't really think you're on the scent of a sale, Jaz?' he says.

Jazmin looks at Lou with her heavily lidded, liner-frosted eyes. 'Oh, I have very highly developed instincts, Adam. They offer a good training here.'

'Ha!' Adam says. 'You wish.'

He and Jazmin kiss each other on the cheeks. As she shakes Lou's hand, Jazmin leans forward and whispers in her ear.

'If you want to talk any more, make sure you ask for me, doll, OK?'

Lou nods. Clutching the penthouse details to her chest and trying not to let Jazmin see her limp, she allows Adam to lead her away to the Rainbow Café for a vegan latte.

40

Then

Drifting back from her ether dream, Louisa makes out the shapes in the room. White, mostly, blurs gradually solidifying, muffled Dopplers forming into beeps and footsteps along corridors.

She tries to move her arm, but she's all wired up to something. Her body feels very, very different, but that's nothing compared to what's going on in her head.

'I think I'm going to be—'

Someone is already there with a cardboard sick bowl to catch it.

'There, there, dear.' A ponytailed male nurse strokes her hair as she settles back, sweating and chilly, onto her pillow. She feels emptied, as if a great hand has reached inside her and scooped out her insides. The nurse holds her hand and dabs at her cheeks with a tissue.

'It's all right,' he says. 'A lot of our ladies are like this when they come round. Do you remember what happened, Louisa?'

She closes her eyes. She remembers being in the garden, September Saturday sunshine that she didn't want to be out in, Poppy playing on her trike. She remembers the whack of the fence as she ran full pelt into it, thumping into her belly, the thud as she flew head first over it and landed on the ground on the other side, Poppy's screams of 'Mummy! Mummy!' and Sam's voice, anger outweighing concern, as he charged across the garden to find her collapsed on the other side of the fence, blood spreading from between her legs onto her white smock.

'What the hell have you done now, Louisa?' he said, as if it were all her fault.

'It's not my fault,' she tells the nurse, her voice still thick from the anaesthetic.

'Shh, honey,' the nurse says, wiping a cool cloth around her face. The sensation is so delicious it brings Louisa back into focus. And then—

'My baby!' she says, trying to sit upright. 'Is my baby all right?'

'He's lovely,' the nurse says. 'A beautiful, strapping little boy.'

'I need to see him,' she says, struggling to get out of the bed. Something is making it impossible for her to sit up, though: her legs feel numb. She wonders for a moment if she has broken her back and is paralysed. For a second the words *that'll make Sam pay* float through her mind.

'Shh, hon. You won't be able to move until the anaesthetic's worn off. We had to do an emergency Caesarean because your placenta ruptured when you went over that fence. We're just checking baby over.'

'Sam . . .' she croaks.

'Hubby's gone to pick up the big sister,' the nurse says.

'Ah, she's back with us. Thanks, Steve.' A doctor appears. She has grey, clear eyes set in a face that has clearly laughed a lot. But right now, the main emotion on show is concern as she bends over her patient.

'How are we doing?'

Steve runs through a series of numbers and acronyms that are lost on Louisa.

'Could we just have a moment alone, please?' the doctor asks him.

'Of course. I'll be just over there, Louisa, dear, if you need me.' He squeezes her hand one last time then moves swiftly off.

'Is my baby all right?' Louisa asks again.

'He's doing really well. He's a proper little fighter. They'll bring him out to you as soon as he's ready.'

The doctor pulls a chair over and sits so that her face is level with Louisa's. Her breath smells of mint, as if she has just cleaned her teeth. Louisa breathes it in.

'Do you remember what happened?' the doctor asks her. 'Going over the fence?'

Louisa nods and closes her eyes.

'I've been looking at your notes from when you came in last year. The stairs thing.'

Louisa nods again.

'It says here that social services were alerted. Have they spoken to you?'

Louisa shakes her head. It's not a lie, not really.

The doctor tuts and rolls her eyes. 'Same old same old. Louisa, if you need help, you must say. You do realise your baby could have died if we hadn't got there so quickly?'

'I know.' Her voice is tiny, fragile.

'And you could have ended up with a nasty neck injury the way you went over that fence. You're lucky in some ways that your belly broke your fall.'

'Lucky . . .'

'How did it happen?' The doctor takes Louisa's drip-wired hand. 'Your husband says he has no idea, that he was in his study and heard your daughter crying. Is that right?'

Louisa looks away and rests the side of her face on her pillow. From where the doctor is sitting, it could be a shake of the head.

'Do you feel safe at home, Louisa?'

Louisa turns her head back towards the doctor and, without meeting her eyes, whispers, 'Yes.' But everything about her other than that one word tells a completely different story.

'You owe it to your children to speak up if anything concerns you.'

'I feel safe.'

'Here he is!' Steve the nurse appears at the doctor's shoulder with a tiny, purple-faced bundle swaddled in waffle-cotton blankets. 'A proper little fighter.'

The doctor presses a button on the side of Louisa's bed and it lifts so that she is sitting up enough to take her baby from the nurse.

'Hello, little man,' she says, looking down at her scrap of a boy. But, inside, she's still thinking: poor, poor, baby. Inside, she feels nothing but a cold darkness.

'I'll leave you to get to know each other,' the doctor says. 'We'll be taking you out to the ward in a while.' She touches Louisa's shoulder. 'Do have a think, my dear. If you need help, we can be there for you.'

Louisa thinks of her dossier at the back of her stationery drawer and how this new, dramatic, pushing over the fence event will boost it. 'Thank you.'

The doctor pauses at the entrance to Louisa's cubicle. 'All you have to do is say.'

Louisa knows this. And she will say.

Oh, she will say it all.

But not now.

Not until she's good and ready.

41

Now

This is going to make Lou late for work, but she hasn't been able to get the idea out of her head.

Up on the ground at Oxford Circus, she ducks into Starbucks. She grabs a coffee and sits in air-conditioned comfort, Jazmin's business card in one hand, her phone in the other.

'Jaz? It's Lou here, Adam's Lou? I want you to keep this between us – yeah, definitely don't breathe a word to him – but could you recommend a solicitor? I'm interested in the penthouse and I want to put a deposit down. It's still free, isn't it?'

She listens to her a while, taking notes on her napkin, which, when she's done, she hides away in the inner pocket of her handbag.

She's going to have to keep this secret until it becomes a fact.

But it's all for the best, and, in the end, Adam will see that, she's certain.

'The client *really* loves the initial ideas.'

Cleo is in a good mood. She didn't even mention Lou's tardy arrival this morning, and now she is sitting on the edge of Lou's desk, dangling her feet, nibbling on one of the *pains au chocolat* she's brought along on a tray of coffee for them both.

'I've never seen such universal excitement. I mean, usually marketing people will get pernickety, and you have to come back with a few changes just because they think they ought to be seen to be wanting them. That's part of the power play. But no, this lot LOVED your work, and, to be honest, so do I, Lou. You've got real flair. I'm so glad we've got you. You're our total star.'

Lou tries to appear cool about this, but she loves doing a great job and pleasing the client. It's what she was made for in this world.

'Did you see the Mumsnet piece?' Cleo asks. She leans over, takes Lou's mouse and clicks through to the page. 'It really works even with just the picture of you. I'm so sorry your ex didn't let us use the children.'

'He's a bit of an arse,' Lou says, tearing off a piece of the pastry and putting it into her mouth. She hadn't planned to eat any, but with the turn the conversation has taken, she needs a prop.

'Aren't they all, exes?'

'Too right.'

Lou shifts in her seat. She's digging herself in deep here with all these stories. And now she's fed Adam a different line to what she's told Cleo. If Lou is going to continue being Cleo's *total star*, she is going to have to keep the two sides of her life apart.

Probably just as well, though. However wonderful he is, Adam is hardly the right type of boyfriend for someone of her professional standing.

'I've worked out those refinements on the engraving effect for the label,' Lou says, moving her stylus across her pad.

Cleo is just leaning in to inspect the artwork when Lou's desk phone rings.

'Excuse me,' Lou says and picks it up. 'Lou Turner?'

But even before the person on the other end speaks, Lou knows that it is Sophie again.

'Nice article on Mumsnet, *Lou Turner*, eh?' she says, her voice even more wired than normal. 'Oh, lovely piece about the difficulty of juggling work and children. Getting a bit cocky, aren't you? Getting a bit smug? Don't you think it's a tad risky putting yourself out there on the Internet again with all these lies? I take it, from the way you describe yourself as a divorcee, that your right-on employer knows nothing about your murky past, about Poor Tragic Louisa, and all the rest, the unanswered questions, the scandal, the—'

'Stop this,' Lou says, horribly aware that Cleo is there, right by her side.

'Be terrible if they found out, wouldn't it?'

Lou turns away, so that she's facing the window, looking down at all the people wading through the hot, soupy afternoon.

'If you dare—'

'You'll what? What? You know what I hate about you, Lou Turner? That you just have it so fucking cushy, when I'm right up against it.'

'You've said this before,' Lou says, trying to keep her voice neutral, knowing that she is being overheard by her boss.

'Your lawyer bitch has served a possession order for two weeks' time, and your arsehole estate agent is lining people up to show around my home. Nice, throwing a woman and baby out into the street. Wonder what the papers would say about that.'

'They'd say you just about deserve it probably. They'd say that you've had more than you're due.'

'More than I'm due? You owe me and my child so much, big time.'

'That's absurd.'

'It's a fact. Legal and moral.'

'Moral? Legal?' Lou snorts.

'It could come to that. Or you could make it easier. Oh. By the way, Celia and Fergus send their love from Shetland.'

Lou recoils as if she has been punched in the stomach. 'What?'

'Celia and Fergus? You know, your parents? Funny how they felt they had to move so far away from you.'

'Just . . .' Lou takes a deep breath and tries to gather herself, to sound cool and businesslike for her audience: 'Thanks. I'll see to it,' she says, then hangs up.

She takes a deep breath and turns to face Cleo, who is busy pretending to look at the label layout on the screen in front of her.

Lou shrugs, tries to keep it cool. 'Like I say. An arse.'

'Wow.' Cleo raises her eyebrows. 'He sounds like a real handful.'

'He is, indeed.'

Lou snaps into work mode. It surprises her how easily she manages to switch gear. But, even so, as she talks Cleo through the minute adjustments she will be making in order to reinforce a heritage feel in a brand that also wants to be upbeat and cutting-edge, she can sense that her boss has a mouth full of unasked questions which, if she were to stop talking for a moment and let her have a word in edgeways, would spill out all over her lap.

42

Then

It's all useless. Louisa has tried over and over to feed Leon, but he just won't take it. Her nipples are sore and the stitches in her abdomen have become infected, probably due to the amount of sweating she's been doing in this overheated dungeon of a hospital. She's got a private side room, but that doesn't insulate her from the constant noise outside, the babies crying, the nurses' and orderlies' incessant, inane, intrusive chatter, the never-ending machinery beeps.

What's upsetting her more than anything is that while she is suffering all this, Sam is out in the open world, free as he likes. Probably getting up to God knows what with 'Soph'. Thanks to the indelible memories of his phone porn, Louisa has a pretty graphic notion of what *that* might entail.

They bring her Leon and a warm bottle for her to feed him with, but she just can't summon the patience or the enthusiasm. Again, she has failed to be the best sort of mother. Again, her life is one of compromise and difficulty. She looks at her little tiny baby boy and feels nothing. All she can think is how many years she has got to wait until he grows up and leaves home, and what kind of damage could be done to him and how messy life might get, what with his philandering, absent father, who deals out nothing to his family but abuse and neglect.

The baby curls his tiny hand around her big index finger and the delicateness of him throbs through her. Along with his sister, he poses a massive, overwhelming responsibility. She should leave Sam right away and set up a new life for herself and her children. But the thought of that, of all the attendant shame and failure, is just not good enough for her. No, there are many, many lengths she will go to before that.

At visiting time, Sam brings Poppy in to see her baby brother. The little girl pushes before her the toy buggy and baby doll Louisa bought her because one of the frightening parenting magazines told her that it is a surefire way to offset sibling jealousy. All well and good, but it hasn't worked, and Poppy barges Leon out of the way to take up her position in her mother's arms. Louisa nuzzles her daughter's hot little head with her lips, but, when she catches the scent of it, she pulls away sharply.

'What shampoo are you using on her hair?' Louisa asks as Sam inspects his new son – as if, she thinks, he were a new toaster or something he is going over for defects.

'What?' he says, looking up.

'It's just I don't want you using anything other than Johnson's on her. Nothing stingy.'

'Grandma wash Poppy hair,' Poppy says, holding one of her red locks up to her own nose and smiling like a twenty-first-century Bisto kid. 'Appley.'

Louisa seethes. Grandma is what Poppy calls the agency nanny Sam is paying to live in the house while Louisa is in hospital. Nothing wimpish like paternity leave for hotshot Sam, oh no. She's surprised he can even find the time to visit his wife and new son, what with all the work and the extra-mural fucking.

At least, with a nickname like that, she assumes this nanny is safely out of the age range for a nookie contender.

She watches him change Leon's nappy and she wants to bat his hands away from her little son's innocent skin.

'I'm coming home tomorrow, and I'd rather we didn't have Grandma around any more,' Louisa says.

'Mummy!' Poppy says delightedly, tightening her grip on her.

'Are you sure that's wise?' Sam says. 'I mean, with your stitches and everything. I mean, do you think you'll be able to cope?'

She looks daggers at him, but he's too busy with baby wipes and tiny Pampers to notice.

'I can cope,' she says.

The following day, Louisa is packed and sitting on her bed ready to go, clutching a white paper bag full of strong antibiotics for her infection. She has a fever, and the doctor said she shouldn't really let her home, but Louisa has insisted, because her daughter needs her.

The sounds of the ward beyond her room oscillate, as if someone is turning the volume up and down, up and down. Everything is a little too white, a little too shining. In the corner of her eye, she thinks she sees rats scurrying along the floor, but, when she turns her head to see them, they are gone. Scampered under the bed, no doubt.

Her toes itch.

Sam comes in alone, with a brand-new baby car seat.

'Where's Poppy?' she asks, as he lifts Leon from his plastic cot and straps him in.

'She's with Grandma.'

'I thought I said I wanted "Grandma" gone for when I got out of here.'

'Yes, and I heard you.' His voice sounds strange, like it is coming from the depths of a cave. 'She's just looking after Poppy till we get home.'

He turns to look at her and his face is dark, blood red. His eyes gleam yellow at her, like the edges of coals. In his hair, which has turned a deep, dark black, she sees them growing: horns, like dirty little rams' horns, but sharp, pointing, like his teeth when he opens his mouth. He speaks, but all she hears now is a sound as if someone is slowly pulling a piece of audio tape through an old spool-to-spool player.

She screams.

He lunges towards her and she jumps backwards, pushing him away. He stumbles against a drip stand, sending it clattering with what to her sounds like a volley of high-pitched triangles shattering to the ground.

'LOUISA!' he shouts, shaking her, trying to make himself heard over the sound of her cries. 'LOUISA!'

In his car seat, Leon picks up her panic and adds his own, desperate newborn bleat to the cacophony.

Sam taps her face, tries to bring her to her senses, but she is only more terrified, because all she sees is that he is moving in to kill her, to bite her neck and drain her blood.

It's only when three nurses come rushing into her private room that Sam's face melts back to normal. Well, normal but for the expression of horror. He had her so strongly by her shoulders that he dug his nails in, made her bleed.

'She just flipped,' he's saying to the nurses, who, ignoring him, are all about making sure Louisa is all right. 'I was worried about the baby.'

The nurses sit her down, check her pulse, take her temperature, look into her eyes.

'I'll talk to the doctor,' one of them, Paula, who has been very kind to Louisa, says. 'But I think you need to stay in another night at least, Louisa.'

'No,' Louisa says, brushing them off and standing. 'I need to get home. I need to see my daughter. Take me home, Sam,' she says to her husband, and, holding her hand firmly over her scar to stop the feeling that it might burst with the effort, she creeps out of the room, leaving him to follow with all her stuff and her baby.

In the car she sits in the back, one hand on Leon's leg as he sleeps tucked up safe in his backward-facing car seat. She rests her forehead against the window and watches the road as it blurs beneath her. Her head pounds.

'What the hell was all that about, Louisa?' She can see Sam's eyes in the rear-view mirror. They are cold, glued on the road, as if he is terrified to move them.

She doesn't answer. She has no idea what it was about, but it has scared her, possibly even as much as it scared him.

43

'I'll see to it,' Louisa says, which is no answer to anything Sophie has been saying, and then she just hangs up.

Sophie puts her own phone down on the bed. Someone must have been listening in. She has got to Louisa, just a little bit. The first crack shows.

It does little to lighten her mood as she turns the possession order over in her hand. Arriving at the same time that she found that self-congratulatory Mumsnet interview, it just about did her in. On top of that, RightMove tells her that Fen Manor has been sold. The home she, Sam and Sami should be in, gone. The wardrobe of Sam's stuff, emptied. The last physical traces of him – outside this bedroom – eradicated. Worst of all, Louisa's already fat pockets gain another lining, and Sophie and Sami still have nothing.

She toys with the idea of calling Louisa's mother again. The first time wasn't all that fruitful. As soon as Sophie stated her business, Celia Turner clammed up, refused to say a word about her daughter, to confirm or deny that she had been injured by her. It was as if she was scared, or hiding something, or both.

Sophie has enough information, however – the fear, the

304

moving away, the pushing down the stairs story – to provide plenty of leverage in her campaign. There's something ugly lurking in Louisa's background. She doesn't have to know that Sophie's knowledge of what it could be is so limited.

She jumps up, strides across the room, and stares out of her window at the gardens at the back of her flat. Even browned and desiccated as they are – thanks to a hose-pipe ban – the sight of them goes some way to soothing her. But any small relief is instantly negated by the thought that, in two weeks' time, she won't be allowed to stand here, by her bed, in this room, in this flat.

And what will she and poor Sami do then, poor things?

She eyes the little mirror on her bedside table. Sitting on the bed again, she licks her finger, wipes it around the dusting of powder remaining beside the scalpel blade and the rolled-up tenner, and rubs it into her gums.

'What do you expect?' she says to the dried-out trees at her window. 'I'm not superhuman.'

It's just a tiny line, anyway. Just to get her out of this pit. She's had that wrap for a whole week and this is just the second or third time she's touched it. Or the fourth. She's done well, considering.

She takes stock. These phone calls are not working. Louisa's never going to give in. There's something not right with the woman. She's written her own version of the truth, and she's sticking to it, no matter what. Sophie is bashing her head against a brick wall.

Now Sami is better, perhaps it's time to actually *do* something, something that Louisa could never ignore.

She sits bolt upright, twitching on her glamorous bed in her beautiful little soon-to-be-lost jewel of a flat. Her heart pounding, her mind working like a spider at its web, she returns to Google and types *how to build a bomb* into the search box.

* * *

305

Fire bombs seem to be quite popular among the DIY YouTube community. There's a kid filling a balloon with lighter fluid and setting fire to it with a piece of paper crumpled over a long stick, but that's too crude even for her own beginner's standards. The most satisfactory recipe seems to involve powdered aluminium, iron oxide and a long strip of magnesium, all packed into a paint tin. With the caveat that this concoction is only published to provide a means of blowing a hole in a hypothetical metal wall, the Milwaukee boy who posted it says that, effectively, the result is napalm.

Napalm. Now that sounds more like it.

Sophie takes one more, tiny, bracing line of Snake's magic powder and scribbles down the napalm ingredients. She pulls a pair of unworn Jimmy Choos out of the wardrobe, throws a tattered kimono over her short vest dress, grabs her little fringed, embroidered, Chinese bag and heads to the Mill Road dress agency. Sami sits upright in her Bugaboo, shaded by a parasol, enjoying a bottle of her mother's pre-frozen milk.

It takes quite a lot of persuasion to get Monica to sub Sophie another hundred for the shoes. She hasn't yet shifted the Chanel dress, and she normally only pays out after a sale. But, thankfully, Monica is softer than that cold-hearted Louisa, and a few smiles from sweet little Sami soon break her down. An ex-model herself – albeit from a much earlier generation – Monica has more sympathy for Sophie than most.

Out on the street, Sophie wonders where the hell you go to buy iron oxide and aluminium powder. It takes three attempts, but she eventually manages to get a taxi to stop for her, and, after having struggled unaided to get baby, Bugaboo and herself inside, she instructs the driver to go to B&Q.

'Which one?' the driver asks.

'The biggest and best, of course,' she says, her jaw working away on a piece of gum.

In a vast, out-of-town superstore that has cost her a rip-off twenty-quid taxi fare to reach, she pushes the buggy along the towering paint aisle until she finds a shade she likes. Farrow & Ball, Terre D'Egypte: an orange that most closely matches Sami's hair, and, by extension, Sam's. It's not cheap, but she always had expensive tastes, so it seems fitting.

She hooks the strap of the tin over the buggy handle and goes off in search of her other ingredients. There's something of an airport about the scale of the shop, with its tannoyed announcements and lofty ceilings. As she and Sami glide over the smooth floor, she imagines that they are Miami-bound on a Heathrow travelator, and when they get there, she will sip cocktails beside an art deco hotel swimming pool as she poses for *Vogue* in Agent Provocateur swimwear.

Turning a corner, she nearly collides with a display of power tools. She's too thin for swimwear right now, though. Too thin, too mad with grief.

A horrific thought strikes her: will she and Sami be forced to return to her parents' Manchester council house and sit there and listen to their Special Brew-enhanced bollocks all day?

Never.

'Not in a million fucking years.'

A passing man shrinks from her and hurries to a different aisle.

She scours the shop, but in all the sacks and bags and pots of chemicals on the miles and miles of shelves, she can't find iron oxide, powdered aluminium or strips of magnesium. She sidles up to a spotty youth stacking shelves in an orange apron, and makes her request.

The kid scratches his head and frowns. 'I'll just ask my colleague, madam.' No one has called her madam for what seems like a hundred years.

He leads her over to an older shop assistant. When he hears what she's looking for, the man clocks her in her battered outfit, her generally wasted air, the one can of designer paint dangling from the buggy, and he laughs.

'Sorry, love,' he says when he recovers, his voice high-pitched, incongruously northern. 'What the heck are you planning to do with that lot, then?'

She pulls herself up to her full height, which, even in flip-flops, is considerably greater than that of either man. She wants to be called madam again. 'Do you stock these items?' she says, very slowly, as if to an idiot.

'No, we don't,' he says, mirroring her tone.

'Then could you suggest perhaps where I might find them?'

The older man sticks out his lower lip in an exaggerated gesture of thought. 'You could try a school science lab?' he says, after a while. He puts his hand on his younger colleague's shoulder and leads him away from her, laughing and shaking his head. 'You don't half get some weirdos in this town, lad,' she hears him say as they turn a corner.

Smarting, humiliated, wishing she had said something witty or insulting or both, Sophie creeps out of the shop, gaining only a speck of comfort from the fact that no one stops her for the paint, for which she hasn't paid.

It takes her two hours to walk home, traipsing along ring roads, jumping out of her skin every time a passing car speeds past her, blasting its horn as if she had no right to be on the roadside. By the time she's back in the apartment, she is thirsty, weary as a starved dog, and well and truly down from her coke ride. She can't believe what she was planning to do. Build a bomb? And do what with it, exactly?

She is also disgusted at herself for being so weak with the drug. She'll not do it again, not even for a face-to-face confrontation. Did she need this confirmation that it sends her too, too crazy? If she's not careful, she'll end up in prison and that'll be the end of that for poor Sami. Jailbird mother, murderer father, skint. Not a great start in life. If nothing else, she has to pull herself together for her daughter.

She turns Snake's wrap over in her hands. She should throw it away, flush it down the toilet. But she's going to keep it instead, as a test of her newly formed resolve. She should be bigger than this.

So instead, she zips it into the inner pocket of her best handbag, one she is trying not to use any more because, even though she loves it, it's Mulberry and she could get up to five hundred for it. Two things she must not use in one package.

Do not touch, Soph.

Sipping on a cup of tea, she sits on her bed and looks at the pot of paint she has bought. Building a bomb was a ridiculous idea. So crude, so frankly fucking weird.

It's time she did something, but not a bomb.

Using a knife, she prises the lid from the paint tin and, not having a paintbrush to her name, she fetches a sponge from the bathroom and daubs Terre D'Egypte all over the walls of her bedroom. Badly, but, she thinks, brilliantly.

That should help Mr M&H estate agent, with his precious clients and his viewings.

When all the paint is used up, she sits and, with orange-stained fingers, counts her money. After the taxi, she has eighty pounds left. If she only spends a tenner over the weekend, she'll have enough to get her to London on Monday.

It is time to get serious.

44

Then

It has taken Louisa three hours to get everyone ready to go into Cambridge. As she changes Leon's freshly filled nappy for the third time – on this occasion having to take off his bootees and unwrap him from his snow suit as well as changing all the layers underneath because of the overspill – she wonders if it is going to be worth it. Is leaving the house for the first time since the birth going to provide the respite she so badly needs?

She had felt so entrenched this morning, so trapped by the many lovely walls of her luxury house. She could feel the pressure building so fiercely that it actually hurt the top of her head. If she doesn't manage to pick up some sort of momentum and get outdoors, she won't be able to answer for the consequences.

Excited beyond measure to be meeting Father Christmas in The Grafton Centre, Poppy is almost impossible to shepherd into the Fiesta. She is too big for Louisa to lift. She tried once, when Poppy was being exceptionally stubborn about going to bed, and her stitches burst. This was painful and annoying, but at least the hospital trip to get them re-sutured gave a convincing medical record for her diary entry for that day.

With some adult shouting, some childish tears and some

further delay, they are finally on the road.

'Daddy, Daddy,' Poppy says as a red sports car passes them on the way into town.

'Not Daddy,' Louisa says. 'Daddy away in America.'

'Daddy in America?'

'Yep. He'll be home in two days. He's bringing back presents for Christmas!'

Louisa has no idea if any of this is true or not, but she is beyond caring.

'Father Christmas! Father Christmas!'

'Yes, we're going to see Father Christmas.'

Louisa eyes her daughter in the rear-view mirror.

With Leon tucked underneath in the baby carrier, the double buggy is a sweaty challenge to manoeuvre. A few hundred yards from the car park, Poppy starts crying for her magic juice, so, swearing under her breath, Louisa finds a bench, sits on it and rummages in the changing bag, panicking slightly that she might have forgotten to pack it.

'Oh, what a lovely big sister!' A grey-haired woman – who, from her patrician tones, heavy dark glasses and tweed skirt, has to be an academic – stops and stoops to talk to the wailing Poppy.

'Want my juice,' Poppy says.

'Mummy's just getting it for you,' the woman says. 'I've got a granddaughter just like you.'

'I don't know what makes you think you are so uniquely placed to shut her up,' Louisa mutters, handing Poppy the beaker of juice which, miraculously, she did actually remember to mix and put in the bag.

The woman straightens, her cheeks aflame. 'I'm sorry?'

'You heard.' Louisa stands, grabs the buggy and, scar a-throb, barges past the interfering old bag and heads off in the direction of Santa's grotto, where there is a long queue of over-excited toddlers straining on the arms of their drained-looking mothers.

Isn't it supposed to be fun, all this child rearing?

'Hello there! Come to see Santa?' Santa's Little Helper – a tiny young woman in green felt and red striped tights – bounces alarmingly up to Poppy, like some eerie child. Poppy recoils in shyness, turning her head towards the back of her buggy, hiding her face behind her beaker.

'Do you have a chair?' Louisa asks as the helper takes her ten-pound note in exchange for a ticket, committing her to waiting here no matter how long it takes. 'It's just I've just had the baby, and—'

Santa's Little Helper's bounce vanishes. Her sigh says everything she feels about the cheek of these mothers demanding luxuries like chairs. Nevertheless, she ducks into the grotto and comes out with a folding camping stool.

'It's all we've got,' she says, eyeing first Louisa and then the stool, as if not quite believing that the former will fit on the latter without some sort of breakage.

'Thanks,' Louisa says with a little too much emphasis.

She unfolds the seat and sits, rocking the buggy. Her eyes blur on the shiny surfaces of the shopping centre as she floats away from the scene and into her own thoughts, which, as ever, turn to Sam and what a disappointment he has turned out to be.

She reaches inside the changing bag and pulls out the water bottle she has filled with vodka, taking a burning sip to warm her guts. At least that's one good thing about having had this baby: she can drink again. Her own magic juice.

A shape flits in front of her eyes. At first she thinks it might be a bird. But what's a bird doing inside a shopping centre? Underneath her winter layers, her expensive ski parka that no longer does up without an unsightly bulge all around her, her flesh creeps. If this is a bird, then it is a bird of very bad omen.

She forces herself back into focus and sees the shape disappear into a shop at the other side of the glossy concourse. There's something about it . . .

She glances at the buggy. Like her brother all wrapped up in the compartment beneath her, Poppy has fallen asleep, sucking on her magic juice – which has done its work – with a sound like a gurgling drain on a repetitive beat. Louisa looks at the ticket in her hand and sees that her entry is not timed or numbered.

'My daughter's gone to sleep,' she explains to the Little Helper. 'I'll be back.'

'You'll lose your place in the queue,' the girl in the elf outfit says, but Louisa is away and through the shop door, following the bird shape. It is only when she is inside that she realises she is in a high-end lingerie shop, full of headless torsos wearing impossibly wispy pieces of lace and silk. The walls are adorned with photographs of the same underwear, sported by women being attended to by men whose presence is only hinted at by the shadow of an arm, the top of a head paying attention around the thong area.

A handful of customers browse the hangers. What, Louisa wonders, are they thinking as they finger the frilly pieces of nothingness? Whatever it is they are picturing is beyond her own imagination. She feels as if she shouldn't be in here with her baggy belly, buggy and babies.

The bird swoops past the edge of her vision. Ducking down behind a circular chrome rack of tiny embroidered nothings, Louisa turns to catch full sight of it, and sees that it is, in fact, a tall, slender woman with long dark hair. She doesn't notice Louisa – or if she does, there is no recognition. Why would there be? Even if she knows of her existence, she has no idea what she looks like. But there's absolutely no doubt who this is. Unlike many people, she – *Soph* – looks exactly the same in the flesh as she does in her photographs. Only, of course, today she's wearing more clothes than in the white iPhone pictures.

She sashays through the shop, adding to the collection of items on her arm. Louisa's not the only one to watch her – so otherworldly are her looks that she also draws the gaze of the other shoppers. Louisa puts her head down and, fighting the humiliation, pretends to browse, trying not to imagine herself in the garments she's looking at, the cutting in of flesh, the hanging over, the bulging.

None of those worries for *Soph*, from the look of it.

'Mind if I try this lot on?' she says to a shop assistant in a husky voice that is trying a little too hard to sound educated, posh, upper class. There's a northern twang lurking there somewhere, too, Louisa notices.

The shop assistant leads her to a purple-curtained changing room, then hangs around just outside. It's unclear whether she's doing this to assist the woman or to prevent theft. For all her external glamour, this *Soph* has a detectably skanky edge to her. Louisa lurks at the racks nearby, earwigging.

There is a brief rustling as clothes are discarded, a clatter as hangers fall to the floor, then a pause while a phone keyboard beeps.

'Hey, baby,' Soph says, her huskiness enriched with a little breathiness. 'What do you think?'

The man's words are inaudible, but Louisa recognises both who he is, and the tone of what he's saying, which is something beyond appreciative.

Soph gives a deep, dirty laugh.

'Is it? Do you think? How about this?'

The man speaks, and Soph responds with a mock-shocked gasp.

It takes all Louisa has not to tear down the curtain and expose her for what she is, to shout to the other shoppers, tell them what this woman is doing to her.

More dirty laughter, more hangers hitting the floor, more provocative sounds.

'Shall I just get the lot?' she says. 'Yes, of course I'll use the card. Yes. Yes. See you in half an hour. Prepare yourself, my sweet. Yes. Love you, baby, yes, kisses.'

America? Ha!

Louisa realises she is now staring at the curtain in disbelief. Through a chink where the two sides fail to properly meet, she sees glimpses of ribs, hipbones, a butterfly tattoo on the rear of a slender pelvis, the improbably generous curve of a breast. As she looks away, she catches the eye of the shop assistant, who raises her eyebrows and gestures with her head towards the curtain as if to say: *Can you believe that?*

No. Louisa really can't.

How can Sam do this?

How can he be carrying on with that – that creature, that caricature of a sexual being?

A hormonally led surge of heat passes through her, drenching her in sweat. Her heart racing, pounding under her hot winter layers, she hangs back and watches as the other woman comes out of the changing room.

'He says buy them all!' Soph cheerfully hands her haul to the shop assistant, as if she knows – is proud, even – that her performance has been overheard. 'He loves the black ones especially, but then that's his thing, black lace on me. Can't get enough of it.'

The assistant makes a surreptitious face as she leads her customer across the shop floor to the tills.

Louisa moves closer, just about managing to spin out her browsing without raising any suspicion. As the cashier rings up her purchases, Soph brags unstoppably about her lover.

'This is such lovely silk,' she says. 'Is that the price?' She giggles. 'Oh but he won't mind. He's so generous. He says nothing's too good for me. Look at this.'

Louisa feels dizzy as her husband's bit on the side holds out her left hand and shows off the big solitaire diamond on her third finger. The shop assistants give a polite gasp of admiration and offer their congratulations.

'Well, it's a long way off, right now. There are a few niggling little details to be taken care of, but it'll happen one day.'

Louisa selects a relatively ordinary-looking bra, in the size she used to take before her breasts expanded to their current unruly dimensions, and takes it up to the till. Just in front of her, Soph continues to go on about her lover – or, as she calls him, her fiancé – about how passionate he is, about how the shop's lingerie is his favourite, about how she plans to buy the whole collection to surprise him every night he is with her. 'I don't know how much more he can take, though. He's been staying with me for the past week,' she says, wriggling her shoulders as she fishes in her purse for a credit card. 'And I've nearly exhausted him!'

Louisa turns sharply and catches Soph's arm with the coat hanger that holds her bra. Somehow it manages to dig into the girl's arm, giving her a nasty scratch. The credit card – *Sam's* credit card, Louisa notices – slips from her fingers.

'Ow! What the—?'

'Oh, so sorry,' Louisa says. But every part of her body indicates the complete opposite. For a moment the two women face each other. Louisa tries to send death rays through her eyes, tries to fire them right inside the woman's brain.

Soph looks down at her diamond-ringed hand, which has flown instantly to her arm. She takes it away to reveal blood, then she looks disbelievingly back up at Louisa.

Louisa turns to the two shop assistants, who are just standing there, mouths hanging open, hands suspended in mid-air. She points to Soph's haul. 'Nice lace on those things,' she says. 'The niggling little details are so important, don't you think?'

She dumps the unpaid-for bra on the counter, swings the buggy round and makes her exit.

Poppy wakes as Louisa is unloading her into her car seat.

'Father Christmas,' she says. Then again, desperately, 'Father Christmas!'

'Sorry,' Louisa says, doing up her daughter's buckles. 'Daddy said we can't see Father Christmas today.'

The little girl puts her hands up to her face in dismay and wails.

As Louisa drives them through the car park barrier, Poppy yells.

'Hate Daddy. Hate Daddy.'

So do I, thinks her mother. Oh God, so do I.

45

Now

Lou's period is now three weeks late.

To smother the explanation for this – because she doesn't dare imagine that it might be true – she concentrates on something worse: those plague-pit bodies. Every time she looks out of one of her windows, she thinks of the dome that contains them, lurking beyond the demolition site barriers and the crane, like some terrible egg sac of death.

She stands there now, cooling in the draught from her fan, binoculars to her face, watching someone – an archaeologist, she assumes – in a white paper suit crossing an expanse of empty space towards the excavation site. The person stops, puts down the bag they are carrying – which looks heavy – and rotates their shoulders, looking round at the sun, up in Lou's direction. Lou's instinct is to duck out of view, but it's highly unlikely she is visible. And even if she were, there's no law against watching what is going on outside your own apartment.

Lou zooms in and refocuses. Her subject is female, with a tiny frame, a pretty face and lovely tanned skin. If Lou were to stand next to her, she would feel pasty and lumpish. She wonders if this might be Adam's tame archaeologist and again she feels the heat of jealousy right there, behind her eyes.

She wants the excavation to finish. Why can't the developers just cart it all away, get on with their work and build their shiny new buildings – her shiny new home – on top? Why does it all have to be raked over and examined and noted? What's the point? Those bodies down there died a long time ago, and that's all they need to know. They should put it all behind them and get on with the future.

And where the hell is Adam?

Rattled by how close two of her worlds came to collision today when she took Sophie's phone call in front of Cleo, Lou needs his solid, reassuring presence more than ever. But, for the first time since he moved in, she has returned from work to find an empty apartment.

Has Jazmin been on to him about her call earlier today? Or – and Lou's fingers tingle at the thought – has he left her already? For one of those younger women, that scruffy little Carly perhaps?

Is it all happening to her again?

The smell coming from the oven – no doubt something nutritious and kind to the planet – might suggest otherwise.

But perhaps it's his parting gift.

It's so bloody hot in this apartment. Perhaps he just put the oven on to be vindictive?

What does he *know*? *What does he know?*

Has Sophie tracked Adam down, as well as her bloody parents?

Sophie. Ugh.

At least, though, she hasn't mentioned anything about the children. If Celia had told her anything about *that*, surely she would have already used it against her.

There's some comfort to be found there.

Closing that box in her mind and locking it tightly again, she bends and scratches at her calves, which have been itching her like crazy all day. She suspects they've put too much chlorine in the pool, it's drying her skin to paper. She'll have to send an email to the building manager to complain.

She presses her face against the window. Over the road, the street party is being set up. The demolition site is secured once more, so the revellers have to stay outside. There are stalls now, with people selling food and drink. Someone has even set up shop offering glow sticks, necklaces, crazy hats, all the summer festival tat. This heatwave is generating its own economy.

Lou runs the binoculars over East Block to her left. It is connected to her own building by glass-walled walkways which, back in the sixties, must have looked futuristic and space age, but which now could do with major repairs and redecoration. It is possible to get to the main entrance through them, but she prefers to take the outdoors route through the central courtyard because she imagines they must be thick with mould spores.

In fact, this building is far, far shabbier than she had thought when she bought her apartment. She can't wait for her tower to be built, to move in above all this, to leave it all behind. The brochure says it will have eco air conditioning, thermally efficient windows and heat-exchange ventilation. No mould in that brave new world.

She passes the lenses over the windows of East Block. Homes of hundreds. Some have neat blinds, others blowsy curtains. One apartment has tinfoil covering all its windows, which could be for insulation against the heat or possibly to deflect FBI microwaves. Who knows what goes on in people's minds.

Lou still enjoys the anonymity of her situation: she is just one set of windows in all of this, and picking her out would be very difficult indeed. Her apartment is her own small planet in a vast galaxy, completely under her control. But sometimes – like tonight, when she's feeling particularly vulnerable – the sheer number of other lives being lived out around her can make her feel insignificant, swamped, outnumbered.

As if by way of example of this, her binoculars find the Dark Man in his East Block window. As ever, he is standing still, gazing out. Something – a glint of sun reflecting in her lens, perhaps – makes him look up and, for a second, once more he stares right into her.

Shuddering, she looks away quickly, scanning past his apartment and on to the windows nearest her own, an apartment whose occupants – a family of three: two mums and a baby – she likes to observe as they go about their everyday lives, performing mundane activities that make her ache for that level of simplicity, something she had hoped she would find with Adam.

But now she has nearly convinced herself that he has left her.

And she is three weeks late.

Where is he?

Down on the street, the party sound system fires up. Right on cue, Steroid Boy upstairs turns his music on, and, in response to the two conflicting bass lines, the baby next door starts crying.

If Adam were here, Lou could cope with all of this. Without him, she's not sure what she's going to do.

To escape, she moves on end-of-the-day weary, limping legs to the far end of the apartment, to the children's room. She checks for the piece of thread as she opens the door, and is pleased to find that it's still there. Whatever else he may have done, Adam has at least respected her wishes about not going in there.

Not that it matters any more because, clearly, he is gone.

She stands in the doorway and stares at the little bed and the cot and all the children's belongings, laid out awaiting their return. Even now, a tiny part of herself still believes that she will one day have them back.

But she won't.

Telling Adam they are dead has broken the spell.

Why did she tell him?

But he knew already. He'd pried and found his evidence. He killed the magic, not her.

Even here, she can still hear next door's baby. Steroid Boy's bass, too, still reverberates in her bone marrow. For one second, she nearly gives in to despair.

'Keep busy, Lou,' she says.

She moves into the children's room and pulls Poppy's duvet from the bed. Folding it up, she piles the pillows on top. She fetches a few of the Bags for Life that Adam uses for the shopping and starts to fill them with the toys and books. Sobbing, she mutters to herself, words that mean nothing.

This is a moving on, a tear-blinded attempt to stave off the darkness of being alone in this apartment with no children and no husband and no Adam and a murderous anger growing towards the selfish idiot upstairs, and the careless, selfish parent next door . . .

The apartment door slams shut, startling her into dropping Poppy's Mary Doll onto the floor.

'Lou? You back?'

Her heart flips in her chest. It's Adam! He has changed his mind and come back to her!

She stands and waits and tries to compose herself, listening to him as he works his way through the apartment. He first goes to the living room and, presumably, on seeing her work bag, figures out that she must be somewhere in the apartment.

'Lou?' He moves along the hallway, first into the bedroom they share, then into the next room, his studio. The bathroom door opens and shuts and finally he knocks on the children's-room door.

'Yes,' she says, her voice tiny.

He opens the door.

'What?' He dashes to her and puts his arms around her.

At his touch, she bursts into tears.

'What are you doing in here, Lou?'

'I thought you'd gone,' she says, sobbing into his chest.

'Gone, me?' He puts his hands on her shoulders and holds her away from him, looking her straight in the eye. 'I will never leave you, Lou. Do you know that? I'm not that kind of boy. I love you. The only way I'd ever go is if you sent me away.'

'I'd never do that,' she says.

'Well, then, we're stuck with each other.'

With his thumb, he wipes the tears from her cheek. 'So what are you doing in here?' he says, looking at the bags.

'I just thought it's time to pack the children away, to say goodbye.'

'Really?' He touches her chin and tries to get her to look directly at him.

She nods, and again the tears come. The recycled plastic bags look so pathetic sitting there half full of toys and books that have not felt the touch of a child in over a year.

'I wish all this stuff would all go away,' Lou says, sniffing. 'Magically disappear. I was mad to put this room together in the first place. It was madness.'

'Oh Lou.' He draws her to him again.

'Where were you, then?' she asks him, as he strokes her hair. 'You weren't here when I got back.'

'I've been at the standpipe. There was a hell of a queue.'

'Standpipe?'

'Remember? I said the other night.'

Lou doesn't remember, but then Adam talks a lot and she doesn't always take everything in, particularly when it's about the domestic side of things, which she's happy to hand wholly over to him.

'As of today there's no mains water except for two hours

every morning,' he says. 'It's a proper drought. They've closed the pool, too.' He leads her out to the hallway and shows her two large plastic containers. 'They were handing them out at the front desk this morning. I wanted to get it all done before you got back – I know you don't like being in here on your own, what with the skellies over there and knob head up there with his music – but I got a bit waylaid today.'

'Waylaid?'

'Filming.'

'What were you filming?'

'Interviews.'

'On your own?'

'No,' Adam says. 'I had my sound girl with me.'

'Carly?'

'Yep. That way I'm free to concentrate on the conversation and the filming. And she's better at keeping an eye on sound levels than she is at filming!'

Lou forces a smile. Carly's footage of the party eviction had presented Adam with a major editing challenge.

'Good news for you, though.' He picks up the two big containers and lugs them through into the kitchen. 'My tame archaeologist says they've nearly got all the remains off site. Just one more day. She's not best pleased, but The Man can force things to roll very quickly if needs be.'

'So the building work will start again.' She follows him through, watching his arms flex in his vest top as he carries the water. 'But that's not what you want, surely?'

'You win some, you lose some. At least you won't have all that death outside your window any more.'

'At least there's that.'

'What makes you happy makes me happy.' He pours water from one of the plastic containers into a saucepan.

'Can we drink that?'

'We're supposed to boil it first; I'm just going to use it for the rice. I've bought us mineral water to drink, if you're OK with that?'

'Sure.'

He moves to the fridge and pours her a glass from a plastic bottle. Lou notes the generic supermarket branding, which is not a patch on the work she is doing for the A.R.K. client.

'This heatwave, this drought, they're just the beginning,' he says as he hands her the glass of water. 'It's all part of a bigger picture. Capitalism can't keep on and on expanding for ever. The world just can't sustain it. We've got earthquakes where we're fracking great holes underneath us, oceans without marine life, the polar ice caps are barely there any more . . .'

He carries on talking as he busies himself in the kitchen. Lou can barely hear what he's saying over the racket going on upstairs, outside and next door, but she likes the rhythms of his voice. They soothe her.

'Can't we do something about that?' she says, suddenly.

'The planet? It's a massive project, but something's got to change.'

'No, I mean that.' She points next door to where the baby is crying.

Adam puts down the vegetable bake he has just pulled from the oven.

'It's bad enough with that psycho upstairs and all his awful music, but the baby . . .' She sits at the table and hangs her head in her hands. 'The baby, Adam. I can't do with it any longer. It brings it all back and I can't stand it.'

'Oh Lou,' he says, going over to her and putting his arm around her shoulders.

She looks up at him. 'Isn't there anything we can do about it?'

'I'll go and have a word right now.'

She follows him and stands just inside her apartment, peering through the partially open front door as he goes down the corridor and knocks on the neighbour's door. The baby's wailing gets louder as the door opens and a young, blonde woman leans out, balancing it on her shoulder, patting its back. Adam smiles warmly at her and they exchange a few words that Lou can't make out over the racket of the child.

Then, surprisingly, the woman invites him in. He nods, steps in after her, and the door closes behind them.

Lou is shocked. What kind of mother is this? When she had children, she would never have let a complete stranger into the house.

She returns to the kitchen and puts the food back into the oven to keep it warm, then kneels up on the sofa and presses her ear against the wall between her apartment and where Adam is right now. The baby's cries subside, and, in the gaps between the sound assaults from Steroid Boy and the partygoers out on the street, she makes out the murmur of voices – one female, light, laughing, the other unmistakably Adam's.

It goes on for half an hour. Lou only moves away from the wall when she hears Adam returning to the apartment. She grabs a book and throws herself on the sofa. When he comes into the living room, she looks up, as if interrupted mid-read.

'Well?' she asks him.

'She was so sweet,' he says, going back immediately to serving up the food. 'Her name's Anna, she's a lone parent and a journalist, working from home. She's been keeping the baby in the living room in the evening to be close to her, which is why we can hear him, because it's just on the other side of that wall. But she knows she needs to change the set-up – it's not good either for her or for the baby. So she's going to start trying to get him to go to sleep in his own room, which is right at the other end of the apartment, where you won't hear him.'

'That's very good of her.'

'She was really lovely.' He brings the plates to the table and Lou gets up to join him. 'She missed the water, too, so I said

I'd go down later and fill a container for her. Miso gravy?' He holds out a jug.

'Thanks. Do you have to do that for her?' Lou asks. 'I mean you hardly know her.'

'I just think it would be a nice thing to do,' he says. 'As she's on her own and can't get down there because of the baby.'

'This is good,' she says, as she tucks into the bake. But, as she looks up at Adam, there's a slight frown playing on the edge of his features. 'What did I say?' she says. 'What?'

He shakes his head. 'Nothing. You said nothing.'

After he's cleared the table, he goes out to get the water for Anna and her baby.

Lou takes herself to bed and hides underneath the covers, running her fingers over her scars. Despite his protestations, she is not entirely sure that she can trust this boy to remain constant to her. He's just too generous with himself.

46

Then

Louisa moves the car seats, sleeping babes and all, from her white Fiesta to the hired silver Astra. The late-afternoon air is finger-numbingly chilly, but thanks to careful magic juice planning on her part, neither child stirs.

She endured a hideous Christmas by taking to her bed. Sam was forced to look after the children, keeping the doors shut on all Poppy's noisy, excited jollity in the living room. He took them out a lot, too, to God knows where. At least the house was quiet with them gone, and Louisa could go to her secret vodka supply in the shed and replenish the innocent-looking water bottle she keeps hidden under the bed.

She also took the opportunity once or twice to go into his study and rummage in his bag. But the white phone was never in its secret pouch – he must have taken it with him when he took her children out. If Poppy were to find those pornographic pictures . . . Her stomach turns with disgust whenever she thinks about it.

Apart from dropping in from time to time to clear away her tray or bring her more food, Sam didn't come into her bedroom. They exchanged perhaps four sentences over the entire holiday period. Even though the surface of what he said was purely functional, there was, as there always is with him these days, an implied judgement in the tone he used, as if all this were somehow her fault.

When, of course, it's all down to him, his philandering, his emotional abuse of her.

She can still see the shadow of that devil in him. He's still there. She has to be careful.

She swings the Astra – which is bigger than she's used to, but as good a disguise as a mask – out of the car-hire company compound. She has tried to stay relatively sober for this journey, but she has her 'water' bottle in her handbag, should she need courage.

She checks the children in the rear-view mirror. They're sleeping as if they have no cares in the world, which they probably don't. Leon has his dummy and Poppy cuddles her adored Mary Doll. It's not fair, really, that they make all this work for her, and just get away with it.

'But that's the contract, Louisa,' she mutters, lowering her voice an octave so she sounds a touch like Sam.

It is dark, yet it is only four o'clock. The heavy frost that splintered itself over the fields the night before has remained all day, and now sits there, impatient for a new icy coat to sparkle over it tonight.

Louisa turns up the car's heater. It's very efficient, and soon her fingers thaw and she can feel the texture of the leatherette steering wheel. She puts on the stereo, which the previous hirer had set to Radio One. An insanely upbeat female DJ reads out readers' tweets in a husky, party voice over a drive time soundtrack. Louisa takes her eye off the road to fiddle with the controls to try to find Radio Three, and the car careers off the edge of the road. She flings the wheel around and manages, just, to avoid ending up in a ditch full of spiked teasels.

Her heartbeat barely registers the shock. What difference

would it have made if she had ended up in there?

No, but she's not ready for that yet. She has more work to do.

And anyway, the children are in the back. She couldn't be that selfish.

With Radio Three finally filling the empty spaces of the car with some grand, mournful Arvo Pärt, Louisa moves south across the flat, dim landscape, heading for the technology park on the edge of Cambridge where Sam's firm has its base. Its UK base, as he now insists on calling it, having established another office in Silicon Valley.

'Good,' she says as she sees Sam's Porsche sitting just outside the door to his company's unit. If he hadn't been here, all her subterfuge and planning would have been wasted.

She turns the Astra into the car park of a neighbouring building and kills the engine, leaving the battery on for the heating and, more particularly, the music, which is reaching a scratching, atonal climax of piano and violin. Louisa listens closely and critically to the pianist – she had once harboured dreams of becoming a professional musician, but failing to get a distinction in her grade six piano had put a spanner in the works. Quite literally, in the case of the Bechstein in her parents' house, which bore the brunt of her fury on the day she found out.

She feels things too deeply, that's her problem. She was born with a skin missing, that's what she always says to herself when things go wrong.

She turns and throws a blanket over the children in the back, so they are not visible, then she pulls a hood over her own head and hunkers down in the car seat, listening critically and sipping from her bottle of neat vodka.

'Just enough', she says, 'to take the edge off.'

She fixes her eye on Sam's unit. It's all very high-tech, steel and grey and glass, lit up by halogen lanterns.

Leon stirs in the back, pushing the blanket from his face. Louisa turns and eyes him, wondering if he could do with the magic milk bottle. But he just stretches, smacks his lips, then settles down again.

She returns to her vigil.

It doesn't take much longer.

As the audience applaud the – to her mind, coarse – pianist, the door to Sam's building opens and he hurries out, a big bunch of roses in his arms. Louise doesn't even for one moment imagine that the flowers are for her, which means her plan is working as she hoped. He jumps into his car and, in almost indecent haste, roars the engine and shoots out of the car park.

She nearly loses him, but thankfully he hits traffic almost immediately. She lurks behind, confident that he hasn't spotted her in her hire car, which she chose entirely for its anonymity. He carries on along around the ring road then heads into town.

Well, he's certainly not on his way home. He did say he would be very late tonight. Dinner with a client, he said.

Ha.

As Louisa follows his car through the clogged city centre, Poppy wakes, pulls the blanket from her face and starts grizzling.

'Shhh.' Louisa reaches with her left hand into her bag and fishes out the doughnut she has standing by for just such a situation. Preparation is all. Poppy takes the offering and instantly it does the trick.

'Look at all the lights, Pops,' Louisa says.

'Lights.' Poppy sits and munches and watches the headlights of passing cars.

Louisa fiddles with her iPhone and the aux socket on the car stereo, and replaces Radio Three with Poppy's favourite nursery-rhyme tape.

'The wheels on the bus go round and round,' Louisa sings, and Poppy joins in.

She's not such a useless mother that she doesn't know what her daughter likes.

Sam heads south then takes a hard left, which almost catches Louisa out. She manages to follow him, causing the driver of the car behind her to brake suddenly and sound his horn. Luckily, Sam has his mind too set on other things to notice this. He turns left again into a narrow, residential street, then pulls in beside a terrace of rather lovely, tall Edwardian houses lined up along a small river. Luckily, Louisa finds a parking place a few cars behind him.

She turns off the engine.

'Where we going?' Poppy says in the back.

'Shhh,' Louisa says. Her little girl knows from her tone that she is serious, so she keeps quiet. Sam runs up the steps to the front door of a particularly fine house, the roses in his arms, and lets himself in.

Louisa sits there, blinking, trying to take this in.

Once he's inside, she opens the door of the Astra.

'Mummy!' Poppy says.

'Mummy won't be a minute, Pops. Would you like another doughnut?'

The little girl smiles and nods and holds out her hand. So easily pleased. It just isn't fair.

Louisa tiptoes up the steps to the front door. There are four doorbells, each labelled with names. One says Williams/Hanley. Louisa mutters the names out loud, turning the conjoined words over in her mouth like a hair she's trying to get out of the back of her throat. She looks up. The house is in darkness, except for the big front bay on the second floor, which, uncurtained, dances with candlelight and what could be the flickering reflections of a roaring fire.

A shadow looms towards the window, massive, blocky, like a bad omen. It has wings, outstretched, black. Louisa steps down onto the pavement and backs out into the road to get a better look, nearly colliding with a speeding cyclist, who swerves, swears and moves on.

The shadow draws closer to the glass, and Louisa braces herself. It is, of course, the tall thin woman, the bragging tart from the underwear shop, *Soph*. Soph Hanley, it is, then. Sophie Hanley. *That's* where she's seen her before. She used to be some kind of model, and then there was a drugs scandal or something . . . Louisa makes a mental note to look her up.

Sophie Hanley is wearing some sort of kimono, her arms spread wide, her hair loose and flowing. She's laughing, standing in the bay of the window, looking out at the river, the streetlights throwing shadows up at her dark red, too-large slash of a mouth. She looks ghoulish, like a zombie who has just consumed flesh.

Another figure comes up behind her, circles her with his arms, buries his face in her dark hair. She reaches up to put her arms around his neck, like a twisted, dark, ecstatic Madonna.

The other figure is Sam. No surprises there. It couldn't have been anyone else. But for Louisa to actually see the living, live, physical evidence is like having a large pair of hands squeeze the breath out of her.

She runs back to her car and hurls herself into the driver's seat.

'Is it Sophie's house?' Poppy says from the back, from behind Mary Doll.

Louisa turns sharply to confront her daughter. 'What did you say?'

The little girl puts her hand over her mouth, as if she has made a big mistake.

'You've been here before, Poppy?'

Poppy nods, her hand still over her mouth, tears pricking her frightened eyes.

'When?'

'Daddy bringed us here for Christmas. She gived me a bracelet.'

Louisa looks up through the fogged windscreen at the bay window. Sophie and Sam are no longer there. No doubt she's already got him tied up and begging for it.

Her fury feels like electricity teeming out of her fingertips. She could point them at the door, make it fall down, charge up the stairs to their perverted little love nest – WITH WHICH HE HAS CORRUPTED HER CHILDREN – and murder the two of them. Just with her fingertips.

How dare he?

'How FUCKING *dare* he?'

'Mummy?' Poppy says. Louisa knows from the sound of her voice that her bottom lip is wobbling. '*Mummy?*'

The wailing starts. The wailing of a child whose mother frightens her.

At the sound of his sister's distress, Leon wakes and squirms, grimaces, cries and fills his nappy. The air in the car is thick with anger, panic and the stench of shit.

'For *fuck's sake*.'

Louisa gets out of the car, opens the back door and leans in, making Poppy cower. She rips the buckles from the baby's car seat, pulls him out, grabs the changing bag and goes to the rear, where she lays him out on the tailgate, removes his soiled nappy – it was another one of his extraordinary, explosive poos – wipes him clean, and puts on a fresh one as quickly as she can to avoid both of them freezing to death.

She is not gentle, and he protests and squirms, as if trying to evade his own mother's touch.

Then sense returns to her. She pauses, picks up her baby and holds him to her. 'She shouldn't take it out on her children,' she tells him. 'What kind of a mother is she?'

'A wronged one,' she answers, as she tries to be more gentle with him, patting his back then returning him to his car seat. She reaches over and strokes Poppy's hair. 'Sorry, Pops. Mummy's just a bit poorly today.'

'Poor Mummy,' Poppy says, touching Louisa's hand and holding it to her lips. 'Kiss you better.'

Something as big as an orange sticks in Louisa's throat, making it hard for her to breathe.

She shuts the car door on the children and goes back to the tailgate, where Leon's soiled nappy sits waiting for her to put it into a scented plastic bag.

'Not yet, nappy,' she tells it.

She unwraps it, exposing its fetid contents. Bearing it like a platter in front of her, she carries it to the three steps leading up to *Soph's* front door, and soils each one with a layer of shit. She briefly considers adding her own bodily waste to the decoration but that is beyond even her. At this point, at least.

As a final touch, she leaves the nappy, soiled side uppermost. Then she goes back to the car, where Poppy is calmly stroking Leon's face and singing him a lullaby.

Much, much later, the hire car returned and exchanged for the Fiesta, the children dosed up and blotto, Louisa pours herself a very large glass of wine, sits at the kitchen table and downs it with a handful of sleeping pills the doctor prescribed during one of Sam's attempts to get her to, as he calls it, *sort herself out*.

He's calling her mad, when, in fact, it's his rogue fucking that is the real problem in this house.

She texts him. First she thinks about sending it to the private iPhone that he has no idea she knows about. But it's too early for that. She wants to string that one out a bit longer, save it for later. So she addresses it, as she usually does when he's out and thinks that she doesn't know where he is, to his normal phone.

Goodbye.

She stands and takes herself over to a bare expanse of wall and hits her head repeatedly against it until she is barely conscious. She slides to the floor and slumps, waiting for him to come home.

47

Now

'It's as if, now I can't hear the baby crying, Steroid Boy thinks there's a gap in the sound level that needs to be plugged.'

The racket from upstairs – something screaming and brash that Lou cannot place – is worse than ever tonight. After a lazy Sunday afternoon in bed together, she and Adam had taken a glorious, cooling wash-down in the temporary shower he has rigged up using one of the water carriers, a piece of hose and some watering-can parts. They were just setting themselves up for a relaxing evening in the living room when the noise started up again, as if the lump of testosterone upstairs were spying on them through a hole in his floor, waiting for his moment.

Louisa scans the ceiling. She wouldn't put it past him to go that much out of his way to annoy her. Yes, she is taking it personally.

'Try to block it out,' Adam says to her from the kitchen area, where he is chopping something green and leafy with one of the new, diamond-sharp Japanese knives he has bought with Lou's blessing, using her credit card.

'With that yogic breathing you taught me? Hah.' She scratches her scalp violently, stands and moves over to the window. 'Shut up!' she shouts up through the tiny gap.

'He's not going to hear that.'

She drags the fan across the floor so that it points at her on the sofa, then she lies down and puts a pillow over her head.

'I wish we could get onto his corridor,' Adam says. 'I'd love to have a word with him.'

'He'd just slam the door in your face like he did mine. He's a nasty piece of work. I don't want us to become his victims any more than we already are.'

'How about we ask Umoh to have a word?'

'That'll only make things worse.'

'Or the police?'

She looks at him with disbelief. 'I can't believe you're even suggesting that, Mr Anarchist!'

He shrugs. 'I just want you to be happy.'

'I know,' she says.

He lays knives and forks out on the dining table. 'You ready to eat?'

'Famished. What we got?'

'Butterbean crumble with spinach salad.'

Lou smiles and looks keen, but she doesn't know if she can face any more pulses. She has taken to supplementing Adam's healthy vegan packed lunches with ready-cooked chicken pieces, or ham sliced from the bone from a deli across the street from the A.R.K. offices. On a couple of shameful occasions, she has binned the lot and furtively taken herself to McDonald's or Nando's and buried her face in something on a completely different level of food sin.

He lays out three pasta bowls and starts to plate up.

'You're not taking food next door again, are you?' she says.

He nods. 'Come on, Lou. Anna's at her wits' end trying to juggle things with the baby and her work. If I can help her just a little with delivering hot food every now and then, well, isn't that a good thing?'

Lou shrugs.

'And you should meet her, you know. You're next-door neighbours, and I think you'd really like her.'

'We just never seem to be in the corridor at the same time. We keep different hours.'

'You should go and knock on her door. She'd be pleased to see you.'

'Love,' Lou says, looking up at the ceiling again and noticing that one of the downlighters needs a bulb replacing, 'I don't think I could cope with spending too much time around a baby.'

Adam hits his temple with the heel of his hand. 'Oh God, yes, Lou. I'm sorry. Of course.'

'I mean, one day, of course . . .'

Adam puts a plate on top of one of the dishes he has served up. 'I'll just run this along the corridor. Do you want to pour the water?'

Lou gets up and pours two glasses of water from the bottle in the fridge. Cold, icy water.

Then she sits at the table and waits for him.

When, eventually, he returns, he looks confused.

'You were a long time,' she says.

'She wouldn't open the door to me,' he says. 'She kept the chain on and said through the gap that I was very kind, but she didn't want my help, that I should find more deserving causes.'

'I tend to agree with her.'

'But it's no bother, just making an extra serving every now and then.'

'Have you thought perhaps she doesn't like charity?'

Adam looks bitten, confused, and very, very young. 'But it's just kindness!'

'And you are, you are very kind. But people can be strange and ungrateful and proud.'

Adam nods. 'It's such a pity. I really thought she appreciated it. You know, she looked almost as if she were scared.'

'Like I say,' Lou says, 'people can be very, very strange.'

Upstairs, the loud, hideous music plays on.

'I left the plate on the floor, outside her door, in case she changes her mind.'

'She won't. I shouldn't think, anyway. Hey,' she says, sitting down to her plate of hard-to-digest food, 'perhaps, she's worried about how it might look, her being kept by you. Perhaps she doesn't want to upset me.'

Adam puts down his knife and fork and looks at her, frowning.

'I mean, she might be a little over-sensitive like that,' Lou adds.

In the morning, as usual, Adam steps out of the apartment to walk Lou to the Tube station. He carries her bag and her packed lunch. Of course, she wouldn't allow it if she weren't so sure that helping and guarding her gives him so much pleasure.

On the way along the corridor to the lift, they pass Anna's door. The dish with the butterbean crumble and spinach is still there, untouched, on the floor.

'You'd better take that away when you come back,' Lou says, 'or it might attract rats.'

Today, watchful as ever that there is no black-clad, crow-like woman on her trail, Lou takes a detour to Boots when she surfaces at Oxford Circus.

Her period is going on for four weeks late, now.

It's not the only sign. She looks up at the clear blue sky and a blackness feathers the edge of her vision, like a Photoshop vignette filter.

She makes her purchase and heads to A.R.K., fully intending to slip straight into the toilets and take the test. But Cleo waylays her, barring her progress like some nightclub bouncer. She pulls her into her office, which, while notionally part of the open-plan scheme, is actually contained within glass walls. Her boss looks completely different this morning, like she's itching all over, in an unprecedented state of stress.

For a moment, Lou worries what Sophie has gone and done to cause this.

'Thank God you're here,' Cleo says. 'I thought we'd decided you'd come in an hour early to prepare for the cat food pitch.'

Lou tries to hide her discomposure. As if she needs another sign that she may be pregnant, she has completely forgotten about the important pitch she is supposed to be leading on this morning.

How can that be? It's as if, over the weekend, it had fallen right out of her brain. But she can't let Cleo know that. An excuse is in order, and it is out of her mouth before she thinks.

'I'm really sorry. I just had a bit of a night with my daughter. She was up vomiting.'

'Oh God, she hasn't got the lurgy, has she? I'm five down today because of it.'

Lou shrugs. 'I hope not.' She hasn't heard anything about any lurgy. But then again, since she digs herself deeper into problematic lies every time she has any social contact beyond work exchanges, she keeps herself to herself so much that she doesn't really notice what's going on with her colleagues.

'You've got something to change into, yes?' Cleo says, signalling at Lou's expensive but dressed-down boyfriend jeans, vest top and cashmere cardigan. 'Like we agreed. For the smoke-and-mirrors effect?'

Lou finally notices that, on top of the change of mood, the other difference about Cleo is that for the first time since she started working for her, she is sporting full killer suit and heels.

'Yep. Just dropped it all off in the changing rooms,' Lou

says, reckoning she can run out and panic-buy something passable in one of the little boutiques in the street below. What worries her more than any of the lies she has had to tell about excuses and outfits is the fact that she had planned to spend the night before running over her pitch, practising it in front of Adam, who would have given her positive, confidence-boosting feedback and the chance to fine-tune any niggling points so that she could be superstar-perfect today.

She had forgotten, though. She wants to hit herself, hard, in the head.

'Good, because we've got *Design Week* coming in, too.' Cleo says. 'They picked up on the Mumsnet piece and they want to do a profile of you as our star woman returner.' Cleo's voice seems higher pitched today, and her hands flutter around her like nervous birds.

'That's great.' Lou is smiling, but inside she's fighting the urge to run out of the office and never come back. How could she have agreed to doing that interview? It's given Sophie so much ammunition. In fact, it is surprising that no one else has cottoned on to her true identity because of it. And now, it seems, there is to be more media coverage, more opportunities for people to draw conclusions, for the trolls to descend.

She is caught in a trap of her own making.

'Still no chance of a pic of you and the kids?' Cleo goes on.

Lou shakes her head. 'Sorry, but he's being very difficult about it.'

'Such a damn pity. Anyway, they'll all be here in forty minutes, so you'd better go get yourself ready.'

Just as Lou is turning to head off downstairs to buy some smarter clothes, Cleo's phone rings.

'Yes?' she says, picking it up, irritated at the interruption. 'Yes, she's in here.' She holds up a finger at Lou, to make her stay. 'What? Oh God, no. Really? Jesus Christ. OK, then, show her up into The Pantry and she'll be down in a second.'

'What?' Lou says as Cleo puts the phone down and looks accusingly up at her.

'Today of all days. You have a visitor.'

'What?'

'Your sister. She says she's in town and thought she'd just "pop in".'

'My sister?'

Cleo looks at Lou. 'I know it's not your fault, and we don't mind family at A.R.K., but it's not really the right moment. Can you go and have a word with her? Tell her to come back this afternoon or something, five-ish, and she can come for a drink or something.'

In no doubt whatsoever about who is waiting for her downstairs, Lou nods, steels herself, turns and heads for the lift.

48

Adam

'They're getting themselves into such a pickle.' Adam takes the final slug from the chipped mug and smacks his lips. 'Man, no one makes coffee like you, Carls.'

'Fairtrade organic Colombian. Nothing better. They're like babies, really,' Carly says. 'They don't really know how to deal with eating without getting it all over themselves. If Heydon was around she'd lick it off them, and they'd learn from her, but, in the absence of Mamma, we're all they've got. Here.' She leans forward and takes a flannel from a bowl of warm water on her bedroom floor and hands it to Adam. 'You do Ron.'

He picks up the tiny tortoiseshell kitten and wipes the food from his fur. 'Man. The food's literally everywhere.'

'Bless them,' Carly says, setting to work on the black-and-white and the ginger. 'Hey, Keith and Sandra, this is your Uncle Adam,' she tells the cats in a baby voice. 'What rescued you from the nasty builder man.'

'Thanks for having them. I wish I could have taken them in, but you know what Roobs is like.'

'Yeah.' Carly snorts. 'He'd have bunged them in a sub and eaten them, most likely.'

'And Lou – well, she's not really a cat person.' Adam looks a little sheepish.

Having finished cleaning Keith and Sandra, Carly closes her eyes and kisses their soft furry heads. 'Nah, it's a pleasure. I love having them here,' she says. 'So long as the landlord don't find out, it's cool by me.'

They are on her bed, which, as her tiny room is in a shared house with no living room, also serves as a sofa. Adam likes it in here. It's full of Carly's bits and pieces, odd things she finds out on the street and brings indoors – a toy bird with real feathers dangling against the purple-painted wall, the top part of a shop dummy, which she uses to sport her vast, tatty hat collection, an old record player and collection of 70s pop vinyl. The room is, like Carly, neither masculine nor feminine – just quirky and warm and welcoming.

'You're a top bird, Carls.' Adam flops backwards, supporting his head on a home-made cushion in the shape of a horse's head. He cradles fluffy little Ron against his chest and touches noses with him.

Carly makes an airhead face and waggles her fingers. 'Tweet, tweet.' She gathers Keith and Sandra to her and turns to face him. 'Is everything all right, Ad?'

'What?'

'Well, you don't look so chilled as normal.'

'Nope. Everything's cool.'

'Everything all right with you and L L?'

Adam smiles. 'Me and Lady Lou? Yeah.'

'You sure?'

He turns a lazy head her way and raises an eyebrow. 'You don't miss much, do you?'

She leans across him and strokes Ron. 'Not when it comes to you, me old mucker.' She moves her hand from kitten to Adam's chest, and lets it rest over his heart. 'Tell me what's going on in here, eh?'

He sighs. 'You won't tell anyone else?'

Carly makes a zipping motion across her lips.

He takes a deep breath and tells her all about how Lou's children are dead and how she didn't tell him, and how he thinks all Poppy and Leon's stuff in the flat is sending her crazy, and how she had started to clear it out but, for some reason, just stopped, and how now it's all there half bagged up, not one thing or another, and it's not only doing Lou in, but it's also breaking his own heart.

'I know it's not about me,' he says, finally, play-fighting with Ron, who bats back valiantly from his safe perch on his T-shirt. 'But I just feel like she needs to move on.'

'Wow,' Carly says, her eyes like circles. 'That's really, really shit.'

'I know.'

'I sometimes wonder what you've got yourself into there.'

He looks at her and frowns.

She puts her hands up in the air. 'I don't mean nothing. It's just – well, you just don't seem like your old self, these days, bruv. It's like she's got some part of you locked up in some pretty little box.' She cracks a smile. 'So to speak.'

'I wish there was something I could do for her,' he says.

'Here, take these two.' Carly places Keith and Sandra on Adam's chest, right next to Ron. She slides onto the floor and pulls her DMs from under the bed.

'What you doing?'

'What does it look like, dur. We're going out.'

'Where to?'

'Your place. L L said she wished all the children's stuff would disappear, yeah?'

'Yes, but—'

'Well, let's do it! She's at work now, right?'

'Yeah . . .'

'So we've got all day. By the time she gets back, we'll have the place cleared out and I'll be on my way, so she doesn't have to get shirty about me being around.'

'She doesn't get shirty about you.'

'Believe me, Ad, she does. Come on.' She plucks the kittens from his chest and takes his hand to pull him to standing.

'I don't deserve you,' he says, steadying himself by placing his hands on her shoulders, and kissing her on top of her head.

Underneath her matey bluster, Carly reddens. ''Course you do. You're the top man, Ad. The best geezer in the SE postcode area.'

He slips on his flip-flops. 'What about these guys?' He points to the kittens, who are displaying good habits learned from their flannel baths by diligently licking each other clean.

'Adam, man,' Carly says, rolling her eyes as she pops a denim cap on her head. 'They're just fucking kittens. You don't need to look after absolutely everything and everyone all the bleedin' time.'

She takes him by the hand and leads him to The Heights.

49

Then

'What the hell were you thinking?' Sam says, two days later, as he drives her back home from the hospital.

She has a white paper bag full of meds, her one concession to the doctors, who wanted to keep her in for further psychiatric assessment. She's not going to take them, though. They're for life's losers, and she refuses to be one of those.

Plus, she needs to hold on to her faculties and her anger for what's coming up. The moment with Sam that she has been holding back for a long, long time.

The Confrontation.

So she doesn't answer his outraged, entitled question. Instead, she focuses on the spikes of rain as they drive into the wing mirror.

It's nearly a week later that she finds the moment. A week when she and Sam barely see each other, let alone talk. For someone who is ostensibly so worried about his wife, Sam has paid very little attention to her since she came out of hospital.

Drunk – for while she rejects prescriptions, she is not, of course, beyond self-medicating – Louisa sits outside in a deck-chair in the cold, frost-sparkled end-of-January night, teeth chattering under the full moon, blanket wrapped around her, waiting for Sam to come home to his family.

She's just nodding off when his headlights turn into the driveway. As he steps out of his car and slams the door, she makes no move to greet him.

'What the hell are you doing?' he says, coming and standing over her.

Almost every time he addresses her now, it starts with 'What the hell . . .' and ends with a question mark.

'You've been away three days,' she tells him. 'You said you'd be coming home about nine tonight.'

'So?'

'It's gone midnight.'

'I got held up.'

'You didn't call.'

'I thought you'd be asleep. Or passed out.'

She looks up at him, holds his gaze.

'Drunk again.' His voice is weary, laced with disgust. 'You could have died of exposure.'

He takes her wrist and tugs her into the house through the front door, which is standing wide open to the icy air.

'This house is a stinking pit,' he says, as he pulls her into the living room and pushes her down on the sofa. 'Where are my children? Are they in bed?'

'What do you think? What do you care?'

He turns away from her and slaps his hand on the wall. 'Louisa.'

'What?' she says, drawing the blanket around herself.

'We can't go on like this.'

'No, we can't.'

He looks down at her, his face shadowed by the stark, overhead light. 'We've got to get help for you.'

'This again.'

'Look.' He kneels and takes her hand. 'You're not well,

Louisa. I thought it would pass, like the last time, after Poppy, but it hasn't. If anything, it's just getting worse.'

She starts laughing. 'You're not being serious?'

He drops her hand and kneels back and away from her. 'What the hell do you mean by that?'

'You're saying this is all down to me?' Her voice is rising.

'You're not well, yes.'

She snorts. 'And it's got nothing to do with you abandoning us all for nights on end, saying you're going away on business?'

'I *have* to go away on business, Louisa. It's what I do.'

'And I'm supposed to just suck it up?'

'Louisa, I—'

'You expect me to believe that every night you come in late, or not at all, you're working?'

'What are you implying?'

'I'm implying, Sam, that you are a liar.'

'I am not a liar.' There is outrage in his voice.

'Coming back late, stinking of cunt.'

'Louisa!'

'You're fucking someone else, aren't you?'

'NO.'

She starts to gesticulate, obscenely, turning her body into positions she remembers from the phone. 'Some little fuck-whore, some skanky slag, some piece of meat.'

He looks at her and lifts one side of his lips to reveal his perfect, whitened teeth. 'You disgust me, Louisa,' he says, his voice as cold as her cheeks had been when she was outside.

'Well, hit me, then. You know you want to.'

He makes to leave the room.

'So no denial, then?'

He stops, his back bristling.

'And', she goes on, 'how come, if you are so concerned about my mental health, my "state", as you put it, you're so happy, so keen, even, to leave our children in my mad, reckless care?'

He stops, turns to face her. 'What are you saying?'

She stands and moves towards him. 'I mean, anything could happen.'

He grabs her wrist. 'What the hell do you mean?'

'I just mean, take care, Sam. If you don't live up to your responsibilities as a husband and father, you only have yourself to blame.'

'If you hurt either of our children, I'll kill you.'

She smiles. 'Is that a threat?'

He narrows his eyes at her.

'You're a bastard, Sam. You don't give a toss about me. You don't even care about the children. They're probably getting in your way, aren't they? You'd be off with your floozy, if it weren't for them. If it weren't for me. The niggling little details.'

'You're crazy. I could get you sectioned.'

'You just try.'

'I could get the children taken away.'

'Oh, yes? And what have you got to prove that I'm doing them any harm? They're healthy, happy, well looked after. More than you seem to be able to say for me, your wife. Yes, your word against mine. That's going to stand up in court.'

'What the hell are you talking about?' he says. 'There is no, as you put it, "floozy". You're just sick, Louisa. You need to admit it.'

'Ha!' she says.

He leaves the room, slamming the door and she hears his heavy footstep on the stairs going up, no doubt, to check on the children he only seems to remember when he can use them to make a point about her.

And still, he lies.

* * *

The next afternoon, Louisa ignores the cooing that's coming at Poppy and Leon from the woman behind the post-office counter.

'First class, please,' she says, putting the medium-sized bubble-wrapped package on the scales.

'What does the name say?' the post-office woman asks, squinting at where Louisa has scrawled the address. Her voice is a little frosty from Louisa's rejection of her grandmotherly advances on the children.

'Soph Williams Hanley,' Louisa says, and the woman makes it a little clearer with her biro.

'May I ask what's in it?'

'It has no monetary value,' Louisa says.

She would like to see this doughy woman's face if she told her what it actually contained.

Later, the children in bed, it is finally time to let him know that she knows for sure.

Louisa sits in her disaster zone of a kitchen. Every surface is covered in half-finished plates of cooked ready meals, puréed pap, baby bottles and their cheesy dregs, three vodka bottles. She gets by. She bloody gets by.

No, she doesn't.

Since she got back from hospital, she hasn't really been able to focus much on anything. Anger gnaws away at her brain like a malignant growth.

Yes, it's time.

She's going to make him pay for making it all end up like this, in this chaos, this battlefield.

Come back now, she texts to his secret, filthy white phone. *It's urgent.*

She goes to her stationery drawer in her studio and pulls out her diary. Finding today's date, she writes: *Broke my arm as punishment for untidy kitchen*. She puts the diary back in its hiding place and sits in the kitchen waiting, listening to the Siberian wind howl over the fen outside. It's so strong tonight that it even rattles the specially made, state-of-the art Swedish windows Sam had installed to keep the elements out.

In just half an hour, his wheels crunch over the gravel of the driveway. Louisa smiles to think how perplexed he must be that she knows his secret phone number. He must be worrying if she's seen the photographs. She has a good old giggle about that.

As she hears the car door slam, she takes the rolling pin from where she had left it by a lump of dough that she'd knocked up in the morning to make biscuits with Poppy. *That* never happened, of course. Poppy was difficult, there was some shouting, she had to be smacked, and her special little baking kit went back into the cupboard, unused.

She sweeps some plates onto the floor to clear a foot or so of worktop, where she lays out her non-dominant left forearm. As Sam puts his keys in the front door lock, with her free hand she raises the rolling pin above her head.

With three successive, resounding whacks, she brings it down again and again on her arm until she can no longer feel or move her fingers.

Sam is standing in the kitchen doorway as she deals the last blow, his face somewhere on the register between fury and horror.

'Sorry to drag you away from *Soph*,' she says. 'But I need you to take me to the hospital.'

50

Now

Lou steps gingerly out of the lift and into The Pantry.

At one side of the room, five geek boys lounge on beanbags, tucking in to morning coffee and pastries.

At the far end, her back turned to the lift as she looks at the display of A.R.K.'s most recent prize-winning branding, a tall, stick-like figure stands in a shabby black silk kimono. Bare, long-boned arms hang at her side, the man-sized hands twitching, fingers working against each other as if rolling invisible thread into tiny balls.

She stands alone. It looks as if the geek boys have deliberately put as much distance between her and themselves as possible.

The professional in Lou wants to back quietly into the lift, zip down to the ground floor and choose a great outfit in a nice little clothes shop so that she can shine at the cat food pitch. This plan is also supported by the more animal part of her, whose instinct is simply to run away.

But what's keeping her there on the threshold of the room is an urge, driven by necessity, to deal with, and finally get rid of, this part of her life. This woman is responsible for stealing everything from her. And it is clear that she is determined to go on and on, drawing out the pain, preventing Lou from moving on.

This is what propels her across the room.

She moves quietly; when she speaks, her tormentor jumps.

'What the hell are you doing here?'

Sophie turns. Something has happened to her face. She's not how Lou remembers her, not even from the last time she saw her, which was way back at Sam's inquest. The pregnant bloom that filled her features back then has gone. Her eyes are sunken and her cheekbones, once so startling, now jut alarmingly. Her mouth still stretches generously across her face, but the full lips are chapped, dry, scabbed.

She has lost her looks.

With Lou's recovered appearance, her sleek new clothes covering the wrecked parts of her body, her reclaimed blond hair, her spirit rejuvenated by Adam, she is now by far the younger-looking of the two, even though she has ten years on her adversary.

Despite the situation, she finds herself with a smile on her face.

'We need to talk,' Sophie says. Her voice is low, and Lou wants to keep it that way. She doesn't want any hysterics in here, not at work. Not in front of the geek boys.

It's only then that the kimono falls away and Lou notices the baby, strapped to Sophie's front with some sort of scarf arrangement.

That black edging appears again, shimmering Lou's field of vision.

How dare Sophie come armed?

Sophie places her big hands on her tiny, sleeping weapon, as if to protect it from Lou. 'Very soon we will be homeless,' she says, the 'we' sticking into Lou like a stiletto blade. 'You will make us homeless. My daughter will grow up penniless, and will one day find out that her father has been branded a murderer.' Her voice is already cracking. She's trying to keep it in, but Lou can smell the unearned sense of injustice that hangs around her like a putrid smell.

'And what do you expect me to do about it?' Lou says. 'I've been exceptionally generous, given the situation. Your baby's born. Now you can make your own way, like everyone else has to in this world, and stop leeching off me.'

'Is that how you see it?' Sophie says, the colour rising in her cheeks. 'I've come here to tell you that I'm starting legal proceedings to get my daughter what she's owed from her father's estate.'

Lou snorts. 'And we're supposed to believe that Sam is her father?'

Sophie pulls back a piece of the scarf she has wrapped around the baby, and, with a look of triumph, reveals a shock of auburn hair exactly the same shade as Sam's.

'That doesn't mean anything,' Lou says. 'You've probably dyed it. I wouldn't put it past you.'

'I'll do a DNA test.'

Lou laughs softly. 'Good luck with that. There was nothing but ashes, and I flushed them down the toilet.'

Sophie gasps. 'You did what?' She stares at Lou, her mouth wide open.

Gormless, Lou thinks. If she's not careful, a fly will get in that big trap of hers.

'You have no grounds whatsoever for any sort of claim.'

'We do!'

Over the other side of The Pantry, the geek boys look up, alerted by Sophie's voice.

Lou moves in closer to her. 'Keep it down,' she says.

'Or what?'

Lou turns to glare at the boys. Embarrassed, they look away. She faces up to Sophie, who, although she towers over her by at least a head and stands more evenly on The Pantry floor, looks so wispy that Lou imagines she might, if touched, collapse into a dry heap. How could she have feared this piece of skin and bone?

'Do you know what Sam put me through?' Lou says, her voice a harsh whisper. 'He was a bad, bad man. Evil. I had to get away, take the children somewhere safe, somewhere better. He wouldn't have it, though. Whatever he told you, he wasn't going to let me escape him. He was so jealous, so possessive. Obsessed. He would rather we all died than escape him. He chased us in the car, Sophie. He tried to murder us all. And it's not like I'm the first of his wives to get the treatment.'

Sophie's lip curls. 'This is all bullshit, Louisa. It's all just a story you made up.'

But Lou forges on. 'Don't you see that, if anything, you've had a lucky escape? Put yourself in my shoes, *Soph*. Have some compassion. How would *you* feel if someone attacked *your* child?'

She reaches out a hand to touch the baby, but Sophie is there, instantly, batting her away.

'Don't you dare touch her,' she says.

Lou backs away, holding her hands up.

'Don't you ever come anywhere near her.' Sophie is trembling now, her cheeks colouring, her hands wrapped firmly around the baby at her front. 'I know about you. I know what Katie's sister thinks of you. I know about what happened to Star and Boy Blue.'

'Star and Boy Blue? Seriously? *Horses?* What the hell are you talking about?' Lou says, laughing at her. 'Have you gone completely mad? Have all those drugs you take addled your mind that badly?'

Over at the beanbags, the geek boys are quietly gathering their bags and phones, preparing to tiptoe out of the room.

'I've been drug free for over three years,' Sophie splutters.

'What do you want? A medal? And what about that poor photographer whose life you tried to ruin with all your accusations? How is he? Don't come all righteous with me.'

'You know nothing about me.'

'Oh no, Sophie. I know *everything* about you. You don't think I had my legal team sitting around doing nothing when I was recovering from the COMA and the HEAD INJURY and the FIFTEEN BROKEN BONES Sam gave me. When you had nothing better to do than sit around and troll your poison over every single article written about me. And now you expect me to forget all that and do something for you and your little bastard brat?'

'And I know about your past, too, Louisa. Louise, I mean. I've had some lovely chats with your mother. Celia has told me all about you.'

Lou stops dead, the speech knocked out of her. She gasps for air. 'What did you say?'

'She's told me what happened.'

Lou's heart thunders so quickly that she is afraid she might take off. Her vision swims as if she is standing in the heat haze on the pavements outside. Everything she has worked so hard to keep buried. How much has Sophie unearthed? 'What did she say?'

'She's scared of you, Louise. She doesn't even want to hear your name.'

'And did she tell you how she brought me up? How she drank and neglected and abused me? And how I couldn't take her attacks for one more day, and had to defend myself? Did she tell you this? Huh? Or did my pathologically lying pig mother make some shit up about me just to save her own bacon? I repeat: you are wrong, and even if you weren't, you have no way of proving anything.'

Sophie snaps her fingers in Lou's face. Her grubby nails come so close they graze her eyelashes. 'Tell you what. Here's a thought: your children's bodies will carry Sam's DNA. How about that?'

Lou snaps. She can't bear it any longer. 'You have no right to be here,' she roars. 'You have no right to be in my life.'

She launches herself at Sophie, reaching up for her hair, yanking it back.

With one arm around her child, Sophie pushes at Lou's face. Lou, her fingers still knotted in Sophie's long hair, grasps at her with her free hand, grabbing hold of the scarf around the baby.

'Let go of her! Let go of Sami now!' Sophie tries to prise her hand from the scarf.

'Sami? You called it Sami? How pathetic can you get?'

'She is named for her father,' Sophie says, clawing at Lou's hand.

'I'll get you put away,' Lou says. 'I'll report you to the police for harassment.'

Sophie forces Lou's fingers backwards, away from the scarf, and manages to partially push her away from the baby.

Lou screams. She loses her uneven footing and topples backwards. Still with her hand in Sophie's hair, she takes her with her as she falls.

'Sami!' Sophie cries as she tumbles forward.

Doing everything she can to save her child from being crushed between them, Sophie crashes messily onto her knees, straddling Lou. She scrabbles to get on top of Lou's arms and pinions her to the ground, leaning over her.

'You will not win this.' She showers Lou with spit as the words fly out of her. 'I will get what my daughter deserves. I will give Sam his good name back. I will not rest until I do so.'

Lou roars. She forces an arm free and reaches up again for Sophie's head. Sophie screams as a handful of long, dark hair is yanked from her scalp. She shoves Lou's arm away, her free hand tightly defending her baby, whose terrified wails rise to meet those of her mother.

'What the HELL is going on?'

Lou freezes, her fingers grasped around the hairs she has torn from Sophie's head, the roots still twitching at the ends. She looks up and sees Cleo standing over her. Beside her are her assistant Fleur, a group of five men in very good suits – presumably the cat food clients Lou is due to impress in about half an hour – and a woman in a shabbier arrangement of skirt and T-shirt – most likely the journalist from *Design Week*.

This doesn't look good.

It is not the behaviour of a London hotshot designer.

Cleo doesn't miss a beat.

'I'm afraid we're very passionate here at A.R.K.,' she says, laughing into the stilled air around the stunned clients. She pulls out her phone and calls security, then she turns to her assistant. 'Would you be a love, Fleur, and make these guys our signature A.R.K. coffee?' She points to the espresso machine at the far side of The Pantry. 'And break out the *pains au chocolat*. They're warm from the oven,' she says confidentially to one of the men, a high-status, dead ringer for George Clooney.

As Fleur ushers the group away, Cleo moves over to Lou and Sophie, who have rolled apart and are still on the floor, like kids caught out fighting at school. 'What are you up to, Lou?' she whispers. 'What's up with your sister? Oh my God. Is that a *baby*?'

Lou scrambles inelegantly to her feet and stands by her boss looking down at Sophie. 'Can we get her out of the building?' she says to Cleo. 'I'll explain later.'

There's a thundering of footsteps on the staircase as two security guards roll up.

Cleo nods to them, and they haul Sophie to her feet.

'She's not who you think she is,' Sophie snarls as the two besuited, muscle-bound guys hustle her out. 'She's a liar, she drove the father of my child to his death, she kills horses, her mother . . .'

Lou exaggerates her limp as she takes Cleo to one side. 'She doesn't know what she's talking about. She's mad. The baby's sent her mad.'

Cleo looks at Lou for long enough to make her feel uncomfortable. Then she sighs.

'Look,' she says, eventually, 'I need you to go, now. You can't show your face at the pitch. Ping the artwork over to me. And then you go home.'

'I can explain,' Lou says.

'Go home, Lou. We'll speak about this tomorrow. Eight a.m. in my office. OK?'

Lou looks over at the suits who are doing everything they can to appear not to be noticing what is going on. She has failed, utterly and completely. She has embarrassed A.R.K., and jeopardised her position. And once again, the fault is not hers. It's that damn girl Sophie.

'OK,' she says, unable to meet Cleo's eye.

51

Then

Louisa covers the kitchen table with a crisp, white linen cloth, and irons it flat in situ to make it look perfect. She sets two places with cutlery from the canteen she picked out as a wedding present.

Wanting to keep the ceremony quiet and discreet after all the noise around poor Katie's death, she and Sam had decided to treat themselves to gifts. It was, after all, Louisa's first wedding, and she had wanted to have her trousseau: the nice porcelain tableware, the good quality, weighty knives and forks, the complete set of Le Creuset. She lingers over the cutlery as she puts it out and remembers the joy, the sense of completion she had felt upon coming downstairs the morning after their wedding to find the pile of presents by the fireplace, each one beautifully wrapped and labelled, as she had ordered, by the John Lewis gift department.

May all your days be sweet!
To the perfect couple!
The fairy-tale wedding!
Let's hear the patter of tiny feet!

She polishes the Dartington Crystal glasses – *Raise our glasses to the happiest couple ever!* – and lays down one setting for white wine, to go with the scallop starter, and one for red, for the steak main course.

From the moment she woke this morning, she has been working her heart out to make the house as beautiful as it possibly can be, given the disorderly influence of the children. The surface of things, at least, appears clean and ordered, even if the interiors of the cupboards and drawers wouldn't stand up to much scrutiny, full as they are of the crusted, stinking, unwashed garbage accrued over the past couple of hellish weeks.

It has not been easy, with her arm in its cast. But, thanks to a fistful of painkillers and an attitude that comes of not actually caring much if she makes the break worse, she succeeds in getting everything done by using it as a lever, platform and thumper.

The children slowed things down, too, but Louisa allowed Poppy to play mummies with Leon.

'Like with Mary Doll?' she asked, her eyes wide with excitement.

'Like with Mary Doll. But remember he's more delicate than Mary, won't you?'

'I'll be a good mummy.'

'And you can watch CBeebies if you keep him happy.'

Louisa gave Poppy a warm magic bottle. The little girl ran gleefully to feed it to her brother, who was in the baby walker in the living room.

At four o'clock, Louisa sends Sam a most civil text. Its tone is in stark contrast to the stream she has bombarded him with over the last few nights, when he hasn't come home at all. In fact, in the past week, she has seen more of him through Soph's bay window than in the marital home. She performs this daily vigil in her own car now, having come to realise that it is more effective conducted in full sight. For the same reason, she now sends all her messages to his white phone.

Please be home by eight. We need to talk. Please don't be late.

He replies tersely that he will be there, that yes, indeed, they need to talk.

At five, she takes the children up to bed. Thanks to her plaster cast, there has been no question of bathing them for over a week now. This speeds things up, and, sleepy with their juice, they are off with the minimum of bother.

Louisa takes a shower – carefully, so as not to get her bad arm wet – does what she can with her hair, puts on the first make-up she has worn for months, and the smartest dress she can get into these days.

She stands at the top of the stairs and takes a moment. Her children sleep in their own beds. She has the semblance of a clean, clear house downstairs. In the kitchen, a jar of home-made dressing waits to be tossed into a salad – made from proper lettuce, not the bagged sort – two fine, organic fillet steaks rest in oil and seasoning, and a grand, fat, expensive Barolo airs. Her husband is coming home to have supper with her.

If only it were always like this . . .

She could almost imagine herself to have finally got where she wanted: 'there', *arrived*. Couldn't she just turn a blind eye? Carry on like this from now on?

'It's too late for all that,' she says out loud.

She takes herself downstairs and sets candles in the contemporary wedding gift silver candlesticks – *May you two lovebirds burn brightly* – pours herself a large glass of wine, and sits and waits for her errant husband to return.

He arrives just half an hour late, which is far better than she had been expecting.

'What the hell is this?' he says, looking at the beautiful

table, the candlelight, the almost-groomed wife, who, the moment he comes into the kitchen, jumps up, pulls a bottle of champagne out of an ice bucket, and pours it out into two long-stemmed crystal flutes.

'It's our make-up meal,' she says, sidling up to him with the glasses.

'Our what?' he says, taking the drink from her at arm's length.

'I'm telling you it's OK,' she says. 'I forgive you.'

He performs that exaggerated double take men do to signal that they don't know what the hell their wives are talking about.

'Forgive *me*?'

'Not for the abandoning me and shacking up with a whore part,' she says, smiling and reaching out to chink her glass with his. 'Cheers, by the way.'

'Louisa . . .' His voice is dulled with weariness.

'No, not all that. It's to say I forgive you for breaking my arm and causing me to want to end my life.'

His mouth falls open. 'I never touched you, Louisa.'

She laughs, short and sharp. 'Oh, you've not touched me since I was pregnant with your second child.'

'I didn't break your arm,' he says, for clarification. His voice is low, serious.

'Didn't you? The doctors think otherwise, I think.' She turns away and moves towards the extra, 'entertaining' hob where eight glistening scallops sit on a kitchen towel, orange corals like fat, soft slugs. She clicks on the gas underneath a small frying pan and, with her bare hand, throws in a knob of butter.

'You're quite mad, Louisa.'

She turns to face him. 'You think so? What is madness, anyway? A sane reaction to an insane world? A line of defence? What are the signs, I wonder, of genuine madness?'

'Perhaps this.' He gestures at her. 'Or this.' Reaching into his leather rucksack, he pulls out the box she sent to Sophie's flat. Handling it with enormous care, as if it contained some sort of deadly virus, he slides off the lid to reveal the test tube full of blood, nestling in its bed of brambles.

'I take it this is from you. What the hell is it?'

She smiles. 'Only women bleed, Sam. That comes from deep inside me. I wanted your little fling to know what she's doing to me. I thought perhaps she might prick herself and join me when she reached in for it. Blood sisters.'

Sam snorts in disbelief.

'Well why not? You've dipped into both of us.'

'Don't be disgusting.'

'Disgusting? Me?' Louisa grasps her breasts and pushes them up and towards him with the palms of her hands in another crude imitation of Sophie in the phone pictures. 'I've seen what she does for you. She's come in and stolen you away from us, broken up our family. Remember how it was when we arrived here? We could have been so happy, Sam.'

She moves towards him, puts her good arm around his neck and says, in her breathiest voice: 'I could give you one more chance if you begged me, you know.'

He stands, rigid as a gatepost, trying to keep his body away from hers. But he can't stop her: she moves in, pushes her pelvis into his, grinds herself into him.

'Is this what she does to you, Sam? Or do you prefer something a bit more extreme, a bit of pain mixed in with your pleasure?'

She reaches down and grasps his unresponsive groin, twisting her hand until he is forced to react, to rip her fingers from him and push her away. She exaggerates the momentum of his shove and flies across the room, slamming herself against the wall. She knocks her head back, whacking it, denting the plaster.

'Ow, oh Sam,' she says, laughing and rubbing her head.

'And after I've made such an effort, been so accommodating.'

She lurches forward and makes another move on him, reaching up for his face, to bring it to hers, but he pushes her away, this time keeping hold of her so that she can't perform the same trick.

He grips her good wrist and puts a restraining arm on her other shoulder. 'Louisa, I've had enough of all this.'

'*You*'ve had enough. What about me? Haven't *I* had enough of all this? You promised me everything, and have delivered precisely nothing. You won't even let me, your own wife, kiss you or touch you. It's as if I make you sick.'

He looks levelly at her.

'I make you sick, don't I?' she says.

He lets her go and dashes to the stove, where the smoking pan full of overheated butter has just turned to flame. He carries it at arm's length to the sink, where he runs the cold tap on it. Fat and fire spit over him as it explodes at the touch of the water. He yelps and jumps away, rubbing the spots of heat from his eye.

The flames subside and Louisa shakes her head. 'That's not how you deal with a pan on fire. You think you know everything but, in fact, you know very, very little indeed, Sam.'

'Louisa,' he says.

'What?' She bustles past him to retrieve the pan, which she sets about wiping with a wad of kitchen towel. 'I'll have to start the scallops dish all over again.'

'Louisa,' he says, pulling the pan from her hand. 'Sit down over there.' He gestures to the armchair where she would have sat breastfeeding her babies, had it all turned out differently for her.

'Why should I?' she says, her hands on her hips. 'I've got to cook the starter.'

'I'm not hungry.'

'You just don't want to eat any food touched by me.'

'Louisa, just sit the fuck down.'

She flings her hands in the air, shakes her head and moves towards the armchair. 'Better do what you say, if that's your attitude. We all know how you can get sometimes, don't we?'

When she's finally sitting, he pulls over a dining chair and places himself in it, facing her.

'Nice,' she says, looking up at him. 'He puts himself above me. Very equal.'

'Louisa, I'm worried about you.'

'Not *this* again.' She purses her lips and raises her eyebrows.

'I know you're very clever and you've convinced the shrinks that you're OK, and all that, but this sort of thing' – he gestures to the box with the blood and glass – 'is unacceptable. Beyond the pale. Sophie's worried—'

'Oh no! Poor Sophie! Worried?'

'Worried that you're going to try to hurt her.'

'Hah!'

'You need a rest, Louisa. You need a break.'

'Yes, and that'll be easy while I'm looking after your children all the time you're off gallivanting with your fuck buddy.'

'I mean a break from everything. I'm worried about you and, more particularly, I'm worried about Poppy and Leon.'

'Oh, you are, are you? I thought you'd forgotten all about them.'

'I don't think you should be looking after them right now.'

She makes as if to get up, but he's there before she can fully stand, pushing her back into the chair.

'Louisa, I don't want you to get into trouble or anything. I don't want to make a big fuss about this.'

'You mean, you don't want anyone to think things are anything but perfect for you, Mr Thrusting Businessman.'

'I want you to move into the flat.'

'The flat?'

'The flat in Cambridge. Brookside Lane.'

'The flat with your bitch in it?'

'I know you know which flat. Don't think we haven't seen you sitting in the car outside.'

'Now you tell me!'

'I bought it a while back. I was waiting for you to get better until – until I told you about it. But I've been waiting and waiting, and everything just seems to be getting worse and worse.'

'Oh, I'm so sorry about that.'

He holds up his hand. 'Louisa, you'll be moving into the flat.'

Louisa's face starts to twitch. Her mouth, it seems, is completely beyond her control. 'Is it big enough for me and the children?'

'No. Just you, Louisa. Like I say, you need a break.'

'I'd like to see that work. How are you going to look after them while running The Best Company in the World, Inc.?' Her hand flies to her brow as she realises. 'Oh my God. You're moving your little bitch out of the flat and into here to take my place, aren't you?'

He squats so that his face is level with hers. 'I've found this very good guy. He'll help you with whatever it is that's wrong with you, Louisa. I can't just stand by and watch you fall apart like this. You'll be seeing him three times a week, and he's just round the corner from the flat. And I've signed you up to this top-notch spa, too, so you can relax and swim, and sauna, and there's a gym, too.'

'I don't swim, I don't sauna. You think I need to go to a gym, is that it? Is it because I'm too fat?'

'You're not well, Louisa.'

'It's her that's too skinny. All skin and bone. All hipbones and butterfly tattoos.' She narrows her eyes at him. 'You're not going to take my children away.'

He shakes his head. 'When you're better, you can see them.'

'You can't do this.'

'I'm afraid I can.' He puts his thumb and forefinger together. 'You were this far away from being sectioned when you broke your arm.'

'You broke my arm.'

'*You* broke your arm.'

Louisa shrugs and cradles her cast. The pain reminds her that all this is real.

'Now, you could do this quietly, or you could choose to make a fuss and you'll end up in a psychiatric hospital, instead of your own little flat with your own life, a nice allowance and proper, private and discreet care.'

'Money no object.'

'Money no object. All I want is to see you better.'

She juts her chin towards him. 'And then you'll have me back as your wife again? When I'm all cured?'

He shakes his head. 'I'm afraid that's not going to happen. Sophie and I—'

Louisa gasps so harshly that she hurts her throat. '"Sophie and I"?, "Sophie and I" what? You're in *love*? Is that it?'

Sam looks at her. Not a muscle of him shifts.

'What are you?' she goes on. 'The fucking king and queen of everything?' She stands and pushes him away from her. 'You think you can just do what you like with me, put me in a cupboard, lock me away? Well, you can damn well think again. Watch this.'

She strides over to one of the big wall cupboards she has stuffed with the day's detritus. As she opens it, everything tumbles out on top of her: rolled-up dirty nappies, unwashed bowls, plates, milk bottles, toys, a saucepan with baked beans crusted to it, mouldy damp washing that she didn't have the time to hang out. She bats it all away as if she is swimming through it, and then turns triumphantly to him. 'See, nothing stays where you put it. It all comes falling out, Sam. Be careful. You shall reap what you sow.' She turns back to her cupboards, hauling out the contents, throwing them around the kitchen.

He picks himself up. 'What are you saying to me?'

'Just get out, Sam. Get out of my house.' She launches herself at him and thumps her cast at his chest. 'Get out; go back to your little whore. Is she still a little lying doped-up jailbird, Sam, or have you put her on the straight and narrow, now?'

'People change, Louisa.'

'No they don't, Sam. They stay the same old bastards they ever were. Look no further than your own rotten self for that. I suppose I should count myself lucky you haven't tried to murder me as well.'

'What the hell do you mean by that?' he says, for the first time really raising his voice.

'YOU KNOW WHAT I MEAN,' she yells, the words scorching her throat.

He swipes at the air with his hands. 'I didn't touch Katie.'

'I lied for you.'

'I was alone. I needed an alibi.'

'I fucking lied for you.' She backs around the room, putting the kitchen table between them. 'Leave me, Sam. Fuck off and leave me and my children alone.'

He looks at her.

'Fuck off, Sam. Or shall I call the police on you?'

'They won't believe you.'

'My word against yours and that jailbird's? Get out of my house.'

He looks at her. 'My house.'

She picks up the knife she had set out to carve the meat with and waves it in his direction. 'GO!'

'I'll take the children with me.'

'No you won't. They're asleep. You will not disturb them.'

'I don't feel safe leaving them with you when you're like this.'

'You think I'd be such a cow as to take it out on Poppy and Leon? Is your opinion of me really so low?' From behind the table, she jabs the knife at him. 'Now GO! Get out of here.'

He holds his hands up in the air and backs towards the door. Before he leaves the kitchen, he stops and looks at her.

'I mean what I said. I'll be back tomorrow and we'll talk about it some more.'

'There's nothing to discuss,' she says.

He shakes his head, turns on his heel and exits the room, slamming the front door as he leaves the house, making the Scandi windows rattle.

She lets go of the knife and it clatters to the ground, narrowly missing her bare foot.

So now she knows for sure there is no going back. And he is going to have to pay the full, no-discount price for the cruelty and suffering he has meted out to her.

Too bad she won't be around to watch him suffer. But, hey, that's the name of the game.

The first step is to go to the study, to pull an edge of his bloodied shirt from the back of the cupboard, just enough for it to be easily found, but not so much that he will ever notice it on his own.

And he will be *very much* on his own.

52

Now

Lou sits on the Tube, folded in on herself. It is only mid-morning, so the carriage is emptier than she has ever seen it. Despite the lack of fellow passengers, it's still as hot in here as the Fen Manor Aga proving drawer that she never got around to using. The open windows at each end of the carriage only serve to fan-assist the cooking effect.

The only other person with her, an unwashed man in too many dirty clothes for the season, sits at the far end of the compartment, goggling at her out of the corners of his eyes and jiggling his hand inside his coat. Such is her mood that this doesn't scare her at all. In fact, she almost pities her masturbating fellow traveller, because he has no idea that, if he gets one centimetre closer to her, she will not be responsible for the consequences – part of her would enjoy the chance to explode. But he keeps his distance up the far end. It's as if she has some sort of force field around her. Earlier, hurrying down towards Oxford Circus, she noticed passers-by shrinking back and parting on the pavement. The way they were reacting, she could have been wielding a pump-action machine gun.

Her head throbs. It's like she has an atonal, experimental electronic score playing in her brain, all discordant crashes and stomach-turning screeches. Seeing Sophie has brought every-thing back: the pain of rejection, the loss of the will to live, the hell Sam put her through. All the broken promises, the shattered dreams, the awful bloody mess.

She was a fool to think she could escape all that.

And now she's probably going to lose her job. Her one chance to shine.

The man's hand is moving up and down furiously now. He shifts in his seat. He's at the edge of her vision, like a wasp caught under a glass. She's had enough.

Her eyes narrowed, she stands and makes her uneven way along the carriage towards him.

In the lift up to the ground level, she works hand sanitiser into her fingers, then scrabbles in her bag for her water bottle. The heat, the dust, the effort of teaching a lesson that will never be forgotten, have made her inordinately thirsty.

'What?' she snaps at the schoolgirl who is staring at her, all big white eyes in an unabashedly curious face. '*What?*'

The girl looks away.

Lou pulls the water bottle out of her bag. Caught up with it is the small plastic Boots bag containing the pregnancy test.

She had forgotten about this. She had forgotten about Adam, about what he means.

A small but not insignificant flutter of hope lights up a corner of her blackly jangling brain. She thinks of her new home, with its sky garden and hot tub and panoramic views, set way above everyone else, where she and Adam will raise their beautiful babies and he will do all the staying at home and looking after them and she will go out and go to work and be important out in the world as well as within her family.

Work. If she keeps her job.

Damn Sophie. *Damn her.*

* * *

Up on ground level, the pavement outside the Tube station is unusually quiet – it's as if the entire population of London has cleared itself out of her way. She turns the corner and passes a group of women with plastic containers, silently queuing at a water standpipe. Set as they are against a dusty backdrop of a demolished waste ground, they could be in some third-world, war-ravaged country. Or extras in a post-apocalyptic movie.

She could join them in that. Survivor of a monumental disaster. She could certainly act that part, no rehearsal needed.

As she passes by, the women shrink back like sunflowers closing under a passing cloud.

Up on her landing, she stabs her finger at the entry pad and shoves open the door to her corridor, where she is stopped in her tracks by Adam, who is moving backwards towards her, carrying something, helped at the other end by Carly.

'What's going on?' Lou says as he collides with her.

'Lou?' He turns to face her with, she thinks, a heavy dose of guilt hanging in his eyes.

'Hi, Lou!' Carly says, just a touch too brightly.

'Why are you home?' Adam says.

'Why do you ask?' Lou's tone is dangerous.

They put down what they have been carrying between them, and Lou gasps as she sees what it is.

Poppy's bed.

She slams her bag down on the ground and plants her hands on her hips.

'What the hell are you doing, Adam?' She points at Carly. 'And what's *she* doing in my apartment?'

'I can explain,' Carly says.

'I think you'd better go,' Lou says. If her voice were the actual temperature of her tone, the windows in the lift lobby behind her would ice over.

Adam holds up his hands. 'Lou. It's all cool. We thought we'd give you a surprise when you got home. We've been clearing the children's room.'

'What? Throwing Poppy's and Leon's stuff out?'

Adam tries to put his hand on her shoulder, but she shrugs him off. 'No, of course not. I'd never do that. I explained the situation to Umoh and he's let us have a storage space in the basement.'

Lou is having some difficulty breathing. 'So let me get this right,' she says. 'Not only have you moved all my children's things out of their room without consulting me, but you've also told Umoh all about my personal life, and no doubt Carly here, too.'

'I'll go,' Carly says.

'Yes, I think you better had,' Lou tells her.

'Can I have the key, Ad? I'll just get my bag.'

Ad. Lou bristles at the abbreviation.

Adam fishes in his pocket and hands Carly his bunch of keys.

'No. I'll get it.' Lou snatches the keys from him and charges along the corridor. She lets herself in and shuts the door behind her so that Adam can't follow her.

First she checks her bedroom.

It is untouched since the morning – the bed made, unrumpled, not even sat upon. In the living room, two mugs stand on the table, both still warm, each with a mint teabag sitting soggily in its dregs. The sofa is as Adam must have left it this morning, cushions plumped and arranged, throws folded neatly over the back. No one has even sat on it.

A canvas satchel slouches on the floor by one of the dining chairs. There's no doubt who it belongs to, because it has CARLY written on it in biro, like a schoolgirl's bag. Lou rifles through it and pulls out a notebook, which she flicks through to find girlish doodles of faces and hearts, notes taken during interviews with past residents of the demolition site, and shopping lists: 'quinoa, hummus, coconut water'. This girl couldn't be more of a stereotype if she tried. Lou also discovers a bag of rolling tobacco, a purse with a couple of coins in it – no cards – a bunch of keys, a clean Moon Cup lurking ominously in a plastic box, and nothing else. Not even a shred of incriminating evidence.

'Calm down, Lou,' she tells herself, speaking out against the backdrop of the clang and thump of the demolition work, which has recommenced at a tilt, no doubt to make up lost time since all that plague-pit nonsense.

She takes a couple of deep breaths, slings Carly's bag over her shoulder and goes to check on the other rooms. The bathroom is pristine, smelling of the essential oil-based cleaners Adam uses daily. She stands at the threshold of his studio and looks around. The only evident activity is the endless editing he spends all day at, chipping away at his magnum opus. This is the one corner of the apartment he doesn't keep well. It's all old coffee cups, piles of papers and Post-its scrawled with notes to himself. She glances at the ten or so he has stuck around his monitor and they are all about timings and possible backing music ideas. On the floor are stacks of the books she saw in his bedroom in the squat and boxes full of old and new tech equipment. A small digital piano rests on a stand, and his old sheepskin slippers lie discarded on the floor by the chair.

And that's what brings her to a standstill. The slippers. They are big, overlarge even for his size twelves, and so worn that they retain the shape of his absent feet. Despite everything she has gone through during the day, the sight of them fills her heart and quashes her agitation. Surely, the man who wears these slippers can't be anything other than faithful, honest and true?

Not all men are like Sam, she tells herself. Adam is different. He would never, ever cheat on her. Look at all he does.

She backs out of the room.

But then she thinks of him, standing hangdog, out by the lifts, with Poppy's bed. How heartless is that, clearing out her children's stuff without so much as a by your leave?

It'll take more than a pair of slippers to put out the fire of her rage.

She storms along the hallway to the children's room. And then she sees them: the Bags for Life that she started packing last week, standing just inside, now full, stacked, ready to go, on the emptied, stripped furniture.

She leans back against the bedroom wall.

I wish all this stuff would magically disappear. That's what she had said.

He was doing it for her. He was magicking it away.

She had all but asked him to do it.

If she had arrived home when he was expecting her, he would have finished the job and he could have explained it all to her sensibly.

Bad timing.

All Sophie's fault again.

She screams, silently, into the half-emptied room.

Adam and Carly are out in the lift lobby, sitting on the bed, talking to each other in whispers, like schoolchildren in trouble outside the headmistress's office.

When he sees Lou, Adam stands, and Carly follows suit.

Lou tries to appear calm, reasonable, dignified, as she holds the canvas satchel out to Carly, who takes it at arm's length. 'Bye, Carly. Thanks for your help.'

'See you, then,' Carly says, keeping Lou at a distance. She summons the lift, which, unusually, and no doubt to her great relief, arrives almost instantly, zipping its doors behind her and whisking her away.

Lou and Adam look at each other.

'I'm sorry,' she says, holding her hands out towards him.

He goes quickly over to her. 'What is it?'

'You were just trying to help me, weren't you?'

Adam nods.

'And I took it all the wrong way.'

'It can't have looked all that good. You were only meant to see the finished part. Carly would have been long gone.'

'I had to come home because I've got this horrible migraine. I've just had a pig of a day, and – you know, well, I have trust issues.'

'Look,' Adam says, 'I'm not that Sam. He's gone. You can trust me. I will always look out for you, whatever happens.'

She steps back and searches his clear, brown flecked eyes. 'Whatever?'

'I love you, Lou. Whatever happens,' he repeats.

53

'You sure you're OK?' Adam asks Lou. 'I'll be ten minutes, tops.'

She nods, and he leaves her in the apartment while he goes to meet Umoh, who is waiting in the lift lobby to help him down with Poppy's bed.

With him gone, she finally takes herself to the bathroom with her little plastic Boots bag.

The blue line appears instantly, before she has even finished peeing.

Her bones knew it, of course, but even so, this confirmation comes as a shock.

Unprotected sex, daily, for a whole month. What did she think was going to happen? That first time, he had asked her if she had it sorted, and she had said yes. She had lied.

Well, what about it? She needs to replace her babies.

She sits on the toilet and hunches over the wand as if it can provide any more wisdom.

'Will he like it or not?' she asks it.

The wand has nothing to say on that point.

He's in tears. On his knees, his arms around her, his cheek pressed up against her belly.

'Our beautiful baby,' he says, kissing her navel. 'Our own little person.'

He likes it, then.

'It's a fresh start for you,' he says, as he pours boiling water onto fresh mint leaves. 'I'm not being callous,' he adds quickly, turning to her, kettle in hand. 'Our baby won't replace Poppy and Leon, but he or she will be a new person, someone for us to share our love with.'

He brings her tea to where he has told her she must rest, feet up, pillows behind her head, on the sofa. 'No caffeine for you from now on.' He hands the mug to her and sits by her side, watching her drink it as if she were God's most marvellous creation. It would make her laugh if it weren't so beguiling.

'You've been let down so badly in the past,' he says, taking her hand in his.

She nods and sips the tea.

'I'm going to stand by you all the way. I'm going to be a better partner to you and father to our baby than anyone else in the world could ever be. I'll always be there for us. I'll never let you down.'

'Come what may?' she says, smiling at him.

'Come what may. Wild horses, hell and high water, the end of days. I'll be here for you, whatever happens.'

'I don't think it'll come to that,' she says, trying not to think of Sophie, of her threats, of her closeness. Of horses. Of what her mother would say if she knew.

But he's right. This is the perfect new start, and with Adam at home looking after the baby she will be able to excel, both at work and as a mother. She'll do it brilliantly this time, though. She'll have more children, rise through the ranks at A.R.K., perhaps take over from Cleo when she retires, and everyone will look at her and wonder how on earth she does it.

If only Sophie would go away, vanish, disappear.

She's that one thorn in her side, pricking the past into her, a constant reminder. At least Lou will soon have a child again. So, whatever happens, she'll be even with Sophie in that way. She'll be able to show her that she really is rebounding. And the more she does that, the less of a threat her old enemy will be.

'My dad left my mum when she found out she was pregnant,' Adam's saying, twisting her fingers around in his. 'He just got up and buggered off. We never saw him again. But she's like you: a strong woman, a survivor. She carried on teaching and brought me up on her own, and I never, ever felt that I lacked a father. But I saw what a struggle it was for her.'

'I want to keep on working,' Lou says, quickly.

'Of course,' Adam says. 'I'll be the one to stay at home.'

Lou nods. 'Good. Yes. And soon the site will be built over and you'll have a lot less to do.'

He frowns. 'But I'll still make films; still keep the spirit of the estate alive. They've just started clearing out another place, a mile down the road from here, six hundred and forty flats, all being emptied, another community ripped apart. The social cleansing marches on apace.'

'But what about our baby?' she says. 'It's a big commitment, Adam, to bring up a child properly, feed it properly, stimulate its mind, its creativity. You're going to have to think really hard about how much else you take on. Believe me, I know from experience. I mean, if you're not willing to give yourself one hundred per cent to this, it's going to be very difficult.'

He lies down next to her on the sofa, and strokes her cheek. 'Of course,' he says. 'Of course, Lou. Don't worry. You and the baby are the centre of my world. Everything else is just details. Hey,' he says. 'We could move to the country: cleaner air, space, green . . .'

'I'm never going to live in the country again,' Lou says. 'Not after last time. It's not good for families to be so isolated, believe me.'

'Of course,' Adam says. 'Just a thought.'

'But perhaps we could get a bigger place,' she says, gesturing at the sky through the window. 'Higher up, fresher air.'

'Dream on,' he says. 'Three million pounds. And, really, that would be like sleeping with the enemy, wouldn't it?'

Lou has not yet told him how much money she has, and doesn't know whether she ever will. She doesn't want to have even the slightest worry that he might be gold digging around her. There's more cash than ever now, too, with the sale of Fen Manor finally having gone through – at a little below the asking price, but not too worryingly. There's also the money from the impending sale of the Cambridge flat, which has improved vastly in value since Sam bought it. That's one thing she can say for him: he had an eye for making a buck or two.

And it's thanks to this ability in her otherwise utterly dissatisfactory dead husband that, when the time comes to pay the balance on the penthouse, she will do it in cash and still have enough left over to live very comfortably for the rest of her days. She clearly has some work to do before she tells Adam about her plans, although the baby will help win him round, she's sure.

'I can't wait to tell my mum,' Adam says, his words intruding into her thoughts. 'She'll be so excited.'

Lou looks sharply up at him.

'What?' he asks her.

'I'd just rather we didn't tell anyone yet. Not until the first scan. Not until we know everything's going to be all right.'

The last thing she wants is Adam's mother, who she imagines will turn out to be an overbearing, overprotective, sensibly-shod busybody, putting her oar in and meddling about with her life. No. This is going to be pure. Just her, Adam and their child. No grandparents involved at all. Perfect. 'It's just that I don't want anything to go wrong.'

'Of course,' Adam says. 'You're the boss. We'll say nothing until you're ready.'

Which will be never, she thinks, as she allows her body to relent and relax against him. He strokes her hair and hums, the soft tune reverberating through his chest. Gradually, she gives in to the fatigue poking around the edges of her after her stressful, eventful day. She drifts into a half-sleep, where she sees herself and Adam with armfuls of smiling babies, who tumble chubbily like putti out of Tintoretto clouds. She's in the middle, a sort of Venus, Adam's at her feet like an archangel. There's a lot of gold, showering down in streamers from the heavens . . .

A massive electric jolt wrenches Lou back into the waking world as a screeching guitar riff pierces her dreams, followed by a high-pitched male scream, soon joined by thumping drums and a bass line that rumbles the ceiling above them.

'Jesus, man,' Adam says, closing his arms around her as if he is afraid the shock might trigger a miscarriage. 'This can't go on.' He kisses the top of her head, slides off the sofa and picks his keys up from the table.

'Where are you going?' she asks him, having to raise her voice to be heard above the onslaught of the music.

'I'm going to get Umoh to put me on the biometrics for upstairs, then I'm going to have a word with our friend. This is seriously not on. Not now, particularly.'

And, like a man, he strides from the room.

Lou hauls herself up, moves to the window and looks down. Her tower is starting to rise. It has a handsome footprint, and her apartment will take up the whole top floor. This is something to look forward to.

But until then, this heat, this noise, is what she has to put up with.

She glances over to the left, to East Block. That Dark Man is there again. He's staring up at her as usual, but under his suit, his white shirt has a big red stain across it, as if he has been shot, or has just stood up from stabbing someone at very close quarters. She gasps and blinks, and when she opens her eyes, he is no longer there.

The front door slams in the hallway. Adam is back. But the music continues, thumping, pounding, making her sinuses reverberate in her skull.

Is he just too nice to be effective? Still, it's better than being a bastard like Sam turned out to be.

Lou continues to look out of the window. She imagines how the sight of the carrier of his child standing outlined in front of the blazing blue sky – a woman who has overcome all sorts of physical and emotional adversity – will uplift him after his failure. He will come to her, put his arms around her and apologise for not succeeding, and she will graciously accept and they will go on to have a beautiful evening, and they won't let Steroid Boy, Sophie or anyone else upset them. After all, the knowledge that soon they will be living on high, with no upstairs neighbours to bother them, makes it far easier for her to block out the sound.

But Adam doesn't come to her. Instead, he keeps his distance. When she hears him sniff, she turns to face him.

His right eye is closed, puffed like a shiny red apple. The lower half of his face is awash with blood streaming from his nose, and he is cradling his right hand in his left, his fingers curled and useless.

'What happened?' she gasps.

The worst part, the thing Lou can't bear to watch, is that he's crying.

'I hit the bastard,' he says, at last. 'He punched me in the eye and the nose, and I lost it and whacked him round the jaw.'

'Wow,' Lou says, not quite sure of what to make of this mood, which is not like anything she has seen on him before.

He looks at her, horror in his one open eye. 'I've never hit anyone before. I don't do that sort of thing.'

'Oh love,' she says, going to him, putting her hands on his poor, beaten-up face. Somehow, the injuries highlight his beauty. 'It's not you. It's him, Steroid Boy. Really. It's him that made you do it. You had no choice.'

'And he's still playing his shit music,' Adam says, jutting his chin to the ceiling.

Lou leads him to the sofa and makes him sit down. She fetches ice from the freezer, puts it in a plastic bag, and wraps it in a tea towel for him to hold over his eye. She pours water from one of the plastic containers into a saucepan and, while it's warming, she grabs a clean flannel and some soap from the bathroom. Tenderly, she washes his face and hand, and binds his knuckles to keep them from swelling any more.

'Take these,' she says, offering him some Ibuprofen.

'I don't take painkillers,' he says. 'Big Pharma.'

'Just take them, Adam,' she says.

And he does. Like a good boy.

Like her good boy.

The music thunders on from upstairs and Lou counts her blessings which, right now, if she piled them up, would outnumber the one pesky problem of Sophie by a good thirty-seven storeys.

Yeah, Sophie can go hang.

Lou has a man who will take a punch for her.

54

Her mouth slightly open, Sami falls away from Sophie's breast, a tiny trickle of sweet-scented milk spilling across her chin. Sophie kisses her finger and wipes it away.

'Don't worry, my little girl. I haven't given up on us yet,' she tells her as she lays her gently down in her basket. 'Not you, not your daddy, not even myself.'

But she has no idea what her next step is going to be. Yesterday has flummoxed her. She had imagined that, by turning up in person, she might be able to get somewhere with Louisa. But no. Louisa is unmovable, stuffed full to bursting with poison.

Sophie can't believe how she lost it herself. She had used every ounce of willpower in her body to avoid opening Snake's wrap again, but even so, meeting Louisa had switched on her coke persona – turned her into someone her sober self doesn't want to recognise.

Is it hopeless? Without DNA she can't do anything for Sami. She knows from her Internet research that, even if she did manage somehow to get hold of some, half-sibling tests aren't at all accurate and can easily be challenged in court, so she'd have to face the law again. And Louisa threatened setting the police on her. She can't risk being sent back inside while she has Sami to look out for.

So it seems that all she can do for her daughter is prove her father's innocence. But all Sophie has is her own conviction on this.

She lays Sami down in her cot, then pulls one of the five remaining LOUISA TELLS ALL newspaper pages from her washing line and burns it in front of Sam's altar, using her bare feet to stamp the embers into the carpet and add another scorch mark. For good measure she repeats the process three more times. She needs all the power she can muster.

She lets each front page drop flaming to the ground, pounding her smarting foot on them, grinding them into the cream wool.

When she is done, only one sheet remains. For a future emergency, should she need it.

But still she feels empty. For the first time, the process hasn't worked. In the same way that phoning Louisa lost its charm, burning her printed features has also now ceased to bring Sophie any satisfaction – beyond spoiling Louisa's carpet, of course.

She sits cross-legged at the altar, in front of the photograph of herself and Sam, her hands knotted in prayer.

'Help me, Sam. Help me,' she says, her eyes closed tight, waiting for a sign.

Nothing happens. He doesn't speak to her.

The little wrap of cocaine, hidden in the handbag in the hallway, calls to her. But she fights it. She needs to keep a clear head, stay calm, work something out.

She casts her eyes around her bedroom.

Today is the day she has to start packing. She has done the research. If she doesn't move her stuff out by her eviction date, the bailiffs will simply tip everything out onto the street. She has a vision of herself and Sami – widow and child – standing by a small stack of paltry possessions like something out of Dickens. It's shot in black and white. She's in something long and black and silk, by Comme des Garçons, perhaps.

'Snap out of it, Soph,' she says.

There's so much to pack. When she arrived here, apart from her designer samples, she brought just one rucksack of belongings. Now she has boxes and boxes of clothes, toys and equipment she has picked up, found, bought for Sami.

Where will it all go? And, more importantly, where will she and Sami go?

She'll have to go and sign on, talk to the council, do all that cap-in-hand bollocks.

No. She straightens herself and sniffs. She's not going to go asking for help when she is owed so much by Louisa.

The anger fizzes again in her brain.

What the hell. It might be better to get busy, keep herself sane.

The possession order Louisa's lawyers sent her contained an inventory of the contents of the flat, taken some time before she changed the locks. When they took the photographs, perhaps. What she suspects, though, is that they did it far earlier, when Sami was in the Special Care Baby Unit.

The heartless bastards.

They reckon every bit of furniture, art and equipment was Sam's, and is therefore now Louisa's. Sophie could argue that he gave her all these things, which he did, but it would just be another massive battle for her to lose, and where would she keep it all, anyway?

She fetches a handful of carrier bags from where she stores them, stuffed under the kitchen sink, and starts to clear her bedroom. The best plan, she reckons, is to see how much tat she has, and then find somewhere to store it. Perhaps Snake can help her. No doubt he's got contacts with lock-ups.

She packs away all but her most essential jewellery and

scarves, stirring up dust, revealing some of the mirror from which they hang.

'Jesus Christ,' she says, eyeing her own reflection.

She decides to leave Sam's shrine until the very end, so that it will be the first thing out when she arrives wherever she ends up. So it's time to tackle under the bed. Her knees complaining from yesterday's Sami-saving manoeuvres on the floor with Louisa, she kneels, lifts up the satin bedspread and surveys the thirty or so shoeboxes that remain, stashed underneath. Along with the five or six dresses still hanging in the wardrobe and a couple of handbags – including the coke-containing Mulberry number – these represent her only significant remaining capital. There is also the diamond necklace and ring from Sam, but she would rather starve than get rid of them.

As she pulls each dust-blanketed box out, she takes a peep inside. But the gorgeousness of the contents brings her no happiness. A pair of ostensibly beautiful Valentino sandals, all points of spiky nothingness, only evoke the metallic, money taste of cocaine dribbling down the back of her throat as The Photographer held the heels like guns while ramming himself into her arse. A shiny pair of platform courts were last worn by her hooked, as ordered, around his shoulders while at the other end her eyes rolled backwards into her lolling head.

Stretching so that her shoulder twangs at the point of a freeze, she reaches towards the back of the bed, under the headboard, to pull out the final box. As she tugs it free from the bed frame, something on top of it falls off with a clunk. Moving the box to one side, she sees, with a rush of blood to her head, what it is.

A white iPhone.

Sophie gasps so loudly that Sami stirs, puts her hands up in the air and, in her sleep, makes her own small exhalation as if in imitation.

Sam's white iPhone.

The phone they were using to photograph themselves when Louisa called him on her landline. She had assumed he'd taken it with him when he left that night, but it must have dropped down the back of the bed. Her heart thumping against her bony ribcage, she holds it as if it is the sword pulled from the stone.

She moves on her sore knees to Sam's shrine, and holds the phone out in front of her, hands flat as if awaiting the sacrament. 'See, look,' she says. 'You did speak to me, Sam. Thank you, my love. Thank you.' If nothing else, she now has the photographs of their last time together.

The phone is, of course, dead. The battery must have run out over a year ago. She pulls over her charger cable, which is plugged in by her bed.

'By Louisa's bed,' she corrects herself. Everything here belongs to Louisa, except herself, Sami, the baby stuff, the clothes, shoes, ring and necklace. And now, this phone!

This phone is all Sophie's.

For half an hour, nothing happens. Sophie sits, staring at the blank screen, willing it not to be completely dead. When finally it springs back to life, Sami is awake, in her arms, having unwittingly joined her mother's anxious vigil at the screen.

Sophie goes straight to the photos.

There they are, she and Sam, on his last night alive. He is so present here in these pictures, so full of life. For a second, Sophie forgets all that has happened. Sami – who she balances in her lap, but shields from the graphic imagery – reaches up and touches the tears on her mother's cheek. Sophie thought she had got beyond the point of denying Sam's death, but here she is again, unable to take the full, awful fact on board. She zooms in on his face and lets Sami see.

'There's your daddy, Sami,' she says softly. 'With your

mummy, but I can't show you that because you're far too little. We're making you, you know.'

She sits for over an hour, crying over her child, looking at every detail of every photo: the gestures that made Sam who he was, the curve of his neck, the look in his eyes that told her she was the only one. Then she remembers that night, and Louisa's intrusions: how she wouldn't let them be, how she kept getting in their way.

With a spike of anger, she remembers how relentlessly Louisa tried to contact Sam, how he had to put the phone into airplane mode to silence her. It was one of his last actions, and the result is still here, in her hands. She is reluctant to change any settings. She wants to keep it as it was when he last touched it. But curiosity gets the better of her: she switches it on to full reception.

At first nothing happens, but then a whole string of text messages pours in. The secret, Pay As You Go account he opened so that they could communicate with each other is, it seems, still active. The first – the most recent – is the message Sophie sent him after his cremation, which she was barred from attending.

I love you and will never, ever forget you, ever in my heart.

The following thirty or so texts are those she sent over those awful three days after he'd gone. He was dead, but she didn't know it, not until she saw his and Louisa's and the blurred-out children's faces splashed over the local paper, with all the vile insinuations about what the police thought he had got up to. All that while she had assumed he had given in, that Louisa had won, had used her sick threats to trap him.

'I'm so, so sorry,' she says. 'I thought you'd abandoned me.'

Sami looks up at her mother and pulls one of those faces that could be either a smile or passing wind. Sophie holds out her finger and the baby curls her little hand tight around it.

But then she sees what comes further down, before her own shameful tirade.

The texts Louisa sent that night, which she and Sam never saw. The words she must have said to Sam when, finally, she got through to him on Sophie's landline, the words that made him blanch and throw on his clothes and run from the flat.

And once Sophie starts reading them, she just can't stop.

55

Adam

The next morning, there is a certain proud spring in Adam's step as he returns to the flat after walking Lou to the Tube station. It's earlier than usual – she said she had to be in at eight to get on with something or other – so he has plenty of time to carry out his plan.

But first, housework. Before he gets busy with the broom, he puts the vintage G-Plan chairs she bought in an online auction on top of their matching table. They go with the apartment, she says, but they're not really his thing – he likes a scruffier, mismatched, less perfect vibe. Still, she knows what she's talking about when it comes to design, does Lou.

As he sweeps the floor, he winces at the pain in his hand. It's bandaged up, but his worry is that some bone inside might be broken. He should probably take it to the hospital, but he doesn't want to make a fuss, not with Lou now being pregnant with his child.

His child.

He stops, leans on his broom, and looks out of the window, his eyes soaking up the endless, vapour-trailed blue of the sky.

This baby is more than he bargained for, yet it seems like incredible bounty. Lou's situation with what happened to her kids is heartbreaking, and he can understand why she is sometimes edgy and a little possessive of their relationship. She has, after all, lost everything. It must be hard for her to believe that this, her new life, isn't going to just vanish as well. His job is to convince her that he's here for the duration. He – and the baby – can fix her, make her whole again.

The start of it, for him, was finishing emptying the children's bedroom for her. The next step is what he has in mind for today.

He brushes up his sweepings into the dustpan and mops down the floor, then he sets out on his search. Somewhere in this apartment, Lou must have some sort of information on her parents that will help him find them. He has this theory that the only way she can start to move on from the damage they have done to her is if he helps her break the wall of silence they have built up against her. They need to know her awful history, the terrible times she has gone through, and she needs to be able to tell them that she is doing fine now, expecting a new baby, happily together with a man who will look after her, despite the shitty beginning they handed out to her.

What a victory it will be for her to tell them that.

He knows there's nothing in the children's room, or his studio – which was completely empty when he moved his stuff in there. Feeling a little guilty, he goes through her drawers in the bedroom, but finds nothing but underwear, T-shirts, jumpers, make-up and hairstyling products. The wardrobe is just full of clothes on hangers. There are no secret drawers or compartments. The space under the bed is empty – he knows that, because he sweeps under there every week.

It makes him happy to find nothing. It means he and Lou have no secrets any more. She has told him everything there is to know about her, and she knows all about him. He is excited that, when she is twelve weeks pregnant, he will be able to introduce her to his mum, who will love her, he is certain. She has been quietly yearning for a grandchild. Her disappointment when Charley went off and left him was almost the largest part of the heartbreak for him.

He searches the shelves in the living room, but there is nothing useful there. A file box only contains service bills and the like. His heart leaps when he pulls out her birth certificate, but it tells him nothing new about her parents, other than that her father, Fergus Turner, was a managing director.

He knows there is nothing in the kitchen cupboards, but something makes him clamber up onto the worktop and reach out Poppy and Leon's box again. He has sworn not to touch it, but what he is doing is for the greater good. If she knew why, Lou would surely understand.

And then he finds it, tucked away behind the box: it's a thick, white envelope, which hadn't been there when he emptied the shelf to clean it.

It has been opened already, so Adam doesn't feel too bad about having a quick look.

Dear Louisa,
I know you don't want me to contact you, but I have
some information that you may find useful at some point
in the future. They are here:

The typed letter, on the headed notepaper of a legal firm in Cambridge, is signed off with love by someone called Fiona. It goes on to give an address for Celia and Fergus Turner, on an island called Unst, in the Shetlands.

So this corner of the kitchen cupboards has become, for Lou, her private place. He supposes she trusted him not to go snooping.

But his happiness at the discovery overrides any guilt he might have felt. This is what he has been looking for! He goes to his Mac and looks at the address on Google Maps. Celia and Fergus certainly put themselves as far away as possible from their poor daughter.

For a second, he wonders if they deserve to have any contact with Lou, but then he remembers that it's not for them, it's for her. No one should be estranged from their parents. We only have one life, and we have to make it work.

He sits at his computer and composes a letter, informing them of who he is, how happy their daughter is – despite their best efforts – and how he thinks, now that she is expecting a child, that they should face up to their responsibility for what they have done, and allow her to take steps to heal herself.

He gives them his phone number, and asks them to get in touch as soon as possible Then he prints out the letter, puts it in an envelope and takes it down to the post office to send, special delivery.

56

'God, you look well.'

It's the first thing Cleo says to Lou when she walks up to her desk at eight a.m.

The early start is a challenge, because Adam spent the night tossing and turning with pain from his Steroid Boy beating. But the whole episode, coupled with his delight at her pregnancy, has filled her with a happy glow that is impossible to hide.

So upbeat is she that it was only when she passed The Pantry in the lift that she even cast a thought to yesterday's scene with Sophie and the fact that today may very well indeed be her last at the agency.

But then Cleo follows up her initial observation with a smile.

'They LOVED it,' she says, moving round her desk to hug Lou. 'And the fight – well, they have no idea that the designer who produced the brilliant work for their brand was the woman squabbling on the floor. To be honest, I think it made the day for those men in suits. It made us look edgy, which suits their brand. Edgy cat food! They want us, they want our ideas, they booked us there and then. And it's all down to your star quality work, Lou. And possibly the little frisson from the fracas.'

'Seriously?'

'Seriously. *Design Week* might present us with slightly more of a problem, but I'll think of a way round it. She didn't seem to recognise you from the photo in the Mumsnet piece, so as long as we make sure that when you next see her you're all groomed and lovely, not looking like you've just been grappling with your sister on the floor, I think you'll be OK.'

Lou nearly asks Cleo what she means by 'sister', but then she remembers that this is the latest lie she's going to have to maintain. And that thought takes her directly to wondering how long she will be able to keep her pregnancy hidden. She wonders how delighted Cleo will be when she finds out that her star, model returner has got herself up the duff just a little over a month after taking up her position.

The note of worry dissipates as she remembers that, thanks to Adam being the carer, she is not going to be taking too much time out. In fact, she can turn the baby into a massive PR coup for Cleo, and she will be happy to pose for photographs with *this* child.

'Have you had breakfast?' Cleo asks.

Lou shakes her head.

'Come on, let's go downstairs.'

They sit on acid-yellow leather armchairs, sip flat whites and nibble at croissants. No one else has arrived yet, so they have the whole of The Pantry to themselves.

'You see,' Cleo says. 'I know what you're going through.'

Lou widens her eyes and waits for elaboration. She has no idea what exactly Cleo thinks that might be.

'My brother David's got mental health issues, too,' Cleo adds. 'I know what it's like. He even turned up at A.R.K. once and caused a not dissimilar scene.'

With the new-found confidence of a star designer, Lou reaches over and puts her hand on Cleo's. 'Poor you,' she says.

'He's living with the parents now,' Cleo says, dabbing her

finger at pastry crumbs on her plate. 'And they make sure he takes his drugs, otherwise he'll just kick off again and it'll be another total nightmare.'

'I wish we had parents Soph could live with,' Lou says, shrugging her shoulders. 'But there's only me, I'm afraid.'

'God, I'm sorry. Poor you. Makes it so much worse. And that poor child of hers.'

'Yes,' Lou says, inventing a history for Sophie that she would actually like to gift to her. 'She's not been well since she was around thirteen. In and out of hospital, sectioned twice. And now the baby, well, it really sent her over the edge.'

'Terrible,' Cleo says.

'She says some pretty hateful things. Makes stuff up about me all the time. It's jealousy, or something. I mean, compared to her, I'm so lucky, despite the bullshit with the ex.'

'You certainly are,' Cleo says. 'I have the same thing with my brother. Guilt.'

'Oh, I'm not going to start apologising because of how my life turned out compared to hers,' Lou says, warming to her theme. 'It's just how things are. I called her hostel – it's up near Huntingdon, a sort of halfway house between hospital and the real world – and she's safely back home. So I'm hoping she's not going to bowl up again.'

'For your own sake if nothing else.'

'Oh yes. But I don't like to see A.R.K. compromised in any way.'

'I'll put an alert on your name. We'll screen all calls and visitors, and only allow clients and anyone you pre-approve to contact you.'

Lou nods. 'Thank you so much, Cleo, for being so understanding, and for being so brilliant yesterday,' Lou says.

'Ah.' Cleo makes a dismissive gesture with her hand.

'No, really. You dealt with what could have been a disastrous situation in a really professional way.'

'It was nothing.'

'With you and me at the helm, this company's going to go the distance,' Lou says, stirring her coffee so energetically that she spills half of it onto the table.

'Here. Let me get a cloth for that.' Cleo gets up and heads for the kitchen area.

Lou notices the slight frown on Cleo's face.

She knew it: she has gone too far. She never knows when to stop, that's her problem.

She takes a bite of her pastry, but a flake gets lodged in her throat.

'Are you OK?' Cleo says, as she returns to find her choking.

Nodding, her face red, Lou flees to the bathroom. The choking is soon dealt with, but as she hangs over the basin and splashes cold water at her face, she glances at the mirror and, dismayed, glimpses a snake writhing out from between her lips.

'Calm, Lou, calm,' she says to her reflection. 'Or we'll never get through this.'

But her reflection's lips don't work, and she doesn't recognise the person staring back at her.

57

Lou kneels on her bed and looks down at the car park where a stretcher is being loaded onto an ambulance. A paramedic runs alongside the body-braced occupant, holding up a bag of fluid.

It is early evening and, for once, no sound intrudes from upstairs: no death metal, no pounding bass, no screeching. Lou is feeling great, if a little on edge. Nothing is beyond her now.

At the sound of Adam letting himself into the apartment, she lies down on the bed, as if she has been resting. With a sloshing sound, he puts down his heavy burden of water containers, one of which, thanks to Steroid Boy trashing his right hand, he has had to carry on a strap slung across his body.

'You back, Lou?'

'In the bedroom.'

She had watched him cross the courtyard with the water on his way back from the standpipe. That was some while ago, thanks firstly to the lift being out of order due to a power cut – coming up thirteen storeys nearly killed her this evening and her bad leg is complaining loudly – and secondly because he was stopped by one of the police officers whose car is parked up beside the ambulance. They spent quite a time with him. With her binoculars, she saw the expression on his bruised face: shock. Horror, even.

He comes into the bedroom.

'Poor you,' she says, holding out her arms to him. He moves forward, takes her hands, and sits on the edge of the bed. 'Lugging that lot all the way upstairs. It's not good enough. This building is so badly run. We should complain.'

'It's an electricity spike caused by all the air conditioners. It's nothing to do with the building.'

'What's the matter?' she says. He's flat, deflated. His usual spark has deserted him. The small, now habitual, flash of panic – *what has he found out?* – prickles across her face.

He looks at her with his one good eye – the other has not yet fully emerged from its purple ball of a bruise. 'Something terrible's happened,' he says.

She brings her hand to her chest. 'What?'

'Look.' He kneels on the bed and gestures for her to join him. They look out onto the car park, where, blue light flashing, the ambulance is pulling away as slowly as if it were carrying a dozen loose rare bird's eggs.

'What's happened?' she asks, as if this is the first time she has seen it.

'Steroid Boy,' Adam says. 'He was found on the stairs. It looks really bad for him. I know one of the police guys – Jake – he grew up on the estate. He says he's broken his neck. Terrible head injuries. They don't think he's going to make it.'

'He told you that?'

'Jake's a mate.'

'Wow,' Lou says. 'Poor Steroid Boy. What happened? Did he trip on his shoelaces or something?'

'You a witch or something?' Adam says. 'That's exactly what he did.'

'I've seen him around. He's always got his shoelaces undone. Thinks it's cool or something stupid like that. And he charges down those stairs. Far too fast.'

'It's horrible,' Adam says. 'Poor guy.'

403

'Adam: he beat you up and made you punch him, and look what that did to your hand.'

'He doesn't deserve that, though.'

'You reckon.' Lou raises an eyebrow. 'Upside, though,' she says, pointing to the silent ceiling above them.

'Lou,' he says. 'Not funny.'

As she turns to look back at Adam, for a brief second her eye catches the man in the black suit in the building to the left.

He's there for just one beat of her heart, and his hands are together and he's applauding her.

And then he is gone.

58

Adam

Two hours before he is due to meet Lou off her train, Adam heads out to meet Carly for a coffee, to tell her that he is not going to be able to give as much time to the project any more. As he passes the Tube station, his eye catches a sign.

CAN YOU HELP?

It says.

> *At approximately 11 a.m. on Tuesday 6 June, an incident occurred on a train at this station during which a man was seriously assaulted. If you can help . . .*

He scribbles down the number. Lou passed through the station about that time – it was when she came home to find him and Carly moving the kids' stuff. Perhaps she could help. He is glad that she escaped the violence, but he also experiences a sensation that has visited him several times over the past week or so: a great shiver working its way down his spine. Someone walking over his grave, his mum calls it.

He hurries away.

He makes his way through the underpass. Just as he is nodding his greetings to Spider and Lucas, the two homeless kids who beg in the middle spot in the mornings, his phone rings. It's not a number he recognises, so he takes it cautiously, expecting some sort of badly targeted rip-off call telling him his PC is out of order when he only uses Macs, or offering to help him with his PPI claim when he's never had a credit card or loan in his life.

'Yeah?' he says, ready to beat them back.

'Is that Adam White?' the voice at the other end says. It's female, cracked with age, posh Scottish. Instantly, he knows who it is.

'You're Lou's mum, aren't you?' he says.

He veers off his path and takes a right into a tunnel which leads down into the middle of the roundabout.

'I am Celia Turner,' the woman says, as he surfaces in the sunken central island. 'Yes.'

Up on the road, lorries, buses, taxis, motorbikes circle constantly, the concrete architecture amplifying the sound.

'So Louise is pregnant again,' she says.

'Yes.' Adam sweeps some cinders from a broken-down park bench and sits, his eyes on the immobile human form in the sleeping bag on the far side of the precinct. After the call he will go and check if the guy is OK – it is far too hot to be comfortable wrapped up like that.

'Oh no,' she says. 'Oh dear God, no.'

Adam blinks. 'What?'

'You know about her other children?'

'Poppy and Leon.'

'Really? She told you what happened to them?'

'Yes,' he says, trying to keep the accusatory tone out of his voice, wondering what this woman can know about Lou's poor babies, when he knows for a fact that there has been no contact for fourteen years.

'Can you let her know that they are fine, then,' she says.

'Who are fine?'

'The children, of course.'

A juggernaut thunders past above Adam's head, and, for a second, it feels like he is out of his body, looking down on the scene: him on one side of the island, hunched into his phone, the person huddled in the sleeping bag on the other, the traffic cutting them off from the rest of the world.

59

Sophie waits in the grimy shadow of a derelict Soho doorway, swigging warm tap water from a plastic bottle. She's wearing more or less the same disguise that got her into Fen Manor: hat, wig and all, and she's determined to keep hydrated through all the sweating, for fear of her milk drying up.

Remembering what happened the last time she encountered Louisa, she has Sami in the Bugaboo. Not having her strapped to her front while they are so far from home makes her uneasy. The possibility of having the buggy handle knocked out of her hand as she negotiates the teeming, sweltering streets on the way to Lou's workplace, or of forgetting and leaving buggy and child on the train – and thereby losing her only reason for remaining alive – chills her heart.

But she can live with that fear, because it means that if anything were to kick off again with her and Louisa, there would be no danger of Sami getting caught up between them. She still shudders to think how close her daughter got to being crushed last time.

With a hungry mewl, Sami stirs under the shade of the parasol.

'Come on, then.' Sophie lifts her out. Sinking to the ground, she sits on the grubby marble step, lifts her chiffon top and holds the hot, plump body of her glorious child – all her own work, against all the odds – to her, skin on blessed skin.

Just as Sami is settling in, gulping her milk in a regular, rhythmic flow, the glass doors of the A.R.K. building revolve and spew Louisa out onto the street.

'Bollocks.' Sophie slips her finger into her daughter's mouth to break the vacuum and prise her away from her nipple. Sami protests, but not too much – it was only really a comfort feed. With the help of a dummy – Sophie can't deny her that solace, however much it is probably frowned on by all those bastards who write the childcare books she has never read – Sami is happy to be quickly swaddled and laid back down.

Just in time, just as Louisa turns a corner a couple of hundred metres up ahead, Sophie is on her trail.

She is not going to confront her out on the street and risk another scene. And, if things did kick off, it would be Sophie who got into trouble, of course. She has no doubt about that. Even from the back, Louisa looks every bit the professional woman – all smooth lines, casual elegance, well-cut hair and, no doubt, perfect manicure. Her limping gait even somehow adds to the sophistication. Sophie looks down at her own bitten, chipped fingernails. There is absolutely no doubt what-soever whose side the police would take if called, even before they found out who the two combatants actually were.

'How we have fallen,' she whispers to Sami, as she pushes the Bugaboo at a discreet distance from her quarry. 'How things turn and turn around.'

She almost loses Louisa on Oxford Street, with its thick knots of slow-moving tourists, ambling with ice creams, Sports Direct bags and bulging Primark carriers. 'Excuse me, excuse me,' Sophie says over and over. 'Buggy coming through', and 'Sorry!' when she inadvertently clips the heels of a shuffling middle-aged woman with the kind of doughnut-calorie hips only found in the Midwestern United States.

'Ow!' her victim complains, with none of the grace or good

humour a more civilised person might show for a busy woman with a baby in a buggy on a crowded pavement.

'Just please get out of my damn way,' Sophie hisses. The woman showcases her outrage as she receives another knock from Sophie's bony shoulder as she passes.

There's Louisa, disappearing with the crowd, down the steps to Oxford Circus Tube station, like dirty water down a plughole.

Sophie grasps the Bugaboo and uses it to make a space for herself in the mass of sweating bodies heading underground.

'Let me help you with that.' A tall, slender man appears in front of her before she gets to the steps. As he holds out an elegant hand to touch the buggy, his fingers brush up against hers. He's wearing a very good watch: a vintage Rolex. For a second Sophie thinks what a wonderful couple she and he would make. Perhaps he's rich. Perhaps he can get her out of this mess and she won't have to worry about Louisa.

But then she remembers that it's not just about the money, the roof over her head, her child's legacy. It's also about the reputation of the father of her child. The words she has in her bag, the transcript of what is on the white iPhone she has left hidden in her bedroom, will be able to kill all those birds with one perfect, diamond-clear stone, while at the same time bringing down the vulture that is Louisa.

And the guy offering to help is probably some kind of hawk himself, out for what he can get from her. She should know better, really. Even good men – like Sam – bring nothing but trouble. Stay away.

'I'm fine, thanks.' She carries on moving, lugging the thing down the steps, accidentally whacking into the people around her, whose complaints she ignores.

In the crowded, gloomy ticket hall, she rips off her sunglasses just in time to glimpse Louisa disappearing through the ticket barrier. Sami has woken up with all the jiggling and is now crying.

'Shh, Sami, shh,' Sophie says, her milk automatically letting down and leaking into her blouse. She steers Sami and buggy through the wide ticket barrier and carries on down the escalator, tipping the buggy back, trying simultaneously to placate Sami and keep an eye on Louisa's neat blond bob as she rides down around thirty people beneath her. She sees her turn left for the southbound Bakerloo. Stuck on the escalator, Sophie starts to panic. She hasn't thought this through. Is she going to lose her chance to bring Louisa to her knees?

60

Adam

The juggernaut passes and, down in the roundabout island, Adam returns to his own skin.

'Poppy and Leon are fine?' he stutters. 'Is this some kind of sick joke?'

'I'm sorry?' There is outrage in Celia Turner's voice.

'Reckon you can speak to the dead, or something?'

'Dead? What on earth are you talking about?'

'How cruel can you get? There's no way I'm telling Lou that. It hurts her even to think about them.'

'She's told you that her children are dead?' The woman exhales noisily. 'For the love of Christ.'

Adam feels the chill again, a herd of elephants trampling over his extremely shallow grave.

'What are you telling me?' he asks, running his hand through his hair.

'Adam – can I call you that?'

'Of course.'

'Let me tell you this. Poppy and Leon are both alive and well. They are on the beach at the moment with their grandfather, and the puppy we bought them.'

'What?'

'Fergus didn't want me to contact you, but I felt I should . . . I don't know . . . warn you.'

'About what?'

'Look. Our daughter was in no fit state to look after her first two children. She told you about the car crash, yes?'

'Yes.'

'So she was in a coma for a month, then incoherent for another few weeks, then in intensive physical, neurological and psychological rehab.'

'I know this.'

'What you clearly don't know is that, underneath their second- and third-degree burns, Poppy and Leon had been fed a cocktail of anti-depressants and alcohol. They were malnourished – Poppy is still undergoing treatment for the effects of rickets – and both of them had injuries that predated the accident and which were commensurate with slapping and grabbing and hitting. Then there were Poppy's psychological evaluations . . .'

'All of that was down to Sam, though . . .'

'No. It was most certainly not. That was the argument that our daughter's lawyers put across in court, and there was evidence that she used – or created – to successfully lead everyone to believe her. But we know her. We know what she's capable of. I am in this wheelchair because of her.'

'What?'

She pushed me down a flight of stairs for no reason whatsoever.'

'You fell because you were drunk!'

'What? Is that what she told you?'

Celia Turner laughs, but there's no merriment in it.

'Look,' she goes on. 'Ever since she was a little girl . . . She's not like you or me. It's as if she is driven by something outside her. She can be very charming on the outside, and she uses it to get her way. But if things go wrong for Louise, watch out.'

413

'But you abandoned her.'

'We moved away because my husband retired and I needed an accessible home. I grew up here, and I wanted to return. We bought her a flat, supported her financially, and she was welcome to come and visit. I even came down to Bristol when she was a student, but she refused to see me.'

'So she knows where you live?'

'Yes! She just chooses not to be in contact with us.'

Adam thinks about the letter he found in the cupboard, with the Turners' address on it. It would appear that Lou had told the Fiona person who wrote it at least part of the same story she had given him.

'How can I believe you?' Adam's shadow hits the concrete in front of him like a shard of glass, a heat haze shimmering around its edges.

'Look. I take it that it's your baby she's expecting, Adam?'

'It is.'

'Then please, watch out. Pregnancy and birth clearly aren't good for her. They make her difficult bits even worse. And when the baby's born, take care. Take care for yourself and the child. We've got Poppy and Leon now. The police tracked us down as next of kin after the crash, and we fostered them initially. But knowing what Louise is like, what she did as a child: horses, other children, me. All of that, plus the physical state of the children . . . We didn't want to make a public row, for Poppy and Leon's sake. But . . . Well, we quietly asked her through our solicitor if she would give them up for us to adopt.'

Realising that he hasn't taken a breath throughout this speech, Adam sucks in a lungful of air. 'And what did she say?'

The weight of Lou's mother's sigh is such that he has to briefly remove the phone from his ear. 'She gave them up. She didn't contest it at all. Once she's failed at something, she wants nothing more to do with it. Believe me. I've seen it: the torn-up reading books, the screwed-up paintings, the essays ripped to snowflakes, the smashed piano, the puppy she failed to train, found drowned in our pond, the burned-down stables, the dead horses. She closed the door on Poppy and Leon – she doesn't want to see them ever again. She wouldn't even let us take any of their toys or books from the house.'

'How am I supposed to believe all this? She says you are a drunkard.'

'I am most certainly not.' The way this is said allows no room for disbelief.

'She said you were terrible parents to her.'

'Yes.' There is a pause, and the woman on the end of the line takes a deep breath that verges on a sob. 'We were.'

'So how am I supposed to believe all this?'

'We were terrible because we never owned up fully to what we feared we had on our hands. Oh, I took her to two different child psychologists, but each time she managed to wangle her way out of any sort of diagnosis. One of the psychologists even implied that I was neurotic, had unrealistic expectations of my daughter. Louise is very, very clever. The truth is that we never let on to anyone how alarmed – how scared – we really were. She was our only child. It would have felt like a betrayal. The scandal with poor Poppy and Leon was that certain quarters in the social and medical services had an inkling that something was going on, but it never got very far, because she presented so well. Nice clothes, voice, money. It's what she does, present well. The social workers had other priorities and the medics were led to suspect her husband of a series of physical attacks that I am absolutely certain she carried out on herself.

'She did the same as her father and I did when she was young. We projected the ability to cope. And nobody asked too many questions.

'We're trying to make amends now, with Poppy and Leon. And slowly, very slowly, they are healing. Poppy's starting at the village school in the autumn. I help out there. It's a wonderful place. We're preparing the other children so that they are ready to see her scars.'

Adam has terrible difficulty finding his words. 'What have I got myself into?' he says at last to this stranger on a remote island at the other end of the country.

'My dear, she—'

He can't hear any more.

He presses the red button and stops the call.

He needs to talk to Lou, to hear her side. Who is telling the truth? The woman he loves, the mother of his child, or this stranger, this person who, until now, he viewed only as a figure to be despised?

There's that shiver again.

Under the full heat of the sun, he buries his head in his hands and wonders what the hell he is going to say to Lou when she gets back from work.

His brain like a plate of ackee, Adam doesn't even register the vibration in his pocket, doesn't see that it's a text from Carly, who is waiting for him in the Rainbow Café, secretly cursing Lou for the spell she has cast over the boy she has always been a little in love with, and wondering where the hell he has got to.

Eventually, at six, he rises slowly, like an old man crippled with arthritis, to head towards the Tube station.

He forgets completely about checking on the guy in the sleeping bag.

61

When Sophie finally gets to the bottom of the escalator, an older man in a suit, who was riding behind her, puts his hand on her shoulder.

'Make way. Baby coming through!' he announces, his voice radiating status and power. He's a man to be listened to. The people part like the Red Sea, allowing Sophie and Sami to the front of the throng. Whilst partly grateful for this intervention, Sophie is also concerned that Louisa – who, thankfully, is still on the platform – might turn and see her. But the train arrives and the noise and the crush are thick enough to keep her hidden. The train doors open and people fall out, bringing with them a magma of hot stale air from deep within the carriage. Sophie lifts the buggy up and into the packed train and turns to thank the man who helped her, but the doors have snicked shut behind her, and he is left saluting her on the platform.

She sticks by the doors – not that she has any chance of getting any further into the sardined train. At every station, she leans out, one hand gripping the buggy handle, to see if Louisa is getting off. At the final stop, there she is, blond hair bouncing along the far end of the platform. She looks nauseatingly happy. Hasn't Sophie managed to bring her down just one tiny peg? Hasn't her campaign managed to evoke just a tiny pang of conscience in her target?

There are two lifts up to the street. Louisa is at the front of the crowd jammed in round the doors for the first. Sophie slips in at the back and uses the Bugaboo to make sure she gets in on the same ride. Once on board, she bends and fusses over Sami so that, should Louisa choose to look behind her, she won't spot her.

Finally, light-headed with the hellish Underground heat, she and Sami are out on the traffic-clogged street, negotiating a poorly formed line of people queuing with plastic containers at a row of water standpipes.

Up ahead, Louisa is greeted by a brown-skinned boy with long, curling hair who, if it weren't for a nasty black eye, would be a dead ringer for Jesus. But this bruised messiah has an air of confusion about him like a black cloud hanging above his head. Flattening herself against a wall, Sophie watches from around the corner as he takes Louisa's workbag and bends to take a kiss from her. All very boyfriend-like, but as he does so his face wears a deep, worried frown. Nevertheless, as the two of them dodge across the busy road, he places a protective hand on Louisa's arm and, on the other side, he guides her along an alleyway down the side of a pub, which, with its wall of plate-glass windows, looks more like a sixties office than a drinking establishment.

They stop in front of a gate set in marble pillars. The boy holds his hand up to a metal plate, the gate clicks open and he holds it back for Louisa. It swings shut behind them and they pass through a revolving door to be swallowed up by the lobby of a vast block of luxury apartments.

Sophie can hardly bear it. What is it about Louisa? How is it she gets everyone looking after her when she, Sophie, has to fend for herself all the time?

She looks so happy. How can she be happy, after what she did?

Sophie closes her eyes and, like a smoker trying to give up, she takes herself in real time through taking down the last of the *Cambridge Evening News* front pages, striking the lighter, holding the flame to the paper and watching the black, charred pieces floating up through the air.

'Louisa, I've got you,' she says, as she grinds the imaginary embers beneath her foot. So fully has she visualised the process, she feels the sting of a burn.

Bolstering herself with the knowledge of what Louisa has coming to her, Sophie crosses the road carefully to avoid the buses, taxis and cyclists dodging along it, every single one breaking the speed limit. This is a very different part of the city to the glossy London she knew in her fashion days. It is a far cry, too, from that deserted house in the middle of Fenland nowhere. With all this, the job, the new man – who looks barely older than Sophie – it is as if Louisa has completely reinvented herself.

Well, she would have to, wouldn't she? Given what she did.

Sophie tries putting her hand up to the metal plate at the entrance to Louisa's building, but nothing happens. To her right is a metal fence with spikes set into the top. Through it she sees four tower blocks sitting around a courtyard, interlinked by glassed-in aerial walkways. There must be hundreds of individual flats in this building. Even if she got into the lobby, she has no idea where she might find Louisa. She thinks about pulling out the sister card again, but that would just give Louisa warning of her approach, and she needs to take her by surprise.

She is going to have to play a different game. If she is going to corner Louisa in her lair, she will have to rely on that top hunter's quality: patience.

She takes Sami to the pub by the gates. Under the bleary

gaze of men with bulbous, purple noses who sit nursing pint-and-chaser arrangements, she spends some of the cash she got for those horrible spiky shoes on a pot of tea and some chips and sets up vigil in the window overlooking the gates.

For the first time in many, many months, she actually feels hungry.

62

Dusk closes in and, even though it's only a Tuesday night, the street outside the pub window has got busier rather than quieter. People in very few clothes stream out of the lobby of Louisa's building, heading off with chilled bottles under their arms into the cooler evening air. They're certainly not the demographic for this rough pub Sophie has found herself in – it seems that the smart block of flats is something of a moneyed outpost in this area.

There's no sign of Louisa yet, though.

Sophie is on her third pot of tea, and the old boys in the pub have now been joined by a younger crowd, South London boys and girls dressed up for a night out, for getting lucky, for getting laid. They're around Sophie's age, but she feels no affinity with them, sitting there in her wig and hat, Sami hidden beneath her blouse, nuzzling at her breast.

In all her life, Sophie has never felt as carefree as this lot seem to be, the girls in their barely there dresses, the boys loose limbed, cocky, confident that they are admired. The only time Sophie ever feels she fully lived was when she was with Sam, in their snatched moments together. Once again, the magnitude of what she has lost hits her, like a well-aimed punch in the solar plexus.

And what Louisa tried to do.

Now she knows it for sure: what Louisa tried to do.

She can't even bring herself to think it while she has her baby in her arms. And yet, soon, she will have to speak it out loud. She is going to have to drive her bargain. It is not fair, what she is planning to do, it is not kind. But Louisa has had more than enough fairness and kindness. And it is kinder, at least, than torture, or a fire bomb.

The thought of the task ahead brings on the addict's pang, the longing that from time to time reaches out from some primordial part of her brain, telling her that she won't be able to face it without her little helper. But the object of her desire is back in the Mulberry bag, hanging on a peg in her Cambridge hallway. She can see it in her mind, like a dot on an Internet map, showing a journey's destination. She should really throw it away when she gets back . . .

She shakes her head vigorously to clear the urge. She will brave this out unaided. If Louisa ever comes out, that is.

She really needs to pee now, but she is torn between relieving her bladder and keeping her vigil at the window – she doesn't want to miss Louisa. If she does get up, she'll have to take all her stuff – baby, buggy, bag – with her, and then she would lose her table to the people who are standing behind her, pointedly waiting for her to leave. She crosses her legs and sits tight.

It's a good job she doesn't succumb, because, just at that moment, there he is. Louisa's Jesus boy. He disappears around the corner with two large plastic containers, heading in the direction of the standpipe by the Tube station.

Which means he will be coming back.

'Got you, Louisa,' she says.

She turns and sees one of the old boys staring blearily at her, purple veins latticing his cheeks.

'What?' she says. 'WHAT? Never seen a woman breastfeed before?'

The old man blinks, turns his body away and swigs his pint of pale ale.

Sophie pours the dregs of the pot into her cup. She just has to wait now, until that doting idiot comes back with Madam Louisa's water.

Forty minutes pass, the light outside fades, and there's still no sign of Jesus. Just as she's wondering whether she should go and check that her assumption that he was going to fetch water wasn't off beam, the lights go out in the pub, the muzak stops and the hum of the refrigeration, air conditioning or whatever it was, cuts out. At the sudden change in atmosphere, everyone stops talking and moving, and for a brief moment the heaving pub is brought to silence and stillness. Even the man with the purple facial veins briefly rouses from his alcohol fog to something approaching alertness.

Then, as quickly as they had stopped, everyone turns back to their conversations and pints and chasers.

'What's going on?' Sophie asks the barman, who is circulating the floor, putting candles on each table.

'Another fucking power cut,' he says, his voice gruff in a pustular face. He nods to Sami, who now snoozes peacefully in Sophie's arms. 'And ain't it time you took the kid home?'

'She's not causing a nuisance, is she?' Sophie says, her chin up.

At once she sees that the barman has taken offence at her voice, her demeanour. She's too posh for this place. She should have reverted to her original accent.

'No kids after eight,' he says, clipping his consonants and nodding at the clock, which reads five minutes to.

Sophie sighs heavily, puts on her sunglasses, and makes a great deal out of gathering her stuff together.

'Just WAIT!' she snarls at the group of lads who are closing in on her table.

All sorts of injustices are whirling through her brain: discrimination against lone parents, discrimination against women, class discrimination in the form of inverted snobbery. Discrimination against innocent widows. She's just wondering if she should form these thoughts into speech, when she sees Jesus returning down the passageway to the gates, lugging the two containers, which, from the look of it, are a lot heavier than when he went out. One is attached to a strap over his shoulder, and she notes that one of his hands is bandaged and he doesn't seem able to use it well. Also, from the look on his face, Jesus is not a happy bunny. Who would be, hanging out with Louisa?

Sophie has a good idea who might be responsible for his injuries.

She runs out of the pub and falls into step behind him, aiming to slip in through the gates with him. But, as it happens, there is no need, because the door opens without him putting his finger on the touch pad.

'Bad, innit,' he says, as he holds the gate open for the Bugaboo. 'Poxy power cut and any old riffraff can get in off the streets.' He's friendly enough, but the way he is carrying himself suggests that he is both weary and wary.

Sophie nods and smiles and, once in, pretends to fuss over the baby to let him lead the way. Far enough behind so that he doesn't notice she is there, she follows him through the lobby, where she greets the concierge as if she passes this way every day. She prays that the power cut will last long enough to let the particular riffraff that she is right into Louisa's inner sanctum.

The boy leads her out and through a courtyard with a carp pond and some sort of Japanese bridge over it. Sophie's fashion-honed taste sensors bristle at how badly thought out all the clutter is. The building sports clean, clear, sixties lines and some idiot has dotted fussy planters and curved wooden benches around. Her burdensome sense of how unfair life is gains weight when she sees the place that Louisa, the Kick Ass Designer, has chosen to live in. All that money and she chooses this? Some visual sense, eh? Some aesthetics. Suburban, corporate values smothering a once clean sixties architectural vision.

'It just doesn't work,' she tells Sami. It is never too early to impart taste to one's child. Especially if they are very shortly going to be in the money.

Jesus disappears into the furthest block and Sophie slides in behind him just to see him go through a double door at the end of the corridor.

She counts to four, then follows. It is a stairwell. Of course, Louisa would live on an upper floor, when the lifts are down because of a power cut and Sophie has a bloody buggy. She takes off her sunglasses and casts around the gloomy enclosure. Under the bottom flight there is a nook that is hardly visible for anyone using the stairs. She could park the buggy there and carry Sami up.

But what, she thinks, if Louisa attacks her again and she has got Sami in her bare arms? What if Jesus turns devil to defend his goddess? What, in fact, is she doing here? She knows now how dangerous Louisa can be.

She can't leave Sami down here, though, on her own. A knot forms behind her navel at the very thought of it. The only thing for it is to carry baby and buggy up the stairs. She looks up and, in the dim glow of the emergency lights, sees the shadow of Jesus making slow progress with his own burden. She has to go now or she will lose him.

As silently as she can manage – she doesn't want any offers of help from her prey – she hoists the heavy buggy onto her bony hip and, tugging on the banister with her free hand, starts her ascent, keeping a careful eye on him as he turns onto each new flight of stairs. She hopes Louisa isn't too far up.

But she is, of course. Sophie follows him up and up until she can barely breathe, until her shoulders seize up, her arms shake, her legs tremble in complaint. It's the most exercise she has done since the all-night, drug-enhanced dancing days. She is not built for this. The hardest part is muffling the sound of her heavy breathing, keeping her curses whispered. At least the stairwell, in the concrete heart of the building, is insulated against the heat of the world outside. Here the air is cool, limestone-scented, hollow. She'd be dead else, she reckons, as she follows Jesus through an exit with the number thirteen stencilled in black on the grey, gloss-painted wall.

As she falls through, panting, the door at the other side of the lift lobby is just closing behind him. She puts the Bugaboo down and, unable to continue, slides to the ground, her back against the wall. She thinks about going back into the stairwell and squatting to take that pee, but her exertions on the climb have sweated out the urgency.

As she catches her breath, she looks out of a floor-to-ceiling window to her left, at a view of acres of spotlit building sites, a sky punctured by cranes, a distant cityscape eclipsed by the smoggy night. The only signs of nature are a few dehydrated trees that appear to have lost the struggle to breathe from all the heat and building work and traffic.

'Ugh,' Sophie says. This is, truly, the landscape Louisa deserves.

A few slugs of water and she is recovered, struggling to her feet. She puts her sunglasses back on and backs the buggy through the door that swallowed Jesus. On the other side she finds a long, windowless corridor, cream-painted and contract-carpeted, only just visible in dim emergency lighting. She looks over the top of her shades. Lined up ahead of her are six maple-wood doors with gold numbers on them.

'Which one, though?' she asks her sleeping baby.

A helicopter throbs by, somewhere close to the building,

but its din is nothing compared to the pounding of her heart in her ears. Of course, if things turn bad, she's done for. Up here, stairs the only way down, baby and buggy.

She has her story to protect her, though. The one Louisa won't dare let go.

63

Sophie works her way along the corridor, knocking on the doors. No one answers the first two, and at the third she is met with a blank look from behind a security chain. The fourth, however, is opened by a pale-faced woman with a crying baby on her hip, who points nervously to the last door on the right.

At least Sophie now has a witness to her being here. Just in case.

She knocks on the door and waits, making sure her wig, hat and sunglasses are in place.

No reply.

Does Louisa know she's coming? Did she watch her trail her boyfriend across the courtyard? Sophie can imagine that she spends a lot of time on guard at her windows, waiting for her sins to find her out.

She knocks again, and this time it only takes a couple of beats for the door to open so suddenly that she jumps backwards.

'Yes?' Jesus greets her, his expression, if anything, more tense than it had been before. Then he recognises her as the woman he let in downstairs. 'Oh, man,' he points at the Bugaboo. 'You didn't have to lug that up all the way, did you?'

'It's fine,' Sophie says. 'I'm used to it.'

'You looking for Anna?'

'Eh?'

'Anna.' He points to the door of the woman with the baby. 'I thought with the babe and all that.'

Sophie shakes her head and instinctively modulates her accent so that it is younger and more urban, peppered with glottal stops like his own. 'I've come to see Louisa. Lou, I mean.'

He blinks, does a double take, rakes his fingers through his long hair. He looks like a man who has just half a millimetre of tether left. 'Lou? What about?'

Sophie wonders if she should warn him right now about the woman he's tangled himself up with. Whether she should just help him to escape.

'About her children,' she says, which is partly true, at least. 'About Poppy and Leon.'

He breathes in, sharply. 'Did her mum send you?'

'Her mum? No.'

'Man.' He runs his fingers through his mop of hair and shakes his head. 'Will this never end?'

'Sorry?'

'Who did you say you were?' he says.

'I'm—' Sophie checks herself. Best not to give too much away. 'Lou and I know each other from a few years back.'

'And this is about the children?'

She nods. Sami, who has woken up, looks up at him with round, curious eyes.

'It's not a great time,' he says. 'We—'

'I really need to see her. We've come a long way, and—'

'Well, I suppose today couldn't get any weirder, after all.' He shrugs and sighs as if he has lead weights on his shoulders. 'You'd better come in, then. I'm Adam, by the way.'

He leads her into the flat, past a row of closed doors and into a large, open-plan living room and kitchen, and gestures to a sixties leather armchair. She thinks she remembers

429

sprawling across one just like it, coked and McQueened up to the eyebrows, for a *Vanity Fair* shoot. The rest of the room is similarly furnished with modern classics. Everything looks very much in keeping with the original architectural intentions – at least Louisa has shown a bit of taste with her interiors. The only odd note is set by the two kitsch little metal vases – one pink, one blue – which stand on the dining table. And then Sophie notices the broken glass and crockery in a swept-up pile in the kitchen area.

'Bit of an accident?' she asks, nodding towards the detritus.

'It was more deliberate, in fact,' Adam says, bending to scoop the breakages into a dustpan.

'Is it OK if I have a glass of water?' Sophie squats down beside Sami to replace her dummy. As she does so, Sami folds her fist around her mother's finger. The touch of her daughter gives Sophie courage for the challenge ahead.

'Of course.' Adam empties the dustpan into the bin, pulls a bottle of water from the fridge and pours it into a tall glass.

'Breastfeeding doesn't half make you thirsty,' she says, necking the water and handing the glass back to him.

'I'll go and get Lou,' Adam says, turning to go. 'She's locked herself in – I mean, she's resting in the bedroom.'

'Are the children around?' Sophie asks.

He stops in his tracks and turns to face her. 'Eh?'

'Just – I'd rather they weren't in the room when I speak to her.'

'You don't know about the children?' He stares at her.

'Know what?'

'What did you say your name was again?'

A voice from the other side of the room startles them both. 'Her name is Sophie.'

Louisa stands in the doorway, her arms folded, her face full of thunder, and instantly Sophie knows who broke those plates. The air is so tight between this couple that it is nearly snapping.

She rises and instinctively places herself between Sami and Louisa.

'What the hell is she doing here, Adam?' Louisa asks, and Adam flinches.

'She says she's here about the children.' He holds up his hands, closes his eyes and shakes his head.

'Did you bring her here? Is this another thing you've "found out" about me?'

'NO. I have no idea what you're talking about, Lou,' he says. 'No idea who she is.'

'And yet you let her into my apartment? A "complete stranger"?'

'How the hell do I know what I'm supposed to do?' It is very slight, but there is a definite whine in his voice.

'So let me tell you who this is, Adam,' Louisa says. 'Sophie here was my late husband's bit on the side.' She strides across the room and rips Sophie's wig, hat and sunglasses from her head. 'His little junkie model. The BDSM sex bomb. And this,' she brandishes the floppy hairpiece like a scalp at Sami, 'is my late husband's bastard child. And you, Adam, you've just let them into my apartment.'

'How was I supposed to know?' he says, his voice cracking. 'I don't know anything about her, or this, or the baby. Or anything at all, come to that.'

Louisa looks at him, her nostrils flaring. 'Really? Really? Didn't she rope you in, though?'

'Like I say, I've never seen her before. Like I say, she told me she wanted to talk about the children.'

Louisa turns to Sophie. 'Ah, so my mother told you too, then?'

'What? I—' Sophie tries to speak, but Louisa cuts right across her.

'You can't do anything to me now with your little nugget of information, though, Soph, because Mother Dearest has also been on to Adam, telling him what a terrible parent I was and how they decided that I wasn't to be allowed to have any contact with my children, when, in fact, I was as much a victim as they were.'

'That's not exactly what she told me,' Adam says.

As if she can't hear him, Louisa carries on. 'We were, in fact, all abused by Sam, but oh yes, blame it on the woman. So it's all out in the open, and none of you've got anything on me.'

'Sam didn't do all that,' Sophie says to Adam, shaking her head.

'You would say that, his little fuck whore,' Louisa hisses at her.

'Lou. Not in front of the child,' Adam says, motioning at Sami.

'It's just a bloody baby, Adam.' Louisa makes a sweeping gesture with her arm, as if brushing him away. The momentum makes her stumble.

'Take it easy, Lou.' He leaps forward and stops her from falling.

'Or what?'

'Your baby—'

'You're not pregnant?' Sophie turns to Adam. 'Say she isn't pregnant.'

His look – a rich blend of fear, resignation and anxiety – says it all.

'Why the hell shouldn't I be?' Louisa says. 'Is it only little toads like you who are allowed to have children these days?'

'Lou,' Adam says.

Louisa swings round so that she is addressing the two of them, as if she senses that some kind of unspoken alliance is being formed against her. 'Do either of you have any idea what it is like for me? Knowing my babies are with those – those – *animals*, who made my own childhood such hell? Poor Poppy and Leon. I can't even *speak* to them.'

'So Poppy and Leon are with your parents now?' Sophie says.

'That's your choice, Lou,' Adam says. 'Celia said—'

'Oh FUCK CELIA! Don't you see? I'd be better off if Poppy and Leon *were* dead.'

'No!' Adam says, shaking his head wildly. 'No, Lou, don't say that.'

'What do you mean, Louisa?' Sophie cuts in over the top of him. Then she sees that Adam is looking at the two metal vases on the table, and instantly she realises what they are. 'My God. She told you they were dead? She told you that Poppy and Leon were *dead*?'

Adam closes his eyes and nods.

'Unbelievable.' Sophie looks at Louisa, then at the urns.

'Oh, don't get your hopes up, *Soph*.' Louisa goes over to the table, pulls the lid off the small blue urn and empties its contents over the table. 'This isn't Sam. I told you the truth about that. He's down in the sewers where he belongs. This is just the leavings from a bonfire at The Pines. It was a little therapy I devised for myself.'

She tips out the pink urn and the dust from the ashes curls into the tight, hot living-room air. Sophie stands there, her mouth open wide, unable to speak.

Adam moves forward and puts a restraining hand on Louisa's shoulder, but she shrugs him off and wheels round to face him.

'Soph here is a devious, sly little slug. She's tricked her way in here because she somehow thinks she's entitled to money for having sex with my husband and turning him away from his wife and children.'

She turns back to Sophie. 'Even though, I suppose, in many ways she was doing me a favour, tempting that abusive bastard out of my life. Except for the fact, of course, that he then hunted us down and tried to murder me and my children.'

433

'That is not true,' Sophie says.

'Oh, but it is.'

The two women face each other in a terrible silence, punctuated only by Sami sucking on her dummy. Louisa's eyes laser Sophie. They are so cold, so icy blue that Sophie touches her cheek to make sure it hasn't turned to stone. She glances, again, over at Adam, who looks like he'd rather be anywhere else than here.

'People know I'm here,' she says, at last, as danger percolates through the dust-choked air.

'Oh, I'm sure they do,' Louisa says.

'Sophie—' Adam says.

'Don't you speak to her,' Louisa hisses at him.

'Sophie,' he goes on, ignoring Louisa. 'You said you'd come to speak about the children. But you thought they lived here, so it wasn't about them being with Lou's parents, was it?'

'No,' Sophie says. 'Although I'm glad they're not here with her. They're lovely kids, they deserve better.'

'You pious little whore, you with your little bastard brat . . .' Louisa makes to jump at Sophie, but Adam grabs her and holds her back.

'Let me go!' she says, struggling to get away from him.

'Calm down, Lou, please,' he says.

'I am calm! Now let me go, Adam. Now. Or I shall start screaming.'

He releases her from his arms, but leaves a firm hand on her shoulder.

Louisa turns to Sophie and digs into her again with those big, cold, eyes. 'So what *do* you want, Sophie?'

'Good question,' Sophie says. With a tenuous appearance of calm, she retrieves her bag from the buggy handle.

'Adam, watch her,' Louisa says, moving now to shelter behind her Jesus Boy, as if she expects a gun to be brought out.

Or a fire bomb, Sophie thinks, smiling to herself, trying to enjoy her own little in-joke.

But her weapon is far, far more powerful than that. Its destructive potential is greater even than an H bomb, an F bomb and a C bomb combined.

'Stay cool, Sophie,' Adam says, leaning towards her, holding up his hands.

As if that can stop her.

As Sophie reaches into her bag, he instinctively stretches a protective arm across Louisa. But the weapon she pulls out is a sheet of A4 paper. On it, in her beautiful handwriting, is her transcript of the texts sent by Louisa to Sam's white iPhone on the night of the crash.

She stands like an actress at a casting and starts to read – in a voice that attempts to capture Louisa's breathy, Marilyn Monroe tones – '"Sam, I can't go on like this. You have to come back."'

'What is this?' Adam asks Louisa, who has folded her arms and is saying nothing.

'Yes, ask Louisa, Adam. She knows exactly what it is. It's one of the forty-five text messages she sent Sam on the night of the crash, the night when she says he tried to murder her and his children. We'd turned the phone off because she just wouldn't give up.'

'"We!"' Louisa says.

'So we didn't see any of them on the night.'

Louisa has affected a look of feigned nonchalance so effortful that her whole body has seized up. She looks like she might, any second, implode.

Taking strength from her discomfort, Sophie forges on. 'You thought the phone had gone up in flames in Sam's car, didn't you, Louisa? Oh, sorry, Lou, I mean. Thought all this was lost. Me too. But, hey! It wasn't. Here's the second text: "Sam, my head hurts where you slammed it against the wall. I feel dizzy. I need to go to hospital." It's pretty artless, isn't it? Sam told me all about this, Louisa, how you were always self-harming. But, of course, then you told him you were pinning it on *him*, what with that diary and all. You made it all up, and after Sam died I *told* everyone you were making it up, but no one believed me. Perhaps they will, now I've got evidence of all your other lies.'

'No one believed you because you're a convicted, dirty little liar. *You're* making it all up,' Louisa says through a mouth that can hardly open. 'There's no phone. It's all make-believe, another desperate little trick to try to get money out of me. Blackmail, Adam. She's blackmailing me.'

'You wish. There are more texts, all in a similar vein, then – oh, this one isn't nice, Adam, listen: "Sam, look what you've done to your children." She attached a photograph of them crying. Just to show him exactly what sort of pain he was causing. Wonder what she did to poor Poppy and Leon to cause those tears?'

Adam frowns. Sophie straightens the paper in her hands and goes on.

'Her next: "You have scared them, and hurt them, and me."'

Still standing in front of Adam, with her back to him, Louisa has her eyes closed and looks as if she is counting.

'And this is where it gets *really* chilling, Adam.' Sophie smiles at him then continues to read. '"Sam, you have driven me to this. The children are quiet now." Quiet. That sounds ominous, doesn't it? How quiet, exactly, we're wondering? As the grave?'

Without warning, Louisa launches herself at Sophie. 'Give me that,' she says, snatching the paper from Sophie's hand and ripping it to pieces.

'You think that'll stop me?' Sophie swings the buggy across to the far corner of the room, out of Louisa's reach. She

436

positions herself in front of it, guarding Sami. 'You think I haven't got them tucked away up here?' She taps her forehead. 'Let me see now. Oh yes, the next one says this: "Sam, I'm putting them in the car and we're driving to Roswell Pits".

'Roswell Pits, you're asking, Adam? Let me tell you about them. I looked them up. They're disused clay pits, flooded to make a glittering, deep lake and a lush reed bed. You can drive right up to them, right to the very edge. Right over.

'Here's the next text, just in case there's any doubt: "This is your fault, Sam. Your cruelty is too much for me to bear. There's nowhere to go. Our blood is on your hands, now and for ever." Very dramatic. Well, she doesn't leave much to the imagination, does she? And here's her final shot: "I covered for you over Katie, but I can't lie any more. The blood-stained shirt you asked me to burn? I didn't. It will be found one day, and you will be found out." It's hard to tell whether she's writing this for his eyes only or for the police, isn't it, Adam?'

Adam turns to Louisa. 'Who's Katie? What shirt?'

'Oh, that's a whole new story for you to hear, Adam, but the point I'm making right now is about the shirt. It's interesting, because the version she gave the police and the press – when she realised that she and the children had survived and he hadn't, and she thought the phone had gone up with him in the car – was completely different to the one she gives here. It served her escape story so much better. *He* kept the shirt, she said, to torment her, to stop her from running away, a threat, she said, to remind her what happened to his women when they disobeyed him.

'If you'd met Sam, Adam, you'd know instantly. That was not him. He was not capable of anything like that.'

Adam stands on the other side of the room, his hands hanging at the end of his arms like dead birds.

Louisa turns to him. 'You know this is all bullshit, don't you?'

437

He can't even meet her eye in response.

'You set Sam up, didn't you, Louisa?' Sophie says, the smile gone from her face as, having stuck her weapon right in, she prepares to twist it. 'You set him up as a wife-murderer, a wife-beater, a bad, bad man, just because he wouldn't do what you wanted. And you were really prepared to do it, weren't you? To kill your own children, as well as yourself, so that Sam would suffer.'

'This is such bullshit. What sort of woman would want to kill her own children?' Louisa says.

Sophie raises an eyebrow. 'Indeed.'

'There's no such thing as a white iPhone. You're making it up.'

'You wish. I have it and it's safe, where you can't get at it. And this time next week, unless you give me the Cambridge flat and enough money from Sam's legacy to ensure that his daughter here has a decent life – let's say, for the sake of argument, one million pounds on top of the flat—'

'One million?' Adam's eyes grow even wider. Any more, and Sophie is certain that his eyeballs would fall out. 'What Cambridge flat, Lou?'

'My Cambridge flat,' Sophie says. 'Ten Brookside Lane, which Sam bought for me to live in and from which your Lou here is now evicting me and my baby. Oh, this, too, surprises you? You should ask your girlfriend here about how much money and property she actually owns. It'll be quite an eye-opener for you. Ten Brookside Lane, look it up on RightMove.'

Louisa looks at Adam and shakes her head, as if to say that what Sophie is saying is rubbish. But Sophie is beyond caring what Adam thinks.

She hooks her bag over one shoulder and takes the brake off the buggy. 'I'll call you next week. If you are still hell bent on not giving me and Sami what's due to us, I'm taking the phone to the police. One week, Louisa. *Lou*. Keep an eye on her, Adam. And look after your baby when he or she comes. Poor thing.' She looks up at his lost, befuddled face. 'What have you got yourself into, eh?'

Her legs shaking, Sophie wheels the buggy around and steers it towards the hallway. She knows Louisa has no choice but to pay up. As much as she knows that, as soon as she gets what is owed her, she will go to the police, anyway. She glances at the ring on her third finger, left hand. Yes, all those birds, killed with one, beautiful stone.

Thank you, Sam.

'Stop her!' Louisa screams at Adam.

'And do what?' Sophie hears him say as, unchallenged, she pushes Sami through the front door of the flat. 'Do what, exactly?'

More satisfied than she has felt since she was last with Sam, she is not the slightest bit concerned about how she will lug the buggy down all those stairs. As it happens, as she arrives in the lift lobby, a loud click snaps behind a cupboard set in the wall. It is followed by a buzz, then a low-pitched hum, then the landing lights flash on and the doors to the lift zip open.

At last. Everything is going her way.

64

Caught in Sophie's jangling wake, Lou and Adam stand and look at each other for a long, long time. The dirty, sultry air percolates around them, but Lou is as cold inside as a plague-pit body.

Adam's throat bobs as he swallows.

Lou yelps, clutches her already discernibly tauter belly and falls to the ground.

When she comes to, she is on her side on their bed, looking down through the window. The empty spaces of the tower that will soon be her new home gape up at her. She turns, thinking she is going to get up and run away, but is surprised to find that Adam has carried through one of the dining chairs and is sitting beside the bed, watching, waiting.

'Well?' he says.

Lou closes her eyes.

'You look so beautiful when you sleep. Innocent,' he says. But he leaves it open, as if the counterpoint to that is when she is awake.

'It's all nonsense,' she says. 'The whole thing is nonsense.'

He is silent.

'You have to understand that the woman who sent those text messages wasn't me,' she tells him.

'What do you mean?'

'She was Louisa. A different person altogether. People can change.'

Again, he says nothing.

'Louisa couldn't see a way through it all. Sam had promised so much, and then he went and took it away.'

'*Did* he hit you?'

'He did things no man should ever do to his wife.'

'He hurt you?'

'So much, so often. In here.' Lou thumps her chest with a tightly clenched fist. 'He was the devil, you know. The devil.'

He swallows. 'Lou, you're frightening me.'

But Lou doesn't hear him. 'She put up with it all for so long,' she says. 'Then he said he was going to put her away, tear her from her children, and she couldn't bear it any more. No way to go on.

'It wasn't like that little junkie back there said it was, Adam, you've got to believe me. The children crying – that was just them. They cried all the time, day and night. It was the air he put around them all, the sorrow, the pain. She gave them medicine to make them quieter, happier, medicine he made the doctor give her, to stop her getting in his way. She took some herself, too. The children slept on the couch like little slugs.'

'Man,' Adam says, shaking his head.

'Look. She made them, after all. They were hers to do with what she wanted, yes?'

He closes his eyes.

'Louisa kept this journal, this record of all the pain she suffered thanks to him. On the last night, she put it in her underwear drawer, somewhere it would be easily found. She drank vodka. On top of the pills. But even that couldn't stop the hurting.

'She sat down and wrote a note: *I just can't go on. We're*

leaving for good, Goodbye – and left it on the kitchen table. Lucky it was so vague, the way things turned out. Lucky that the white phone was lost. She tried to call Sam, she texted him again and again. She called the whore's landline, and finally got through to him and told him what she was going to do, and that it was all his fault. She wasn't religious, but she knelt in the middle of the kitchen floor and said the Lord's Prayer.

'She strapped the children into the back of her little car, not so much for safety but to keep them in place. The girl – Poppy – woke, and started crying again, so she offered her chocolate if she took two more tablets. She was a good girl like that. Anything to please her mother.'

Adam shudders. Lou reaches up, touches under his cheek and feels wetness.

'Don't cry. It's a sad, sad story, but don't cry. It turns out better than you'd think, so it's all right.

'Louisa sat in her car and sent that one last text to Sam the devil. About the shirt and the alibi and poor, poor Katie. But she'd taken too long. She hadn't reckoned on how fast a man can drive in a red Porsche, wanting to save his own skin.'

'And his children,' Adam says, but Lou doesn't hear him.

'As she pulled out of the driveway of the house in the middle of nowhere, he appeared out of the dark and the mist, roaring his engine. She tried to escape – the cold, dark water was calling her. She just wanted it all to stop. But when they got to the narrow track that led to her release, he was right on her, forcing her off the road . . .'

She scrambles to her knees and faces him, smiling.

'Adam? Adam? You see? It was true. He did try to kill them! He did try to kill her, he was wrong, and she was right. No one lied. Intentions are one thing; acts are another. Like the people out there.' She points to the building site. 'They think they're making things better, but they've killed a community, wiped out a civilisation.'

'It's not the same,' Adam says.

'But it is! Don't you see?' She puts her hands on his face. He doesn't shy away, but, ever so slightly, he flinches at her touch. 'It might never have happened. She might have changed her mind.' She strokes his cheek in the way she knows he likes, in the same way Louisa used to stroke Poppy's.

He takes her hand and moves it away from his face.

'And it was a different woman who did all that, Adam. She doesn't exist any more. The moment he died, she was remade.'

'But the children. The children, Lou.'

'Yes. The poor children.' Lou is crying now, too. 'Once he had gone, Louisa knew she could save them, that they were free. She fought and she was burned, then blown backwards.' She thrusts her forearms before him, showing him the scars he knows only too well. 'These are the proof. She fought for her children.'

Adam doesn't move.

'And then they wouldn't let her have them back, not even when she was better. Her evil parents, took them away, told lies about her.'

'They weren't lies, Lou. They were true. They were true. You've just told me yourself that you drugged them.'

'*She* drugged them.' She lets her arms fall, then tumbles back to the bed, lying there, looking up at the ceiling.

'Man, this is so fucked up,' Adam says.

'And Sophie?' she says, at last. 'Sophie's just greedy. She's blackmailing me. She's making my life hell. And why? If this is anyone's fault other than Sam's, then it's hers. Not Louisa's.'

'And what about this Katie?' Adam says, his voice tiny, like a little boy's. 'What happened to her?'

Lou shrugs and continues to look at the ceiling. Her voice

flat, she speaks. 'Poor Katie was killed with a log as she walked her dog in the woods near her home. No witnesses. Sam told me he was in my flat all night, waiting for me to come home from Edinburgh, where I'd been at a conference. I got home around midnight, later than he'd been expecting me. When the police called in the morning, when her body was found, I said I'd come home earlier, and we'd spent the evening in together. He would have been the prime suspect, being the husband and all. I was his alibi.'

'And the shirt?' Adam says. 'Which of your stories is true? Did he ask you to burn it, or did he keep it to threaten you?'

Lou shrugs. 'Whatever you want to believe.'

Adam begins to say something, to ask a question, or to argue. But then he stops. 'I don't know what to think, or to say.'

'You don't have to think or say anything.'

'I don't know what's true and what's not any more.' He hunches in his chair and looks down at his feet, as if some sort of answer can be found there.

'*This* is true.' She grasps his hand and places it firmly on her belly. 'Feel that? Our baby's growing inside me. It's going to be different this time,' she tells him, her voice hoarse. 'It's all good. You're going to stick with us whatever happens, remember? You swore.'

'Us?'

'Me and the baby.'

'And if Sophie goes to the police?'

'She won't. And if she does, they won't believe her. She's not a reliable source. She could have made it all up. She's been in prison before, for lying, you know.'

'I don't think you can pretend text messages came from somewhere else.'

'Oh, she'll be all right. She'll see sense.'

Adam falls quiet but allows her to keep his hand pressed to her belly.

Gradually, the weight of deceit at last off her shoulders and her mind set on what she has to do, Lou, or Louisa, or whoever she is, falls asleep.

65

Lou shines a torch around the dark, stinking alleyway. All she sees is a pile of crap that could be canine or human in origin. Satisfied that the coast is clear, and holding her big tote bag close to her – how ironic would it be if she were mugged at this point? – she steps around the turd and hurries out of the boarded-up block of flats, past the pebbledashed seventies maisonettes.

Good job her hunch had been right and Reuben and mates in the squat were still up partying – if that is the right description for lying around in a stupor twitching to overloud drum and bass thumping out of knackered speakers.

'Roobs' had stumbled towards her and suggested – quite graphically – that she could pay for her purchase another way, involving her mouth and his penis. Stepping away she instead handed him a hundred quid in notes. Even if Reuben weren't so utterly repulsive, she couldn't be unfaithful to Adam.

A hundred was probably more than the going rate, but what the hell. And she'd needed him to set it all up for her, too, after all, and provide the extras which, as he was quick to point out, was 'really putting me out, man'.

She steps out into the dim, pre-dawn light of the main road and hails a passing black cab to take her north.

At King's Cross, she pays the driver without leaving a tip. Trying her hardest to minimise her limp, she crosses under the soaring latticework dome of the concourse, holding her mobile phone to her ear like a proper businesswoman, leaving a message on the A.R.K. voicemail.

'Hey, Cleo! I'm not too good this morning. Might be that lurgy that's been going around. I'll work from home on the cat food project and hopefully I'll be in tomorrow.'

She's nothing if not professional.

There are more people here than she would have expected at six in the morning, but then the world of business starts early. Men and women in summer-weight suits stand like pale statues, chins lifted, eyes fixed on the information boards above them, waiting for trains to whisk them to York, Edinburgh, Leeds, to lunch with clients, seal deals, open prospects. Oh yes, she knows the language very well from the days Sam used it. From before it became nothing but lies and excuses for being away from her and the children. The flash of anger stirred by this thought brings her to a brief halt, halfway across the concourse, but she is soon on her way again.

After nipping into Boots to buy a pack of pre-sterilised, ready-filled baby bottles, she makes her way past the Harry Potter photo opportunity and a closed bookshop to the toilets to indulge her new morning pregnancy habit of throwing up. She's not desperate quite yet, but it's better to get it out of the way now, than to suffer indignity on the train. She squats over the pan and sticks her finger down her throat, bringing up black, stringy bile.

She rinses and spits, rinses and spits. In front of the mirror, taking inspiration from Sophie, she winds a grey headscarf around her hair and dons a pair of sunglasses. It's not a complete disguise, but it tones down her look sufficiently to make identifying her from a remembered chance encounter, or a piece of CCTV, more of a challenge.

The Cambridge Express flies through North London, blurring the Emirates Stadium into Ally Pally, zipping past Edwardian suburbs, brown-lawned parks, sun-scorched trees, the cracked, dank mud-bole remnant of a river. Lou presses her forehead to the window and thinks how beautiful Adam had looked when she woke before dawn and slipped out of bed. Surprisingly, given all that happened last night, he was sleeping soundly beside her on the bed, his hand still resting on her belly, only a small frown creasing his brow.

She had half expected to find him gone, or on the sofa. But no. What constancy her boy shows. She will win him back. She will make him believe her over her cow mother.

When he wakes, he'll not know where she is, and he will worry, both for her, and for his unborn child. She could text him, let him know that she and it are safe, but she won't. Let him find out how much he needs her. Let him search the streets for her. Sooner or later he'll call A.R.K. and come up against the impermeable receptionist who, knowing nothing of Adam, will, under Cleo's instructions, block any unexpected calls for Lou. She is not even allowed to confirm whether she works there or not.

Poor Adam. But it's all for the best, for their future together, that he realises just how much he needs her.

Just as she's settling into her seat, the train pulls in to Cambridge Station. Forty-six minutes! Extraordinary. It really is very handy for London. In fact, she could see herself moving the family up here in a year or two. She steps out of the train and breathes in the cleaner air. It would be a lovely place to bring up the children, a happy medium between town and country.

But, as she reaches the ticket barrier, she remembers that,

thanks to the bad memories lurking all over the city, she could never live here. Her eyes darken. Yet another possibility Sam snatched from her life. Again, she has to pause to allow the fury to pass through her.

It is as hot here as it is in London, but the blue sky lacks the big-city grey haze. Lou could go straight to her destination, but she decides instead to take a turn through Cambridge. It's a little early, after all, to be paying surprise visits.

She walks into town then heads down towards the river. She's not going anywhere near The Grafton Centre and that lingerie shop – to do so would be as painful as scraping flesh from her bones – but she does pass the market square, where the traders are unloading for the day. It's gratifying to see that there is no sign of Jammin's awful whimsy. If there is any justice in this world – which Lou doubts – she has gone bust.

Her bad leg starting to complain, she makes her way to The Backs, just as the morning bicycle rush hour kicks off. Here, the imperatives of tourism – or perhaps just the privileges accorded to the elite – have earned the greenery a reprieve from the hosepipe ban. Ignoring a sign that tells her the fenced-off area is for King's College members only – what makes them think they're so special? – she climbs over a gate, thinking how pleased Adam would be at her adventurousness.

She puts her heavy bag down and sits beside it on the bank of the depleted, stinky Cam, basking in the shade of the first living green she has seen in months. Above her, a towering willow rustles in the faint breeze, and whispers to her that soon she will find the peace she so badly needs.

'I know that,' she tells it. 'State the obvious, why don't you?'

She puts one hand on her belly and lies back in the cool grass, which is still damp from its morning watering. She can breathe here. She knows what she has to do.

With her free hand, she strokes her bag, tracing within it the outline of one of Adam's sharp, Japanese knives. So lethal is the blade that she has wrapped it in a tea towel to avoid accidentally doing herself a damage. She shivers to think what its honed steel edge would do if she ran a finger along it, but she hopes she won't have to use it and make a mess. It's only a back up to the main idea. This involves the purchases she made from Reuben, which nestle at the bottom of her bag, carefully wrapped in the spare summer dress she brought along should a change of clothing be needed. She has also packed a handful of carrier bags, a roll of duct tape and a pair of soft, clean cotton gloves.

'All you need to add now is nerve,' she tells herself.

The long willow leaves dance above her like gossiping tongues. 'You've got plenty of that,' they whisper back at her.

Satisfied, she closes her eyes and dozes in the morning heat.

Somewhere towards the north, a church bell strikes nine. It is time.

She stands and has to pause for a second to ride the pregnancy-induced, low-blood-pressure dizziness that moment-arily threatens to floor her.

Falling down in a faint. Now that would never do.

Some time after Sam died, Detective Sergeant Pam handed Lou a small Ziploc bag containing the very few items salvaged from the charred remains of the Porsche. Inside were his wedding ring – cleaned, she was relieved to see, of any remnants of him – his watch, which no longer worked, but which fetched a good price anyway, and a keyring full of partially melted keys. Two of the survivors of the bunch were for the flat, so Lou had copies made, keeping one set for herself and giving the others to Fiona so that she could get someone in to make the inventory before handing them over to the estate agents.

This is the first time Lou has personally entered the flat. Until now, it was the last place she would have chosen to visit. She has, however, looked at the photos and floor plan on RightMove, so an added benefit to having to make this journey is that she will see first hand what she's got on the market.

She puts on the white gloves and uses the bigger key to unlock the front door, which opens easily to reveal a hallway which, she notes, could do with a lick of paint and a new stair carpet. She steps over the pile of free sheets and leaflets which always manage to accumulate, no matter how upmarket the communal hallway, and edges silently up the stairs. But when she tries to open the door to the flat, her key doesn't even fit into the hole. The little junkie must have changed the lock. Surely, without the owner's permission, this amounts to criminal damage? And how is the estate agent supposed to get in and show prospective buyers around?

She presses her ear to the door. There is a movement inside, a gurgling, a soft singing; Frank Sinatra plays in the background.

So Sophie is up. Lou had thought her the kind of lazy princess who lies abed all morning. But, of course, she is no more immune to the tyrannies of a small baby than she herself had been.

There's nothing else for it. She knocks softly on the door.

'Who is it?' Sophie says from the other side.

'It's me, Lou,' Lou says, her lips right up to the door. 'Louisa.'

'What do you want?' Sophie says.

'To come to an arrangement.'

The door opens a crack, still on its security chain, and Sophie's dark, doe-like eyes peer out, sideways. Lou lifts her sunglasses and smiles.

'I want to buy the phone off you,' she says.

'Are you on your own?'

Lou nods, but still Sophie hesitates.

'Look,' Lou whispers, mindful of the neighbours. 'I just want this part of my life over and done with. I've made my mistakes in the past. I wasn't well when all that happened with Sam. I was drinking, my judgement was clouded, I had the baby blues or whatever. But the facts remain. He tried to kill me and my children, and he failed. It has been decided in a court of law. No matter what was going on in my mind back then. I just want to draw a line, put the past in the past, and get on with my new life.'

'Do you now.' Sophie remains where she is, her eyes on Louisa.

'Look. I'm pregnant with Adam's child,' Lou says. 'I just want to give you what you need so I can move forward.'

The door closes. For a moment, Lou thinks she has blown it, that she's going to have to somehow force her way in. But the chain rattles, and shortly the door pushes open and Sophie is there, her baby in her arms.

A sheen of sweat blooms on Lou's forehead. She forces a smile as she notices the way Sophie is eyeing her white cotton gloves.

'It's for the burn scars,' she says. 'I have to wear them as much as possible. To help the lotion soak in.'

Raising an eyebrow, Sophie ushers Lou into the flat. 'That way.' She points down the hallway, keeping Lou in front of her. 'It's a bit of a mess, I'm afraid,' she says, as they pass a stack of packing boxes. As they enter the sitting room, Sinatra launches into 'I've Got You Under my Skin'.

A bit of a mess is no understatement. Lou has a faint memory of the difficulty she had keeping things in order when Poppy and Leon were around, but this is something else. Are prospective buyers being shown the flat in this state?

'Take a seat,' Sophie says, which is a bit rich, seeing that this is Lou's flat and Lou's sofa.

Pointedly, Lou moves a washing basket full of dirty linen to clear a space so that she can sit down. She looks around the room, which she knows well from RightMove. Of course, it's smaller than it appears in the estate agent's photographs, but it's still a good size with plenty of natural light. The big bay window looks out onto a view, which, in any other summer, would be bosky and leafy. Under Sophie's junk and detritus, the broad, wooden floorboards are partly covered by a lovely pair of Bokhara rugs, which Lou recognises from photographs taken for the inventory. They will look nice on the engineered oak floors in the penthouse, she thinks.

'Well, what's your offer?' Sophie says, perching on the edge of an armchair, still holding the baby, who gurgles in her arms.

Sweet little thing, Lou thinks. Despite its parentage.

'I'd like to see the phone before we go on.'

'Oh, I can't do that. You'll just have to take my word it exists. You know those text messages weren't made up, don't you?'

'It's a pity you won't show it to me,' Lou says.

'What's your offer, then?'

'Could I have a cup of tea, please?' Lou asks. 'Peppermint, if you've got it.'

'Fuck off. This isn't a café.'

'There's no need to be uncivil.'

'Oh, I think there is, Louisa. I'm not waiting on you.'

'A glass of water, then? I'm feeling a little faint. It's been a long journey. And you get so thirsty with the baby, don't you?' She taps her stomach with her white cotton hand. 'Peppermint's so good for the heartburn, too. Did you find that?'

'Fuck's sake. I'll make you a fucking tea.' Sophie sighs, stands and, backing out, her baby in her arms, leaves the room.

The minute she is gone, Lou pulls the duct tape from her bag and tears off three long strips and one shorter length.

She sticks two of the longer pieces loosely to the back of the door – which Sophie has left open – and fixes the other to her index finger. The shorter tape she sticks temporarily over her forehead, like, she thinks, a pore strip, or part of a face mask.

Yes, she has thought all this out. She is, after all, a hotshot designer.

She turns up the volume on the crooning Sinatra and takes up her position behind the door. She has one chance, and it all relies on taking bold, decisive action at just the right moment.

So, the minute Sophie comes into the room, Lou slams the door into her, causing the two mugs of tea she is carrying to fly back, straight, as Lou had hoped, into her face.

She's glad to see the little baby isn't still in Sophie's arms. It would have been a pity to have got boiling water all over it. A pity, yes, but it wouldn't have stood in her way. Needs must, and even great nations acknowledge that collateral damage can sometimes be a sad necessity in the face of a greater good.

Lou deftly hooks her foot into Sophie's instep and, grasping her shoulder, trips her stunned, scalded adversary forward, splaying her, face down, on the floor. Straddling her back, she binds Sophie's hands behind her, using the duct tape she had hooked over her index finger. Before Sophie can find the breath in her to scream, Lou has the tape whipped from her forehead and slapped over her mouth. Then she just has to wind one of the other pieces around Sophie's ankles and use the final stretch to hog-tie her arms to her feet.

'Wow,' Lou says. 'That went well.'

She winds more tape, straight from the roll, around her captive, then stands back and admires her handiwork. It's perfect. There's no chance of Sophie going anywhere.

She turns the music up another notch. There's a sort of

bleating sound coming from behind Sophie's gag, and you never know how nosey neighbours are going to be about a bit of scuffling heard through the walls or the ceiling.

'Shut up, *Soph*,' Lou says, giving her a kick. It's gentle, but it's in the throat, and it does the trick.

'Did you think I'd really do a deal with you?' she goes on. 'All of this is actually your fault. You know that, don't you? If you hadn't fucked my husband, none of this would have happened, so you've only got yourself to blame.'

She squats beside Sophie and pulls her hair backwards so they are both looking each other straight in the eye – Lou's cold and blue, Sophie's set in her wet, scald-reddened face, black and wild with terror.

'Yes, you've got that look, like Sam had, Soph. Something of the devil in those pretty eyes of yours. I should have noticed that earlier in him, before it was too late. Did his demon perhaps slip into you alongside his dick? He liked being tied up like this, didn't he? Oh, I've seen the photos. On the phone. But you're not so keen on being at that end of things, yeah? Oh, poor, poor Soph. Sorry about that. Girl's gotta do, et cetera.'

Lou gets up, moves to her bag and tugs out the knife, which she carefully unwraps and lays on the sofa, on the patch that she cleared for herself earlier.

Sophie makes a tiny, high-pitched noise in the back of her throat.

'So, Soph. You have to tell me where the phone is.'

Sophie shakes her head and struggles with her ties.

'Oh, don't waste your energy. You'll never get out of all that tape. I've done too good a job on it.' Lou sits on the arm of the sofa and faces her. 'You'd better tell me, or I'm going to have to take this place apart to find it, and it'll end up an even bigger mess, and I don't like mess. Also, there's this . . .' Lou picks up the knife. With her teeth, she pulls the glove off her free hand then runs the blade along her finger. She just can't resist it any longer. Blood beads on the tiny cut, then bubbles and dribbles down into her palm.

'Oops. Potential for DNA.' She licks her hand then plugs the finger in her mouth and sucks on it. 'Better keep it all inside, eh? Don't want to leave any traces.'

Once again, Sophie bucks against her restraints.

'You really have to keep it down, Soph,' Lou says, the knife still in her hand. 'Or I might have to take matters into my own hands, and I really don't want to do that. So look, I'm going to take that tape off your mouth and give you a chance to tell me where the phone is. If you make a sound that anyone outside this flat will be able to hear above the sound of Ol' Blue Eyes, then I'm going to have to hurt you.' She squats close to Sophie, not caring that she is practically pushing her crotch into her face, and lets the knife hover near her throat. 'Or your baby.'

Sophie's head jerks up. It would have been impossible to imagine that she could have cast a wilder-eyed look than previously, but she manages it.

'Yes. I'm afraid needs must, Soph. So are you going to be a good girl, or not?'

Sophie nods her head.

'Good.'

Lou takes hold of the tape and rips it from her face. Sophie gasps at the sudden tearing, which strips a layer from her top lip, leaving it bleeding, like a horrible cold sore.

'Where's the phone, Soph?'

Sophie looks like she is going to be sick, so Lou backs off a little, still holding the knife close to her victim's face.

'Come on, Soph.'

'It's in the bedroom,' Sophie says. 'Under the cot mattress.'

'Oh, under the baby's bed. Nice move. Classy.'

'Please don't hurt her.'

'Oh, Soph. What kind of monster do you take me for? Of course I won't hurt your little baby. Not if you behave yourself. As if. Oh no. Now keep very, very quiet, yes?'

Sophie nods wildly as Sinatra launches into a leisurely 'Come Fly with Me'.

Singing along, feeling calm now that she has everything under her control again, Lou floats to the bedroom, pulling her spare glove back onto her hand. On the threshold, she stops and takes in the bedroom, described quite accurately by her estate agent as a generously sized master suite. Her full lips tighten into a thin line at the layer of dirt and decadence Sophie has spread over the space: walls daubed with orange paint, a blanket of dust, a mirror barely visible through the scarves, necklaces and feathers draped over it, a phalanx of expensive perfume bottles guarding its bottom edge. She tries but fails to eliminate the image of Sam stretched out here, on the bed, tied up to the rings bolted onto the four corner posts.

While she was stuck back in her Fenland hell.

Taking a deep breath, she moves across the room to look more closely at a pathetic collection of artefacts on a small table in the far corner. She runs her gloved fingers over a picture of Sam with Sophie on that tacky bed, a bunch of dead roses, a cinema ticket. She takes the lid off a bottle of Eau Sauvage and, as she expects, one sniff brings him back in front of her, all devil eyes and laughing at her.

'Well,' she says to his photograph, 'I've got the better of you, Sam, and no two ways about it.' She swipes the whole load of shit off the table and grinds the crispy dead flowers into the cream carpet which, she notes, is also riddled with burn marks. She doesn't even want to start imagining where they came from.

Then she spots the shirt, hanging from the wardrobe door. She tugs it down and examines it, holding it right up to her eyes, sniffing it, running her fingers over it. Without a doubt, this is Sam's shirt. Paul Smith, little flowers on a cotton lawn, his size and, detectable even under the whore-stink, his smell. It could even be the one she bought to replace the bloody version. Smiling as she recalls how Sam never noticed a thing, she puts it on and rips the scarves from the mirror to look at herself. Yes, she thinks, doing up the buttons. She really got a lot of mess on that other one.

She turns to face the rest of the room. An empty washing line with pegs on it is sluttishly suspended across the corner.

'What's wrong with the bathroom for drying your washing?' Lou says, scorn in her voice. This girl has no idea how to live like a civilised being.

Finally, her eye is drawn to the baby, sleeping on its back on top of the sheets in a cot placed right up against the bed. Attachment disorder, Lou diagnoses. Poor little Soph can't differentiate between herself and her child. It's a recipe for disaster. The baby sighs, its arms flung up either side of its head.

Trusting, tiny thing.

Lou goes to the cot and bends over so close that she can blow on the baby's cheek and make it pull a little face. Its eyes can be seen, moving from side to side underneath delicate, blue-tinged eyelids. Lou hates to admit it but, looking at its face, it could be no one else but Sam's child. She is surprised to register that she is less concerned about this than she might have been. Perhaps it's down to the new life of her own, thrumming inside her.

'Sweet baby,' she says to it.

She feels around underneath the mattress until she discovers the phone, tucked far away, right in the middle. Doesn't Sophie know about the dangers of mobile phones? That you shouldn't put them near a young child because the radiation can get through their thin, pliable skulls and into their brains? To have your baby sleep right on top of one, even one with, as Lou discovers quickly enough, a worn-out battery, can't be any good at all.

Really, this girl knows nothing.

She puts the phone in her pocket and lifts the baby out of its cot. 'Poor child,' she says, cradling its head against her chest. The baby smells of milk and sweet sweat, a combination that makes her stomach heave, but it's not the child's fault. It is the stench of its mother.

She carries the baby through into the living room. 'You really shouldn't—' she starts to say, but is stopped by Sophie's growl.

'Put her down,' she says from the floor. She has clearly been trying to work herself free. Lou is not impressed.

'I've got the phone, Soph, but really, you haven't been looking after this baby very well. It needs a change, and it certainly needs a bath.'

'PUT HER DOWN!' Sophie yells, and starts frantically working her way across the floor, jack-knifing her legs against the carpet.

Lou lays the baby – who is awake and looking around her wide eyed – on the sofa, a little distance from the knife. Then she moves over and kicks Sophie in the head. Again, it's enough to shut her up.

'You think I'm not serious about you being quiet?' Lou says. 'I want you to know that I don't take rubbish from anyone. I take a stick to anyone who gives me grief. I bring it down on them again, and again, and again, until they can't cause any more trouble.'

'Like you did with Katie,' Sophie croaks. 'The shirt,' she says, clocking what Lou is wearing. 'Oh, Jesus.'

'Like I did with Katie,' Lou says, fingering the buttons on her front. 'Yes, in a shirt very like this one. You can't imagine the trouble she gave me. Her sister coming up to me and Sam in a restaurant and shaming me in front of everyone. Really, really horrible letters. She just couldn't see that Sam and I were in love and there was nothing she could do about it. Katie refused to let the divorce go ahead. She had to be stopped. She had it coming. She had no one to blame but herself.'

Sophie looks at Lou, opens her mouth to speak. Then her eyes flick over towards her baby and she thinks again. But Lou has clocked her intention.

'Oh, you're thinking that's just like you and Sam, aren't you, Sophie? And I was like Katie? But what you don't see is that it's completely different. For one thing, I am a woman and you're just a little junkie wee piece-of-shit of a girl. But the other thing, Sophie, the big difference is that THERE WERE CHILDREN INVOLVED.' Realising she has just shouted out loud, Lou clamps a hand over her mouth. 'Oops.'

Sinatra moves on, to 'Strangers in the Night'.

'And, oh dear, I've said too much, haven't I? That's the trouble. It's the first time I've had a chance to tell anyone about Katie, and once you pop, you just can't stop, can you? Oh God, sorry Sophie.'

'What do you mean, sorry?' Sophie says, her eyes darting wildly from Lou to Sami and back again.

'Oh, don't worry. I won't hurt your child. I couldn't, like I said. But you really were a very, very poor mother. Dragging her all around with you while you did your dirty work, having her stuck to your side all the time. You really were making a rod for your own back.'

Lou moves to the sofa.

'LEAVE HER ALONE!' Sophie yells and, with an almighty heave of her long, bony body, she manages to separate her arms and legs and somehow bring herself to standing.

'What did I tell you?' Lou holds the knife, blade pointing downwards, over Sami's chest.

The child gurgles and reaches up at it as if she is being shown some sort of shiny new mobile toy.

'Be QUIET, Sophie,' Lou says.

Sophie freezes. 'Please . . .'

'Sit DOWN.'

Sophie collapses to her knees, tears and snot hanging from her overlarge features. 'Please don't hurt her.'

With one hand still holding the knife over the baby, Lou rummages in her bag with the other. She draws out her rolled-up spare dress and unravels it onto the sofa. Three capped hypodermic syringes fall out, each one full of an amber liquid.

'What's that?' Sophie says, her voice barely a squeak.

'Hmm now,' Louisa says, holding one of the syringes up to the light, marvelling at the colour of its contents. 'What do you call it? Skag? Horse? Shit? Anyway, it's the finest, shittiest, most adulterated no doubt, heroin money can buy.' She turns sharply and pitches the knife, blade first, towards Sophie, who instinctively flinches and cowers. It lands, however, where it was aimed, halfway between the two women, its pointed tip – not yet blunted by its encounters with vegan food – piercing the wide, fine floorboard, its steel handle vibrating with the force of the throw. Before Sophie has time to recover, Lou is onto her, a syringe in each hand, a third between her teeth. Like a pirate boarding a ship, she launches herself on to Sophie, pushing her face-down onto the floor, sitting on top of her so that, once again, she is immobilised.

'You'll just feel a tiny prick,' she says. 'Might remind you of Sam! My, what lovely veins you've got.' Sophie screams as Lou stabs a needle into the skin behind her knee. She pushes the plunger down and the golden brown liquid flows into Sophie's long, slender body.

Almost instantly, the struggling ceases beneath Lou. She feels the tension held beneath her relax as the heroin travels through Sophie's blood and into her brain.

'Nice, eh?' Lou says. 'You done this before?'

'No. I—' Sophie slurs, gags and throws up violently, all over the floorboards.

'Ugh. Disgusting,' Lou says, using the sleeve of Sam's shirt to wipe away the flecks of vomit that have splashed onto her.

'Just in case you've got rid of some of it through the puking,' she says, as she thrusts a second needle into Sophie's thin, vein-traced thigh. There is little resistance this time.

After a few moments, Lou steps off and rips away the duct tape binding Sophie's arms and legs. Liberated, her limbs just flop to the ground.

'Sami,' Sophie says, trying to move. Her voice is slurred, distant, as if coming from deep inside a dream. Lou rolls her over onto her back, noting how her head lolls, her eyes roll. It reminds her a little of the porn photos on the phone, except that Sophie's lips, so full and red in the photographs, are taking on a bluish tinge.

'Oh, Soph. Soph,' Lou says. 'You should have just let it lie, Soph. You were just too greedy, weren't you?'

With her gloved hands underneath Sophie's clammy armpits, Lou manages to haul her to a sitting position and prop her against an armchair by the coffee table. She is like a rag doll, but far heavier than Lou had imagined. Who knew that all that skin and bone could result in such a weight.

'Sami—' Sophie manages to say again, her face now greying, her head, her whole body, too heavy to hold up. It takes all her remaining strength to keep her eyes open. Lou stands and looks at her. She doesn't know why, but she decides to offer her one comforting thought.

'You don't worry about your baby, Soph. I'll make sure she's all right.'

The applause from the Sinatra concert fades and Sophie

finally gives up her battle to remain conscious. Her eyes roll back in her head until only the whites show, then her leaden eyelids close over them.

Working quickly, Lou rips what's left of the tape from Sophie's limp body. Then she pulls the remainder of her Sophie obliteration kit from her bag – the spoon and lighter Reuben used to boil the powder and liquid, the baggie that contained the heroin, and one of the shoelaces he uses for a tie. He threw this lot in for the hundred, so Lou supposes she got quite a bargain, all told.

She lays the paraphernalia out on the coffee table in front of Sophie, adjusting the arrangement a couple of times for maximum realism, then takes one of Sophie's long, floppy, pale arms and ties the shoelace around it. There are no veins to be seen now – it's as if her system has retreated deep inside the shell of her body. Lou checks for a pulse. It's there, but very, very faint. She's certain that the two full syringes she has shot into her have been enough to do the trick.

'It's a pleasant way to go, apparently,' she whispers to her now insensate rival who does, indeed, seem to be smiling slightly. 'I did my research on weights and amounts. It might take a few hours, but now you're asleep, it'll be quite gentle. Sweet dreams, *Soph*.'

She squirts some of the liquid from the final syringe and sticks it into the inside of the girl's elbow, where it hangs like a limpet with commitment issues. Stepping back and admiring the scene, Lou can't help congratulating herself. If the design work ever goes tits up, she could consider a career in set dressing for film.

On the sofa, the baby has started crying, kicking her feet and thrusting her fists into the air, as if she knows what is happening to her mother.

Poor baby.

Lou hurriedly peels off the sick-splattered shirt and bundles it up so that no stray hairs or fibres spill onto the floor. It is a pity that it isn't covered in blood like the other one – that would have provided a lovely symmetry. But it is better, really, that she didn't have to use the knife. She stuffs the shirt first into a carrier bag and then into her shopper. Her dress, she is pleased to see, is unmarked, so she has no need for the spare. She uses it instead to wrap up the knife, and then puts everything back into her bag.

She takes off her gloves and unwraps one of the sterilised, pre-filled bottles, then she sits and feeds the baby, adding songs and cuddles, until she falls back asleep. After setting the child gently down on the sofa, she puts her hands back inside the gloves, and sets about trashing the flat as if she were a burglar looking for valuables. She finds very little any opportunistic, murderous junkie would consider worth stealing except a diamond on a gold chain round Sophie's neck and Sam's bloody ring on her finger, which, she realises makes a set with the necklace. She rips both pieces from her body.

In the hallway, she discovers an impressive Mulberry handbag – and Sophie had claimed to be skint! She tips its contents out on the floor and finds – along with an empty purse, three tampons, four clouded dummies, a pack of baby wipes, two spare nappies and a crumbled cellophane pack of rusks – a paper wrap about the size of a razor blade. On it is written, in an almost indecipherable scrawl, the word SNAKE, followed by what looks like a mobile phone number. Lou carefully unwraps the package – a folded-over corner cut from *HEAT* magazine – to reveal Joey Essex's face, mostly obscured by a crystalline white powder.

'Hah! Serendipity,' Lou says. 'Silly little junkie.'

Back in the living room, the Mulberry over her shoulder as if it's already hers, she spills the powder – which, she guesses, might be Sophie's drug of choice, cocaine – onto the coffee table beside the other props, and positions the wrap with the phone number uppermost. The final, authentic touch.

This Snake came round with some coke and said, 'Hey, Soph, try some of this heroin.'

Yep. That's a good story.

Very much later, on her way back to London, Lou flushes the diamond jewellery down the train toilet, which, she supposes, from the sign forbidding its use in stations, empties onto the track. With regret, she leaves the covetable designer handbag in the baby-change room at King's Cross, certain that an opportunist finder will keep it.

Then she changes the baby's nappy and takes her back to The Heights.

She thinks she might start calling her Poppy.

66

Opening her apartment door, Lou recoils at the burst of heat that assaults her from within, furring her nostrils with the smell of dust baked through windows by relentless, scorching sunshine. The first thought that strikes her is that she can't go on living in this atmosphere. Not with two babies to take care of.

'Adam?' she calls, backing into the hallway. 'Adam?'

He emerges from the living room, with, she notes, the air of a man nearly ripped apart by worry. He doesn't, however, come up to her and kiss her with relief; she is disappointed by this.

'I didn't know where you'd gone,' he whispers.

'I'm fine.' Lou straightens her shoulders. 'I just had to speak to Sophie about stuff. You know.'

'You've been to Cambridge?'

'Maybe.'

She pulls the buggy through the door, and he jumps as if he has just received an electric shock.

'What's that?'

'You mean who, surely?' Lou reaches into the buggy and strokes the baby's chubby little chin.

'Who, then?' Adam says. He is as still as stone.

'It's Sophie's baby, of course. Sami. But we'll call her Poppy from now on, won't we, Pops?' she says to the baby, who grasps her finger and smiles. 'Aw look. All gums.'

'You took her away from Sophie? You kidnapped her?'

'What? No, of course not!' Lou laughs and pulls the buggy into the apartment. 'Sophie can't look after her any more.'

'What does that mean?' Adam says, pressing his back to the wall as she wheels the baby past him. He hurries after her into the living room. 'What does that *mean*?'

Lou parks the buggy, puts on the brake, lifts Poppy out and turns to him, smiling, the baby in her arms.

'It means I finally had it out with Sophie, and we agreed that she's really in no fit state to be raising a child. She has no money and she's taking far too many drugs. Far too many. You saw the state of her. She's too selfish, really, to be a good parent. We decided that this child would be far better off with me. With us, Adam. I got that white iPhone from her too, so we're all cool there.'

'I don't believe this,' he says, shaking his head.

The baby starts crying. Lou takes her to the sofa and sits down.

'Would you mind heating up one of the bottles from my bag?' she asks him. 'They're ready filled and I got enough to see us through until we're set up. Wash your hands first though, won't you?'

Dazed, Adam does as he's told, fixes up a bottle and passes it to Lou. As she gently holds it for the baby to feed, he finally finds his voice.

'You can't just take a baby away.'

'I've *told* you what happened.'

'When I was out looking for you, I ran into Carly.'

Lou raises her eyebrows. 'Did you, now.'

'She'd bumped into Reuben and he said you'd been round the squat, buying stuff.'

'Ha. I told him to keep quiet about it. Never trust a junkie, I suppose.'

'Lou. You're not – you don't use that shit, do you?'

'Me?' Lou snorts with laughter, disturbing the baby, who grabs at the bottle for fear it is going to be removed from her. 'No. Not me, Adam. I'm pregnant apart from anything else, and I'd hate anything to harm our baby. Wouldn't you?'

'Yes, of course. But then what—'

Lou sighs. 'If you must know, it was a gift. For Soph. She likes that sort of stuff. Greedy for it.'

'Ready made up with all the works?'

'Reuben gave Carly *all* the details, then.' Lou tuts and looks up at Adam, who hovers in the middle of the room as if he has no idea where to put himself. 'Call it gift wrapping.'

'What have you done, Lou?'

Lou looks down at the baby, who has slowed right down on the bottle to an occasional, drowsy suck. 'Ah, look. She's sleeping again.' She stands and puts the child back in the buggy. Then she turns to face Adam.

'I have saved this child,' she says, looking up, her eyes beautiful, blue pools. 'That is what I have done.'

'Where is Sophie? I've seen how she is with her baby. She wouldn't just give her away.'

Ignoring him, Lou turns away and goes to the window. 'Look, Adam. There's our crane. Remember when we first saw each other? You were up there, I was in my bedroom window. It was only a few weeks ago. But it seems like a lifetime, doesn't it?'

He goes to her, grasps her upper arms, twisting her to face him, and he shakes her. 'What has happened to Sophie?'

'Are you going to hurt me, Adam?' She flinches and cowers. 'I thought you were better than that. Remember: our baby . . .'

He lets go of her and steps backwards, his shoulders hunched, looking at his hands as if they belong to someone else.

'Of course you wouldn't hurt us, would you? You're not

like Sam.' She touches her belly and turns back to the window. 'See down there? Come. See.'

She beckons him over and, reluctantly, he moves to join her.

'That's the start of the tower that will soon be up there, even higher than our crane.' She points up into the sky. 'Can you imagine our view from the penthouse?' She turns and smiles at him.

'No, Lou.' Adam shakes his head wildly, backing away. 'No.'

'It'll be glorious, the perfect future. What a wonderful symmetry – our crane is building our new home. We started off on the thirteenth floor and we'll end up on the thirty-seventh, up in the sky, in our hot tub, you and me, like the couple on the model in the developer's office. What a vision, eh? A perfect life for you, me and our babies. Sealed off from the horrible outside world and all the terrible people who live in it, we'll sit right at the top looking down on this puny, shabby old building.'

He goes to her and wheels her round to face him. 'YOU HAVE TO TELL ME WHERE SOPHIE IS.'

'She's at home, of course.'

'In the flat? Ten Brookside Lane?'

Lou blinks. 'Well remembered.'

'I had this feeling you'd— I looked it up, found it on a property website. Rang the estate agents.'

'Tracking me down.'

'I was WORRIED, Lou. Our baby—'

'Oh, our baby. Don't worry about *that*.' She smiles and takes his hand. 'I know what you're really worrying about, in fact. And of course some people *will* be sniffy about you living up there, when you did all that protesting. But we can make new friends, start again, start our perfect new penthouse lives from fresh.'

Adam takes a deep breath, puts his other hand around hers and lowers his voice. 'We need to call Sophie; she'll be worried about her baby.'

'You'll come round,' she says, drawing away and smiling at him. 'It'll take a while, but you'll come to see that it's for the best. You have to, because if not, then, well, I don't think I want to have a baby here, in this place with this bad air.' She touches her belly and looks at him. 'It's not too late to do something about it, you know.'

'Lou. Stop this,' he says, and she notices that there are tears in his eyes.

'Oh, poor Adam. Don't worry,' she says, laughing, bringing a hand up to his face. 'I couldn't do *that* unless I was *really* forced to. I'm very pro-life, you know.'

Adam steps away from her and pulls out his phone. 'Tell me Sophie's number.'

'Don't bother. She won't answer.'

'Why not? What have you done to her, Lou?'

'For God's sake, Adam. You have to help me,' she says. 'If you don't – if you don't stop asking all these questions then, instead of everything being perfect, it could all go horribly wrong. We can hide Poppy from view until everything blows over. It's easy, here in the city. And I've been really careful. There'll be no questions asked about Sophie. It's an overdose, pure and simple, a sad junkie story.'

'An overdose?'

'So long as you keep quiet, everything will be fine. It would be terrible for both the children if I were, say, taken away from them.' Again, she touches her belly. 'If things came to a head, like I say, something could be done about this one. I couldn't, for example, bring myself to give birth in prison. I just couldn't. But what about poor Poppy, here? To lose one mother is devastating enough. But two?'

'How long ago did she take it? How much?'

'Sophie's locked away in the past now, Adam. You can forget about her.' Lou reaches up, puts her hands on his shoulders and turns him to face her. 'You have to help *me*, now,' she says. 'Together for ever, remember? Whatever happens.' She stands on tiptoe and kisses him on the cheek. 'What do you say, Adam?'

He blinks and, in her omnipotent mood, it looks to her like assent.

'Good. Good.' She pats his hand. 'I knew you'd see it from my point of view. Now, me and the baby inside are tired. We've had a busy day and I was up in the middle of the night, as you no doubt know, thanks to that little blabbermouth Reuben. So I'm going to have a sleep. Could you get me a peppermint tea? Leave the bag in.'

She leaves the room and closes the door behind her.

67

Adam

Adam remains, alone but for Sophie's stolen baby, who sleeps on the other side of the living room, sweetly oblivious to what might be happening to her mother.

He hears the bedroom door shut.

His heart thuds into the empty space left by Steroid Boy's missing bass lines.

Who *is* that woman he shares a bed with?

She has taken him over.

As he stands there, doing nothing, she is growing his child.

His child.

But what has she done?

He looks out of the window, at the blur of the building site. But he can't get beyond his own image, reflecting back at him from the dusty glass.

What has he become?

He pulls his phone from his pocket, and punches in three nines.

Acknowledgements

Thanks to: Ronnie at Hutcheon Law for much appreciated legal advice on inheritance; Nigel Burstow, Police Constable with the British Transport Police, Brighton, and Lisa Burstow, Case Administrator in the Criminal Justice Unit at Sussex Police for their insights into police procedure; Camilla Harrisson at Anomaly for her generous insider info on design and advertising agencies. Anything I have got wrong is my own doing. Thanks also to Simon Trewin for talking me through the story, Leah Woodburn for being my guide and champion, Vicki Mellor for her incredible editing, Katie Brown for her fizzing publicity and PR energy, and Patrick Insole at Headline Art Department for the beautiful cover – as Lou would say, don't forget the designer.

Thanks also to Tim, Nel and Owen, my diligent first readers, to Joey for putting up with late suppers and an occasionally absent-minded mother, to #Keith and #Sandra for keeping my feet warm while I write, and to my friends, most particularly Hannah Vincent and Emma Kilbey for coffees, wine, cake and wisdom. Finally, thanks to a certain secret Facebook group, where all questions may be asked, all FTSs aired, and all YAYs fist-bumped into the air. How did I ever manage before?

If Adam has got you interested in the politics of urban

regeneration, have a look at https://southwarknotes.wordpress.com/, which has been documenting the regeneration and gentrification in Southwark, South London, for nearly a decade. Quite an eye-opener.